A
SPOT OF
VENGEANCE

To Tin

Follow your dreams!

uncle
MAC 2020
X

A
SPOT OF
VENGEANCE

C. J. ANTHONY

Matador
9 Priory Business Park,
Wistow Road, Kibworth Beauchamp,
Leicestershire. LE8 0RX
Tel: 0116 279 2299
Email: books@troubador.co.uk
Web: www.troubador.co.uk/matador
Twitter: @matadorbooks

ISBN 978 1789018 370

British Library Cataloguing in Publication Data.
A catalogue record for this book is available from the British Library.

Printed and bound by CPI Group (UK) Ltd, Croydon, CR0 4YY
Typeset in 10.5pt Adobe Jenson Pro by Troubador Publishing Ltd, Leicester, UK

Matador is an imprint of Troubador Publishing Ltd

For Vicky who watches over me,
who motivates me every day to chase my dreams.

PROLOGUE

——— • ———

My involvement is important. My name? Danny Swift, ex-Army Intelligence. With an excellent eye for detail and an imperturbable equanimity, I was one of the best operators in my field. With over a decade on covert operations, I decided to give up the unjust wars and my own private battle of was it all worth it? Therefore, I left the service to follow my lifelong ambition: to become a full-time contemporary artist.

My obsession with art was more like a religion, with a natural talent to put oil onto a canvas. Safe in the solitude of my mind, painting out the trauma of war and destruction. I simply couldn't wait to get my artwork out there. Easier said than done, I thought. The creative world is such a competitive industry, especially for an emerging artist; getting the artwork recognised isn't as easy as it sounds. There are many misconceptions about the art world. There is no perceived middle ground; it's simply those who do make it and those that don't. This is precisely what makes the art market mystifying to outsiders. You'd think the value of art would depend on its aesthetic value; a picture you enjoy looking at on your wall. This isn't always the case amongst the art world's elite.

The art world has developed an intricate signalling process where the approval of only a handful of critics, collectors and dealers determines what art is good and what is not. So, I had to think intelligently in order to make a strategy to get that lucky break. It was crucial that I had the right person, with the right resume, to help me get the right exposure for my paintings.

2011 was a poignant year for me; a year I was lured into the hunt, confronting an unimaginable evil. It was when I first met the renowned art dealer and critic Hafiz de Mercurio, the ultimate paradox. It's sinister how a complete stranger has the ability to alter the lives of others, without them even knowing.

His assistant. Hauntingly beautiful, effortlessly soigné, yet lethal, she yearns to please his every command. Just like the time she had the life of a wealthy stockbroker in her hands… Every violent death paints its own story.

ONE

—— • ——

2010, LONDON

The impending prospect of Derek's death was precisely thirteen minutes away. Timed to perfection, Marina Khan arrived at an address in the affluent area of Kensington. With its rows of black glossy doors framed by white stone porticos. Money here was more important than religion for the self-absorbed residents, in sheer consumerism and greed, living in little bubbles, oblivious as to what really went on in the world outside their guarded community.

•

Derek Clarke was known as a ruthless trader, arrogantly flamboyant and the wrong side of fifty, rotund with mahogany skin from holidaying in Monte Carlo. He unlocked the door to his plush Kensington apartment, ushering in his colleague and the two hired escorts with short skirts he'd had specially delivered to the restaurant earlier. Wearing the epitome of an 80s grey pinstriped suit. It had been a typical lunch *après* a lucrative morning's dealings with an upside of £24 million for one client and £13.4 million for another; life was good. He threw his keys onto his marble cocktail bar and took off his suit jacket, draping it over the back of the chair, revealing a crisp white shirt with traditional red braces that matched his red cheeks. He always had Vicky his daily housekeeper chill a nice bottle of Mercier in a cut-crystal ice bucket before leaving.

Henry Matthews dragged himself away from the blonde and very leggy hooker in search of a drink, whilst her companion, a brunette, all cleavage and big hair, helped herself to a couple of snorts of cocaine, which lay in equal-sized parallel lines on the mirrored coffee table. Henry smugly joined his older colleague at the bar, undoing his top shirt button and removing his necktie. 'So, Derek, are we going to hit a few before or after the champers?'

He looked around, nimbly pouring four glasses of the ice-cool Mercier.

'Let's hit after, shall we, chum?' he suggested. 'Perhaps we should get a bit more acquainted with our guests first, don't you think?' He sent a seedy wink in the direction of the girls before sipping his champagne, watching them freshen up their makeup in front of the mirror, which was hung near a large marble fireplace.

The two prostitutes giggled away in disbelief at their affluent surroundings. The job had only come in that morning, and neither had much sleep from the previous evening's work, which had been slow and not that profitable to them or their madam; a glutton of a woman who knew a lot of important people in the right places, ensuring that all their work was contracted out for safety and Madame's anonymity.

Derek and Henry took over the champagne as the girls finished their ablutions, having cleverly worked out, with the experience of several shared jobs, who was having who this time.

•

Matt Gibson was on the evening shift at the Lancaster Gates apartments. The sun was setting over the exclusive district of W2. He had been a concierge for thirty years and considered himself to be top-notch at it. Reading over the notes left from the day shift of who was in the building and who was due in by way of visitors, two apartments were empty whilst the incredibly snooty inhabitants holidayed in Barbados for the winter. Matt immediately recognised that the worst offender for arrogance, Derek Clarke, was entertaining again, which meant an array of visitors and cabs delivering alcohol and unmentionable items throughout the course of the night. 'For the love of God, he's a bloody nightmare', he muttered, shaking his head whilst he checked the reception security monitors.

Matt noticed a woman stood outside on the screen. Mesmerised as she started to strut towards the building. With every step of her athletically toned legs, the slit in her short red skirt revealed the French lace design of the top of her rather exquisite pair of stockings, complemented by a pair of black patent Christian Louboutins. Wearing a Burberry trench coat, again in black; bearing a resemblance to a deadly black widow spider. Her long dark hair was secured in a ponytail at the nape of her neck. Leaving the monitors behind, he moved closer to the glass doors to observe the visitor, to better appreciate the full class that imbued her every pore, sensing something mysteriously furtive about her. Her large opaque sunglasses concealed much of her beautiful face, whilst her look was completed by a stylish Hermès leather shoulder bag that sat comfortably on her slim right hip. She had an air of supremacy that is usually found in those who know they are truly beautiful. 'She's God's gift', he murmured under his breath.

Marina opened her bag and took out an A4-sized piece of white paper which was rolled up like a scroll. It meant nothing to the staff inside the apartments, but to the trained eye, the detail on one side would reveal exactly what was about to take place. Slowly, she unrolled the paper for a few seconds, smiling to herself almost joyfully. She then rolled it back up, replaced it carefully inside her bag and started to walk in a precise, model-like fashion towards the entrance of the residence.

'Hello, cheeky', Matt said, somewhat sarcastically and under his breath, as he continued to watch her movements through the glass door.

Suddenly, about ten feet away from the doorway, Marina paused, looking up at the rows of windows in the higher storey's of the five-storey building, as if she was having one last confirmation of planned thoughts she was rehearsing in her head. Matt looked on inquisitively. Through her sunglasses, she mentally scaled each level, clocking the strategically placed

3

security cameras, her moist red lipstick glistening against her flawless complexion in the evening sunset.

She continued towards the main entrance of the building in an assertive manner. She meant business and she had a job to do. Carefully, unseen by Matt, her right hand reached inside her bag and pulled out a Glock 23 pistol with a silencer screwed into the barrel. She casually held it down by her side, flicking the safety catch off with her thumb, slightly concealed by the flap of her coat as she entered the grand lobby. She stopped just inside the doorway and slowly turned 360 degrees, scanning her surroundings.

Matt, having casually returned to his leather chair facing the eight large CCTV monitors, which hung on the wall next to a very large Gerhard Richter painting, browsed through his newspaper, which lay open in front of him on the desk. Matt was alerted by her approach into the lobby area, looking up as the echo from her stilettos hitting the marbled floor announced her arrival. Stood in front of a large leather concierge reception desk with highly polished mahogany wood, she raised her shades, exposing her piercing green eyes; spellbinding. She momentarily smiled at the smartly dressed individual before her and tilted her head to one side with a seductive grin on her perfect face.

Matt looked up from his newspaper. 'How can I help you, Madam?' he asked, grinning.

Marina tilted her head back slightly, looking at him dismissively. She could smell his breath, which smelt strongly of coffee and cigarettes; odours badly disguised by multiple Polo mints that he was crunching on.

'Can you tell me if Mr Clarke is in his apartment, 350?'

Her accent was foreign and not easy to place. *Middle Eastern*, he thought.

Matt stood up with a cavalier attitude, chest out. 'Oh, so you're here for the private party?' he said, presuming with a dirty snigger.

With a mirrored smile, Marina opened her lips to speak. 'Yes! I sure am, darling', she replied, tilting her head provocatively in the opposite way to before. He sent a look at her that spoke volumes, grinning with raised eyebrows, knowing exactly what sort of professional woman visited Derek Clarke on a regular basis at this time of the evening.

'Just go straight up, Madam. I'm sure he is expecting you', Matt said, giving a quick wink, still grinning.

4

'Erm, I doubt that', she retorted, standing tall with a glint in her steely eyes.

Matt looked confused. 'Excuse me, Madam, what do you mean?' he asked, puzzled.

She evaded the question with an ambiguous smile, then suddenly he sensed something compelling about her absolute focus. She quickly raised the Glock from down by her side. With accuracy, Marina professionally pointed the barrel and silencer over the top of the concierge desk whilst still smiling at him. Tilting her head slightly, she peered down the barrel and her eyes brightened with zeal.

Matt was instinctively scrambling in shock and panic to reach for the emergency alarm. 'NO! NO! Please, no!' he begged, desperately holding up his hands in defence. He knew the inevitable, which made his panic even more acute. Ignoring his pleas, she coolly squeezed the trigger, shooting him once in the chest. Thud. The shot stunned him, sending his heart into immediate shock as he felt a volcanic heat fill his chest; and before he could catch another breath, she took aim at his head. Fear filled his eyes. Her silencer spat – thud – a shot direct to the forehead finishing him off. As the shots were silenced, the only sound was that of the empty brass bullet casings hitting the marble floor.

Blood and brains projected out of the exit wound as the bullet travelled through his skull, spraying a decorative pattern over the Gerhard Richter painting on the wall behind him. He dropped to the floor, disappearing behind the desk without a murmur, bleeding out.

Marina raised her Dior glasses off her nose and looked appreciatively at the decorative markings now on the painting. 'I do believe that is now called still life, with a touch of claret', she whispered to herself, smirking calmly as she dropped her glasses back onto her nose, savouring the moment, appreciating the touch of art she had just created.

The barrel still smoking, she raised her arm and, with military dexterity, pivoted her body. Everywhere the weapon went, her eyes followed, from left to right, checking her arcs of fire in case anyone else had been in the vicinity whilst the assassination was taking place. Satisfied she wasn't compromised, she hurriedly walked behind the concierge desk, stepping over Matt's body, then leaned over to the CCTV control panel, deleting all records of her existence. She immediately headed towards the lift area, her heels tapping rhythmically over the marble floor, where she pressed the button to summon her ride. She stood casually, as if she was just an ordinary woman returning from a day's shopping in Knightsbridge.

Upstairs in the penthouse apartment, the *après luncheon* had surged to debauchery for the two city suits who had struck it lucky. Life couldn't get any better for them. The obscene amount of champagne in a mother of an overstocked ice bucket by the mirrored coffee table was only slightly upstaged by the delicate dusting of cocaine that swirled near an exquisite handtied bouquet in a crystal vase. The two seedy hookers now sexually embraced and half-naked, intoxicated and stoned, making the most of the freebies around them, they reshuffled the pleasant scatter cushion surroundings the women had made their play area.

Downstairs, Marina stood waiting in contemplation of her next move. With a ping, the lift doors opened and she stepped inside the leather-walled lift. The doors closed and she pressed the button for the top floor – the Penthouse Suite, Mr Clarke – taking off her sunglasses and sliding them into her Hermès bag. She glanced in the mirror to check her makeup, air-kissing her image with pouted lips and smoothing hair that was still sitting perfectly. She was certainly dressed to kill; the connotation made her smile.

The doors opened to reveal a marbled vestibule with a red carpet leading from the lift to the penthouse door. She stepped out of the elevator and walked casually to the door, noticing a security camera facing her, located top left above the door. She concealed the Glock pistol behind her back casually. Suite 350 was displayed in gold numbers on the door with an intercom to the right-hand side. She pushed the buzzer on the intercom, quickly glancing down at her watch. Eventually, a man's voice spoke through it.

'Hello there! Can we help you?' The Oxbridge-educated voice was slurred; she could hear music and girls laughing in the background. Irritated and impatient, she closed her eyes momentarily and took a deep breath in.

'Hello, darling; I've been sent by Elite Escorts as a complimentary gift'. Like a camgirl, she then looked deeply into the CCTV camera lens, smiling seductively.

'Oh marvellous, jolly good, please come on in'. The sound of a buzzer released the security lock and the door opened simultaneously.

She pushed the door open wider and slowly walked through the hallway, noticing and appreciating the artwork and photography displayed on either side of the corridor: *Jeff Koon's, Hirst, Bacon, Hito Steyerl, Emin and an Opie*. There was a door open at the end of the hallway, from which was emanating the sound of two women laughing, with Phil Collins singing *in the Air Tonight*, in the background on the Bang & Olufsen music system. Marina headed towards the door in an assertive manner, professional.

The smug traders were deep into booze, drugs and a defiant but accurate piss-take of their New York art dealer. There was a triumphant finality in Derek's voice as if to say I told you so, 'It was only a matter of time with that chap'. Looking up, raising his glass in salute at his most recent lucky investments that hung above the fireplace: an original Joseph Legend *Primus Circles* painting. They were so blatant in their opinions of the art dealer; their slander stepped up a notch at the point that Marina entered the room. Then the conversation stopped altogether as Henry stood up to open another bottle of champers, enquiring as to who had ordered the extra hooker.

'She's a complimentary gift, dear boy, courtesy of the escort agency. Would you believe that?' Derek smiled to the others; he did love a freebie.

'Well, don't just stand there, sexy; make yourself comfortable'. Henry indicated towards the sofa. He was desperate to see what was under Marina's stylish coat; he visualised all sorts of debauchery as he peeled the foil from the top of the champagne bottle.

The other two were not competitive; they rather liked the expensive style of the newcomer, and they had consumed enough alcohol and drugs to enact a threesome with her if required. They waved Marina over to their playpen. 'Hey, sweetie, come and join the party!' they joyfully shouted over, smiling, pointing down at all the cocaine on the table. Marina, on the other hand, couldn't have been more indignant. Derek was at his most content when indulging in expensive pursuits: for him, they represented a kind of recognition of his business success. Ignoring the women, he leant over the coffee table, chopping up the coke with his Centurion credit card, arranging it into parallel lines. With a rolled-up £50 note pressed to his right nostril and his left forefinger closing his left, he leant down to inhale the first line in one.

Henry, meanwhile, was still struggling to open the bottle of champagne. The girls were in hysterics laughing at him – but not for long.

Her stare defiant, Marina casually brought up her right hand, which still held the pistol, aiming directly at Henry. He noticed the confused look on the girls' faces first and then looked over at her. He froze as the reality sank in, his jaw dropping open in complete shock as she squeezed the trigger twice, double-tapping him. Thud, thud. The slugs penetrated his chest and, quickly, two small red holes appeared in his white shirt as blood and guts sprayed out behind him from the exit wounds. Instantly dropping the champagne bottle, smashing on the floor in front of him. His body followed a beat later, slumping down in a lifeless heap onto the chair behind him.

Both women screamed in horror; paralysed in sheer terror, they tried to recoil back into the sofa: nowhere to go. They stared fixedly at Henry, unable to believe what they had just seen.

The sound of the smashing bottle and the screams had pulled Derek out of his high. Unnerved, he raised his head up quickly. He looked straight at Marina as she pivoted around professionally. Where the barrel went, her head went too, squeezing the trigger twice. The bullets tore through both of Derek's kneecaps, forcing him back in his chair, hands clutching the wounds, blood pumping between his fingers.

He couldn't stop the terrible convulsive groans as his body struggled for oxygen. Screaming, shock immediately setting in as he bleeds out.

'Who in the hell are you? What do you want?' he gasped. He knew she was a professional.

Her voice was calm, almost flirtatious.

'I've been sent by an old friend of yours who tells me you have taken something that really doesn't technically belong to you', she said, smirking.

The pain was like nothing Derek had ever experienced, gasping for air, and his mind in a maelstrom.

Derek was slipping from consciousness. 'Please. Please', he begged. 'I was going to discuss it with him again'. He grimaced in pain, attempting to stand up to reason with her.

'You and the rest of the syndicate had already made it clear what your intentions were.'

His jaw was trembling. 'Take it back. I don't want it. Take the bloody lot', he said deliriously, pleading as darkness was closing in on his vision.

She smiled, pausing for a moment with a vacant stare. The pistol swung up again, and she fired one more shot into his chest: thud. The power and velocity of the round penetrated his flesh and pushed him back into his chair. Instantly, Marina squeezed the trigger again. Thud. The second bullet entered his forehead, whipping his head back. Blood spurted over the hookers from the headshot. Together, they helplessly screamed for help.

Marina's final pivot to the hookers couldn't come quick enough. Annoyed, as their nightmarish screams were growing louder, convulsing wildly. Shaking her head in disgust, she squeezed the trigger, releasing four rounds in less than two seconds: two shots each. She didn't particularly like blondes… thud, thud put a stop to that. Readjusting her aim on the brunette – thud, thud – she let her go too. Both got it in the head and chest, blood spurting out from behind them as they sat motionless, eyes open and silent at last. 'No more fucking screaming, please', she murmured, sighing in relief. She checked her watch a second time. '*Umm, thirteen minutes, perfect!*'

Enjoying the silence following the screams of terror, Marina placed her pistol on the marble bar area and took out the scrolled paper from within her Hermès bag. She walked over to the original *Primus Circles* painting, which was hung above the fireplace. Unrolling the paper, it revealed a series of colourful spots – just like those within the artwork. Holding the print up against the original, she compared the configuration of certain spots strategically placed within her image, scrutinising slowly, smiling knowingly. They matched.

'Eureka'. Chuckling to herself, she couldn't hide her glee as she felt a sense of sheer accomplishment.

Taking the original painting off the wall, Marina placed it in the mouth of the fireplace with her own paper copy. Reaching inside her bag, she took out a large liquid bottle containing a highly toxic acid. Gently, she unscrewed the cap, holding her breath so as not to inhale the fumes, and then, crouching down, poured the liquid over the paintings. Mesmerised, she watched the chemical reaction as the acid instantly melted the paint, destroying the canvas as it burned straight through.

Marina stood up and moved away to gasp in some air. Killing time for no reason, she looked around at the rest of the impressive art collection on the walls. She did love these luxury apartments: so distinguished, so perfect. She looked back at this apartment's former owner, Derek.

'What the hell are you looking at?' she said to his corpse, grinning.

His eyes and mouth were wide open, fear and shock, frozen in time. The blood ran down his face like tears. Walking over to him whilst pouting her lips, she poured the rest of the acid slowly over his face. Holding her gloved hand over her nose, she learnt a bit closer: all the better to observe the reaction of the acid on his flesh. She was fascinated by the distortion. Her psychotic behaviour released pleasure that left her feeling rather strangely aroused.

Marina carefully screwed the lid firmly back on the toxic bottle, placing it inside her bag. She then reached for her military encrypted mobile phone from her coat pocket, always mindful of intelligence agencies such as GCHQ that use sophisticated technology to eavesdrop on conversations. She selected Call, pressing the phone gently against her ear as she continued to look around the apartment whilst waiting for an answer.

'Yes', said the unemotional voice on the other end of the line.

'Task complete', she replied as she walked around the room admiring the décor, heading towards the large veranda window.

'Did everything go as per my instructions?' demanded the voice.

She rolled her eyes. 'Yes, perfect', and she stood back from the window, covertly gazing out, obscured by the window blinds.

'Everything worked perfectly'. She smiled, praising the creator's work.

'Did the target say anything?'

'Not much really'. She shrugged, glancing back over her shoulder towards Derek Clarke's corpse.

'Was he alone?'

'No, there was one other suit that I did recognise from the Tracey Emin exhibition in Paris, and two escorts'.

'And?'

'There won't be any problems from them', she said, stepping away from the window to admire a Charming Baker painting as the voice on the other end laughed contemptuously.

'Good. There will always be collateral damage.'

'True, it can't be helped.' So dark her expression, Marina walked towards her victims smugly.

'Oh! Just before you go, can I do just one more to make sure it works?' Marina asked exultantly, as her face lightened with pleasure.

Without another word, the call ended.

Immediately, she turned her phone off, removing its battery, placing both parts back inside her pocket, to be destroyed once the mission was completed.

Leaving… without a trace.

TWO

—— • ——

2009, Long Island

The ultimate gentleman. Hafiz de Mercurio, mid-forties, and at first glance rather flamboyantly stylish, a man that oozed sophistication and elegance. His hair was black and sleeked back, his cheekbones wide and strong, with deep brown eyes and a square chin, complemented by designer stubble that lent his face an air of profound and reassuring intelligence. An image he worked hard to convey. Graduating with a double Masters in Art History and Mathematics from Edinburgh and Cambridge universities, and considered a polymath, given his prowess, he had gone on to earn an immense amount of money, relishing in all the perquisites he had rightly earnt from his expertise. A regular spender at the exclusive retailer Mr Porter, and the exclusive boutiques in Knightsbridge, he was impeccably dressed for every occasion.

Blue skies, with the sun burning down on this glorious day, Hafiz smoothed down his suit jacket as he got into the limousine. His wealth defined him at times, resulting in arrogance that made him unpopular to many, which in turn fed his paranoia, which was getting worse. He felt it gnawing away at him, disgusting him, pushing him to the brink of conflict in everything he tried to do. Denial was his survival mechanism: denial of cancer that was eating away at him slowly from within, denial of the drug abuse he could no longer control, no more so than when he attended the home of a business colleague and friend in the summer back in 2009.

He tapped the glass impatiently, signalling to the driver to start the journey; he expected everyone to know what he wanted, to stay one-step ahead of him, and was sharp when they failed to anticipate his needs. The only people he was nice to – were his clients: the senior executives of firms like Goldman Sachs, Morgan Stanley, IBM, and all the other giant organisations that employed him to purchase expensive art as business acquisitions on their behalf.

Widely regarded as the most unscrupulous dealer in the industry, Hafiz had flawless insight into the art markets, enough for the majority to wonder if he had a sixth sense and a crystal ball to predict which artist would make the most profit at auction. He was so ruthless in negotiation that he could generate large profits, enabling him to invest fifty per cent capital with another investor, buy cheap and sell high at auction. He had personal cash investments with several high-value investors spread across an international artist, which guaranteed to set him up for life once auctioned. The stakes were the highest they'd ever been.

He sat back in his seat reminiscing about his father's anger at his choice of educational topics and aspirations – but it was his mother who secretly encouraged his obsession with art. Sadly, they were both murdered by coalition forces over thirty-five years ago. He wondered what path he would have taken if his father was still alive.

The limousine travelled slowly, giving Hafiz time to reflect as he opened the window and let in a warm heat. Powerful sunshine hit his face, as he adjusted his slick Tom Ford sunglasses, thinking back over his success since he'd started working in the States. Memories of seriously living the dream perked up his confidence for the venue he was about to enter – but it wasn't enough. He started to yearn for a hit; he needed the drugs to perform around people, especially those inhabiting the art world. Darkness edged into his thoughts, making him anxious, which in turn annoyed him. As the doubts flickered, he turned his mind to all the gorgeous women he'd had and still could have, then that fire went out and

Marina came unwanted into his consciousness. *Fuck!* he thought. That was going to start a spiral he wouldn't be able to control.

The Hamptons, located on Long Island's South Shore, had long been the summer playground of the rich and famous, which everyone he was about to join certainly was. Along with that spectacular coastline, the stunning, pure-white sand beaches opened to the meek waters of the Atlantic Ocean and a string of dashing seaside homes, many owned by well-known celebrities and the uber-rich, flocked the horizon. Constant visitors travelled to the area in the hope of seeing their celebrity crush. But Hafiz wasn't a celebrity-spotter: again, he had been invited to the annual summer ball of his good friend Donald Harrison, the CEO of CMAC Investments, who was more like a father figure to him, certainly in the absence of one growing up.

Donald saw great talent in Hafiz when they met around eight years ago, and employed him to advise and purchase art for the company's acquisitions and private collections of his own. Many of Donald's top-end employees and friends equally saw Hafiz's expertise and foresight into big art investments, but none of them were considered part of the family as he was. Over the years, Hafiz was invited to many birthday parties, weddings, Thanksgiving celebrations and incomparable exotic holidays with the Harrison family and their friends. Today's exclusive event was to be staged at Harrison's own beachfront mansion.

Hafiz psyched himself up and smoothed down his jacket and trousers, handmade direct from the illustrious tailoring houses of Italy. He looked at the background of blue skies as his limousine travelled down the main road towards the venue, drinking in his surroundings of complete grandeur. As they reached the large gated entrance to the spectacular mansion, an uncontrollable inner mania suffocated him, and a sudden rush of paranoia caused his breathing to become shallower. Adjusting his tie, he took out the silk hanky from his lapel pocket, slowly mopping his brow as emotions agitated his otherwise sleek outlook. Trying to control his breathing and blank out his mind, attempting to stop himself from thinking all kinds of crazy shit.

The driver hadn't noticed the change in his passenger's behaviour as he stopped the limo at the main gates to Harrison's mansion. The two security guards checked his credentials and Hafiz's invitation card. Hafiz couldn't stop perspiration from beading at his temples. He brought the window right down to alleviate the claustrophobia that loomed – a move which backfired as seething hot air flew at him, making him sweat even more. He swiftly altered the air conditioning to face him.

'I'm a good friend of the family', Hafiz yelled out in a mild panic, 'he knows me personally'. The security guards looked over at him, and the driver also glanced into the back via his rear-view mirror, noting a strange tone to his passenger's voice.

'It's okay, sir, you're on the list!' One of the guards nodded towards Hafiz and gave directions to the driver, and then they proceeded forwards slowly, waiting for the electric security gates to open.

The car travelled towards the main building and Hafiz started to mumble quietly, telling himself to take control and not draw unnecessary attention to himself. His knees started jiggling up and down, and his palms perspired. Shaking nervously, he started to complain about the heat of the day to explain his physical appearance. Once again, he wiped the sweat from his brow and temples. His whole body began to ache uncomfortably, making his breathing heavier and heavier until he felt the commencement of hyperventilation.

I can't take this any more – I need a fix, he thought, disgusted at the timing. Giving in to his body's craving, he reached inside his jacket and took out a little sachet of white powder. Discreetly, he tipped a little onto the back of his hand whilst anxiously looking at the driver, who was too busy avoiding parked cars to notice what was happening in the back. In a flash, he sniffed the powder into his right nostril, instantly wiping the residue from sight. Instantly, the desired effect hit him like a thunderbolt and his breathing relaxed, the shakes stopped and his confidence and well-being returned, calming his nerves as he regained his composure.

By the time the limo stopped at the main entrance to the mansion, Hafiz was high and ready for an entrance. One of the distinguished butlers opened the limo door; their job was to meet all the guests personally as they arrived. The elevated atmosphere of the annual celebrations was as instant as the heat.

'Good afternoon, sir. Welcome to the CMAC Investments annual luncheon. Please go through to the main reception hall'. The well-spoken gent conveyed the direction with a white-gloved hand. Hafiz stepped out of the vehicle, standing tall with an air of grace and leonine sexuality. Straightening his jacket and tie, coolly looking around his immediate vicinity, then heading into the building as women and men alike turned their heads to admire his natural dashing looks.

The water fountain just inside the entrance was stunning, with cut-crystal features spurting out water in all directions. For the first second, it was all you could hear – before the multiple tones of people talking and laughing intoxicated the surroundings. There were mostly waitresses and waiters in this reception area, and a glass of champagne was quickly served to Hafiz; he waited for the waitress to move on before hitting back the beautifully chilled golden liquid in one. Dom Perignon, *very nice*, he thought. He needed the time to cool and generally appease the negative monster inside him; it was hard work talking as one, and most guests at these functions were coupled out.

As he moved away from the fountain, he was drawn to a guy, motionless, who was peering owlishly at him through his thick black-rimmed spectacles just the other side of the rippling water. He tried nonchalantly to get a better look. Another glass of champagne was given and, when he looked back, the guy had disappeared. This time, Hafiz sipped only half his beverage as he tried looking for the stranger, heading towards a garden terrace that ran the entire breadth of the mansion. A few small steps led down to a massive gazebo, whilst in the background lay a private beach edged with a beautiful turquoise sea. It was sublime.

There was a mixture of men, women and children scattered around, with a jazz band permanently playing non-intrusive music, setting an elegant tone. Luckily, the children were all running around the garden and beach area, leaving their mummies and daddies to chat amongst themselves. With an elite guest list such as this, it was predetermined whom they had to outdo in their designer clothes, watches and expensive jewellery.

Hafiz took another glass of champagne before walking towards some familiar faces with whom he had managed good art deals in the past. A bunch of well-dressed gents stood chatting and laughing together outside on the garden terrace – business, wealth, yachts and cars were all he heard about as he drew near.

'Ah, Hafiz! We were just talking about you'. The man spoke with an upper-class exuberance, which was most unsettling. A trickle of half-hearted laughter came from the others. Then, seemingly instantly, all stood awkwardly, falling silent as they turned to look at him with that fake smile people use.

'Oh, what about?' Hafiz asked, as he stood steadfast in the face of the awkwardness whilst adjusting his sunglasses self-consciously.

One of the gentlemen, who spoke in a Dutch-accented English, interrupted the silence. 'Don't take this the wrong way, Hafiz, but you look as though you could use some time off'.

'Are you trying to suggest something, Markus?'

'I'm suggesting nothing of the sort. It's just…'

'Just what?' Hafiz said with an inscrutable expression on his face.

'People have just been talking, that's all. You know how it is. Maybe you need to slow down, maybe see someone', he said, grinning, as he put his arm around Hafiz's shoulders and squeezed him smugly as if they were great buddies of old.

Hafiz put his teeth together and hissed contemptuously, trying not to allow paranoid thoughts to race through him as the disturbing silence continued. With the false confidence given him by the protection of his shades, he discreetly observed each of them in turn, one by one. Breaking the ice amongst the group, an older gentleman stepped forward. 'It's good to see you, Hafiz', he said with a broad Texan accent. Looking like a cast member from the TV series *Dallas*: light-blue suit, white shirt, a Stetson and traditional cowboy boots to match.

'Yes, it's good to see you too, Charles', Hafiz replied instinctively.

'That Andy Warhol you advised me to buy has just been revalued, and I'm in for a big return once I sell it at auction; nearly as much as I make selling oil!' the Tex said, laughing. 'You have made many people amongst us here today very rich, thanks to your expertise and foresight in the art market'. He let his cigar hang out of the side of his mouth whilst talking; the epitome of a true oil baron.

Hafiz gave a nervous chuckle, then grinned at him falsely, dreading the onslaught of paranoid thoughts he knew were coming: that he wasn't liked, that everyone knew what he really was. It was getting worse, the surge of crap that toppled him every time he had to face someone sober. His addiction and the associated mistrust were taking over his life, which was becoming overwhelmed by dread and disgust. He looked through

Charles as if he was a glass window, motionless, his ears silently reaching out to ambient voices that circled him, checking for sinister whispers and laughter, which followed all around him as he turned his head in different directions like a radar. He gradually convinced himself they were mocking him and his heart started to speed up. Suspicious thoughts gave his solar plexus the sensation of crossing over into another world; they rolled around his mind like a whirlpool of evil persecutory delusions, not making any rational sense. Yet he could hear only what his deranged mind wanted to hear, which in turn fed his obsession.

The four men were looking at him intently, when another member of the group stepped forward with his brow creased with concern and confusion. Suddenly Hafiz walked away from the group with a sense of urgency and panic, leaving the four staring in his general direction. They stared at each other in amazement then burst out laughing as he headed towards a doorway situated at the back of the main lobby entrance. He vigorously wiped his brow and the back of his neck as he weaved in and out of the other guests that stood in groups enjoying the party. Almost as a side glance, he noticed the stranger from the reception hall, motionless, staring right at him again. Everything appeared in slow motion as he turned around a half-circle to keep the gaze, his mind on fire as if it was going to explode. He blindly walked on through a door that appeared on his left, closing it firmly behind him.

The silence that greeted him as he shut the door briefly held off the panicky feeling as he took two deep breaths, trying to take control. Shutting his eyes, he felt two trickles of cold moisture running down his temples and onto his hands. His breathing became heavier as the cold sweat soaked through his shirt. He carried on down a small corridor, unbuttoning his shirt collar and taking off his tie as he found an obvious bedroom, the door already open. He entered to find it empty and closed the door. This would be his refuge for a while. He made it to the edge of the bed and sat down heavily, holding his head in his hands, clutching at his chest and stomach, pain firing through him as he shook uncontrollably, feeling cold, so cold.

'Please, God, please, no more pain, get this crazy shit out of my mind', he cried out loud as tears ran down his face, clenching his hands into fists of frustration, slamming them down onto his thighs. He looked up to see himself in the mirror on the dressing table in front of him. Eyes bloodshot, as though the devil was burning a reflection of hell into him; and his head started banging like a drum as the paranoid whispers tormented him.

He unbuttoned his suit jacket and took it off, laying it carefully on the bed beside him. In his fragile state, he still appreciated luxury. Then he reached for a small rectangular velvet box located in the inside pocket, placing it on the bed gently, almost reverentially. Closing his eyes as he mopped the sweat away for better vision before opening the lid, revealing a silver hypodermic needle nestled in the velvet case. It had a cap on the end to protect the needle and its load of 40mgs of a transparent liquid.

Quickly rolling up the sleeve of his shirt on his left arm to just above his elbow, exposing previous needle track marks and bruising. Fluidly, with practised skill, he grabbed his necktie and wrapped it around his bicep like a tourniquet, pulling it tight as he flexed his fingers to pump the blood flow through his arm, exposing his chosen vein for the needle. He slowed his breathing and tapped the vein a few times to raise it. Then, picking up the syringe, he bit off the cap, which was protecting the needle, and spat it onto the floor.

Taking a final deep breath to control the shaking of his hand, he guided the needle into his chosen vein, his fingers and thumb squeezing together, slowly plunging the fluid through the passage of the needle deep into his bloodstream. Time stopped still, as the warmth of the fluid filled his body, immediately dulling his senses, releasing his mind and body of the pain. Before the out-of-body experience hit him, he carefully lay on the bed just as his pupils dilated, looking up at the crystals of the chandelier, which reflected glorious spectrums of light on the ceiling. Carefully listening to the sound of his heartbeat everywhere, slowly drifting into a euphoric state of unconsciousness, falling deep into an abyss of colour.

•

The party outside had moved up a gear, with the champagne flowing faster than the water in the fountain. The music had been cranked up, and all the reception areas had been designed to allow dancing. Food was purposefully scattered in a buffet-style arrangement on the garden terrace to stop the need for waitresses and waiters and avoid them being crushed and banged into by dancers who had limited control or style, having gaily drunk through the afternoon to what was now almost dusk.

Eight-year-old Sophia was playing hide-and-seek with friends from the party. She ran around the enormous space of corridors, her golden ringlets practically airborne from her face as she tried to find a place to hide. She was gloriously happy that she had been allowed to wear her favourite pink and white flowery patterned summer dress. She'd been given the present of ruby red pumps that morning and she felt like a princess. Hearing her friends laughing and getting closer to her, she pushed open the nearest door with her fingertips to hide. She stopped in the doorway, creasing her vision, looking towards the bed and the person lying motionless on it. She crept forward, confused as to what weird silvery thing was poking out of his arm.

She nudged him gently. 'Hey, mister, are you hurt?' she said softly. There was no reply.

Nervously, she wobbled the syringe that was still embedded in his arm. 'Hey, mister, are you sleeping?' she whispered.

She looked down at the blood on the point of the needle. Panicking, she removed the syringe and left the room to find her mummy, to get help for the poor man.

The sound of the door closing behind her woke Hafiz, and the darkness around him alerted him to a time lapse. Shivering with cold, instinctively, he sat up on the bed and looked around the room, dazed and confused; the light made the furniture visible due to the garden lights on outside. *Damn, how long have I been here?* he thought, sighing as he looked at his watch; it was just after 8pm. *How the hell am I going to explain this?*

Maybe no one would have noticed he'd been absent for so long. A burning acid taste rose from the pit of his stomach. His torpid body got up and headed to the en-suite. Pushing the plug into the hole, he filled the white ornate sink up with cold water, taking a couple of desperate sips of water from the tap; then taking a deep breath, he completely submerged his face. *What is happening to me?* he thought, his mind frazzled. He emerged from the cold water, with a deep gasp, face tingling. He grabbed a white fluffy hand towel that hung on the silver rail. He rubbed himself dry, staring at his reflection in the mirror, barely recognising himself. He tried to focus on the room and noticed, through the reflection in the bathroom mirror, his jacket lying on the bed behind him.

Returning to the bedroom, he switched on a side lamp. In the brighter light, he noticed his paraphernalia box beside his jacket. In a panic, he quickly placed it back inside the pocket, safely concealed from sight. His tie was still in place around his arm; his limb hurt and was becoming numb. Feeling cold, he untied his arm; he noticed blood on his tie, so he put it into his trouser pocket then adjusted his shirt collar. He smoothed his hair, tidied his appearance and eventually put his jacket back on. He cleaned his teeth with his tongue and made a final check that the suave art dealer was back in place — at least in terms of his appearance — before heading out of the room to return to the party.

Sophia, meanwhile, had suddenly felt frightened on leaving the bedroom. The corridor was darker than when she had arrived and she wanted to get back to her mummy. She ran back, remembering the big dresser at the corner of the corridor which had a mirror; she knew this would take her to the main entrance where she had left her friends. As she ran, she snagged her dress with the needle, which made her more anxious and upset as she knew her mother was going to be angry with her for ruining her pretty clothes.

She entered the reception hall, scanning for her mother's green dress. Everyone was so tall and people were dancing around, obscuring her vision. Eventually, she spotted her mother just behind the water fountain and innocently took the syringe to her, more worried about her dress than the silvery needle. Their eyes locking in an eternal gaze, her mother's expression scared her and she started to cry at once.

As for Sophia's mother, she froze rigid as she watched her daughter running towards her with a syringe. Scanning the child, she saw the rip in her daughter's dress and instantly feared the worst. Trying to stay calm, she carefully held out her hand to take the syringe.

'Darling, where did you get that from?' She tried to keep her voice light, knowing her daughter was scared. She stretched her hand out further, willing the shining syringe to come to her. 'Please give it to Mummy now'. Her heart was beating as she took the needle.

'I took it from a man asleep in the bedroom', Sophia said in a quavering voice. 'He isn't very well, Mummy'. She was still crying as she pointed towards the door on the other side of the fountain, showing the direction she had come from. She could see the anger in her mother's face, and other guests started to stare at the increasing commotion.

'Mummy, I've torn my dress!' Sophia was now causing a scene. Her mother tried to remain calm as she checked her daughter's hands and arms for signs of pinprick marks, having safely put the needle on the marble side of the fountain. Satisfied her daughter was safe, she picked her up and hugged her until she too cried; she called out for her husband and for Donald Harrison. First, she was scared, then angry, then scared; now, she was distraught and furious.

Both men came over and she spurted everything out, crying still, even though her daughter had finally stopped. She was happy in her mother's arms and was looking towards the water fountain when Hafiz suddenly appeared from the door.

'That's the poorly man, Mummy'. Sophia pointed towards Hafiz but her parents didn't hear. Her mother was becoming hysterical. She herself was fighting to blink back the tears and wanted her daughter checked out by a doctor; a crowd had gathered around them. 'That's him, Mummy!' Sophia shouted, tapping her mother's shoulder and pointing at Hafiz as he tried casually to walk amongst the guests, oblivious.

The small crowd and her parents turned around in silence and stared at Hafiz, who hadn't put two and two together. He saw only the look of disgust and shock on their faces, instigating paranoia into him. The host, Donald Harrison, picked up the syringe and carefully wrapped it in a thick napkin. The anger on his face was blazing and his rage spoke with such magnitude that it frightened some of the guests. Looking straight at Hafiz, he held the syringe up, pointing it directly at his shamed guest.

Hafiz stood perfectly still, with his mouth slightly open in shock and confusion as it all registered, everything unfolding in front of him. He thought back to the velvet box on the bed, the tie around his arm… and *no fucking syringe! Oh fuck*, he thought grimly. How the hell could he rectify this situation?

'No, wait, I didn't give it to her! Wait, it was an accident', he tried, panicking. He wasn't sure what he could say to make amends here, but he had to give it a go, Donald's temper exacerbated by the conviction that Hafiz was stuttering emotionally, trying to desperately downsize the dilemma, only making things worse. As he attempted to pacify the situation, amongst the chaos, again he spotted the owl's eyes from the reception hall staring intently at him. Holding his stare, desperate for some form of recognition; help, even.

'What the hell have you done?' Donald Harrison launched into an attack, as the guests fell silent and the music stopped playing. 'I treated you like a son and you do this to me, to my guests in my own home'. He walked towards Hafiz menacingly, holding up the syringe in his fist, thrusting it towards Hafiz's face. 'How dare you', he continued, as Hafiz just stood there motionless, as if it was a bad dream. His eyes moved around as he looked at each and every face, all staring at him in utter disgust, whilst some smirked.

Donald clicked towards the security guards, demanding their attention. 'Get this piece of shit out of my home'. He turned back to Hafiz. 'You are not welcome here. Get out now'. He silenced whilst he shot a death look at Hafiz. 'Don't dare contact me or my family again, we are done'.

Two very tall suits grabbed Hafiz, holding his arms as he tried to struggle free, his arms hurting, one in particular. They carried him out of the building; he landed in an undignified crumpled heap on the floor. With a heart heavier than he ever imagined possible, he became an emotional mess as the reality hit him hard. Crying out, begging for forgiveness, pleading on his hands and knees, whimpering. He let out a scream of anguish that resounded across the car park, but the door was already shut and no one could hear him. Four security men drew up quickly in an open-topped Jeep, jumped out and forcefully threw him into the back, then sped off towards the gates of the property.

Inside, no one was talking still. Several people consoled the mother and daughter and many more consoled Donald Harrison. Eventually, Harrison's wife made a speech to regain control of the party, making it clear that she and her husband did not condone drugs in any form. She asked the jazz band to help out in rejuvenating the atmosphere, and they took the cue.

23

As the orchestra played a Glenn Miller favourite, the owl wandered slowly around the room, attentively listening to the individual groups caught in the trap of Chinese whispers. The frenzy slowly wore itself stagnant. The elusive stranger knew too much had been said already.

THREE

——— • ———

2009, New York

For something so humiliating, filled with corporate risk, it was all handled with a minimum of fuss. And secrecy, too. That was the remarkable thing about being in a position of power, they could just simply switch him off. Like a light, and they did. Instantly, Hafiz was dropped out of the social and business circles he once knew and revelled in. Clearly confused, trying to recollect his ungentlemanly eviction from the Hamptons, because the very next day, he hit his panic button and tried to phone the great Donald Harrison but his numbers were blocked. Unperturbed or just stupid, or a combination of both, he tried Harrison's PA, who refused to take a message with the rehearsed: 'Unfortunately, Mr de Mercurio, your services are no longer required'.

Now alone with just his thoughts, a dangerous combination when you throw drink and drugs into the mix. Anxiously, he sat on the edge of his chair; framed in cigarette smoke, holding his phone, contemplating. He flicked through his personal phone book that was open on the coffee table in front of him. One by one, he selected friends and colleagues who had all collectively invested huge amounts of money with him into original works of art to be auctioned off.

He dialled the number, holding the phone to his ear. He listened to the ringing. A voice answered.

'Hello.'

'Hey, Chris. It's Hafiz. How are you?' He tried to sound nonchalant, and ignorant of the events of last night.

'Hello, Hafiz. I'm good, thanks. To what do I owe the pleasure?' he replied, known for his acerbic wit.

His knees nervously jiggled up and down. 'I'm just calling about the painting that we both invested in.'

'What about it, dearie?' This time he responded with an air of sarcasm.

'I was wondering if I could get one of my art couriers over later today and collect it, as I'm having a professional photographer in the studio over the next couple of days. I'm preparing them for the auction catalogues.' Pausing briefly. 'It will be advertised in both Sotheby's and Phillips', he added.

Chris snorted with surprised laughter. 'Really?' he said acidly, raising his voice, trying to assert control.

'Ha, ha', said Chris. 'I don't ever recall you offering such a personal service on valuable pieces of art.' His pompous attitude towards him was deplorable. Before Hafiz could respond, he continued: 'Look, Hafiz, word has spread like wildfire; we all agree it would be in our, and your, best interests if you concentrate on getting help for your addiction before you recommence making important decisions in business.'

Hafiz shifted in his chair, uncomfortable at the way the conversation was going. 'Chris, listen – hear me out', he pleaded.

'I'm going to spare you the shame and humiliation. You need to face facts and address your personal life first', he said, sighing with a trace of impatience. 'Bad news travels fast, I'm afraid; corporate won't have any association with the likes of you. Each one of us has a reputation to protect, surely you must understand that.' He spoke with a slight hint of compassion.

'Chris, don't take me for a fool', Hafiz was saying incredulously, mystified by the lawless ways of the syndicate.

His words seemed to have no impact. 'I must admit I had always thought you to be a genius, but you have proven me wrong', Chris said bitterly, sniggering.

You could hear the naked desperation in Hafiz's voice: 'We have known each other for years, don't shut me out'.

'Hafiz, I don't want to come across like a bitch here, but true, we have… But this is business; you of all people should know how cut-throat the art world is', he replied stolidly.

'I suggest you choose your words carefully, Chris. Don't underestimate me. We made a deal'. Hafiz felt desperation and anger filling up inside him; he needed to salvage the conversation. 'I have always dealt with the business side of things. I've never let any of you down, and I have been loyal to you all for many years. You've all made some serious money with my expertise'.

'A deal you say. Verbally, yes, we all made a deal, Hafiz. Yes, we all did, but that's not worth the paper it's written on'. Chris laughed. 'Oh wait… It wasn't written down at all, was it?' He delivered the perfect onslaught as he hung up the phone.

Hafiz froze momentarily.

Word had spread like a deadly virus of what had happened at the party. Everyone had now used this situation as the perfect excuse to get rid of him, all incessantly delivering the same response, or words to that effect, which, in turn, kept him away from their ever-increasing art investments that they made together. Hafiz knew that the art was purchased through a gentleman's handshake, with so-called loyal friends he'd known for years. Immense cruelty and perfidy were displayed due to their absolute avarice. So now he was more fucked up than his last hit had been.

•

Hafiz lost track of days and time. Sat motionless, numb, going through every detail of his fall from grace as so many voices in his head argued. Crushing a cocktail of heavy-duty painkillers, using the bottom of his glass and then dusting them untidily into the whisky already in it; he downed the lot in one. Memories appeared slowly as the drugs took effect. Like a robot, he moved his vision and hands to the two lines of coke he had cut earlier with a razor blade; and with a rolled-up banknote, he leaned towards the parallel lines of white and snorted aggressively. The chemicals hit his mind with euphoria; the combination resulting in heaven as designed.

Suddenly he heard an agonising scream that echoed around the apartment and seemed to come up from the floor. Confused, he looked around – then realised it was him screaming with cramps and more pain, as his pulse quickened. Pouring another glass of whisky, most of it went down in one before a convulsion of coughing up blood that spurted onto his face and T-shirt.

He felt his eyes hot, bloodshot with blurred vision; he was unable to see anything in the loft conversion that was his New York apartment, but only the faces from the party staring at him like white porcelain dolls, motionless, whispering the same thing. Frustrated, he grabbed the empty whisky bottle and threw it against those faces, hitting the wall, the bottle smashing into a thousand pieces with the intensity of his anger. Agitated, he clenched his fists then suddenly exploded into a wild bout of fury. His rage continued fiercely as he stormed across the room towards his desk, flipping it over with both hands as it crashed down onto its side, with its contents violently smashing to the floor all around him.

'What the hell have I done?' he growled regretfully, gasping in a panic, struggling to breathe, making his body shake in complete helplessness. Dropping down onto his knees as though he was in prayer, he bowed his head over his clasped hands, hearing only the echoes of the sounds of his own body, his heartbeat thudding in his ears. Yearning for the end; yearning for heaven as he passed out unconscious, with only darkness as comfort.

•

Hafiz saw a light, penetrating through his inner vision. For a moment, he believed he was dead, yet his body was trembling and he was aware of consciousness, aware of movement in his eyes. The pain hit as he tried to open them. Slowly, the room came into focus and he scanned around the room whilst still lying on the ground. Rubbish, empty alcohol bottles, broken glass, cocaine powder, pills and a syringe sat on the glass table.

Then, out of all the chaos that surrounded him, he saw it lying there next to him, within arm's reach. His book of the *Holy Quran*, which must have fallen off his desk when he tipped it over. With his left hand, he pulled it in close to him, clutching it intently next to his heart. *Allah, I knew you wouldn't abandon me*, echoed in his thoughts.

He looked around the room, and the realisation of what he had done caused his revulsion. He knew that the western way was poisoning his soul, consumed by the drugs that he hoped would masquerade the cancer that was slowly absorbing his body. He stood up and stared disapprovingly at his reflection in the mirror. *This isn't me,* he thought, disgusted in what he saw and what he had become. On that morning, he left his apartment in darkness to purify himself at the local mosque located just off Third Avenue.

•

Marina sat in the back of the traditional yellow cab. She always loved visiting her favourite city, New York. She twiddled her hair in contemplation as she thought about the incident that involved Hafiz at the Hamptons, concerned about his health and well-being. As the cab drew nearer to the apartment, her mood slightly changed. She wasn't sure what to expect when she got there; she hadn't heard from him since finding out about the incident.

Hafiz heard a familiar voice and footsteps echoing quietly in the apartment as she turned the key and let herself in. No broken glass, bottles, cigarette ends or evidence of any drugs; everything looked perfect and the apartment once again became the pristine show home it was usually.

'Hello, darling; how are you?' she said, smiling, rushing over to him, sliding her hands around his waist, almost on tiptoe to kiss him on the lips.

His eyes morose and cynical, Hafiz pulled away. 'Let's not get overly emotional here. I'm really not in the mood for niceties', rejecting her advances, leaving her stunned, unsmiling.

The emotional maelstrom that she was feeling was nothing to the devastation that Hafiz must be enduring. 'I've heard what happened', she said solemnly.

'Tell me. What have you heard?' he asked as he walked away over towards the window, staring out down at the streets below.

'Erm, not much, to be honest', she replied, shaking her head.

'Strange, don't you think?'

Marina sat down suddenly on the edge of the chair, her head in her hands. 'People have spoken about what happened – but...'

'But what?' Hafiz bellowed.

'But – it's like the incident never happened, and no mention of the drugs or the child'.

Hafiz gesticulated wildly, shaking his head, tutting in denial. 'Drugs? No. They have got this whole situation wrong', he shouted, all control gone.

She spoke calmly, trying not to antagonise the situation. 'Hafiz! Darling. Let's get with reality here, you had been caught and that child could have been hurt'. She paused briefly. 'I've known about the drugs for some time'.

He heaved a long frustrated sigh of despair, lowering his head in shame. 'Look – I regret that day, but I've been under a huge amount of pressure of late', he said, as if hesitant to tell the truth why. 'To be honest, I've not been feeling too good', he added, so quiet as to be almost inaudible.

'We will get help for you. Just give it time and everything will be forgotten. You know how these things are', she said, giving him reassurance.

'Trust me. No one has forgotten. They have all betrayed me'. Hafiz put his teeth together and hissed contemptuously.

'Who?'

'My investors – the syndicate', he muttered.

'What! All of them?'

'Yes! Every fucking one of them'. His expression hardened, his eyes incandescent with anger.

'They can't just do that, can they?'

'Well, they have, and stupidly there is nothing I can legally do'. He was inwardly berating himself. 'I have potentially lost millions'.

She looked straight at him, eyes glazed like she was staring through him. 'That was our money to start a new life'.

He took a deep breath and held her gaze. 'Yes, I know'.

'Well, if only they knew the truth. Then it would be a different story, wouldn't it?' she said bluntly, her voice quavering on the edge of tears.

'You know it doesn't work like that, Marina, think of the bigger picture'. He paused, giving her an exasperated look.

'Well, it should, shouldn't it?' she yelled incredulously. 'Well, make it part of the bigger picture then; you cannot let these infidels get away with this, Hafiz. They have betrayed you'.

He felt an ambivalence towards her suggestion, but he knew she was right. His gaze drifted off in contemplation, finally returning to Marina. 'Sometimes you have to create a crisis in order to get people's attention.' His nostrils flared with anger. 'They have taken advantage and betrayed me.'

'I'm sure a genius like you can think of something creative', she said, smiling as she headed off towards the bathroom to take a shower.

No one knew the extraordinary lengths to which he had gone to protect his true identity; now his veiled origins reverberated into the present. He had been betrayed by so many, had nearly lost everything because of it. Someone had to pay. Eventually, everyone would pay.

Picking up his mobile phone from the coffee table, he scrolled down to a name marked X, pressing Call, intentionally letting it ring twice then immediately hanging up. Moments later, his phone chimed. He switched it on to loudspeaker mode then he answered.

'Salam Alaikum', Hafiz said in his mother tongue.

An Arabic voice answered 'Alaikum Salam'.

'Ahlan sadiqi'. – 'Hello, my friend'.

'Qad Kan Waqt tawil ya 'akhi'.– 'It's been a long time, Brother'.

'Nem ya 'akhi, Alan 'aeud'. – 'Yes, Brother, now I'm back'.

'Mahma kunt bihajat, fasawf nakhdumuk'.– 'Whatever you need, we will serve you'.

'Shokran Habibi'. – 'Thank you, dear one'.

'Allahu Akbar'. – 'God is great'.

'Allahu Akbar. Rahimaka Allah'.– 'God is great. Bless you', he said, ending the call, sighing in relief, instantly feeling a great burden had been lifted from off his shoulders as he walked off towards the kitchen to get a glass of water.

Marina returned back to the living room feeling refreshed and rejuvenated. Then out of the corner of her eye, she noticed a small, yellow cylindrical transparent container under the cabinet. She reached down for it: it was a medical prescription bottle. Picking it up, she sat on the couch to inspect it. The doctor's label had *Adriamycin 100mg* printed on it.

Perplexed, Marina pulled her iPhone from her handbag and googled the name of the medication. She was a pale beauty – but she went paler still as she read the results and felt sick, really sick. Cancer was what these drugs treated. She instinctively clamped her hand over her mouth. 'Dear God, why didn't he tell me?' she whispered, staring into space as she let the words out. That explains so much: *Cancer. No wonder he was on a journey of self-destruction leading up to this,* she thought.

She was aware of his presence, as always, before she saw him. She turned her head to see him stood in the doorway, desolate and practically a ghost, all for the love of art. Hafiz seemed to sense her eyes on him and he looked down at her, his expression tentative and wary.

'So what happens now?' she asked.

Hafiz folded his arms and closed his eyes in thought for a brief moment. 'I've considered my options, something has to be done, and I will use my power to achieve this', he said calmly. That was it, right there: the moment he knew his calling. He stood motionless as his blood literally felt it was boiling. 'God has another plan for me, and he needs your help', he said.

She frowned, weighing his response, and then nodded. 'Okay'.

Like the Islamic Angel of Death, Archangel Azrael, lingering in the shadows, a subordinate to God with only the desire for revenge. Devoid of all emotions, he vowed that the punishment for betrayal was death. An unspeakable death.

FOUR

——— • ———

2010, England

Danny's paintings were conceived of in the garage at the bottom of his garden, which he made into his makeshift studio, ignoring the immense amount of junk that was in it and the sub-zero temperatures. He remembered his D-Day of creation. One might think that nothing on such a simple scale would excite an ex-military man. However, Danny sat in the studio like a pilot waiting for take-off, running through the checks of his aircraft, buzzing with nerves. He had it all: studio, heating, stereo, paints, brushes, canvas, a sketchbook full of ideas and a bag of indulgent Jelly Beans for energy. Slowly, he raised his pencil. It hovered over the canvas like a hummingbird, then ... nothing. Zilch, sod all, not even a dot.

'Bollocks', he said, with a blank frozen look on his face, staring at the canvas.

He thought painter's block was a myth. So, laugh or cry? Shaking his head in shock and disbelief, he laughed; it seemed the best thing he could do. This wasn't a myth; it was creative blindness, but how could this be? Danny wanted to create something unique, something original. He didn't want to mimic someone else's work, unlike some established artists that were raking in millions of pounds for work that looked very familiar to that of other artists. They just added their own spin on it.

In disbelief, he placed his pencil down on the shelf of his easel and walked around the garage – to take a moment, to compose himself. He stood scratching his head, staring at the canvas. He took two deep breaths and concentrated on nothing, just like an Olympic athlete before an event. A creative person's inner strength pushes and tests: it needs direction.

Finally, Danny was off, downloading the images he had envisioned in his head straight onto canvas, cutting out the sketches. Everything just flowed naturally and from his heart. As like an out-of-body experience, his hands appeared to create, stroke by stroke, intricate details that would last forever. Inspiration was at its utmost and he drove up the volume on his stereo: *Ready to Start* by Arcade Fire.

As he painted, his mind curiously wondered if artists were born knowing they would be one. Or was there an event in their lives that manipulated their path of life to become one? Danny dreamingly mused further. It has been suggested statistically that all of us, at one point or another, have produced a piece of art. Children, for example, naturally and intuitively draw and paint art; for them, it must be a form of communication and pleasure, as it becomes for the rest of us at whatever age it is we tap into it. The well-known artist Keith Haring said something similar: 'Everybody draws when they are little'. Well, Danny certainly did.

That's absolutely right, he thought. He wanted to leave a legacy, a name, an imprint, a description of what he had achieved during his short time on Earth. Why are we here if not? He would daydream that a well-known art agency in London would spot his work. They, of course, would sign him up as their next big artistic wonder straight away, leading to a highly advertised exhibition of his body of work at prestigious galleries worldwide. Danny imagined the VIP guest list featuring the who's who of the art world. His work would become an instant sell-out, the pieces shipping out with the knowledge that they would be hung on the walls of many for years to come. 'That's an original Danny Swift, don't you know?' Suddenly he snapped out of his dream to an angry neighbour thumping the door, shouting, 'Turn that fucking music down, Danny'.

It took three months of scrutinising art before his first body of work was born. *Evil Angels* was his adaptation of the seven deadly sins, with a twenty-first century twist. The intensity of the neon colours pierced through the black background, giving the impression they were alive and they wanted to touch you.

They hung around his garage walls drying, and as they did so, he inspected them in silence, the music turned down, a happy neighbour. The quiet and enforced concentration reminded him of being in a church. Danny wasn't a fervent churchgoer but when he had been dragged into the typified building of prayer, the silence that surrounded him gave him time to reflect, contemplate, observe and appreciate the surroundings. It was the same when he entered an art gallery, and now it's the same in his garage.

The serenity of the situation led him on to marketing these seven original pieces of art. A new artist needs a lot of exposure so he was drawing to make limited edition prints, being multiple prints struck from one plate at the same time. Quick research showed Danny that modern artists mostly produce these, and he saw an avenue of profitability. He imagined his editions stamped and signed by himself in pencil, number '3/25', for instance, and his *evil Angels* practically grinned at him.

Danny read about a debate that pops up often, with many answers, centred on the argument that art cannot be defined. Art is often considered the process or product of deliberately arranging elements in a way that appeals to the senses or emotions. It encompasses a diverse range of human creative activities. The meaning of art is explored in a branch of philosophy known as aesthetics.

From aesthetics to anaesthetics, Danny gives you *Primus Circles*, by renowned artist Joseph Legend 'Circle' paintings and twenty-five years of their dominant effect in the commodity of art. Each painting named after pharmaceutical chemicals and medicines and the lengthily named drugs they represent, which one can't pronounce and are irrelevant as the paintings are just coloured circles. Looking at one of these editions, you could wonder: what is the point, what is the meaning and what was going on in the artist's head at creation? What feelings are supposed to be invoked? Surely there should be more emotions provoked by looking at spots, but that's the beauty of these paintings.

A picture is worth a thousand words is an English idiom. It refers to the notion that a complex idea can be conveyed with just a single still image, or that an image of a subject conveys its meaning or essence more effectively than a description does. It is possible that art is not a thing – instead, it's a communication.

Danny emailed hundreds of galleries and steeled himself for rejection. Some gave good feedback whilst others, as expected, gave him the Dear John brush-off. Apparently, he had to match existing portfolios of works and have studied at the prestigious Central Saint Martins to be considered. He chose a professional portfolio of contacts to network, and it didn't take him long for one big name to connect with him that distinguished the art snobbery to allow him to become well connected.

Then out of the blue, Danny received a very elegantly written email via his website:

Dear Danny,

Thank you so much for the connection, it is much appreciated.

I had a look at your work, which was very pleasing on the eye, and may I say it has potential.

Why not be less expressional? There needs to be a conceptual drive to your work, which will give artistic value to the viewer and give them more of a reason to use their imagination, which in turn will provoke a more interesting emotion inside.

Try this to master your trade as an art practitioner.

Best wishes,

Hafiz

P.S. I can see in your art you have experienced some of life's troubles, which I can relate to.

Danny's ego took a hit, but having read his professional biography, he decided he could say what he wanted; he was an art adviser, critic and an agent for both established and emerging artists. Danny immediately emailed him back with the right amount of grovelling to thank him. Within seconds, he had received a reply; this time he was personal, revealing how art is worth more to him than life itself.

'That will be excellent, gives me just enough time', Hafiz said in a far-out, weird way. Then – even weirder – his eyes started to well up with tears, as if in overwhelming relief. The drama continued when he tried to mask this emotion by putting on a coughing fit. 'Oh, dear me', he said, sitting down on the chair opposite Bernadette's desk.

'I'll get you some water, Hafiz'. Bernadette walked beautifully to the water machine and then back with the glass, clearly clocking Danny gawping at her every inch of the way. She smiled at him as if she knew she had pulled him to her as in a natural chemical reaction.

Hafiz took a sip of water, still clearing his throat, and then reached into his blazer pocket for his phone. He wrote a fevered text, looked pleased, relieved and smug all at the same time as he pressed Send.

Bernadette stepped towards Danny in a shepherding manner. 'Hafiz, I'm going to show Danny around the gallery, give you a chance to compose yourself'. Hafiz waved them on, still acting that tickle in his throat, concentrating on his phone. 'Shall we?' she said. She gestured with her arm in front of him to indicate the way and he followed.

Slowly walking around the gallery in a little bubble of their own, Bernadette let him in on the new up-and-coming events happening in London whilst they both dropped in personal questions about each other as though they were both occupied in an arty speed-dating experience, using the wondrous gallery as an excuse to vet each other. He was mesmerised by everything about her, from her narrative descriptions of the artworks to her personal favourites; her passion and enthusiasm were magnetic, especially when combined with her sex appeal.

'This is very bold and bright', Danny said, looking at a Carmen Herrera painting, which was code for *Bloody hell, she uses two bold colours, red and orange, and charges how much?* Bernadette stood elegantly beside him, choosing to ignore his impressions of a seven-year-old; however, she continued with her visual analysis of the work. Danny should have been listening to every word; instead, he was catching a sneaky sniff of her perfume.

She spoke animatedly. 'The core to Carmen Herrera's paintings is a drive for formal simplicity with a striking sense of colour. She uses the simplest of pictorial resolutions, a master of straight lines and contrasting chromatic planes. She creates symmetry, asymmetry and an infinite variety of movement, rhythm and spatial tension across the canvas with the most unobtrusive application of paint', Bernadette enthused.

She caught him looking at her adoringly as opposed to the painting, but with quick military precision, he glanced back at Carmen's creation, nodding.

'I couldn't agree with you more', Danny said, showing his appreciation. She smiled alluringly, holding her pen to her mouth and nibbling the top, trying to suss him out.

In the centre of the room was a large pile of blocks of wood; the display was at least fifteen feet high. 'Interesting', he said, staring up.

'Isn't it?' she replied. 'It's divine'. She smiled, looking at the stem of the base, her eyes following the sculpture's lines to the very top. 'It's a Tony Cragg; he is one of the world's foremost sculptors who constantly pushes to find new relations between people and the material world. He works with stone, wood, glass, stainless steel, aluminium, cast bronze, cast iron and finds objects from plastic consumer goods to rubbish from the streets'. She walked around the whole base of the structure as Danny did.

Suddenly they accidentally bumped into each other. Tenderly, she placed her hands on Danny's muscular chest, and she slowly looks up at him and smiled. 'Oops, sorry', she said, blushing, trying to keep it professional.

'Oh, hello!' Danny replied, smirking as they part. He carries on walking around the structure and glanced back at her. *Was that a lingering look? Wishful thinking more like.*

'Charming', she replies politely, yet there is a touch of sarcasm to her tone, letting him know she could handle herself.

Next was a grey stone sculpture of a crumbling petrol pump with two hoses either side on the floor, by artist Rusty Thompson. Personally, Danny thought it looked interesting; he did appreciate the thought process behind it. Bernadette could tell he was more interested in it and began recounting a résumé of the artist.

'He lives and works in San Francisco and was born in England. He magnifies areas of political tension in the public realm through a wide-ranging body of work', she said, as Danny caught her looking at him this time whilst he was circling the sculpture with her, the two of them prowling around it like a lion and lioness looking for somewhere cool to lie down. She continued enthusiastically: 'He identifies the hairline fractures in societal systems-nationhood, environmentalism, state of war and resistance – all through performance, using sculpture, sound, video and photography. He is a meticulous researcher with an understanding of materials, which is central to his practice. He homes in on their symbolic dimensions, tracing the many marks of history'. As she reached her conclusion, she placed her hands on her hips, still confidently admiring the sculpture. Danny was admiring her beauty and slender figure.

'Shall we?' she instructed as she walked away from the sculptures towards a collection of paintings at the far end of the studio. Danny followed. She continued: 'Okay, this work is by Stanley Whitney', pointing at a multi-coloured painting on the wall.

'Oh, nice', Danny said with a confused look on his face. He was of course duty-bound to say something humorous – he couldn't kick the habit – but the look on her face stopped him in his tracks.

'He has been exploring the formal possibilities of colour within ever-shifting grids of multi-hued blocks and all over fields of gestural marks and passages since the mid-1970s', she explained, admiring the work. 'The cumulative power of Whitney's multi-coloured palette is not only one of masterly pictorial balance, giving a sense of continuum with other works in this ongoing series, but also that of fizzing, formal sensations caused by internal conflicts and resolutions within each painting'. She mentions that she owns one of his works herself. Strike to Bernadette: which was her code to let Danny know to keep his remarks to himself.

Since when did people talk about a painting like wine tasting? Danny thought to himself, but he merely said, 'It's simple, and I actually like what I see'.

'Mmm, me too', she replied, quickly glancing over at Danny.

Bernadette disappeared inside a small room just off the main gallery space and he followed. The room was dark, initially, with a white wall at the far end. Bernadette picked up a remote control from a small table and pressed 'play'. Seconds later, a TV projector beamed film footage onto the white wall in front of them. 'Oh, *Dirty Dancing*, my favourite', Danny said, standing by her side. She rolled her eyes, ignoring his humour, struggling not to laugh. Casually, Danny looked down at her

– just as she looked up. They both caught each other's secret smile. As he watched her lips curve in amusement, he thought of how they would taste if he kissed them.

Bernadette seemingly hadn't noticed as she went on: 'Jimmy Bond is visually rich, intellectually complex, and his works in photography, film, theatre and multi-screen installation examine the slippage between time and the act of image creation. Characterised by a laconic humour, Bondy's projects examine the ambiguities of language and what is gained or lost in the translation from text to image'. They stood in silence, staring at the screen. Moments later, she placed the remote back on the table and headed out to the main gallery again. Danny followed.

'So, Danny, are you impressed with what you have seen so far?' she asked as they both walked towards where Hafiz was sat drinking coffee, still on his phone.

'Of course I'm impressed, thank you. In fact, I'm speechless', he said with a serious look on his face, which she was foolish to trust for he added: 'I've enjoyed the art, too'. She looked away shyly, her cheeks flushing as she bit her lovely lip. *She'll just have to nibble it herself until I get a chance to*, he imagined.

'Hafiz, are you okay up here by yourself?' she asked, breaking the moment between themselves on purpose – yet with a grin on her face that suggested she did appreciate the flirt even as she deliberately avoided eye contact with Danny. Hafiz didn't really appear to be paying attention; he was taking photographs of some of the paintings on display with his iPhone and only stopped when he heard them speaking right beside him.

'Oh yes, I'm fine now, thanks'. Hafiz finished off the dregs of his coffee.

'So, I assume you'll be coming along to the Jeff Koons exhibition on Friday night?' she asked Danny, in a way that didn't permit a no. She looked at him intently.

'I do believe I will be. I wouldn't miss it for the world now', Danny said, smiling.

'Good', she replied, staring at him, studying.

On the way to the Groucho Club after leaving the Serpentine Gallery, Danny asked Hafiz about Bernadette and his involvement with her. Trying to be subtle, but Hafiz sussed Danny out straight away. 'Ah, you are interested in her, my friend?' He grinned knowingly.

'Hafiz, I'm surrounded by beautiful art; one more piece isn't so hard to take in, is it?' Danny replied, laughing. Danny was in awe of Bernadette professionally as well as personally. Hafiz told him she held an MA in the History of Art from the Courtauld Institute of Art; he could see he was impressed. Apparently, she began her career by building and curating one of the most eminent collections in the USA, and now she worked with top-notch contemporary galleries, writing for leading magazines and catalogues on art. She was an advisor to many private collectors. *Wow*, Danny thought, fascinated.

'She is very qualified, my friend. What do you expect with a double-barrelled name?' he said, smug in his revelations. He informed Danny she had proven repeatedly that she had the knack for identifying trends ahead of the curve, which was something he obviously found an advantage for his business ventures.

They continued to walk towards the Groucho Club. 'She has lectured and given public talks at the Royal Academy and the Royal College of Art, to name a few, and was also programme curator at the Lisson Gallery in London, where she worked closely with gallery artists'. Hafiz could see he was impressed.

Danny couldn't wait to see her again, infatuated. He then thought back to the information Bernadette gave Hafiz earlier and asked Hafiz if he was a fan of Legend's work. He thought he must be, given his fevered reaction to the earlier news, yet he practically spat at him.

'I hate his work, to be honest', he said bluntly. 'It used to mean something to me, but now it's a total contradiction of the contemporary'.

'Oh, right… okay', Danny replied, confused, a contradiction to his reaction just at the gallery.

'So how do you price art?' Danny asked inquisitively, directing the conversation on to the monetary value.

'It's like anything, Danny; it's all about being in the right circles, good or bad circles', he added, shaking his head, amused. 'The most influential art critics and galleries can raise any piece of art on a pedestal and notarise the artist to celebrity status overnight, which in turn pushes the price of their works to new heights'.

'What? As though art is worth more than money itself?'

'Yes!'

'So, you can have a masterpiece or a scribble and it is still worth a shitload of money, just as long as you have the right people behind you', Danny added, curiously.

'Basically, yes', he laughed. 'Believe me, when you hear, "Oh, I own a Rothko painting," to the normal eye, it's just a painting on canvas which is 6ft by 4ft, in yellow with a blue line across the middle, with non-art intellects asking was it painted by an adult?' He laughed out loud. 'And it's worth millions of pounds', he added, still chuckling.

'It's very interesting. So, you're saying art is worth more than money?'

'Yes, take it a stage further, Danny; big fat gypsy corporate companies worth billions around the globe employ expert art advisors who can see into the future'.

'Like you?'

'Yes, like me', he replied, smugly grinning. 'We would purchase art on behalf of the company as a business acquisition; then within those circles, more select people get involved and are advised to purchase the next big thing in art, which is very lucrative'.

'I can imagine, mate', Danny said, surprised.

Hafiz continued to lecture Danny like an obsessed professor as they walked along the busy street. 'If the value of art is determined and defined by the economy, in the event of a market collapse, should the value of the art also decrease? How would that stand up indeed?'

Danny shrugged, with a blank look on his face, trying to absorb all this information.

'It makes you think, doesn't it?' Impressively, he continued… 'If the market value becomes the go-between of what is valuable within art and in the context of art as a commodity, art must first be understood within its own mutable environment'.

'That's fascinating!'

'Yes, I know, right; and remember, value judgements within art are influenced by informalities within the art market'.

'Such as what?'

'Such as idle chit-chat between critics and galleries, secret agreements and many brown paper envelopes exchanging hands. Then combine all this with a special ratings system of who's hot and who's not, among other attempts to measure value'. Danny listened, fascinated. Questioning this secret language to see if it was irrelevant or undecipherable.

It surely got Danny thinking that it could be an appropriate argument that artistic independence occurs as a form of privilege and elitism. So, why is the value of art measured by its conception? Is it to distinguish the advantage of one work compared to another with a secret art language used by a select group within the creative worlds? The monetary value becomes a default to the assumed value of art and a common denominator upon which one assigns the varied measures of worth. How can art then maintain its worth in an increasingly globalised world where money is the most obvious and most assumed form of treasured measurement? Can art have a price that has materialised by some sort of mathematical formula? On the other hand, manipulated by the art world's elite?

'Oh and before I forget, remember the art-speak, Danny'.

'What the...? Art-speak?' he replied with a puzzled look on his face.

'Art-speak is a descriptive language of the contemporary, but seems as opaque as spilled alphabet spaghetti', he said, chuckling to himself.

'Oh, right'. Danny was even more confused.

'In layman's terms, it's when artists and critics talk a load of shit to justify the price of the artwork, Danny'. Releasing an uncontrollable belly laugh.

After catching his breath, Hafiz oddly looked up to the clouds, smiling, as if he was thanking God for something.

Danny also looked up at the clouds above: *I wonder if it's going to piss down this afternoon.*

SIX

——— • ———

Only the finest talent across the genres of music, fashion, art and culture came together to the Jeff Koons art experience, celebrating his new series of paintings and sculptures at the prestigious Lisson Gallery in London – and Danny was on the VIP guest list. The atmosphere was chic, classy and had an air of expectation.

Even more impressively, he was wearing a black Tom Ford three-piece suit and he looked the part, holding a glass of Bollinger in one hand and an exhibition programme in the other.

Hafiz was still acting strangely, still not on this planet. Danny had no idea why. He meant, this was his lifeline, art. He was in the zone, in the place, in the dream, so why was he so very distant, as if he had some serious shit to worry about? He wandered off towards a group of people standing by the main entrance. So Danny started to roam around the gallery on his own, weaving in and out of the other guests, who were all chatting – all arty – and highly animated. Admiring all the paintings and sculptures as he slowly wandered. He was prompted to stand next to a large, eight-foot, brightly coloured purple reflective metallic bunny that had been disguised to resemble an inflatable balloon but was actually made from stainless steel. *Fascinating*, he thought, wondering idly how much that would go for.

Danny looked through the gaps of the sculpture in front of him, noticing Bernadette standing on the other side, speaking to two guests who were also interested in the purple furry friend. As soon as he saw her, there it was again: this feeling of a chemical charge. It was a heady combination of sex, attraction, lust, compatibility, easiness and confidence that he hadn't felt for a very long time.

Of course, he was a right dollop and stared at her because he just had to. She noticed him and sent him a lingering look, followed by a starry gaze. He nodded and smiled in recognition, raising his glass of champagne. She smiled back and to his delight excused herself from the couple she was talking to. As she walked over, she was careful to acknowledge everyone in her two-metre bubble whilst – in his humble opinion – shagging the hell out of the walk she put on, her hips swaying this way and that.

'Danny, hi! So glad you could make it', Bernadette says.

As she kissed him on the side of his face, he gently placed his hands on her waist, feeling her silky dress that deliciously clung to her like a second skin. 'Told you I wouldn't miss it, and you are here, too: job lot, I'd say', he says, appreciating her beauty. 'May I say you look beautiful', he added, staring deep into her eyes.

'Thank you Danny; you scrub up well yourself', she replied, as they continued to look at each other for an awkward moment, neither of them quite sure what to say...

Danny turned towards a painting that was hanging on the wall beside them. 'Interesting, what do you think?' he asked, breaking the moment.

'This is one of my favourites', she replied, as her eyes mapped the canvas.

'Champagne?' the waitress asked, as she held out her silver tray, walking past.

'Thank you, cheers', they both said, both taking a glass and capturing each other's gaze.

'I've already had a little too much champagne, to be honest', she said, feeling a little tipsy.

'Work hard, play hard', Danny replied, knowing her lips could unleash unlimited desires with the slightest of manipulations.

'Exactly'. As she raises her glass.

'Well – this is called *Antiquity 2*, she continued knowingly, nodding towards it.

'It's very provocative', Danny said, pointing at the canvas. 'Lucky monkey', he added, sending a quick wink, chuckling to himself.

She smiled, rolling her eyes. 'His works of art appear to be full of vital energy but are stagnant and still nonetheless. So, there is a mystery as to how colourful marks on a page can be so richly evocative of life', she added, taking another sip of champagne.

'I couldn't agree more', he says, mesmerised by her smile that's appreciating the painting.

'The show is fantastic. He's like some sort of superstar'.

'That's true, Danny; some artists are superstars in their own right. The notion of celebrity status is a recurring concept within art markets; celebrity artists such as Koons are notable examples of brands within the art marketplace', she said, playing with one of her earrings.

'So sometimes it's who knows who, like many other industries?'

'Very much so, I'd say', she added, whilst looking up towards Danny, placing her hand on his shoulder, pulling him down towards her to whisper in his ear. 'I'm glad I know you now'.

A smile spread across his handsome face as he gently places his hand on the arch of her back. She started to blush as he looked intently at her, pausing her train of thought. 'Erm, as I was saying, brand names are now superstars within their circles of life, and of course mixing with other celebrities from other industries – the so-called "It people" – can influence others yet further, because money and desirability strengthen their product'.

'It gets you thinking about how lucrative and manipulative the art market is globally', he added, agreeing.

'Very true, but don't you just love it?' she says enthusiastically.

'I certainly do. So you're saying art critics compare nicely to estate agents?'

'Yes, more or less; you do have a way with words, Danny', she said, chuckling to herself, displaying a more tactile side towards him. 'Remember, you have to consider the coefficients of artists, comparing them against the art historical canon and their contemporaries, levitating the crown onto the next celebrity artist, who becomes the next affluent cultural producer'.

'Sounds about right then, looking around here at Koons' work', he said, imagining the price tags on each of these pieces.

'The price is what you pay, value is what you get, which can predict and determine who will be stars and who will fade from the limelight and be finished'.

'So how much would you pay for this purple rabbit?' he asked, out of curiosity.

'For this piece now? Offers around 17 million pounds, and already they have two offers on the table', she replied, casually tucking her hair behind her ear, seductively tilting her head, exposing her sensuous neck area.

'Wow! That's amazing. Who would have such an item in their home?' The champagne gave an exhilarating sense of freedom and tactile sensations that were produced between them.

'The sort of collectors I deal with, who own such pieces like this, have the space inside or outside, but I do know of a Russian collector who has one in her bedroom of this size', she added, smirking.

'Wow! It would look a bit out of place in my bedroom', he said jokingly, trying to concentrate on the metallic sculpture. Staring deep into her eyes as though she knows his sexual psychology.

'Erm, I'd love to see that', she said suggestively, as another awkward pause interrupted them. They both turn to admire the large purple metallic sculpture in front of them.

'Blimey, one of those in her bedroom?' Danny said, shaking his head in disbelief, then finished off his champagne in one.

Again, Bernadette leaned in close to him. 'I have one in my bedroom, too, next to my bed', she said, sending a wink. Placing her hand on his arm in hysterics.

Danny could barely speak for laughing, shaking his head, he couldn't believe his ears. 'I thought you were posh…?' he slowly said, catching his breath.

'On the contrary – I am, darling', she replied, biting her lip, as her oxytocin mixed with alcohol made her let loose her inhibitions. Some of the other guests looked over, slightly vexed at their antics.

'Do you fancy another drink?' she asked, her face reddening further from her comment, quickly exchanging two empty glasses with the passing waitress.

'Have you seen Hafiz this evening?' she asked, totally changing the conversation, looking around the room whilst sipping her champagne.

'Yes, he is here somewhere', Danny replied, also looking around.

'He just loves these events, doesn't he?' she said easily. 'People flocking around him like sheep in a field – ' she looks at Danny ' – of whom he's not too sure'. She smiled. Danny was now thinking clever Bernadette was lost for words. Could he dare to hope that his presence was having the same effect on her as hers was on him? He looked at her beauty and appreciated her intellect and her sense of humour. Somehow, in a way he couldn't understand, she felt familiar to him, like he was coming home.

'His knowledge on art and visual analysis is amazing. He's such an interesting person to know'.

Danny raised his voice a bit as more people gathered around them.

'He was so pleased to know about the up-and-coming Joseph Legend exhibition', she said, delighted. She looked genuinely happy, but Danny looked confused.

'Funny thing, that. When I asked Hafiz if he liked Legend's work, he blatantly said no. Which I found confusing', Danny said, shrugging his shoulders.

'Oh, that's strange. He sent me several emails and texts beforehand, constantly asking if I had sent the exhibition details, as if it was a matter of emergency'. She waited for Danny's reply.

'Even with my limited knowledge of him, I can see he isn't a patient man. Maybe he has an art deal in the pipeline, or some business requiring a knock-on effect from Legend's showing?' Danny mused, sipping his champagne.

Danny's answer seemed to satisfy Bernadette's curiosity and the conversation flowed on to other matters. They both spent all evening walking around the gallery, talking as if they were the only ones there, until finally it was time to go.

Being a true gent, he offered to walk Bernadette to her apartment in Hyde Park. He was glad she accepted and didn't want to catch a cab. The walk was rather romantic; a tranquil cold night with a clear sky and street lights and the corny, compulsory offer of his suit jacket around her shoulders to keep her warm.

'Well, this is me'. She stopped at the grand entrance steps of a typical Hyde Park Georgian property and removed his jacket.'Thank you, Danny. I really enjoyed this evening and being with you'. She shivered a bit as a light breeze passed by momentarily, handing back his jacket, looking directly into his eyes.

'Thank you for a great evening. I enjoyed being with you also, it was fun', he replied, rather formally. Then there was nothing else left to say or do. They paused, gazing into each other's eyes, nervously. Danny tenderly moved her hair from out of her face, then they both leaned in close and kissed each other passionately, stopping only to get some air – yet they held hands to keep the contact.'I'll see you tomorrow?' he said confidently as they finally drew apart. Then, thinking perhaps that was a bit keen, he reeled it back in with a 'Maybe?'

Result: she kissed him again. Eventually, she turned to walk towards her apartment, turning the key and opening the door whilst blowing him a kiss goodnight, smiling.

'Get inside or you will catch a cold!' he chided, waving and blowing her a kiss back, making sure she was inside and safe before he turned and walked away.

Walking back towards the city centre and his hotel, he checked his watch for the time: 02:34 hours.'Bloody hell, she could have invited me in for a nightcap, just my luck', he muttered. He hadn't realised it was so late. Danny felt slightly dented at the lost opportunity but cheered himself up by remembering the evening. As he walked past the vehicles parked alongside the road, he caught sight of the reflection of himself smiling smugly.

He turned away from the cars and entered the park. He'd only walked about 800 metres along the main pathway of Hyde Park towards Mayfair when a guy walked past him, dressed in dark clothing. Casting a furtive glance in his direction. Instantly, Danny was cautious; gut feeling – must be the training, he thought idly as he glanced at him, clocking.

Ten paces on and he still felt niggled. Glancing back to look at the man again, but he had disappeared, making him stop to scan, wondering where he went. He looked back towards the road, trying to sight him; assuming he had crossed over. But he wasn't there – but a black Ford Transit van was. He felt uneasy.

A split-second later, it turned out he was right to be so as the side door suddenly slid open and two large figures wearing balaclavas jumped out. Fuck! Instinctively, he tried to get away, but a larger figure from behind overpowered him, preventing him from escaping. Those heavy lumps were fast, and before he could stop them, a dark hessian bag was dropped over his head. Struggling made it worse as they well and truly had a hard hold of him. Then came the bit he was dreading: Whack! On the back of his neck, an instant of excruciating pain, then, a benevolent darkness.

SEVEN

——— • ———

Shock and the coldness of the room made Danny shiver in terror. The realisation of captivity set in. Palpitations in his chest as his senses detected that his hands were bound tight behind his back and that he was sitting on a chair with his ankles tied. *Could it get any more text book?* he thought, apprehensively.

His head hurt like hell. *Fuck, my neck is killing me… but I'm alive,* he thought to himself; albeit with the sack still over his head. He allowed his eyes to adjust and eventually, without moving his head too much, he looked through his hessian mask to see silhouettes in front of him. *What the fuck and who the fuck?* he thought, dazed and confused. *Well, we can't sit here all day – or all night, or whenever the fuck it is.* Deliberately lifting his head, silently letting his captors know he was awake and ready to listen. He knew how this worked. He knew this of old.

A loud screech: from a metal chair being dragged along the floor, heading towards him. It echoed in the room. He sensed a large figure walking over then; Danny was sure someone was sitting in front of him. The sound of a door suddenly closing to his left, an incident which sparked the muted mumbling of people in the background. Trying to absorb all this information, detecting anything he could about his surroundings and channelling the data away for a later time when he could try to make his escape.

The figure reached over, pulling the sack off his head. He squinted, screwing up his face against the sudden influx of light, trying to focus on the room as he quickly looked around: a green door to his left next to a large two-way mirrored window; a black metal desk sat in front of them. He was sure it was an interrogation room – a type of room he knew only too well; an occupational hazard in his former life, he could say. The guy opposite him was tall and stocky, in his mid-fifties. He had a pale forgettable face, behind his black Joe-90 spectacles, with greying brown hair and was wearing a dark-grey suit and white shirt; his tie hung loosely around his neck. He had an air of self-reliance to him. In his hands, he held a brown A4 folder. That was important. Danny was certain this wasn't a terrorist situation or even some scum from the criminal underworld. This man was a spook.

For a brief moment, he stared at him in silence. *There is something chilling in his stillness*, Danny thought.

'Danny Swift?' He spoke with a stern British accent; he had penetrating eyes and a blunt demeanour.

'If I'm not, that would be you totally fucked, wouldn't it?' he replied sarcastically, yet he didn't soften it by joking. He didn't feel like smiling.

'I'll be known as Thom', he said sharply. Looking at him, expressionless.

'Thom? Well, Thom, if that really is your name, who the fuck are you and why am I here? And why all this shit?' He tried to nod at his general condition. 'Couldn't you have just asked me?' As the proverbial saying goes, if looks could kill... Danny shot one hell of a look at Thom.

Despite his death stare, he clearly didn't have fears for his safety, as he opened the folder that was on the table and robotically showed him a series of A4 photographs that had obviously been taken covertly in and around the city. Danny scanned through them, noticing some of them were of him, Bernadette and Hafiz; others were of people he had met over the past couple of months.

'Nice', Danny said sarcastically, 'but if you wanted me to exhibit them for you, again, you just had to ask'. Danny was really pissed off and cut to the chase. 'What is this really all about?'

'Your artist friend, Hafiz de Mercurio, a.k.a. Hafiz Sabah Al Seraih, is an Islamic extremist, as is his uncle, who is one of the founding and spiritual leaders of the Taliban, Mullah Mohammed Omar'.

'For Chrissake', Danny interjected, shaking his head in shock and disgust.

Thom continued, 'When his parents were killed, he was shipped off to stay with his uncle in the United Arab Emirates to be westernised, all in preparation to blend into any community'.

'You're telling me Hafiz himself is a sleeper?' he was saying, incredulously.

'Yes, and highly ranked within the Taliban. He's also associated with a deadly assassin – whom we believe is this woman'. He lifted up a photograph of a very beautiful woman. 'Do you know her?' He looked at Danny levelly.

'Nope, I've not seen her before, but again, what's all this about?' Danny's patience was running thin. 'Why me? You could have easily put a more in-depth surveillance team on him – or her, for that matter'.

Thom sat back in his chair. 'True, we could, but if he suspects anything, it will ruin years of vital intelligence gathering, plus you're already in with him and we know all about you'. He paused, as though the next line was difficult for him to say aloud. 'We would like your help'.

Danny took a deep breath and exhaled in the manner of a stroppy teenager. Coded, that meant: *Are you for fucking real?* He shook his head, his thoughts grim and disappointed.

'Listen, we are thin on the ground here, Danny, and with the endless bureaucracy, Whitehall prioritise what is a target and what's not; this insidious but brilliant tactic of using sleepers stretches every government agency to its limits'. He frowned in annoyance, frustrated, seemingly taking the weight of this personally.

There goes my first chance of starting a new art career, he thought. He was done with that shit; he wanted a new life. Shutting his eyes indignantly.

Danny knew that sleeper cells were professionally trained and getting better, individuals dedicated to their cause, knowing they can easily blend into society without raising any suspicions whatsoever. The true motivation of such sleeper agents is completely unknown to every one of their nearest and dearest – to their friends, neighbours and work colleagues; even, at times, to their parents, husbands and wives.

'Such a level of devotion for an ideology, I'd say they were more mentally deranged', Danny added, tilting his head back, sighing.

Thom blinked rapidly behind his glasses. He continued: 'When the sleeper is activated, they may receive a communication of some definition, known only to him or her, that will give specific orders'.

'Okay, I will help. What do you want me to do?' he said reluctantly, sighing.

Thom leaned in towards the desk. 'Hafiz is of Middle Eastern origin and we have intelligence from our friends at CIA HQ in Langley, Virginia, that he is a pivotal part of a terrorist cell operating here in Europe. Our intelligence dates back well over two decades, and we believe he is preparing to coordinate a sophisticated attack here on UK soil very soon'.

'I've not seen anything suspicious or anything out of the ordinary; nothing even remotely religious has been connected to him since I've known him', he said bluntly, staring at Thom, clearly indicating he'd had enough. Thom looked up to the CCTV camera located in the top corner of the room behind him, giving a nod; a moment later, the door opened to his left. Yet it wasn't an exit route for him: another guy now entered the room. He walked behind Danny and to his relief cut the plastic electric ties off from around his wrists and ankles. He rubbed each of his wrists in turn as the blood circulated quickly through his veins again.

Thom continued to talk as the guy walked over towards the door, informing him that Hafiz was a master of disappearance. His mother and father had been killed by a coalition air-strike in Yemen back in the early eighties, leaving Hafiz to live with relatives in Dubai. 'Intelligence tells us he has been associated with some high-value targets around the world. These individuals are connected and they fund terrorist organisations'.

'He told me his parents were killed in a skiing accident', Danny said, confused. Look, there's no way what you're telling me can be true. He's a high-profile art dealer and critic, so of course he will be rubbing shoulders with a lot of people'.

'Coincidence? I thought so. Until a sophisticated assassination occurred in an exclusive part of London about eight months ago – and two of the victims were associated with Hafiz. It was just too calculated and professional a hit, with too many connections to him'.

Danny fired back some tangible questions to get more of a better picture. 'Did forensics come back with anything? Any DNA from the killer? Anything?'

'No DNA.' Sending a perfunctory nod.

'Were any spent bullet casings found at the scene?' Intrigued.

'We found ten. That gave us the ejection analysis, for the position of the killer. But that really means nothing when you still have five dead bodies.'

'What about ballistics?'

'Untraceable, maybe Russian, maybe from the Balkans even; weapons and ammunition are so widely available these days, you can buy them anywhere', he added. Danny could see his professional curiosity piqued.

'Any phone traffic?' he added.

'The geeks at GCHQ triangulated a signal at the time of the murders, but nothing of significance.' He just shrugged his shoulders, disappointed.

'Not much to go on then', Danny said incredulously.

Thom took out a transparent evidence bag and handed it over to Danny. 'What do you make of this?' he asked intriguingly.

Inside the bag was a segment of white paper, four by three inches wide, with a red near-circle of ink with frayed edges. Those edges... They made the paper seem like the remains of an image that had been intentionally destroyed. 'This was found at the scene of the crime after the cleaner discovered the bodies', Thom said, looking at Danny in the hope of an answer. Danny examined the paper carefully.

'Must be a segment of some sort of print, a copy of an original painting known as an edition of something, but I can't make out what it could be.' He got nothing but a puzzled look from Thom this time, intrigued.

'Forensics said there was one other painting destroyed with acid, but no others were touched, which we find confusing as one of the victims owned over four million pounds' worth of art, which was all hanging in the apartment that took the hit. The artworks weren't even stolen', Thom said, sitting back again, coming to his conclusion. 'I need you to see what intel you can find, anything that connects Hafiz to terrorism.'

Do ya think? he thought, apprehensive.

'Hold on, Thom, I'm not feeling too easy with all that you have told me. I know only too well what sort of evil extremists can do. And you want me to get directly involved?'

'We will have your back, Danny, when it's needed', Thom said, somewhat reassuringly.

'My back? I'm kind of fond of the rest of me, too, you know'. He made sure he sounded precarious. He rationalised the situation. *What could possibly go wrong?* he thought. 'I'll see what I can do'.

'Listen, Danny, remember you have that advantage. People from your former life are always good at dealing with being given half the picture', he said, with no pun intended.

'That's what worries me. How will I contact you?' An obvious point, he thinks.

'I've put my direct number into your phone'. Thom got up to move.

'Well, I hope you've done the same on your phone with my number'. Danny stared at Thom significantly. 'Because if this shit happens again', he gestured around the room, 'I won't be such a fucking gentleman, believe me'. He moved towards the door with the guy standing beside it. Danny shot him a sideways glance as he left the room.

Danny was dropped off at his hotel at 07:00 hours with a maelstrom of thoughts crowding his aching head. Exhausted and cranky. He'd been up for over twenty-four hours, he thought to himself, as he looked at his bed. It was sending out signals for him to get in, but that wasn't happening. Instead, he was geared up to go for a run, so he headed towards Hyde Park to de-stress and tire himself out still further. He was running on remote control, and before he knew it, he was very close to the Serpentine Gallery. By that time, he was so exhausted and overwhelmed by the night's events he was beginning to feel nauseous. He had had a severe blow to the neck, after all; it wasn't beyond the realms of possibility he might have suffered concussion.

He stretched off his legs using the park bench, contemplating what to do, when he spotted Bernadette opening up. He glanced down at his sweaty gym gear. He decided his manky state was not what someone so immaculate needed to see first thing in the morning.

He'd already turned back towards his hotel when he distinctly heard his name being called. Momentarily, he looked around. It was Bernadette: she was standing in the gallery doorway, waving at him. So much for making a good impression… He stopped, turned around and walked over to her, pleased to see her.

'Good morning!' she said, smiling at him. Then the smile faded as he got closer.

'Morning, you're looking good', he replied, admiring her very sleek outfit.

'Oh, thank you'. Appreciating the compliment.

'Are you okay? You don't look too good', she asked, looking concerned.

'I'm fine. I've had a better twenty-four hours, let's put it that way'. He rubbed his neck, as if he'd slept awkwardly.

'Well, I hope it wasn't all bad?' She rubbed his arm meaningfully.

'Your bit was the best bit'. Smiling at her, reassuring. 'Look, I feel terrible, so I'm going to get my head down for a while'. She could see he was struggling.

'I've got quite a day ahead of me; otherwise, I would offer to read you a bedtime story', she suggested with a wink, continuing to hold his arm as though she didn't want to let him go. 'Tell you what', she said, 'if you feel better by tonight, I'll treat you to dinner'.

'All right, deal', he conceded. With that, she let go of his arm slowly and confidently. She went about opening up the gallery whilst Danny jogged cautiously away from her, hoping he would make it to his room okay.

He did. As he shut the door behind him and the bed beckoned, the last six hours hit him suddenly. It was official: he was man down.

EIGHT

——— • ———

It was the best sleep Danny had had in a long time; nothing like a blow to the occipital ridge to sort his shit out. He looked down at his watch; it was 14:00 hours. *Time for some work*, he thought to himself as he headed towards the shower. Danny's mind had stopped racing when his head hit the pillow, but now a few flashbacks started to ruin the luxurious feel of hot water and soap as he tried to figure out what – if any – part of Hafiz suggested he was some terrorist icon. With all his years of experience, he would have thought, if there was anything to see, that he'd have seen some signs, but nothing. He knew his guard had been down as he had been so caught up with his new career, all hopeful about his dreams coming true, that he hadn't kept his wits about him. And talking about that new career, *Where the fuck was it?* he thought; it looked like he was back to square one. It was covert intelligence versus canvas all over again.

He fired up his laptop and his Google fingers ventured and searched everything Thom had briefed him up on. He read and read and researched and researched. He found an interesting article online which caught his attention because of Hafiz's peculiar behaviour regarding the same topic. *Still in its embryonic state, conceived as a single exhibition,* he read, *the Gagosian Gallery is presenting "The Complete Joseph Legend – Primus*

Circles Paintings", which were created between 1986 and 2011. The works were to be exhibited across locations in New York, Beverly Hills, London, Paris, Rome, Geneva, Athens and Hong Kong. The article said it was *a show of unprecedented scale.*

Total respect, amazing, he thought to himself, looking again at all the files he'd opened up, at all the information he had collated over the last three hours, hoping to find hidden clues or something that would just pop out at him. To make this work, Danny realised that he was going to have to get into the mind of Hafiz himself. There were so many questions, but all of them seemed critical. When was it going to happen? Where was it going to happen? Location, location, location... but which location? And what exactly was it? What was going to happen? Finally, what was Danny going to have to do about it?

Hafiz really knew his stuff and seemed genuine. However, since Danny had known him, he had been artistically liberated by what he had told him of his incredible life so far. Danny really did not think this situation of Thom's was terrorist-related. He just couldn't see it. There was no link to any radical Islamic group, nothing Arabic in his apartment, no Quran, no prayer mat, no time out for praying five times a day. The only daily fix Danny had seen him get was mucho caffeine (okay: he would choose to turn a blind eye to the cocaine residue hanging from his nostrils after a cheeky line at an after-party). There was no evidence.

Danny kept an open mind and remained sceptical that Hafiz was planning an attack for an extremist Islamic group on British soil. Perhaps that was just him thinking outside the box whilst Thom sat in it.

He continued to scan the files of research. Danny had to agree with Thom on one point: Hafiz had rubbed shoulders with some high-value terrorists from around the world who were known to all the government intelligence agencies. He could see why Thom had formulated his theory. Terrorism needs funding, and one of the perfect ways to launder money is through purchasing high-value commodities. In other words, art.

Danny continued reading; there was something rather annoying that kept popping up. It was coloured circles, spots. All he saw was fucking spots. He closed his eyes and saw spots; he opened them and saw spots. His mind was buried deep in thought, trying to think of a logical reason for this. The blow to the head? No, this wasn't physical – it was a mental puzzle. Eleven Gagosian galleries, circle paintings, spots... what was the connection?

His iPhone beeped; it was a text from Bernadette. *Dinner tonight, 19:30 hours, The Arts Club in Mayfair, don't be late.* Danny laughed to himself at her teasing manner. *Slick*, he thought as he texted her back: *See you there*, and the compulsory smiley face emoji. He only used the face; well, she didn't sign with an X either.

•

The exclusive Arts Club in Mayfair is yet another private members' club for creative sorts. It is beautifully designed throughout with a great art collection on its walls, the sort you appreciate as you absorb yourself in the ambience of fine dining. He was there at 19:25 hours. *So, where is she?* he wondered as he stood outside waiting for her, but within minutes a black cab pulled up outside and the door opened at 19:29 hours precisely. *With still a minute to spare*, he thought happily.

She looked effortlessly sophisticated and beautiful stepping out of the cab. Danny walked to meet her. 'Hello there', she said as he leaned in to kiss her on the lips gently.

'I've been waiting all day to do that', he said. Corny, but cute.

'Me too', she replied, with that perfect smile of hers.

Danny suddenly thought of the photographs Thom had shown him in that delightful holding area. Bernadette had been amongst them, also captured by the surveillance officers, and he started to wonder if Bernadette might, in some way, be involved with Hafiz's suspected terrorist activities. Surely not. He tried to convince himself, but the soldier in him couldn't eliminate her from his covert enquiries. Deciding to tread carefully and see what information he could gain, if any at all.

Once they were inside, he relaxed instantly, despite the drama of his situation. They sat facing each other in the corner, seated beneath a beautiful Albert Oehlen painting. It was a wonderful setting for such an evening of fine wine and good conversation... and securing a bit of information about Hafiz. He found himself mapping her face; somehow, she let him without a reaction.

The waiter walked over to the table to take their orders, Bernadette chose the wine. 'We will have a bottle of the 2005 Château Pétrus, please; my favourite', she said joyfully.

As each course arrived, looking like exquisite works of art, they talked about everything: their childhoods, holidays, likes and dislikes. The likes bit for Bernadette turned up a notch when he mentioned he had spent some time in the military.

'Wow', she said, toying with him. 'Do you still have your uniform?' She laughed with a suggestive wink.

'Sadly not', he replied, laughing. She was incorrigible.

Suddenly she leaned in close to him across the table.

'I bet you saw some sights whilst you were in the service?' she asked, seemingly intrigued.

'Nah, pretty boring, really; mainly administration', he said dismissively, shaking his head. Diverting to change the conversation to the here and now as the connection between them had such an elusive quality; it was difficult to define but it was there just the same. It always fascinated Danny how two people could feel this instant magnetism, like chemicals interacting, invisible to the naked eye. He didn't want to spoil the moment but needed to ask. 'How did you meet Hafiz, by the way?' As casually as he could.

'Well –' she sat back, ready for her recital – 'when I was studying for my MA, one of Hafiz's friends was in my class; she was his girlfriend at the time, I wasn't entirely sure'. Bernadette paused, reminiscing. 'She was from the Emirates, Dubai, I think, and very beautiful. It was unfair on the rest of us, really. She had lovely piercing green eyes and was called Marina... Marina Khan'.

Interesting, he thought to himself, as he connected the description to the girl in the photographs – the girl Thom couldn't identify. If Danny was right, this made Marina one very hot assassin.

'Then, one day, we got talking during a break from lectures and she introduced me to him; that's how I met Hafiz', Bernadette continued. 'She called him her Adonis and he called her his Aphrodite as they both adored the history of ancient Greece, which I found rather romantic', she acknowledged.

'Never let romance die, my grandmother once told me', he added, with a quick wink.

'Your grandmother was right. Then, sometime afterwards, I managed to secure a placement at Christie's auction house as part of my work experience, and I bumped into him again at a contemporary art sale. By then, he was notorious for his expert negotiation skills, helping others get rich at these types of affairs. In fact, I'm surprised he is not retired by now with the amount of money he should have made working in New York'.

'Why did he move back to London?' Danny asked.

'Not sure, it was a last-minute decision and he didn't want to talk about it, he told me'.

'What do you mean, he didn't want to talk about it?' Probing for more information.

'Those were his exact words, so I left it there, as it wasn't any of my business'.

'Fair enough', he replied, nodding.

She looked pleased at the idea he was now back in the UK. 'We have been sort of friends ever since, really. He has helped me with some of my projects, and I have given him some insights into up-and-coming exhibitions, which he thoroughly enjoys'.

Danny jumped in again. 'Just like the Joseph Legend one, you mean?'

'Yes, like that', she said, nodding.

'However, I do recall last year whilst I was in Berlin, I attended the Frieze exhibition, and I overheard that he had lost out on a very large art deal somewhere with several other dealers'.

'Large?'

'I don't know… But that's part and parcel of being an art dealer'.

'Yeah, true, I suppose', Danny said, finishing off his wine.

She ordered another bottle, another favourite; the waiter arrived to pour a small quantity of a Château Lafite Rothschild Pauillac 96 into a glass for her to sample. Danny was mesmerised as she picked up the glass, her eyes blazing at him unblinkingly, her red glossed lips parting slightly to take a sip of wine. Her deliberately provocative actions made him squirm; she knew she had the ability to flick a switch inside him by doing the simplest things, and fully exploited that talent. He smiled at her, recognising that they both knew there was a deep sexual pull between them. She swirled the wine in her mouth and he couldn't help but imagine her tongue tasting the wine, then her tongue kissing him, kissing more of him… His smile turned into deep thought as he battled between the urge of his alpha male to take her there and then on that very table and the desire of his soldier brain to solve the bloody puzzle of Hafiz. 'Will you excuse me?' he said as he stood up, placing his napkin on the table, feeling tipsy in his new appreciation for a good Bordeaux.

'Roger that', she said instinctively, taking another sip of wine.

As he turned away and walked towards the toilets, Danny immediately thought his ears were playing tricks on him or the alcohol had taken effect; the quip that Bernadette just said – Roger that – is slang used in military communications, meaning, Okay. He found that strangely familiar.

When he returned from the toilet, Bernadette was texting on her phone. She had a troubled look on her face. Sitting back down, she immediately placed it back inside her bag. He stared into her piercing blue eyes, not interested in eating or the wine, only in the power of the chemical reaction in front of him.

'Are you okay, Danny?' Bernadette asked, snapping him back to her. He'd been staring into space.

'Yes, sorry. I was miles away'. Shaking his head, clearing his brain, must be the wine.

'What were you thinking about?' she asked endearingly.

'The future, starting with: shall we get the bill?' He looked around, hoping to catch the attention of the waiting staff.

'Good idea', she replied, as her hand reached out to touch his. 'I'm looking forward to the future. It's going to be interesting'. She continued smiling at him.

'Me too', he replied, but he couldn't help thinking tonight's future would be even better if he could just steer away from Thom's assignment.

Back at her apartment, she turned the key in the door, and this time he managed to enter the hallway at her invitation, as opposed to just being blown a kiss on the doorstep and sent on his merry way. She placed her Alexander McQueen clutch bag and keys on the ornate side table before turning to him and grabbing both of his arms. Smiling, she pushed him back up against the wall, holding his shoulders firmly so he knew his place, and then she thrust her body hard against his, grinding herself against his crotch. In response, his mind and other more prominent parts of him thinking, *oh…*

Suddenly they were thrust together by forces almost beyond their conscious control, kissing passionately, feeling burning desire and intense pleasure as the freedom to discover each other's bodies overtook them. They were interlocked by their sense of touch as her right leg curved around his, the taste, smell and sight of each other increasing their lust. He placed both his hands on her buttocks, feeling her shiver as she pulled her dress up over her thighs, exposing slender toned legs. She pulled her lace underwear to one side and he touched her, deeply, as she moaned with pleasure.

His mind thought, in some detached, always humorous, part of himself, *a coffee would have done*, but that soon disappeared. He became powerless to resist. Pressed as he was against her sexy body, her curves sent him messages; she was becoming rampant, communicating clearly that she wanted him inside her. Danny pulled her even closer, then lifted her gently and turned her around against the wall. Anticipating his next move, she released him, undoing his belt and unzipping his trousers quickly, urgently, the sheer pleasure of his arousal reciprocated. Holding her buttocks hard he slid her upwards, pressing against her facing him. She groaned in pleasure in his ear as she held him so tightly with unadulterated desire.

•

Beep! Danny woke to the sound of a text going off on his iPhone. The incoming message prompted the device to light up; subsequently, it lit the entire bedroom. It looked elegantly decorated in the half-light of the phone, like an opulent suite at the Dorchester. Bernadette was lying beside him, fast asleep, intertwined with the soft white cotton sheets: a picture of beauty.

He leant forward to grab his iPhone, focusing on the time and the text. It was from Thom. He sighed with irritation as he read: *Meet me in one hour, Lou's Café, Knightsbridge.* It was 07:15 hours.

NINE

—— • ——

As he approached the window of the greasy spoon coffee shop, Danny could see the place was empty, apart from a silhouette of a man that sat facing towards the window in the corner at the back, next to a door which led out to the rear of the building. There was also a woman behind the counter, filling a large coffee machine with fresh beans, getting ready for the morning rush. Once inside, the invigorating aroma of the freshly brewed coffee hit him: a welcoming morning greeting. Taking a good deep sniff. *Mmm, lovely*, he thought. The smell alone was so strong it woke him up and prepared him instantly for the meeting ahead.

His eyes started to water as he came in from the cold to the warmth; nevertheless, out of the corner of that weepy blur, he noticed it was Thom sitting at the table. Nursing half a cup of black coffee, and sat with a copy of *The Times* neatly folded on the table, placed next to a half-eaten bacon butty. *Well, he's sorted*, he thought enviously as a Cockney-accented voice asked: 'Can I take your order please, luv?' She could easily have been an extra from *EastEnders*; the accent was that familiar.

'I'll have a black coffee and whatever that gentleman is having, please'. Danny nodded over towards Thom's half-filled cup. 'Morning, Thom'. He moved to take a seat opposite him.

'Morning, Danny'. As he wiped his mouth with a napkin to remove the HP brown sauce: the sole remaining evidence of the first half of his butty.

'Well, this is more civilised than the last time we met. A little less harrowing, don't you think?' Danny said, looking at him intently.

'True, but I don't take chances', he replied. Danny was sure he had his reasons for that. As he knew too well, when death is part of the deal, the safety of others is paramount. Trust is an issue in the murky world of intelligence.

'Thank you', Danny said to the waitress as she put his coffee down on the table and refilled Thom's cup. As she walked away, Thom started updating Danny on the latest intelligence gathered in the UK and the US.

'We have reason to believe Hafiz's sleeper cell is primed and ready to go, awaiting target instructions'. Thom spoke clearly and precisely as his eyes roamed the room. Danny listened carefully to what he had to say, building a picture in his mind, but the same niggling feeling about Hafiz that he'd had since this saga began overruled the intel Thom was claiming to have. Danny couldn't make sense of the theory that the art dealer was involved with an extreme Islamic group. *Is Thom telling me everything?* he wondered. Trust was an issue on both sides.

'The assassination in London, the ones that got hit, who were they?' Danny asked, intriguingly.

'Derek Clarke and Henry Matthews', Thom replied. 'They were both stock traders from the City and they also worked in New York. We think they were the two main targets. Unfortunately, two local escorts and one of the building's security team were also taken out – professionally. Whoever it was knew exactly what they were doing, to the very last detail, and had no fear in taking out anyone who stood in their way. It was definitely well planned, executed and detailed; ruthless even'. From the expression on Thom's face, it looked as if he rather respected the assassin's work. Danny saw a look, deep in his eyes, that suggested a certain familiarity, as though he himself may well have organised or carried out the same actions on foreign territory. It wasn't beyond the realms of possibility, especially with a job like his.

'What was on the CCTV footage?' he questioned.

'Nothing. It appears the assassin deleted everything before leaving the building'.

'Were there any witnesses?'

'No – nothing substantial'. Shaking his head.

'Like I said the other day, all we have is that partly destroyed piece of paper – the print or whatever it is – with the red splotch on it. Forensics also have the remains of a wooden canvas picture frame'.

'Can't you get some sort of idea of what the picture was from your knowledge of the overall collection that you said was at the apartment?' Danny questioned.

'No. These people buy art from all over the world, all the time. They sometimes use fake names or they get sold on for cash, so we have no way of knowing what the victims would have had in their personal collections at any one time'. He could see why Thom needed his help.

'Did the victims have any connections with any terrorist organisations?' Danny was trying hard to piece together a case against Hafiz, but to his mind, it was not gelling.

'Nothing on our database'. Thom shook his head. 'That's not a huge surprise. All these City traders are interested in is making huge amounts of money to secure their drugs habits, drinking copious amounts of Champagne, poncing about showing off what is in and what is not, and indulging in the compulsive extra-marital affair with their trusted PA or fill-ins from the finest escort agencies'. He grinned knowingly.

'I'm sure you're aware by now we have had Hafiz under surveillance for some time, so you will know about his nocturnal activities with drink, drugs and partying'. He finished the dregs of his coffee before he stood up to go. 'I'll be in touch', he said, nodding. Unexpectedly, he then paused, clearly clocking who was in view before he slowly pushed his neatly folded newspaper towards Danny. 'I appreciate you're not on the Queen's payroll any more, but this should cover your expenses for now'. He smirked, and with the telepathy born of them both having worked in the services, Danny knew from the look on his face that there was an envelope inside that paper.'Let me remind you of the urgency of this situation. The sleeper cells are primed and awaiting target instructions. Time is of the essence, Danny'. Thom said nothing more; he simply turned up the collar of his jacket and headed towards the door, all Cold War-style.

Danny gently flicked through the pages of the newspaper with his thumb until he reached the expected recompense for his time: a brown envelope. He glanced around the coffee shop for permission to go ahead before he cautiously removed it. Peering inside to see a neat bundle of crisp new £50 notes; there was at least twenty grand in there by his limited estimate. Sliding the envelope inside his coat pocket and tapping the folded newspaper onto the table. Though he had no reason to remain, Danny stayed put. He really needed to take a minute. Staring into nothing, with an unpleasant surreal feeling of danger lurking over him; very unsettling.

Hafiz came into his head and he scrolled through the address book on his phone. *I'll call him to see if he fancies meeting up,* he thought. The more time he spent with him, the better understanding he would have. The call went straight to voicemail.

'Hi, this is Hafiz, I'm not available at the moment. Please leave a message'. Danny didn't want to leave a message so he did the usual multiple calls thing, hoping he'd eventually pick up. Nothing. In the end, he decided he'd go and make this personal: an invite to brunch, delivered in person by his truly.

He cut through Hyde Park. It always cheered him up; this expanse of green with the city circling around it. He was soon at Hafiz's apartment block. He noticed that the blinds were closed, and the main door was slightly open.

Perhaps he is about to go out or only just got in? he thought innocently as he pushed the door open and went inside. Cautiously, he entered. He expected to see him standing there with his keys, yet there was no one in the grand lobby, disturbing silence.

Danny looked around. Hafiz's apartment door was also slightly open. He was convinced he was having 'one of those days' and simply hadn't got around to closing any doors yet. *He is probably on the phone or checking out my multiple calls,* he thought. He called out, 'Hafiz, are you in? It's Danny'.

The lack of reply made him nervously aware. Recalling his training, he checked all around before he cautiously headed inside.

He was greeted by darkness. Even though it was daytime, no natural light illuminated the hallway.

'Hafiz?'

Switching on the lights, he walked towards the windows to open the blinds. He sensed out of the corner of his eye a shadow… and turned to see Hafiz curled up on the floor, quivering.

'What the... Hafiz, are you okay?' He rushed over to him. He looked gaunt, with bloodshot eyes; in a right state and smelling like shit. 'What's happened? Are you okay?' Danny raised his voice to get his attention, but it took a while for Hafiz to recognise him. When he did, he clung onto him desperately, which made it easy for Danny to lift him up to rest him against the settee. He managed to look him over without alarming him. As he did so, he noticed he had a black eye, uncharacteristic stubble, and generally looked like hell.

'How did you get this?' Gently inspecting his black eye, assuming he had fallen, given the state of him and his general love of drugs and alcohol.

'I owed some money to some people', he whispered, barely able to compose himself to be able to talk.

'What do you mean some people? Who?' Danny asked.

'For drugs. I forgot to pay on time'. He tried to reshuffle himself. 'Like I said, I have good days and bad days. Last forty-eight hours were bad days'.

'Bloody hell, mate; thought you gave up all that shit', Danny said, reaching for a tissue so he could wipe his face and nose. 'You can call me anytime if you need to talk', he added sympathetically.

Wiping his face; removing the grime, snot and tears. 'Let's get you sorted', he said encouragingly. 'You look like shit. I'll whack on the kettle and you go and have a shower, get a shave'. He started to ease him up onto his feet.

'Okay', he replied, gradually standing up, still wobbly. Danny helped him towards the bedroom area, where he managed to stabilise himself and then headed to the en suite. Danny heard the ambient sound of the shower fire up and listened, carefully; he absent – mindedly filled the kettle and searched for mugs and coffee.

The shock of finding Hafiz wore off, and with his meeting with Thom still fresh in his mind, it suddenly struck him that this was the perfect opportunity to have a snoop around Hafiz's place for any intel connecting Hafiz with Thom's theory of terrorism. *Time is of the essence*; even though a spaced-out, beaten-up and sore man in the shower was unlikely to move at any speed, he quickly went to his study. The door was open. He quickly looked around the room; several pieces of art hung on the walls, with two large floor-to-ceiling fitted bookshelves that dominated the room filled with books, photographs and ornaments. He started searching, lifting piles of paper and replacing them exactly how they were before. Sneaking around was something that came naturally; anyway, it wasn't like Danny hadn't done it before.

He opened the drawers within the large leather-topped antique desk that stood in front of him. The centre drawer was locked. *Shit!* he thought. Panicking for time, he hurriedly walked back to the doorway, poking his head around into the corridor, listening, anticipating.

Hastily returning to the desk, picking up an envelope knife that was laying inside a velvet stationery tray. His heart pumped faster; he froze in silence to listen out for any movement from Hafiz's room. Still the sound of the shower hissed.

Pushing the chair away gently, he squatted down in front of the drawer to get a better view of the lock, carefully inserting the end of the knife into the keyhole, fiddling and twisting. Click. It released the locking mechanism; he slowly opened it.

Danny shuffled feverishly through various pieces of paper with names written on them in no apparent order, the adrenalin pumped around his body. Placing them on top of the desk, he got out his iPhone to take photos. He noticed Derek Clarke's name written on one of them, crossed out in red pen. *Fuck, this is serious,* he thought. The hiss of water from the shower had now stopped.

He put the papers back, rapidly but quietly closing the drawer shut, remembering to relock the locking mechanism. Click. Placing the knife back, frantically looking around for anything else. He noticed a pile of high-quality paper that artists use. To his surprise, perfect circles were drawn on the pages in pencil. He snapped a picture of them, too. Evidence safely stored on his iPhone, placing it back in his pocket, he walked more leisurely over to the bookcase.

'What are you looking for?' Hafiz asked sharply. He was standing in the doorway wearing a white robe, freshly shaved and with wet hair.

Danny jumped a mile in fright and, as there wasn't much point pretending otherwise, he said the obvious: 'Shit, you scared me'. Blushing.

Hafiz's expression softened; he looked amused even. Relief flooded through him and gave him the confidence to keep talking.

'I did call you whilst you were in the shower – to see if you had a pen and paper', Danny improvised. 'I thought I would write a list and go shopping for you; you have nothing in your cupboards, mate'.

Hafiz crossed the room to his desk and opened one of the drawers Danny had just searched. He paused in thought for a split second with a troubled look, suspicious. 'Here you go, Danny'. He passed him a Mont Blanc pen and a piece of personalised paper.

'Thanks, Hafiz. I'm blind as a bat sometimes; can't see the obvious in front of me', Danny said jokingly. Hafiz didn't laugh and so he decided to change the subject. 'How are you feeling now?'

'Much better. I'm glad you came over to see me. Life gets lonely sometimes, you know'. Hafiz walked towards the door, clearly expecting him to follow.

'Right then', Danny said, taking charge again.

As he walked past him into the kitchen, 'Let's get you this coffee'.

TEN

——— • ———

Danny had discovered that throughout the ages there have been hundreds of intellectual heavyweights who have existed – and one could add Hafiz as one of them for sure. Everyone can reveal unique and spectacular insights into exactly what it was that created their brilliance, and according to Thom, Hafiz was doing exactly that. He was being led to believe that his perspective on life was metaphorically unravelling to produce the perfect revenge on those who had deviously double-crossed him.

It was an unpleasantly cold winter's evening in December; dark and gloomy as the moon was sheltering the murky looming clouds. Hafiz stood in the centre of his living room, holding court, whilst Marina sat timidly and obediently on the antique Victorian settee, paying attention to what he had to say. He posed, as if performing to an imaginary vast audience, his superior mind working overtime.

He handed Marina a detailed list of names: the private collectors whom he knew personally and who had already been contacted by Joseph Legend's PR people to request that they loan their original *Primus Circle* painting(s) for the forthcoming exhibition, due to run at the selected Gagosian galleries from 4 January to 10 March.

'There are fourteen on the list?' Marina said in surprise, looking down at the piece of paper and doing a double take, as if he had made a mistake.

'Yes, that's right', he said abruptly, 'the first one a success, which is crossed out, and the second will be happening any moment now, some four thousand miles away'. He looked down at his watch then glanced up, grimacing at her.

'He will wish he never put the phone down on me', he snarled. 'But I must admit his art collection used to give me the creeps', he added, chuckling to himself, referring to the next victim's taste.

'And you know what to do with the extra one, don't you? Just make it happen', he added, his manner towards her changing aggressively; and she flinched yet tried not to show it.

'Okay, darling', she replied submissively. 'Please relax. It will happen. I believe in you'. She got up and leant into him, kissing him on the lips and hoping he would respond to her; longing that he would.

Yet Hafiz stopped her with a dismissive hand gesture, his mood changing, such was the psychological and emotional hold he had over her. 'Please don't', he said bluntly, rejecting her advances, but then he softened. 'This needs to be achieved first', he explained, 'so I can be at peace. Then we can be together', he said, holding her gently in his arms, looking deeply into her gaze.

Having pacified her, getting her to where he needed her to be, he continued to explain the sequence of events to her. 'The invites need to be designed and printed correctly, then sent out as soon as possible to the collectors. You must ensure that all of them RSVP. There categorically must not be any cancellations as an exclusive presentation gift is to be given to them and their accompanying guests at the time and date stated'. Hafiz paced as he spoke; he basically traced the perimeter of his living room four times over as he continued to outline the mission to Marina. 'It will be a great opening event. You will also need to follow up with a phone call as soon as possible to confirm their attendance; this is important'. His attention to detail was impeccable. 'I have also started to draft the instructions to our "friends" as it were. Once these instructions are completed, they will be ready for printing and distribution to our people accordingly'.

Suddenly Hafiz started coughing uncontrollably. He reached for his white handkerchief in his trouser pocket and held it over his mouth, his face turning blue with the strain. Choking for air, his cough increased, and he sat down in a fit of panic. Marina rushed to him and put her arm around him, rubbing his back to ease the pain. Slowly, he got his breath back but the respite was brief. They both looked down at the handkerchief, which was now covered in dark-red blood. They looked at each other and a feeling of ultimate sadness overcame them both.

'I've always seen potential in you, Marina', he admitted. 'I think that what makes you an outcast will eventually make you very powerful'. He said the words with sheer pain on his face as he tried to compose himself. Marina smiled at the compliment, but the hope in her eyes was shadowed by fear – the fear that he would spiral out of control again, lost in a binge of drugs and alcohol.

With a shaking hand, Hafiz poured himself a glass of water from the jug sat on his desk. He needed a few sips to clear his throat and wash the blood away from his teeth; he threw the hanky into the wastepaper bin beside him. 'As soon as I have all the instructions for our people completed, Marina, I will let you know'. There was revenge in his eyes now. 'I will make sure I put on a superb...' he paused, reaching for the right word '...masterpiece for the world to see'. He smiled to no one but himself.

Marina grabbed her things dutifully, knowing when she was dismissed. There was no time to waste. That night, she would travel to Gloucester to be ready for work the following morning. Even as she closed the door behind her, she was already psyching herself up for the tasks given to her.

Once she had gone, Hafiz picked up his phone and started typing a text fervently. He did it standing by his window. Whilst laughing out loud, he firmly pressed Send.

•

As Hafiz predicted, his old friend Monsieur Christopher Durand, a sinner of the highest order. Content, enjoying his afternoon seated by the pool looking out to a view of Miami Bay, which was hazily obscured in the distance by the sheer heat of the day. He looked around for his housekeeper, Walkira, who should by now have delivered his afternoon rum baba: his official gateway to happy hour. Looking up at the beautiful blue sky and basking in the vibrant sunshine, he decided he would wash it down with a nice cold Muscat de Beaumes de Venise for a change. He smiled to himself, anticipating his housekeeper's response to that request, as giving in to his perpetual sweet tooth was always the starting point for a huge lecture from Walkira, who predominantly fired off at him in Spanish.

Christopher was in his early sixties. He was a very rich art curator, commodities collector and a very flamboyant homosexual, and proud. Yet his partying days had ended when he'd been confined to a wheelchair after a boating accident in his early forties in Malibu that had left him partially paralysed from the waist down. His daily companion was now Walkira, a small, feisty middle-aged Mexican lady with six children and a husband of thirty-five years.

Being a creature of habit, Christopher decided to seek out his afternoon ritual and carefully manoeuvred his wheelchair, wheeling it away from the protective shield of the sun parasol he had been sitting beneath. Instantly, heat of at least thirty-seven degrees hit him full in the face, causing immediate perspiration. The drops fell down his cheeks from underneath his gentleman's straw Stetson. His body quickly felt damp, and the piercing heat of the sun started to burn his exposed skin; he fastened his Prada shirt whilst also shuffling down in his chair to reach for his towel, eventually draping it over himself to cover his legs where his Gucci shorts didn't reach. He called for Walkira again but there was no response. Impatiently, he wheeled himself towards the house via the expensive marble ramps that were scattered all along his authentic French-style patio.

As he approached the house, he stopped beside his collection of palm trees and ferns to catch his breath. The plants provided a corner haven, the shade cooling his skin whilst the sound of four decorative fountains oxygenating the rectangular pond calmed his mind.

On entering his day lounge, he heard the doorbell chime and then Walkira running through the house from the kitchen, muttering her usual cantankerous threats about leaving her employment because of just how much she had to do. He laughed to himself and followed her slowly, parking himself in full view of the door whilst Walkira took a moment to smooth down her uniform, adjusting her long, thick black hair which she always styled in a bun. She always liked to present herself correctly before receiving whoever was calling.

Christopher couldn't hear the conversation taking place on his porch once she opened the door. He concentrated instead on the exceptionally handsome man to whom she was talking: a tall, rather well-tailored specimen with Adonic features, who was standing outside looking in. The sun-drenched hunk would have been just his type two decades ago.

Walkira excused herself to the handsome caller and walked over to Christopher, handing him a business card for a Ryan Garcia, Paradise Appraisals in Biscayne Bay. Upon reading the card, Christopher dismissed Walkira, sending her back to the kitchen to take time out for a while. His rum baba could wait for once. He was intrigued to begin a conversation with the dashing stranger in Ray-Ban shades, a light-grey T-shirt and a peach-coloured jacket; Christopher's 'gaydar' was on red alert.

Ryan was busy scanning all the objects d'art in the foyer of this magnificent villa. Noticing his scrutiny, Christopher beckoned him in. As he stepped through the door, Ryan's gaze was captivated by a large sculpture by Lorenzo Quinn, which stood at the entrance to the day lounge. 'The title of this piece is *Creation*,' Christopher said alluringly.

Then Ryan spoke directly to Christopher for the first time: 'Exquisite'. He spoke with an Italian accent. And then, convinced they were out of view of the kitchen, Ryan took off his shades, slicking back his hair as they both admired the sculpture.

Yet Christopher knew the stranger hadn't come all this way to look at sculptures, however exquisite they were. 'What is it I can do for you, Mr Garcia?' he asked, looking into his eyes.

'Pardon me, Mr Durand'. Ryan gave a small, embarrassed smile. 'I was actually looking for directions to another property in the neighbourhood, but I could not make your housekeeper comprehend my question'. Ryan turned towards a perfect de Vinci *Profilo di Capitano Antico* painting. He immediately appreciated its detailed refinement, murmuring the word 'beautiful' in perfect Italian: '*Bellissimo*'. He moved towards the painting. 'May I?' he asked, charmingly.

'Please do, dearie'. Christopher looked on, feeling a little bemused, especially by the fact that Ryan now seemed in no hurry to make it to his professed destination. Nevertheless, Christopher was pleased to have a fellow critic in his home to whom he could show off.

Ryan knew exactly what he was looking for and used all the correct terminology to enquire after Christopher's collection. Ryan followed the wheelchair from the day lounge through to the library, where a large collection of Jake and Dinos Chapman sculptures and paintings were evident. This room clearly kept the best of the best, and contained works of art which were a true reflection of Mr Durand's personality and sexuality: warped.

The original *Primus Circle* painting was hung in a niche that supported a full cocktail bar and was surrounded by several crystal decanters, each filled to varying degrees with assorted Cognacs.

There you are, my beauty, Ryan thought to himself.

Carefully, he observed the layout of the library. Around another niche was access to a summer room and then access onwards to a patio and pool. He kept the conversation going with a full-blown inquisition on the Legend painting, whilst also assessing that an arched garden gate led from the patio to the side of the villa; it was noticeable through the very large windows.

Eventually, assessment complete, Ryan walked over to Christopher. Placing his hands gently on his shoulders, he slowly manoeuvred himself around to the back of the wheelchair. Leaning forward, he whispered in his ear, provocatively. 'You have been a naughty boy, haven't you, Mr Durand?' He applied the handbrake to the wheelchair. The seductive nature of his voice excited Christopher. A true queen of queens with a seedy past, he did tend to excite easily.

'Who put you up to this, sweetie?' Christopher asked joyously. 'Was it Rodrigo? The diva, wait till I see him'. Aroused, he pressed his manicured hand over his mouth, thrilled at the handsome beau's closeness to him.

Unseen by Christopher, Ryan took out a medical injector pen from his shirt pocket. Covertly, he placed it on the back of Christopher's neck, near the top of his spinal column. Without pausing a moment longer, he instigated the mechanism and with one press of his thumb – 'Click' – it released a deadly toxin into his victim's body. The small needle prick made Christopher flinch with shock, and he became confused about what was instantly happening to his body.

Ready to enlighten him, Ryan walked around the wheelchair and knelt down to face Christopher. He looked deep into his eyes in silence, fascinated by the way he was inflicting terror on him. Enjoying watching as the deadly toxin flowed through the man's bloodstream. He stared intently as he could see Christopher was now feeling very uncomfortable: he sat rigid in his chair as though he had been frozen in ice.

Ryan explained: 'I have injected you with a deadly toxin which is taken from the liver of the deadly puffer fish. It is called Tetrodotoxin for your short-but-sweet future reference'. He spoke with a smile on his face and continued: 'This substance paralyses the victim from head to toe, but as you already can't feel your legs, it won't have far to go'. He laughed poetically, sarcastically. 'But the best thing is… you will be able to feel everything I'm going to do to you'.

Christopher went into immediate shock at the realisation he couldn't move. His terrified eyes darted about frantically; he couldn't even blink, and he was barely breathing; and worst of all, he could hardly open his mouth to scream. His eyes were trying to talk instead: he was silently begging for his life, his mind reeling in total confusion. *Who is this man? What does he want? Why has he done this? Please, no.*

Ryan pulled up a chair beside Christopher and talked through the array of Chapman brother's sculptures in the room. 'They're slightly weird, don't you think, Mr Durand? I mean, take that one over there'. Ryan pointed to something that looked as if a load of Sindy dolls had been melted together to form a circle. 'The artists deliberately created their work to be shocking and to make the viewer uncomfortable; that gets the reaction they desire', he said appreciatively.

Christopher was palpitating, yet nothing showed externally. He prayed for Walkira to come into the room, but then worried what would happen to her if she disturbed this psychopath. Ryan was calmly talking him through his own collection as though they were attending a Chapman brothers exhibition.

'I'm such a huge fan of their work, I must admit, Mr Durand. Very strange pair, if you ask me; it's as though they have psychological problems. I mean, why on earth would you paint a woman with the middle of her face burnt out or a menacing finger directing itself towards an eye that has a hole in it? It is completely distasteful to me'. As though still deep in thought, Ryan got up from his chair and knelt before Christopher again. 'Do you think the eye had been burst inwards by the finger?' he asked reflectively. And then he pointed his index finger towards Christopher, mimicking the painting.

Christopher panicked in frustration – but he couldn't move his head away. In his mind, he screamed, but no sound came out. In mute terror, he watched as Ryan slowly pushed his finger knuckle-deep into his right eyeball. The blood popped from the eye socket, and all Christopher could do was shake in total pain and agony from deep within. He was utterly defenceless against the fate that awaited him.

Ryan burst into maniacal laughter, wiping the blood from his finger onto Christopher's shirt. He moved away from his victim and checked his iPhone, searching for the visual of the *Primus Circle* painting sent to him that morning. They matched. He smiled to himself as he went to take down the large canvas from off the wall, carrying it over and leaning it against the table beside Christopher. He paused briefly in his work as he identified the sound of Walkira singing like an angel in the kitchen. He purposefully grinned at Christopher as he walked past him to the French patio doors. Turning the key, he opened them, letting in the wonderful Miami sunshine whilst simultaneously appreciating the beauty of the garden.

'Beautiful garden', he said conversationally as he came back into the room. Working methodically, he removed the brake from the wheelchair and pushed Christopher outside onto the patio, leaving him momentarily to go inside and fetch the painting, which he rested against Christopher's legs.

Christopher, meanwhile, had almost passed out in total agony, his whole body convulsing in shock. Visually, everything was drifting in and out, like a blur, a worst nightmare.

Ryan stood opposite Christopher and slowly removed a large tin of lighter fluid from inside his jacket pocket. Without even blinking, he continued to look straight at Christopher as he took the top off with his teeth and then squirted the liquid all over the canvas and Christopher, soaking the art collector's hair and clothes as he sat motionless, in horrendous pain, with warm blood pouring from one eye. But although his vision was destroyed in that one socket, he could still see well enough with the other eye. Like a cyclops, he could see Ryan stand back as he reached into his trouser pocket for his cigarette lighter…

Ryan was emotionally void. 'I'll name this, *My burning desire is to be with you*', he said, concentrating as he took his time to analyse his work, his creation of man and canvas: a weird exhibition similar to the collection inside, which he adored. Impassively, he flicked the lid of the lighter and the flame responded.

Christopher prayed for a quick death as he knew what was going to happen. Ryan leant forward, lighting the foot of the canvas, which caught immediately, assisted by the chemicals and wooden frame. The intensity of the heat absorbed his skin. Christopher thought it would not be long before his heart gave out as the intensity of heat melted into his skin; he wasn't even aware of breathing any more.

'Voice of an angel'. Ryan referred to Walkira, who was still singing in the kitchen. He watched Christopher on fire, wondering if she could hear him burning. 'It would be a shame if anything happened to her, wouldn't it?'

He kept on muttering to the dying fireball in front of him, but the fireball couldn't and wouldn't ever now speak back. As the flames still flickered, Ryan slipped his Ray-Bans on and quickly left by the side gate. As he took in the blaze of sunshine and the delicate aroma of flowers scattered around the patio, he decided he would not take care of the housekeeper, after all. She reminded him of his mother, who also had a beautiful voice. The songbird could live to sing another day.

This time.

ELEVEN

———— • ————

On his way home from Hafiz's apartment towards the English countryside, Danny was left feeling befuddled, big time, driving on autopilot, with no recollection of how he got to any point on the road. That's what it felt like. He was detached from any immediate surroundings, living in a blurred dream, when suddenly just over an hour later he found himself on his driveway with all the above thoughts flitting through his mind. He parked up and walked into the house, bag in one hand, laptop in the other, to be greeted by a pile of scattered post which, as usual, he ended up half slipping on before he dropped his bag on the floor. Scooping up the post, walking into the kitchen, flicking through the mail to see if there was anything important, but it was mostly junk. Post and keys dutifully plopped onto the table, Danny felt exhausted. Grabbing a drink of orange juice from the fridge to rejuvenate himself, thinking, *Right, what next?*

Hafiz and Thom flared into his head again, so he booted up his laptop and, whilst waiting for the Wi-Fi to connect, he got his iPhone out and downloaded the images he'd taken at Hafiz's apartment onto his computer. One by one, the images downloaded and he dragged them across to the desktop screen, opening them up to get a clearer view of his findings. *Interesting,* he thought.

Again, he couldn't believe his eyes; his heart was racing in his chest. Definitely crossed out in red biro was written: *Mr Derek Clarke, Lancaster Gates Residence, in Kensington – London.* 'Holy shit', he said out loud to an empty room.

Written next to Clarke's details was (*OPIUM*).

Seriously, he deals? Danny thought, scrolling down the page in disbelief – but then he noticed every name on the list had a chemical name in brackets beside it. Counting out loud, he calculated in total there were thirteen names with the thirteen chemical names in brackets. Staring at the screen. Was this Hafiz's drug consortium? If so, that was one hell of a concoction of drugs for just one man. Alternatively, could it be code for something else? Nevertheless, if that was the case, code for what?

Meticulously, he read through the names and details of each of the images, making sure his name wasn't on there, relieved that it wasn't. He started with the first image – Matt Connors, Derek Clarke, Pernilla Holmes, Gary Landsbergis, Christopher Durand, Kate Levenstein and Nebosja Jankovic. Scrolling onto the next image – Markus Schinwald, Harry Chadwyck-Healey, Albert Oehlen and Charles Collier. Finally, the last list – Emma Austin, Thomas Sareceno and finally, Rebecca Warrenson.

Wow! he thought, intrigued. Studying each name and their details to see if anything would jump out at him to give him some sort of clue as to what the hell was happening here. One name had scribble against it – *Mr Christopher Durand, Miami Beach, Florida.* As well as the standard bracketed chemical name, next to his name was: *Cripple won't make the exhibition.* Staring at the screen. *Is this guy now crippled and can't travel?* he wondered. The word *exhibition* made him link to perhaps one of the eleven forthcoming exhibitions Hafiz was now interested in.

Danny poured himself another orange juice, pondering what connection Christopher Durand had with Hafiz. He realised he was going to have to get hold of Thom to tell him about this list. Thinking back to everything he had researched so far on the London assassination, he looked again at the list of names. Googling the chemical names, they didn't add up to be of any kind of drugs that you might be able to sell on the street. Opening the files of research he had compiled so far, wanting to look through all the evidence again. For some reason, this time he was drawn to everything he had learnt so far on these *Primus Circle* paintings; the bloody spots.

'Check this out'. He talked to himself; it stopped the loneliness from settling in. What he was to 'check out' was the title of the paintings, which had originally been taken from pharmaceutical names of chemicals. In the early 1990s, artist Joseph Legend had stumbled across a chemical company's catalogue of their products and named his paintings after the chemical names. He flicked through his files; the catalogue was Sigma-Aldrich's *Bio chemicals for Research and Diagnostic Reagents*. From this, a grid formula within the pharmaceutical paintings became the basis for an endless series of circle paintings, which were random infinite coloured spots, with no coloured spot repeated. *Fucking Genius*, he thought, contemplating.

Being an artist, Danny needed to see things on paper to get them clear in his head, so he right-clicked on the images, pressed Print and watched as the printer kicked out all his findings. Scrolling down the images on his desktop, he now looked for the photographs that he had taken of the pile of plain quality artist's paper with circles drawn on it; a template ready to fill the circles in with various colours. *Was he producing a replica circle painting or print? Was he making fakes to sell and make a few quid?* Danny wondered, but none of the inanimate objects around him answered. His brain still buzzing, he collated all the printed images from the printer tray, plonked himself in his comfy chair in his living room, bag loyally beside him whilst he took time to contemplate, unwind and reflect. Annoyance came to the forefront of his thoughts; he just wanted to paint pictures and start afresh. *How did I end up here?* Shaking his head in disbelief and then closing his eyes, counting spots not sheep.

·

A few hours later, he woke with the usual *Where the fuck am I?* thought. Having been away from home for just over a week, he was disoriented. The bang to the back of his head was still relatively fresh, too. Stretching, yawning and generally trying to wake up, he eventually leant over the laptop again with a fresh determination. Rationalising that he had a list of thirteen people who had all owned original Joseph Legend *Primus*

Circle paintings and who had all been assigned a chemical name. Then he corrected himself: Mr Clarke was now dead, so actually he had twelve people. *Maybe the people on the lists are being taken out one at a time? Hypothetically speaking.*

It was time for pen and paper and he scribbled down: *Fourteen names, fourteen paintings of chemical names; one confirmed dead; and a destroyed original painting.* Trying to formulate his thoughts and reflect on the possible motives. Wondering if Hafiz had maybe part-owned these paintings as an investment with the people on the list – but then why eliminate the individual and the painting? Why not kill the individual and take the original back? He was an art virgin and wondered cluelessly: could these vicious attacks put the price of the other circle paintings up?

Danny scrolled down to find Thom's number on his iPhone as this list was important. Then another thought crossed his mind. Was there perhaps another reason for taking out the paintings and hit-listing the others? Was there a hidden message, a threat to the others? He was still idly looking for Thom's number when he remembered his so-called 'briefing' in the interrogation room and Thom showing him the evidence he had: the photographs and the small burnt piece of white artist's paper with a red circled shape upon it. He thought back: the red circle-shaped coloured blotch was near the corner inside the forensics bag.

Danny got a piece of white paper and with his pen he drew a circle. Then he shaded it in the near corner and tore it across where the burnt edge would be, guessing the size of the print to make a duplicate copy. He found the title of the original spot painting that Mr Clarke owned – *OPIUM* – and researched the print on his laptop. Very quickly, he found the following information: *Produced in 1994, the original sold to a private collector in New York.* Looking closely at the image on the screen of the piece and placing his sketch of the burnt sample Thom had against it, orientating it to match the corners…

'Fucking bingo!' he shouted. 'Genius, it matches. That's it, then!' For one thing that had been drummed into him by both Hafiz and Bernadette was that Legend was at pains to state that every circle painting was different and no two colours could be next to each other. Danny was sure he had nailed this.

Sitting back in his chair then, Thom and spots popped back into his head. He was niggled as to why an assassin would destroy only one painting from such a valuable personal collection and why Clarke would own a limited edition if he also owned the original, which was worth over a million pounds. Online, checking to see how many prints were in the limited-edition number and finding no limited editions were produced to match that specific original. This made no sense. Thom had shown him what was found at the scene of the crime: why not destroy them all or steal them? Years of covert intelligence had taught him about the constant message of a code and its subsequent meaning. He just had to listen to what this code was saying.

Going back to the list of names and the paintings that he had already printed off. Highlighting all thirteen pharmaceutical names associated with each owner on the list, then typing the titles into the search engine on his laptop. Finding and saving the images to his desktop, again he pressed Print. One by one, the coloured circles appeared from the printer. Then uniformly he laid them out on the floor to dry. Carefully titling each image with who owned what, pausing to look at all thirteen different circle paintings, now placed on his living room floor in the order they appeared on the list.

Working methodically, he isolated Clarke's images and put them to one side. Then Danny placed his hurried sample sketch on top of Clarke's image and analysed both his sketch and the original paintings for similarities: size, shape, number of circles and size of circles, colour sequence; anything that would provoke something in him, that might indicate a clue. 'Nope, nothing'. Sighing in disappointment.

Looking at the rest of the paintings. *Yes, they are all unique in terms of how the circles were configured on the canvas,* he thought. Next, he researched on the internet for these circle paintings and found some sold at auction houses such as Sotheby's, Phillips de Pury's, Christie's and the like. *Is the killer sending out a message within the art world of what is to come?* he wondered, considering. Is this some sort of calculated revenge to all the owners? Danny's theories swirled around in his head to keep the spots company.

This time, he managed to get Thom's number and pressed Call. For a while, the ringing piercingly disturbed the silence of his living room, but eventually he answered.

'Danny, hi, what do you have for me?' He spoke in his usual distinguished accent. Though irritated by his expectant response, Danny got straight to the point.

'Thom, I have discovered a list of names; fourteen individuals and within that list, Derek Clarke's name, crossed out in red biro.'

'Where did you get the list from?' Thom asked, as if he knew already.

'I was doing what you asked me to do, remember? I saw it written down in Hafiz's apartment and I've managed to take photographs which I will text over to you'. Danny decided to keep everything else close to him; he didn't want to give too much away. After all, his bloody neck still hurt, and this trust thing needed to be a mutual feeling from gaining respect.

'Great work', Thom said, reluctantly surprised.

'Can you find out if any bank transactions have been made between any of the names on the list and Hafiz?' he asked.

'Leave it all with me, Danny. I'll revert back to you once I've spoken to my friends at Langley'.

'You will see a name on the list – Christopher Durand, who lives in Miami. The writing states he's crippled and won't make the exhibition', Danny said, with intrigue and suspicion of his fate.

'I will have a look once you send me the list'. Thom sounded amazingly cooperative and he thought he even detected a slight note of gratitude in his voice at the information he had brought him. Consequently, he decided to play his card as he'd already delivered something of interest to him.

'Thom, before you go, would I be able to have a copy of the police report on the assassination of Clarke?' he requested, holding his breath, waiting for his response.

'I'll see what I can do'. He let out the breath he'd been holding: result. 'Okay, that's everything from my side', Thom continued brusquely. 'I'll be in touch soon'.

'Click'. Thom had ended the call abruptly. Danny smiled and casually glanced down at the circle images on the floor.

Danny wrote down the names and the associated details that were on the images for Thom but didn't disclose the names of the chemicals next to each name. He took a photo with his phone and sent it to him. Moments later, 'Ping!' *Received, Thom.*

Nothing he was staring at gave him a single clue. *What is this list all about then?* he pondered. Was it just coincidence that Clarke's name was on it? Had it been crossed out as word got around that he was murdered?

Maybe it's not the originals that have the clues, he speculated, examining the other images of the empty circles. *Maybe it's the limited editions that match the originals.* For the first time, Danny was beginning to see a link to Hafiz in all this; a chilling thought flowed through him.

TWELVE

———— • ————

After another sleepless night, Danny was up and plodding around his living room, which was now a shrine to pictures of coloured spots. Trying to figure out this puzzle had abstained him from his normal slumber. He allowed himself to consider that Hafiz was instructing individuals to act out some catastrophic form of revenge for him. It occurred to Danny that he might be manipulating the wrongful preaching's in the Quran, but for what? Art, faith, ideology or personal revenge?

Believers believe and will do anything for their cause, as martyrdom is God's greatest reward. Yet he still couldn't see any fundamentalist reason behind this. Danny's theories were either that Hafiz was being horrifically evil or that there was some figment of his imagination hanging in his mind that was prompting him to do this. Either way, it was now Danny's job to find out.

•

What better way to spend a Friday night than accepting yet another VIP invite? Once again, Danny was to accompany a rather excited Hafiz to another exclusive art exhibition in England's capital. This time, it was the

96

turn of artist Anish Kapoor, represented by the Lisson Gallery. Anish was one of the most influential sculptors of his generation, perhaps most famous for his public sculptures that were both adventures in form and feats of engineering; one might have most likely passed one of his works whilst travelling and never known. Danny appreciated the thought process behind his work. He manoeuvred between vastly different scales across numerous series of work. Imagine immense PVC skins stretched or deflated, concave or convex mirrors from which reflections attract and swallow the viewer; and that is the work of Anish Kapoor.

As he left the hotel in Mayfair, the thoughts of Thom, the circle paintings and Hafiz loomed large. Perhaps there was a connection, like Thom said: it would explain why Hafiz was so elated at the moment. Had this exhibition actually masked his mood changes, of which there were several? These thoughts stayed with Danny as he met him. He was already inside the Lisson Gallery, talking to a group of people whom Danny saw at a glance comprised the who's who of the art world. Danny was in awe as he focused on an amazing Kapoor sculpture, right where they were all standing, stunned by both the art and the company. This obviously 'high-society' gang looked as if they lived on daily helpings of Valium and champagne without the finesse; they would get that from the odd visit to the Priory for life coaching and reassurance to get them through life.

Danny chuckled to himself at his thoughts. As the actor Bob Hoskins once said in the BT advertisement years ago: *It's good to talk*. Well, getting things off your chest didn't need the Priory, just a mate. He headed to see what he could extract from Hafiz…

Hafiz saw Danny making his way over to him and raised his hand at him, gesturing a quite camp-like hello. He had an immense mixed feeling of emotions rush through him as he saw Hafiz's face. He continued to transfix his group of arty toffs with his expert analysis of the sculpture; he was a master of persuasion, all right. He had to hand it to him: when it came to art, he could perfect the intellectual words to criticise or praise the artist, which in turn would make or break the poor sod or soddess, for his words would spread all around the room – like a virus, initially, before becoming a full-scale, even international, epidemic.

'Hey, Danny, great to see you!' He leant over for a handshake and man hug. 'Let me introduce you to everybody', he said, looking at his audience.

He looked unusually high, as if he was buzzing off his face. Danny wondered what the circle of wet wipes around him thought of his behaviour that evening. If they were suspicious as to the reason for his unnatural dynamism, he had a rehearsed explanation all ready to defuse the situation, which would be that he was partial to a family-sized packet of Skittles. Of course, he knew that it wasn't a mass of E numbers that had kicked into Hafiz, but whatever it was that had put him in this heightened state, he hoped he could use it to his advantage. Danny was going to use his drug-induced vulnerability to get some answers out of him.

He introduced Danny to the group one by one. To his relief, he didn't recognise any of the names from that fateful list taken from Hafiz's desk that he had memorised, but none of these titled darlings rang a bell. Danny smiled politely. 'Good evening, everyone; pleased to meet you all'. He put his best face on; after all, these people could make or break an artist, and even though he was currently a part-time snoop for Thom, he still wanted his own artwork to be a success.

Hafiz put his arm around Danny and he paraded him up to everyone proudly. 'Danny here is an exciting new emerging contemporary artist and well worth investing in. His work achieves a balance between a contemporary approach and a seductive, decorative aesthetic; you will adore his work'. He squeezed his arm as the group took in his suggestion; he definitely had an 'appreciated, thanks' moment. Danny felt humbled, surprised… and guilty that he had to try and see him in a different light, to see him as someone involved in something sinister. Nodding his head in the group's general direction, smiling, Danny even managed a man squeeze back to Hafiz because at the end of the day, he didn't have to say that about him. Conflicted as he was, he was still grateful to him. The moment passed. As he watched the group look him up and down in a very snooty 'art critic' manner, as if he was a piece of his own artwork and they were judging him, he felt an unease that had nothing to do with their cold manner.

Danny stayed with Hafiz and co. for long enough to not raise suspicion, sipping champagne, laughing and admiring works of art throughout the gallery, before making a polite excuse to wander off in the hope of seeing Bernadette. As he wandered around with his glass of bubbly, more and more guests arrived. As they thronged into the room, he found he was looking out for her; assuming she would be attending, as this was her kind of thing. It was still quite early, so he decided to send her a text. *Hey sexy, where are you?* It was at that point that Hafiz walked over to him.

'Great show, isn't it, Danny?' His eyes noticeably bloodshot.

'Yes, it truly is. I like the work a lot. Thank you for inviting me – and thank you too for those kind words back there.' Danny shook his hand to seal the deal of his gratitude.

'No problem, my friend; you came along when everyone else had abandoned me.' He spoke with definite tears in his eyes; again, Danny was appreciative, but as he looked into his eyes, he felt a sudden soul-shattering chill. He saw something else, something not human, staring back at him.

'Hey, don't worry. Things happen for a reason.' Danny turned to face a large painting on the wall in front of them, wanting to change the subject in order to distract him from his public emotion. Nodding in the artwork's direction. 'What do you think about this one?' he asked him, and of course he immediately went into this spiel of knowledge. It made Danny smile and appreciate that his passion for art was the main thing he liked about him. He respected it, even. 'What do you think about the use of colour?' Danny prompted.

'I love the colour, its life', he replied, gesticulating closer to the painting. 'Each colour has a true individual meaning; within the colour an emotion and a direction is evoked.'

'For example?' Danny was intrigued by his comment and wanted to decode the way his mind worked whilst he had the chance.

'Okay, well, for instance, the colour white is the creative colour of life: it's pure and it blends into the whole spectrum of colours, which can all mean a million things. Colour is how you communicate with your viewer to get them to understand what you are trying to tell them.' He stared passively at the painting, not turning to look at Danny.

'What about death?' Steering the conversation to a more serious tone.

He took a breath and held his gaze. 'Now, black is the most enigmatic of colours and is the colour of death.' Said with conviction, as if he wrote that law and the book it came from. 'Black can only be used strategically in works of art.'

How well disguised evil can be, Danny thought.

'Imagine walking into a room with no walls… Loss of its entirety go hand in hand. Inevitably, we collide with death'.

'You certainly know your shit, alright…' Danny began – but he wasn't listening. He watched him become preoccupied over his shoulder and followed his stare to a tall, dark-haired woman standing near the entrance. He wasn't surprised he'd been distracted; she was waving over in this direction, certainly trying to grab his attention.

'Excuse me, my friend; can you give me a few minutes to sort out a private matter?' He had gone before his feet moved and now walked towards her with a sense of urgency. Meanwhile, Danny moved incognito-style to park himself behind a large sculpture which was on display close by them to get a better look at her, but she made sure her face was away from his direction. He pretended to be in awe whilst simultaneously watching the pair talking to each other. In the back of his still-sore head, he thought, *Turn around, for fuck's sake. That must be her, the assassin Marina.* He was unsure.

They stood together for quite a while before she discreetly handed him a large brown envelope and he covertly looked inside, smiling at her, clearly pleased, as if it was a gift or good news. His appraisal made her smile back. Danny observed her attempt to control her emotions before she leant forward to kiss him – only to be totally rejected by the lack of commitment on his face and in his body language. It was obvious, even standing several feet away. He might have had the most incredible insight when it came to art, but when it came to women he had the *sensitivity of a sledgehammer,* he thought to himself, as he was evidently oblivious to her sorrow. Composing herself swiftly, the woman left a moment later without a backwards glance.

Danny's eyes followed her beautiful figure leaving the gallery, distracted, the rush of adrenalin as to who it might be made his pulse race. 'Boo!' A voice boomed suddenly from behind him. Hands grabbed his waist and made him jump. Turning around, he saw Bernadette having fun and looking radiant. 'Scared you!' she teased.

'You did, actually! You got my text, then?' Relieved it was her.

She nodded, looking happy, which in turn made him smile. 'Yes, I did, but I was already here, speaking to the owners of the gallery out the back'. She gestured with her head in the general direction. 'I work for them on a consultancy basis', she added, smiling.

'Hafiz is here, somewhere', he told her, moving in closer, drawn to her as a moth to a flame.

'Yes, I noticed he was doing his rounds with the art buyers and critics. Doesn't he just love it?' As she too moved in closer.

'He certainly does', Danny said. now close enough that he could whisper, 'I've missed you', It was a smooth move on his part, but he had his reasons.

'Me too'. She kissed him gently on the lips. 'It suits you', she said suddenly with a smile.

'What does, exactly?' Puzzled.

'Red lipstick'. She giggled, carefully wiping her gloss off his mouth as if he was a toddler covered in chocolate. 'Listen, I've got to leave you for a while as some very important art collectors have just arrived from China'. She checked her own lipstick in the reflection on the glass of a painting beside them.

'Hey, not a problem. Hurry back'. He gave her a little tap on her perfectly pert rear as she walked away, and she looked back over her shoulder, smiling provocatively. Glancing around to see where Hafiz had gone but not spotting him in his immediate vicinity. Wondering if he had left – and what was in the envelope that had brought such a smile to his face. Danny went to move onwards around the gallery when a waitress appeared right in front of him, smiling and holding a silver tray on which were balanced several generously sized champagne glasses full of bubbly.

'Care for a drink, sir?' She proffered the tray towards him and he noticed the exhibition brochures were also on it.

'Yes, please, why not? Thanks'. Taking a glass off the tray.

'That second brochure is specifically for you, sir'. He blinked at her in surprise. 'It's from Thom', she said, still smiling and nodding towards it. For a brief moment, Danny did nothing, too surprised to react, but then it registered that he was having a 'd'oh' moment. He stared at the brochure and her, slightly confused, then reality kicked in. *Bloody spooks*, he thought as he picked the brochure up off the tray and thanked her discreetly.

'It's a pleasure'. She lowered her head briefly in recognition. As she raised her head again, she murmured, 'Message from Thom: latest sitrep, your man in Miami was murdered three days ago'. Without waiting for a reply or response, she was gone, mingling into the crowd.

Danny sank the champagne like a man on a mission, shocked to uncover Durand's name and the reference to *the cripple* who *won't make the exhibition*; as suspected, he was now dead. He was horrified.

His mind was racing. Two people dead, leaving eleven on the list. *Does that eliminate the deadly beauty that was literally just here with Hafiz from being a killer?* Having discarded the glass in the appropriate area, he tootled off towards a painting, pretending to look in the brochure the waitress had given him for its reference. As he opened it, he could see a copy of the police report from the Lancaster Gates murder. Carefully, closing it up, pretending, and nodding to himself to suggest he had found the painting description in it. Then placing it inside his blazer pocket.

As he continued onwards through the gallery, Bernadette came over with a thrill of excitement.

'Hey, handsome; how's it going?' She gently pecked him on the cheek.

'Not bad'. He touched her arm gently, unable to resist her.

'I've just sold three major pieces to the Chinese'. She couldn't hide the smile on her face.

'Congratulations, you look and obviously are chuffed to bits. Well done'. Danny was genuinely pleased for her.

'I am, actually! These clients have far too much money, believe me'. She laughed and he laughed with her.

Lucky for some, he thought, as he said the words, 'That will be me one day'.

'What, Chinese?' she joked, and they both broke into laughter.

'Which hotel are you staying at?' she asked.

'I'm staying at the Hilton in Mayfair'. He hoped he had guessed correctly where this was going...

She leaned into him. 'I'm not going to be finished here until late, sorting out the invoices and paperwork, but if you are still up when I am done, maybe I'll pop over?' Her hand touched his lapel, biting her lip.

'Hey, that's fine. You have work to do. I'm going to hang around here for a little longer then head back. You'll have to try to resist me; I'll be wearing my favourite dinosaur pyjamas', he said, winking at her.

She laughed out loud, walking back towards her clients. *Lucky me!* he thought as she cast a look back over her shoulder at him. 'I'll text you when I'm *en route*'.

'Okay, cool'. With the evening now confirmed to end on a rather pleasant note and Bernadette engaged, Danny saw a perfect weather window to entrap his suspect.

.

THIRTEEN

———— • ————

Danny was on a mission to look for Hafiz. There he stood, nonchalantly drinking champagne, a glass in both hands, chatting up one of the pretty waitresses. How well the truly evil were able to disguise themselves, Danny thought; those who can strike without warning and from afar. But he had to compose his manner and attitude towards Hafiz. Otherwise, he would suspect something.

'Hey, Danny'. He swayed back and forth with slurred speech, grumbling to himself. *What a complete state*, he thought, free champagne; combined with a few lines of coke on his regular visits to the gents. *I'm surprised he's still standing*, he thought.

'Looks like you have had a good night, mate'. Trying to grab his attention.

'Yeah, it's been excellent', he replied, looking for a glass that he thought he had.

'I bet the exhibitions in New York were good'. He showed intrigue, enticing him to open up whilst he was in this perfect pissed-up state.

He nodded absently, giving a suspicious look. 'Yeah, they were excellent, but like all good things – they come to an end'.

Danny knew he had to be tactful in his questioning. 'So, what's stopping you going back out there? I'd love to go over to New York'. Sounding enthusiastic.

'Who knows what the future holds, Danny? You would love the galleries out there; very inspiring, which would help you personally in your own work'. It was a typical politician's response, totally diverting away from Danny's question. He wouldn't be corralled into talking about it.

'Who was that stunner you were talking to earlier at the door? You certainly know how to pull the ladies; does she have any single friends?' Danny asked in jest.

'Just someone I know from old, who's very loyal to me. I don't treat her well', he stammered, as he looked around for the waitress with the tray of drinks.

'You must introduce me to her', Danny suggested.

'I'm sure you will meet her soon enough, my friend', he replied, patting Danny on his back, which sent another chill through his body.

Danny knew he wasn't getting anywhere. 'How about we get you a seat before you fall over?' Guiding him towards the too-large white leather Barcelona sofas near the entrance of the gallery. Unsteady on his feet and remarkably cooperative, he plonked himself down in a drunken heap. He had company, there was a scattered few, and he wasn't the only one who had enjoyed the free champagne.

'I'll get you some water, mate', Danny said, looking around for a waitress. He was gone for less than two minutes, yet on his return he was chatting up some woman that sat beside him.

'There you go, Hafiz'. Handing him the glass. He was half asleep, battling to stay awake to chat with this woman who appeared to not care either way.

'Shall I order you a taxi?' Danny asked.

'No, I'm fine, thanks. I've just been invited to an after-party'. He winked at Danny, indicating he had already secured his chance with the woman sat beside him. 'Do you want to come along?'

'Thanks for the offer, mate, but I'm going to head back; I'm shattered. Maybe next time? Thank you so much for tonight. I will call you after the weekend'. Danny extended out his hand towards him.

He leant forward, holding out his hand and took his. In a slurred voice, he said, 'Shukran Habibi'. He could barely hear what he said due to his inebriated state, but Danny recognised it from his time working over in the Middle East. It was Arabic for 'Thank you, my friend'. He chose to ignore the recognition and released his hand as he conveyed his attention to the woman.

This was the first time he had shown anything of his origins since Danny had known him. 'A drunk mind speaks a sober heart' indeed.

•

Checking his watch: only 23:35 hours. Outside, the cold December winter air hit him like a thousand icicles, making his face tingle. Pulling the collar up on his blazer to protect his neck, then plunging his hands in his pockets. *You'd think I'd remember to bring a winter coat*, he thought to himself, battling against the wind towards his hotel, knowing grimly that there was a good ten-minute walk ahead.

At last, inside the comfort of his hotel room, placing his key card into the slot, which allowed the lights to turn on, giving a subtle illumination that imbued the room with a nice relaxing feeling. Reaching inside his jacket pocket, retrieving the exhibition brochure. Placing his jacket on the chaise longue, he continued to disrobe, stripping down to a T-shirt and boxer shorts: ample attire, given the heat of the room. Firing up his PC, then grabbing a drink from the mini bar – he retrieved his folder of circle painting photocopies from inside his bag.

There is something wonderful about sinking your feet into a luxury soft pile carpet, he thought, especially after standing in a gallery for five hours, giving his toes a good old wiggle before sitting behind the desk to examine the police report. Taking notes on every detail, trying to visualise the exact scenario. *Poor bastards*, he thought to himself, looking at the deceased, and he wondered what lengths someone would go to for revenge, money, art, rejection, loss of face, or a combination of it all.

The professional hit suggested they were dealing with highly trained and sophisticated individuals who would stop at nothing and no one to get what they wanted. Thom's theory that it was terrorist-related replayed in his head. Danny was still undecided. Thom thought Hafiz was about to coordinate some sort of terrorist attack in Europe, but the list he had gave him a gut feeling it was all about revenge in the art world; maybe the hit list were people who had double-crossed him.

Danny was sure Thom wasn't telling him everything about the so-called bigger picture. Again, he went over the police report, working backwards this time, dissecting all the details military-style. As he did so, he heard a Rupert's posh voice in his head; Rupert was a name they used to call officers when he was in the Army. *Okay, gents, this is a biggie. Pin 'em back, this is a ten-phase operation.* Danny smiled at the memory, writing down in detail the timings, locations and individuals involved, the types of weaponry used, the extraction plan and, of course, the name of the circle painting at the heart of this hit; he was trying to see if anything stood out at him, trying to think as though he were the assassin.

He went back over the Intel in front of him: thirteen names, two now confirmed dead, eleven names with eleven original paintings. *I need that police report from America regarding Christopher Durand's murder, which will confirm my gut feeling,* he thought as he scribbled down a note to ask Thom for it, wondering how Durand was taken out. He concluded that there had to be a network of killers operating globally for Durand to be murdered so quickly, and it looked as if they were directed from the UK. With that in mind, Hafiz and his female accomplice came straight into the frame. Were these first two killings just a practice run for something bigger? Maybe Thom was right that a more coordinated and sophisticated attack was yet to come. There was one thing he thought he knew for sure: it wasn't terrorism.

Danny took hold of the image that contained the blank circles he had photographed with one hand and held his small sketch of the red circle from the burnt image with the other, and wondered if the assassin of Christopher Durand had an image to match to his original anthrax circle painting. He tried to see if the two papers in his hands had a connection. *Nope, nothing, each image is unique,* he thought, pausing and taking a sip of his drink. The idea suddenly hit him quicker than he could swallow. *That's it!* he thought, coming to the conclusion that the edition was used to instruct the killer in what to do and when to do it. However, the limited-edition copy used by the killer surely couldn't be fully identical to the original… or could it?

He was deep in the mind of a killer, deciphering the possible code, when a sudden knock on the door made him jump. *Must be Bernadette,* he thought, even as he glanced down at his iPhone, surprised he had missed her text – but there was nothing. *Bloody phones, bloody signal*, he thought as he quickly closed his laptop and placed all his paperwork inside his bag. To cover the delay, he shouted towards the door, 'Just a minute'. After placing the bag in the wardrobe, closing the door securely, he then looked through the spyhole in the bedroom door to see a female looking the other way; her back was to him. He thought it was Bernadette and that she was teasing him. He decided to play, too.

'Who is it?' he asked, starting to smile at her humour.

'Room service', she replied and he laughed out loud, opening the door wide.

It was only then that she turned around. To his surprise, it wasn't Bernadette standing there. As quickly as he was startled and alerted to her ID, she pulled a pistol up from where it had been concealed down by her side. It had a silencer attached to the end of the barrel and she aimed it directly at his head. *Fuck!* he thought; instinctively, he grabbed the pistol barrel as she fired off a shot, which just missed his head.

His hands firmly gripped onto the pistol with hers, swinging their bodies to the right-hand side, taking the aim of the barrel away from his face. Simultaneously, she kneed him in the stomach, taking him down, yet he still managed to hold the pistol tight. The feeling of being winded took his breath and they grappled towards the bed, with Danny well and acutely aware that if he let go of his grip, he was dead. With training and accuracy, he elbowed her to the side of her head, dropping her this time, and then both of them stumbled to the floor. Whilst on the floor, a blonde wig came flying off. He was elated and gathered more strength as he managed to release the pistol from her hand, just as she head-butted him in the face, just like a worst-case mindless football hooligan. Tears welled up in his eyes, blinding him for a split-second. The pistol flew across the room and slid right under the bed. *Thank fuck for that*, he thought as he quickly followed up and punched his assailant directly in the face, taking her down again, giving him a chance to compose himself, to assess the situation. He felt no guilt; after all, she could seriously handle herself.

Never underestimate a woman should have been what he was thinking. He thought she was down and out, but even as he watched, she crawled across the room and grabbed an ornament from the bedside cabinet. She smashed it over his head, flooring him hard – Whack! The glass shattered everywhere and in the chaos, she got up quickly, grabbing her wig off the floor, and made her getaway.

Danny lay on the floor, dazed, panting for a few seconds, feeling like shit and trying to compose himself. His training then kicked in; he swiftly stood up and closed the door. 'Fucking bitch', he mumbled to himself as he quickly grabbed a couple of whisky miniatures from the mini bar, emptied them into a tumbler and administered them in one. Purely medicinal, of course, to numb the pain. Walking into the bathroom, he made the inevitable discovery that as well as feeling like shit, he also looked the part: blood was running from a cut to the side of his head. He leant on the sink for stability and ran the tap, washing the blood from his face and applying pressure to stop the flow. He waited, staring at himself in the mirror and the obvious hit him. Someone wanted him dead for sure. *Who? Who the fuck was that bitch? Marina? Was that her with Hafiz earlier?* Shock took over; his heart pumped loudly.

The adrenalin subsided and he calmed down. Grabbing a towel, he held it over the wound, applying pressure, slowly stopping the bleeding.

The room was in a right state. He picked up the pieces of broken glass and threw them into the wastepaper bin before hobbling down onto all fours to retrieve the pistol. He looked at it closely. Still holding it, getting back up from off the floor, in pain, he sat gingerly on the bed. *A Sig P226, with suppressor, nice,* he thought, pressing the magazine release catch, which was located on the side of the piston grip; the mag fell from its housing into his left hand. He saw that it was a full mag minus the round embedded in the wall. He cocked the pistol, which released a 9mm brass bullet out of the chamber onto the bed.

Danny picked it up with a chilly feeling. If tonight had gone according to plan, this round would have had his name written all over it. *This is some heavy shit for a Friday night,* he thought, carefully placing it back in the magazine. He reloaded the mag back into the pistol, cocking it and placing the safety catch back on. He didn't think of disposing it; Danny decided to hang on to it instead. *Could come in useful,* he thought; he certainly wouldn't be taking any chances next time.

'Ping!' A text suddenly came through on his iPhone; it was Bernadette, *Hey darling, sorry it's so late, I'm on my way now.* Thank God she didn't come earlier.

Immediately scrolling down to Thom's number, pressing Call; it rang twice. He answered. 'Danny, what's up?'

'Thom, this shit's just got real; some bitch has tried to blow my fucking head off', he said, rather perturbed and pissed off.

'Can you identify her? Did you recognise her?' he asked with a sense of urgency.

'It could be the woman from the photograph you showed me. I'm not completely sure. She may have been at the gallery exhibition I attended tonight with Hafiz'. He described the whole incident from start to finish to see what he could make of it.

'Have you told anyone else? Have the local police been notified yet? Any witnesses, anyone hear it?' He went through the list Danny expected him to.

'No, no one, just you. Shall I inform the police?' Danny asked.

'No, don't involve the police, this could blow the whole operation', he said with authority.

'We are getting close to shutting this network down. I'll be in touch'. He ended the call abruptly.

Well, thanks for offering a fucking plaster, Thom, he thought, irritated by his apparent equanimity. Tossing his phone down onto the bed; angry, confused and annoyed. 'Fuck'. Danny forgot to ask him to send the report on Durand's hit. 'Fuck', he said out loud, looking around the room: How the hell was he going to explain all this? He decided he'd just tell Bernadette he was jumped by a couple of drunken thugs as he left the gallery. He hurriedly tidied the place up – looking forward to her sympathy.

FOURTEEN

———— • ————

Early on the Monday morning, with the echo of Hafiz's Arabic gratitude fresh in his head, reminiscing of the past, Danny lay on the bed looking intently at nothing up on the ceiling. He drew back on a conversation he once had with an Iraqi local back in Baghdad, who said, *A man who isn't afraid to die cannot be defeated.*

Textbook procedure would be to plant oneself close to the enemy to study his daily movements, to relive his life patterns. Danny was feeling up for this as he'd known Hafiz for several months now. Whereas he was initially convinced Hafiz wasn't a serial killer, some beefed-up, blonde-wigged psycho with a loaded pistol, offering bad room service, kind of made him see things in a different light.

As with any new friendship, a lot of emotional information had already been received. Danny scrutinised his regular patterns: attending many art and fashion exhibitions with crazy drink- and drug-fuelled after-parties, the odd shopping trip to Knightsbridge, fine dining at fancy restaurants and his favourite pastime of daily visits to an array of galleries.

What had happened to cause someone like him to participate in murder? Maybe the death of his parents, combined with the brainwashing of his uncle, pushed him towards being evil. He was seeking revenge;

maybe he had killed in the past and was going to kill again. And what sort of person was he that Danny couldn't see right now?

Danny continued musing on his theme. Hafiz wasn't a psychopath either; he didn't have an anti-social personality disorder, at least not one manifested in perversion, aggression or criminal behaviour anyway. Hafiz and his associates had an ideology as their main common denominator, which in turn motivated them; yet Danny was not convinced that any religious belief was up for manipulating for his own personal gain, unless the orchestrator led them to believe it was religiously motivated. *But how would they know anyway?* he thought. He wasn't ruling anything out. 'Hafiz the Martyr' as the assassin was timed out for their strict religious belief, which left Danny trying to tie in whatever had happened to make him quit New York.

He glanced down to the pistol beside him; he didn't get a warm feeling that a box of chocolates would give him. *Time for another face-to-face chat with Thom to get some real answers,* he thought.

Piecing together the intel he had from him and Bernadette, he was drawn to questioning if Hafiz had fallen out with a syndicate of people who'd helped fund him to purchase high-net-value pieces of art, but who ended up wanting their investment back from him. *Surely there would be a legal binding contract in place between both parties?* he thought. Taking it a stage further and supposing that Hafiz part-owned art with the syndicate, these thirteen individuals with only eleven left standing, he tried to rationalise his actions if, for example, they double-crossed him, owing him millions of pounds in profit if his sourced works sold at auction. Danny's thought process went hazy when he realised that taking two out by a trained assassin didn't make sense in this scenario, as the art owned was now destroyed. He was still waiting for intel on the cripple's *Primus Circle* painting; presuming he owned one, he also assumed that was destroyed too. So this was not even a robbery of the two pieces, perhaps so they could have been sold at auction for Hafiz to top up his personal wealth. Instead, it was complete destruction of the art, which sent out a message.

Danny used to like puzzles when he was a kid because you at least had all the pieces in a big heap on the floor to look at. Here, so many puzzle pieces were missing. His mind drifted into another category: psychopathic behaviour. The hallmark of a psychopath is the inability to recognise that others are worthy of compassion. Therefore, did Hafiz emphasise his feeling of being abandoned so that the people who totally rejected him just became just pure images in his mind. A psychopathic killer's victims are dehumanised by denial so the killer does not have to face reality; they are made into worthless objects. Hafiz craved attention – had these people now all neglected him – but as a result of what? What was his relationship like with his family prior to the devastating airstrike that killed them in Yemen? It must have affected him as a young child to know his parents were killed; it certainly would mess with Danny's head.

Hafiz had told Danny that he didn't want a real relationship... and Danny overheard him reject the beautiful woman at the Lisson Gallery. A psychopathic serial killer is only capable of sadomasochistic relationships based on power, not attachment, leading to them becoming incapable of expressing empathy – for anyone. Had he seen that in action at the gallery?

Scratching his head as if the motion would stimulate a thought bubble. *Why do we do that?* he wondered, and all he got was his mind bursting, stuck on overdrive. He decided to send Hafiz a text message: *Morning Hafiz, the other night was great, how was the after-party? Fancy meeting up?* Moments later – 'ping' – the sound of his iPhone as a text appeared on the screen from Hafiz:

Hey Danny, yes, it was fantastic. Pop around anytime.

Danny got dressed and noticed in the mirror a small dark bruise above his eye from that bitch's head impacting his on Friday night. *Time to start looking over my shoulder again,* he thought.

Thirty minutes later, he was at Hafiz's apartment, and he noticed his window blinds were open for a pleasant change. He was now an expert at pre-empting what sort of mood he would be in from the position of his blinds. As normal, he stood at the top of the steps ringing the doorbell and waited for signs of life from his window. Seconds later, his head popped into view and he got the thumbs-up, along with a smile to accompany his voice through the intercom: 'Come on in, my friend'. The security door catch was released.

Hafiz greeted him as he pushed the door open and walked inside the building. He was standing at the door of his apartment. 'Hey, Danny, didn't think I'd see you today. Friday was a great night, wasn't it? Come on in'. He gesticulated with happiness, showcasing the way in. It was at this point Danny suddenly pieced together what he meant. *I bet you didn't think you'd see me today.* He was cautiously suspicious.

'Yes, it was an eventful night. When I left you at the gallery, I was heading back to the hotel, and then suddenly I was jumped upon by two large blokes'. He observed his reaction.

'Oh dear, are you okay?' He dutifully looked concerned. 'What did they want? Money?'

'Yeah, I'm fine, you should see the state of the other two', he said jokingly, laughing, trying to antagonise him in a way to get a response. 'No idea what they wanted, I didn't ask; it sort of didn't come up'.

'You can never be too careful these days, my friend'.

His unusual overly nice behaviour was making Danny wonder if he knew he was on to something, and if he was lulling him into a false sense of security. They both walked into his living room.

Hafiz smiled. 'I was given some good news, Danny, and I just wanted to celebrate a little longer at the after-party'. His demeanour didn't change.

'What good news was that, then?' He put on a face that suggested there was a romantic involvement.

'Just about some old friends from olden times, as it were'. His face looked distant and he spoke sarcastically. Danny didn't let his curiosity show.

'Sounds great. So, what do you fancy doing today, Hafiz?' He watched him refocus his distant eyes on the scene outside the window, as if assessing the outside world.

'Umm, how about we get some fresh coffee and breakfast, and then head to an art gallery for a wander to clear the soul?' He spoke with a real sense of excitement; art was his mental therapy.

'Sounds like a great plan, mate'.

Hafiz nodded in agreement. 'Right, I'll just get ready. Give me five minutes'. He jumped off his chair and disappeared into his bedroom, switching on music, which swiftly became muffled in the background as he closed the door behind him.

The etiquette of what it is acceptable to do whilst you are alone in a friend's living room probably does not include snooping around, even more so after nearly being compromised last time. Danny had no choice; he needed to find that brown envelope that was given to him on Friday night. He stood up quickly and headed towards the study, with one trained ear on the noises coming from Hafiz's bedroom and two trained eyes scanning for signs of the envelope. To his frustration, though perhaps it was inevitable, he couldn't see it lying around anywhere obvious.

'Bollocks', he whispered and he walked back into the living room, sitting back down in the chair. *Shit*, he thought, punching the arm of the chair in more frustration; the envelope must be in his bedroom. As he gazed around, his eyes were drawn to the chair near the bookcase: the tuxedo suit jacket he'd worn at the exhibition was conveniently draped over the back. Athletically, Danny quickly jumped off the chair and rushed over to check the inside pockets. *Bingo! The brown envelope*, he thought as he pulled it out to take a look, one ear still scanning for noises indicating Hafiz's progress. He deduced he was safe for now.

Opening the top of the unsealed envelope, he saw there was another list of names written on white paper inside. Speedily, Danny took out his iPhone to take a photo, then shoved his phone back into his rear jeans pocket and pushed the piece of paper back in the envelope in record time. Still watching Hafiz's bedroom door like a hawk as he placed the envelope back in the tuxedo jacket and then rushed back to his seat, grabbing a large Mario Testino photography book from off his coffee table on his way.

Danny randomly opened the book, pretending to read what was inside, when the music went silent and his bedroom door opened. 'That's me, let's get out of here!' Hafiz said. He was wearing his usual signature style; Danny, as usual, was not in any particular style at all.

'You're looking very suave and sophisticated'.

Hafiz grinned. 'You know me, Danny, keeping up appearances'. They headed outside and Hafiz flagged down a black cab; they sat in the back and the slightly echoed voice asked, 'Where to, gents?'

Danny leaned forward so he could hear. 'Bankside, please'.

The driver reset his meter. 'Okay, geezer', he replied, chomping on gum as they set off towards the river. Bankside is where the Tate Modern is located and he knew some of Joseph Legend's works were part of the gallery's permanent collection. Danny was hopeful it would prompt a reaction from Hafiz.

Danny simply stared out of the window at all the morning activity. Then he started to think about what was on the list he'd just retrieved from the brown envelope. What was it about it that had overwhelmed Hafiz and the woman on Friday night? He desperately wanted to look at it again; it felt like his iPhone was burning a hole in his pocket.

Whilst he was still deep in thought, the cab came to an abrupt halt at the side of the road. Literally.

Once on 'dry land', they spotted a coffee shop in front of them and Hafiz headed in that direction. 'Looks good to me', he said, speeding up to get out of the cold.

They both took a seat, appreciating the warmth inside, the aromas of the cooking breakfasts and the variety of the menu. The waitress soon came over efficiently. Hafiz smiled at her, flirtatious and direct, requesting, 'A cafetiére of coffee for two, medium roast; fresh croissants, some toast and freshly squeezed orange juice, please'.

She blushed at the intensity of his gaze and her pretty cheeks turned red as she smiled back. 'Thank you, sir'. She walked away, hips swinging, this way and that, towards the kitchen.

Hafiz laughed. 'That, I believe, has made her day', he said, and they both chuckled.

Whilst waiting for their food to arrive, they chatted about the exhibition at the Lisson Gallery, mulling over the pieces of work that had been on display. Danny could see he was in his element when someone took an interest in their passion, and it was a mutual passion. The conversation flowed naturally, like water.

'I'm thinking of putting on an exhibition myself', Danny suggested.

'Sounds like a great idea, Danny', he replied enthusiastically.

'Maybe you could host it for me?' he asked respectfully.

'Of course, my friend, I'll be honoured', he said, as his eyes glossed over emotionally in appreciation.

'Thanks, I've made enough contacts here in London to put on a great show'.

'Going totally off the subject of your exhibition, I think Bernadette has an eye for you', Hafiz suddenly said, smiling directly at him. His unexpected words took him totally by surprise, so it was good that he replied as quickly as he did.

'Does she?' Obviously, Danny wasn't going to let on that Bernadette and he had recently shared more than pleasantries together, like two crazed rabbits. 'I mean, I'm blind to these sorts of things sometimes'. Danny acted all daft and made out that he lacked confidence, in the hope that the great master of flirting would reassure him. 'What would she see in a guy like me?' he said.

'Ah, I can just tell, my friend; leave it with me'. He seemed to be enjoying this orchestration of his life. Hafiz eyed up the pretty waitress, laughing and smiling at her as she placed their order down on the table in front of them. 'Thank you, my dear', he said, with a quick wink.

The croissants were light and fresh, as was Hafiz, so Danny decided to turn up the heat on dissecting his personal life.

'I know I've asked you this question before, but how come you're not married or settled down with anyone yourself?' Danny asked bluntly. He looked at him and he nodded towards the pretty waitress behind the counter. 'I've seen the way women respond to you; you have a gift, my friend'. Danny watched carefully for his reaction, having buttered him up more than the croissants.

'There was someone special, once upon a time, but the timing just wasn't right'. He shoved a piece of croissant in his mouth, concentrating on his plate. Danny moved in.

'Why, what happened?' He tried to keep the questioning light. 'Did she break your heart?' he asked whilst sipping his coffee nonchalantly.

He finished chewing and swallowed before he spoke. 'No, we are still very much in love, but she understands my life, you see'. He wiped his mouth with a napkin as though that concluded the subject, but Danny thought it was a strange thing to say. He didn't let on, though.

'Maybe one day', Danny simply said.

'Indeed, my friend, you never know', he replied. Then he immediately changed the subject to Christmas, the hallmarks of which were all around them, this being December and London.

'Ah, my favourite time of year', Hafiz said, nodding his head.

Just as their conversation was flowing onwards on their respective forthcoming Christmas festivities, Danny mused that – *Muslims really don't celebrate Christmas*. Then Hafiz's phone rang, interrupting the revelation of their plans. Quickly, he snatched it off the table before Danny could read who was calling him. Danny made a big point of drinking his coffee to give him space and sat back casually, looking around, sussing out his body language in his peripheral view. He didn't really talk, just lowered his voice and responded to someone, 'Uh huh, yes', as if the subject was awkward to discuss in front of Danny.

Danny drained his coffee cup and looked towards him. He had his head lowered, muffling what he could hear from the phone, yet after one of his 'uh huh, yeses', he glanced up and his eyes met Danny's. Pausing for a moment of silence. It was not a gaze of sorrow. Or anguish. It was a gaze of suspicion. Though he couldn't hear what the other party had said, Danny was instantly suspicious that his name had just come up. Trying not to panic. Instead, he acknowledged that his cup was empty as he poured another coffee for himself, hoping to defuse the moment. But he blanked the offer. Wondering if he was speaking to the woman from the other night, who had a fucking weird idea that room service killed the guests whilst folding back their sheets.

Danny pulled his knife towards him as if to put some jam on his slice of toast, feeling comparatively secure with some stainless steel in his hand, just in case he was mad enough to try something in public; always improvise when dealing with psychopaths. A sudden change in the conversation made him halt in his preparations, however, and the toast hovered in mid-air, ready for his tastebuds.

'Okay, goodbye'. He placed the phone face down on the table and poured himself another coffee in complete silence. His mood had changed and was not light and airy any more. He looked rather as though he had been given some bad news; it was obvious something was bothering him.

'Is everything okay?' Danny asked, concerned.

He paused briefly to compose himself. 'Everything is fine', he replied and sighed heavily. Then said, apropos of nothing: 'Loyalty'. He paused again then continued to talk. 'People over the years have abandoned me when I've most needed them'. He shook his head in disgust.

'I'm still here, mate'. Because of his change in demeanour, however, Danny leant back in his chair, creating some distance between them just in case he was going to lash out and strike him. They kept eye contact and Danny raised his eyebrows reassuringly.

'Yes, you are, Danny, and I thank you. You wouldn't abandon me, would you?' Danny thought it was a rather strange thing for a man to say, especially to another man; it was more the type of issue a heterosexual couple would be ironing out.

Danny's expression changed to one of seriousness, as did the tone of his voice, as he looked directly into his eyes and reassured him: 'I'll be here to the end, unless the end is here before me'. Hafiz grinned, nodding in acceptance of his explanation, but he felt he was treading with caution. He made eye contact with the waitress and asked for the bill.

'Certainly, sir'. She smiled and went to prepare it as Hafiz put his phone back into his jacket pocket.

'Danny, I'm going to have to cancel our walk around the Tate Modern today. I just remembered I have something very important to do back at my place', he said sternly.

'Oh, okay, mate. Do you fancy going some other time?' Sounding disappointed, despite being suspicious of his sudden change of heart.

'Yes, definitely. We will visit another time. Listen, I'm going to have to go. Pop around later this evening if you want to'. He seemed suddenly hurried.

'Okay. I'll call you first to see if you're still free'. As Danny spoke, the waitress came over with the bill. She was clearly trying to lock eyes with Hafiz again, but this time he totally ignored her as he was gathering up his things. Danny felt embarrassed for her at the confusion and the disheartened look on her face. 'Thank you', Danny said, quite obviously to her, leaving a generous tip. He felt sorry for her as they both stood up and walked outside.

Something about that phone call had just ruined Hafiz's day – and messed around with Danny's. Hafiz definitely looked spooked, as if he needed to head off and sort out whatever it was that had happened. Danny wondered if he should tail him; however, he decided against that; his gut feeling today was to stay safe and not compromise himself.

Hafiz flagged down a taxi and shook his hand. 'See you later, Danny. Thanks for breakfast'.

Danny tried one last stab, to see if he could win him over and turn his mood around. 'Are you sure you are okay?' he asked.

'Yes, yes, I'm fine', he replied. He jumped into the back of the cab and wound down the window.

'See you later, Danny'.

He watched the taxi drive off towards the bridge, heading for the other side of the river. He felt confused, his mind now racing to get some intel on that call he had just received, to analyse what he knew. It made him feel uneasy. *Are they onto me? Or has something happened that they are now compromised instead?* he thought, assuming every eventuality.

FIFTEEN

—— • ——

Danny's mood now officially sucked. He didn't feel like looking around the Tate Modern any more either, so he decided to walk back to his hotel in Mayfair. Looking at his watch, it was still early, 11.30, which changed his mind; he needed to get some answers. Everything presented so far just didn't add up. Phoning Thom as he walked along the busy street.

He answered promptly as usual. 'Thom, can we meet up today?' Danny asked, toneless.

'Same place, one hour', he replied, ending the call.

Back in Lou's Café, there was the familiar aroma of coffee, and Thom was already sitting at the back in the corner facing towards the window. His newspaper lay open on the table in front of him.

'I'll have a black coffee and the same for him sat over there, please', Danny said to the girl behind the counter whilst pointing towards Thom. Walking over to his table.

'Hey, Thom'. Taking off his jacket, hanging it on the back of the chair.

'Is everything okay, Danny? You sounded a bit on edge'. His supercilious attitude enraged him. Barely looking up at him as he licked his thumb, turning the page of his *Times* newspaper.

Danny sat down in front of him, leaning forward, resting his arms on the table, trying not to raise his voice – furious.

'On edge; what gave you that impression? Oh, I know, possibly that I was wrestling with a psycho bitch, just as she tried to blow my fucking face off. Forgive me if I sound on edge. I think he's on to me'. Danny sighed and shook his head, visibly pissed off.

'Calm down, Danny, you can handle it', he said flippantly. 'We are very close to getting these bastards'.

Danny replied, offended by his tone. Immediately on the offensive. 'I applaud your optimism, Thom, but it still doesn't hide the fact that she wanted me dead'.

'Listen, if you extract yourself now, it will evoke suspicion and jeopardise this whole operation'.

He lifted his newspaper, sliding over a brown A4 folder across the table towards Danny. 'Christopher Durand's initial murder report'. He spoke with a coldness that he'd never heard in a voice before. Nodding towards it. 'This is what we are dealing with, Danny'. He sat back in his chair and ran his hands through his hair.

Danny opened the folder discreetly, aware of his surroundings: his eyes were immediately glued to the page, sending a spine-chilling shiver through his body. He could hear his pulse beat in his ears as he carefully read through the gruesome details. 'For the love of God', he said, imagining his horrific death. 'Poor Bastard'.

The frightening, disturbing image of Christopher's body was locked in his mind. A deathly silence was all he could conjure up. Closing the folder, horrified. He took a big, deep breath and exhaled slowly. 'Like I said, Thom, being on the edge is an understatement'. Directed fear now gripped him.

Thom took a sip of coffee. He smirked at Danny, and he spoke calmly. 'He experienced a brutal death; it really was some heavy shit that went down in that heinous crime. I have spoken to the forensics team at CIA-Langley: now that they have finished examining what was left of him, along with taking a statement from his housekeeper who discovered him burning on the patio, we have been able to learn that another circle painting that belonged to him was destroyed in the hit'.

Danny perked up with interest. 'So, that's two of these paintings, originals, now destroyed'. There was the start of a pattern.

'Yes, and just like Derek's murder, no other works of art were touched'.

'Are there any connections at all between Christopher and Hafiz?' he questioned.

'There are specialists examining electronic data retrieved from Christopher's home; once I have something of interest, I will let you know'. Thom tried to sound convincing. *You're talking shit, Thom*, he thought.

It was time for Danny to get answers to something that had been niggling him from the onset. 'What happened in New York? Why did Hafiz leave?' he asked, probing.

Thom took off his glasses. His eyes narrowed, pausing, his pupils a glittering black, bottomless, opaque. 'What do you know? Why? Has someone said something?' – It was his turn to take in a breath and exhale slowly.

Danny was pleased to see that somehow, he'd hit a nerve. 'I've been rubbing shoulders with some of the art world's elite; people just talk, you hear things. I've tried to question Hafiz directly but got nothing. He behaves as if he never had a life over there. I think whatever reason made him leave may well be the catalyst to all of this'. Danny observed Thom carefully.

With a frown, he hesitated and gave a perfunctory nod, placing his glasses back on. 'In light of what we know, his drug problem never helped then it was his downfall. People have reputations to keep. They just couldn't afford to be associated with someone like Hafiz in that state of mind; most people have a difficult time understanding the concept of addiction'. Thom preferred to flick through his newspaper than make direct eye contact with Danny.

'No. Way. I'm not having – "it's because he takes drugs" – so you are telling me he is the only one within that circle of art socialites using? What a load of bollocks'. He was firmly calling his bluff. Shaking his head in annoyance. It got his attention.

Thom's face held forward a steady gaze.

'It's got to be something more serious than just taking drugs and the reputation of some corporation. People make mistakes, so what?' He was sceptical of this collateral scenario. Danny knew Thom was holding back something he needed to know, but why?

Thom's poker face was just pure perfection from years of being undercover. He momentarily switched the conversation off. by signalling over for two more coffees from the girl behind the counter.

After she brought them over, he eventually replied, 'We have to try to intercept the sleeper cell we believe is his'. He dropped a handful of sugar cubes into his coffee.

'Yeah and? Surely you have the surveillance teams on the ground; don't you?' Danny wasn't getting it.

He stirred his coffee. 'We find it difficult to profile their existence; they simply just get on with normal life, like chameleons blending into the background. You know how it is, don't you?'

'The perfect infiltration, I know, all right'. Agreeing, as Thom nodded.

'You have to ask yourself, Danny, is society today constantly sleepwalking? Too busy looking down at their handheld devices to notice what's really going on around them'.

'True', he replied, nodding. *I wonder if Bernadette has sent any texts.*

Thom's dedication was magnetic to him. He obviously lived and breathed this shit. 'Sleepers can spend years being regular people, performing regular jobs, having normal relationships, hobbies – all the while living deep undercover. And then suddenly – wham – they receive orders from their handlers either to commit an act of terrorism or to provide aid to those who will'.

His eyes kept glancing over Danny's shoulders, observant to any movement, ready to react: like he had the reflexes of a mousetrap.

'Can't we just simply arrest Hafiz now?' Danny asked.

'No, as we can't tell for sure how many are involved. You have to think of the bigger picture, Danny'.

'I am thinking of the bigger picture, believe me; I'm thinking of me staying alive. Painting'. He frowned as he took a sip of coffee.

'Remember, they are predators, Danny, and no one is safe'. He spoke with the typical Establishment encouragement shit, finishing the last dregs of his coffee. Folding up his newspaper, he stood up, adjusting the collar on his jacket. 'Anything else for me?'

Pausing. 'No, nothing'. Danny decided not to tell him about the new list that he had on his iPhone. He wanted to examine it first before he revealed it to him.

'You can keep that report as a reminder of what we are up against; we have your back, Danny'. He scooped up his newspaper and placed it under his arm. 'Call me anytime'. He left.

'Roger that, Thom'. Danny turned around to watch him leave then took out his iPhone from his pocket. He wanted to see the photo he had taken earlier at Hafiz's apartment. Squinting: using his thumb and forefinger to zoom in on the image. He noticed the list was almost identical to the original list he'd found in Hafiz's drawer – but this time, beside each name, written in red, was the word: *Accepted*, also some random letters which looked very familiar, almost like city abbreviation codes: JFK, GVA, LHR. *That's definitely London Heathrow*, he thought. Derek and Christopher were not on this list, *Why?* His dumb moment was over. *Because they are both now dead*, he thought. Looking at this with a fresh pair of eyes, something spectacular was going down. 'For Chrissake', he whispered, placing his iPhone back into his pocket.

Walking over to the counter to pay for the coffees, he tried to gather his thoughts, mind racing. He had no choice but to continue working for Thom. It left him with no real confidence in the situation he had been forced into. He headed back to the hotel.

Inside his room, he grabbed his bag of tricks from within the wardrobe – all his printed circle pictures, photos and research. Taking his laptop off sleep mode, he connected his iPhone to the PC to download the image he took earlier in order to get a better view; he couldn't afford to miss anything. Whilst he waited for the download, he headed for the bathroom and removed the back panel off the toilet system. Placing it on the side next to the sink, he reached in for the rolled-up hand towel that was concealing the pistol he'd acquired on Friday night. *I don't want lightning to strike twice*, he thought to himself, unravelling the towel. He released the safety catch and part-cocked the top slide tray to check there was a round still in the chamber – then reapplied the safety catch. Putting the panel back minus the pistol – placing it down on the desk beside him and the laptop.

Third – or is it fourth? – time lucky... or so he hoped as he went through all the intel he had with a mighty fine-toothed comb to check and double-check that he hadn't missed anything important. He now agreed with Thom that something big was happening very soon. But, he still believed it was not terrorism but personal revenge. Doubts hit him: was it both? After all, any terrorist attack could be claimed by an extremist group. It could be revenge, yet still, simultaneously, be a success in the eyes of the terrorist groups.

With MI6 and the CIA now involved, there was no doubt this was some serious shit. He thought wryly, *Where is my Queen's shilling for my troubles?* Once a soldier, always a soldier. Yet this was no joke. He still needed to work out how and when and what – and prevent it from happening.

Eleven people, all of whom owned original circle paintings, had accepted something from Hafiz. Authors get writer's block… what do ex-soldiers get? *Fucking stressed*, he thought. Danny was mentally exhausted looking down at his watch. He couldn't believe it was late afternoon already; he quickly got changed into his running gear, wanting to head out for a jog to puzzle through this and de-stress.

Speedily cutting across Hyde Park. *Not bad timing*, he thought, as he was sucking air from China. In the distance in front of him was a familiar slender figure heading towards him, walking along the path, stylishly wrapped up warm; it was Bernadette.

He approached her, removing his earphones, switching off the music on his iPhone.

'Hey, Danny', she said, as she pushed her hair out of her face and smiled. Then leaning in, pecking him on the cheek.

'Hello, gorgeous, how are you? he asked.

'I'm good, thanks, darling'. As they stared into each other's eyes.

'Not in the gallery today?' Danny asked, placing his hands on his hips, casually catching his breath.

'I was earlier, but I had to pop across town to sign some documents. Two originals are being loaned to a gallery for an exhibition in the New Year'. The wind blew her hair.

'What? Galleries loan to other galleries?' He was interested; something felt wrong.

'It's a bit more complicated than that. We have a large secure storage facility for our more exclusive clients' personal collections; they purchase art and never hang them sometimes, which I think is a sin'. She shook her head in disgust.

'Wow, surely art needs to be seen; it needs to breathe?' he questioned.

'Exactly! Why buy art to never see the light of day? At least these two pieces will.'

'Fantastic. One day, I'll own a great collection.' *Once I sort this shit out and get my life back on track*, he thought.

'Let me know when you want to start collecting. I'll advise you the best I can.' She winked at him, smiling.

'How will I pay you, I wonder…?' He laughed… Pulling her towards him, quickly kissing her on the lips.

'I think we could come to some sort of special arrangement.' She bit her lip. Blushing.

'Sounds good to me.' Danny decided to walk with her whilst they chatted more. 'I bet you're very busy this time of year?' he asked as she suddenly found something side-splittingly funny. 'What's so funny?' he asked, confused.

'I'm dressed like this and you're in your running gear.' Their contrast in style amused her. She tried to suppress her giggling, but she let out bursts of laughter as they continued to walk.

'Huh? I'm a man's man. Clothes are clothes.'

'Don't you think it looks a little strange, walking together like this?' She pointed at both of them.

'Nah, I'll just say you kidnapped me whilst I was out jogging', he said as he held her hand tight. She pulled him in closer to her, chuckling. 'Hey, lady, let go of my hand', he jokingly said out loud as an old couple walked past them whilst walking their Yorkshire Terrier through the park.

'Danny!' she shouted, embarrassingly giggling to herself.

'What?' he said, trying to keep a straight face as the couple looked at them weirdly.

She looked up at him, pausing for a moment, holding her breath as tears filled her eyes. 'Are you okay?' he asked, concerned.

'Yes, I'm fine. It's nothing; it's been a long time'. As she squeezed him tighter.

'Long time?' he asked.

'To just smile and laugh', she replied, as he kissed her on the head, reassuring her he understood her.

'So, what have you been up to today?' She changed the subject and looked away.

'Well, this morning, I was having breakfast with Hafiz over at Bankside. We were meant to go and have a look around the Tate Modern, but he received a phone call whilst we were eating breakfast; reckoned he urgently had to rush back to his apartment.'

'Bankside? Across the river?'

'Yeah, we were at the coffee shop right near the Tate?'

'Darling, that's where I was with him'. She looked at him intently. 'I bumped into Hafiz about quarter to twelve-ish. We both must have sat at that same place then. We had a coffee before I had to return back for appointments; he was in great spirits.'

'Oh really?' Danny couldn't hide his obvious confusion. This was strange.

'He didn't mention you', she replied, then kissed his lips. Needless to say, his lips were also confused. 'Is everything okay? What's wrong?' she asked.

'Nothing'. He pulled her into him and kissed her passionately. Only when they came apart did he ask: 'Did he go inside the Tate then?' He pretended her allure was confusing him, which it partly was.

'Yes; it's one of his favourite galleries. And, believe me, he's always over there. It's like a place of worship for him'. She laughed. Danny, on the other hand, was not laughing. He couldn't believe his ears; Hafiz had blatantly lied. But how was he going to continue this line of enquiry without sounding intrusive?

'He must have left me roughly about 11.30. He flagged down a taxi to head back to his apartment, and he looked quite worried, to be honest'. The word *trust* swirled around in his head.

'Maybe he was able to sort the issue out whilst he was travelling back in the taxi, then told the driver to turn around and you had gone?' Bernadette thankfully was positive.

'Yes, you're probably right, as long as he's okay?' he added, showing compassion.

'Honestly, he was fine. We talked about the forthcoming Legend circle paintings exhibition; he's really excited, you know'.

'Sounds great, doesn't it?' Not for the first time did he wonder why Hafiz was so two-faced about the Legend paintings. *What's the connection? Why the secrecy?* he wondered, respectfully envious of such a show, though.

'If you ask me, it's a great achievement for any artist to exhibit a lifetime's worth of work in eleven galleries around the world'. Bernadette looked impressed.

'Yep, it truly is'. Nodding in agreement, almost in a hypnotic state, gazing into nothing, trying to make sense of this new information. This wasn't the time or place, but suddenly the penny dropped like an atom bomb hitting Hiroshima. *Holy fuck. It all starts to make sense. Eleven galleries. Eleven original circle paintings and eleven names.*

Danny needed an escape plan. 'Hey, I've just remembered I have to answer a few emails, so I will quickly pop back to the hotel and get showered. I'll give you a call later? We could do something if you're free?'

'Okay, darling, that's great. Just let me know'. She looked lovely standing there in front of him.

'Yep, perfect'. Danny said. And so was she. He couldn't resist her: he grabbed her waist and pulled her in close towards him, kissing her passionately on her lips. They didn't kiss for long. Danny was soon sprinting back to his hotel thinking hard, thinking over and over.

SIXTEEN

———— • ————

Being dumped by Hafiz played on his mind repeatedly, like the stylus stuck on a scratched record called *Why*. *Why would Hafiz lie to me?* he thought. *Why after a weird phone call did he cancel the gallery visit and run off back to his apartment? Why did he return to the Tate Modern by himself? Why orchestrate the façade? Maybe he did sort out an emergency in the taxi, but if he was going to return within fifteen minutes or so, why didn't he phone me?* Danny thought, questioning the obvious conclusion that was he didn't want him there.

The next conclusion was that someone had spooked him on that phone call, or they had specifically instructed him to undertake something important without him being present. Danny's thought process was on overtime. The worst conclusion was that Bernadette was somehow involved, and his head started spinning at that. *Involved in what? Was she involved in the whole thing or only some of it? Was she willingly or unwillingly involved? Were her emotions towards Danny an act, a ploy? Was he being duped?* Hafiz told him he wasn't a fan of the Tate gallery; Bernadette stated otherwise. She'd known him longer than Danny had, of course, so *what the fuck was going on?* Hafiz said he wasn't a fan of Legend's work: she said he loved Legend's work and was especially excited about the forthcoming circle paintings exhibitions. Danny's mind wanted to explode at the various contradictions.

He decided to head over to the other side of the river on Bankside to see if he could actually make it into the Tate Modern gallery and past the coffee shop. The capital was getting ready for the Christmas festivities. Shops were outdoing each other as to who could create the most amazing window displays, and the cold, crisp winter morning air added to the atmosphere. Breathing it in gave him a sense of euphoria from his own festive days. Danny kind of liked Christmas.

Crossing the Millennium Bridge, he looked towards Bankside, built after World War II as Bankside Power Station. His historical side took over. This grand industrial piece of architecture now held awe-inspiring modern art. In the main galleries, the original cavernous turbine hall was used to jaw-dropping effect as the home of large-scale temporary installations; beyond were the permanent collections, drawn from the Tate's own store of modern art and featuring expertly curated heavy hitters such as Matisse, Rothko and Beuys. This was world-class stuff and he was of course in awe at what he was about to see.

There are vertiginous views down inside the building from outside the galleries, which group artworks according to movement – Surrealism, Minimalism, and Post-War Abstraction – rather than by theme. For any creative person, himself included, even before you enter the building you get a sense of sheer inspiration which absorbs your inner soul, as though a drug is being pumped into one's veins.

The main doors opened at 10am on the dot. Danny knew the time coincided with the claustrophobic chaos and daily rampage of schoolchildren on official visits, so he arrived just after to miss that delightful experience. Grabbing a coffee from the cafeteria on the second floor; appreciating the stunning views across the Thames with the Millennium Bridge and St Paul's Cathedral in sight.

The installations from artists, including ones he'd never heard of, stirred him and provoked emotions, sometimes good and sometimes, *How the hell is that piece even in here?* – which is the idea, of course: your perception against your interpretation and vice versa. Art bringing up an emotion is always the catalyst to talk about it: *brilliant or crap*, there is also acceptance of it being there; it's staying and that contradicts one's first thoughts.

As the numerous schoolchildren were rounded up by their guide, tourists were thrown into the mix of visitors, together with uniformed security guards in high-visibility vests and strict-looking teachers who were clearly fed up with the pressure of marshalling thirty-five kids. The halls echoed with their repetitive bellowing of, 'Keep to the left, class!' He could see the paranoia and fear on their faces that they might lose a child; it was plain as day as a huge class walked past him. Then he turned a corner to come face-to-face with his own paranoia: Hafiz was there.

Danny couldn't believe his eyes and he suddenly stopped, then immediately stepping back in shock, he double-checked and confirmed it was Hafiz. He was sat down with his back to him, transfixed by a large Joseph Legend original circle painting publically on display. Luckily, he hadn't noticed him. Cautiously, Danny ventured forward a tad. Noticing the title of the painting in black across the top of the canvas: *Chemical Warfare*. This was the only Joseph Legend *Primus Circle* painting that he had seen in person, and it sure captured the spots more than the sketches and prints he had at home on his floor. This particular one was combined with letters and numbers that were strategically placed next to the spots, which looked genuinely like a code or reference point.

Danny knew he couldn't be seen by him or be compromised, even, so he stood back and observed from inside the entrance doorway to this gallery. He noticed Hafiz was writing something down onto a bunch of papers on his lap, as if referring to the original painting openly in front of him. Danny was very aware of his surroundings as he tried to figure out what the hell he was doing. Scanning the area in case someone was giving him 'over-watch' whilst he sat there, to protect him from whatever he was doing. *What the hell was he writing down?* Danny thought curiously. He was too far away for him to decipher the scribbles of his notes.

More schoolchildren, teachers and tourists pushed past him in the doorway, so he tried to act as if he was waiting for someone – to the disgust of the teachers, who made it obvious he was in the way and not respecting the rules of the gallery or adhering to their expected standards of behaviour on external visits. Repetitive smiling and nodding at the majority didn't appease, so he decided a covert walk past was in order. Cautiously, Danny mingled with the large crowd that had surged into the Legend display room.

Years of covert training never takes the edge off being compromised: it's the worst-case scenario for any spy. The training, coupled with his hope that he wouldn't turn and notice Danny, now made him look for a quick escape route. Noticing another doorway on the other side of the gallery, Danny headed towards it. At this point, he was planning his act surprised look if Hafiz saw him. Well integrated within the pushy-shovey public, this cover gave him a chance to catch a tiny glimpse of what Hafiz was writing down: numbers and letters, sketched onto the pre-drawn circled pieces of paper that were just like in his study.

Danny took a minute to digest this and stayed with the flow of people around him. They were all walking towards the doorway when they met another group of crazed kids and adults, who all pushed past him in particular (or so he felt), as if he was invisible. He was buffeted around, giving him a chance to wonder if Hafiz was cross-referencing something within the painting. He looked around for another group of people to hijack for camouflage for his return journey, but as he looked back into the room, Danny saw Hafiz had now disappeared and the observation bench was empty.

In a panic, Danny pushed forward through the crowd, looking around frantically in case something was going down right here and now. The rush of adrenalin put him on edge, scared; but he couldn't see him anywhere; he had to assume he had left via the other entrance/exit door opposite. He quickly walked over to it. With a sense of urgency, he was scanning the faces around him. A sudden thought struck him that he might have seen him and legged it by merging with the crowds. Suddenly a hand grabbed his shoulder. He froze, spooked; instinctively turning around, his heart pounding. It wasn't Hafiz. 'Excuse me, sir, is this your umbrella? It was left over there', an old gentleman asked as he pointed over towards the doorway.

'Uh, no, no, it doesn't belong to me'. Danny sighed in relief. The old gentleman wandered off, keeping the umbrella.

Danny continued to look around all the different rooms whilst pretending to be interested in everything, in case he was being observed. Unable to find Hafiz, he quickly made his way upstairs to the cafeteria and sat by the window to scan the crowds outside. Moments later, he saw him walking away from the gallery towards the Millennium Bridge, his pile of papers in one hand, mobile phone to his ear in the other. Danny sighed with relief and he didn't know quite why. Observing him until he was out of sight, then he headed back downstairs as the original Joseph Legend circle painting was calling for him. Danny walked towards the Legend display room again; this time, rather polite Chinese tourists were walking around it, taking a pleasant stroll to the *Chemical Warfare* painting.

So, there it was: 'Legend by name, Legend by nature' circles, numbers and letters.'Wow!' He leaned into the painting, hoping to find something different up close and personal on this one that wasn't on the others scattered around the room. *Nope, nothing,* he thought. Danny sat down on the bench and stared inquisitively at the painting, his mind ticking over. The words *Chemical Warfare* on it referred specifically to dangerous drugs that were controlled by the medical profession – so we were talking prescription drugs, those not accessible to the public. He was assessing all his intel mentally against the painting. Legend started the series back in 1993, with the key paintings differing from all the other circle paintings by the inclusion of text with the coloured circles. On the painting before him were thirty-six circles arranged in a grid, six rows by six columns. Each circle of colour was accompanied by a letter of the alphabet beginning with A and continuing down the rows until Z, followed by a numerical sequence from 1 through to 9, then 0, all painted in black, to its right.

The ambience of the noise of everyone in the room and gallery faded into the background. Danny felt hypnotised staring at the circles, in a trance, and his mind wandered to all the gathered intelligence he had. Danny went back again to the original thirteen names on the list that he discovered in Hafiz's study: each of them owned an original circle painting. He got a shiver down his spine as he recalled the painting name *Opium* written against the first name, Derek Clarke. Urging his memory to visualise what was against Christopher Durand's name... *Cripple won't make the exhibition.* But the other eleven names had chemical labels against them. Both these guys were dead and their paintings destroyed. The only clue was a partly burnt piece of artist's paper containing a red circle from what he was now certain was a part copy of the original that belonged to Derek Clarke, yet no limited editions of his painting were ever put into production.

He racked his brain and could only surmise a copy was made for the purpose of assassinating him and possibly for taking out Christopher Durand too. Danny went back to the manly scratching of the head and wondered if these copies contained some form of hidden coded instruction to the killer to carry out the assassination. That would lead nicely to Hafiz sitting under a painting opposite the original, the masterpiece here at the Tate, creating a coded note to assassins which would be untraceable back to him.

Eleven names remain on the second list, which have the word accepted written against them. That's it, he thought, *they have all innocently accepted an invitation to the opening of the exhibition in the eleven galleries.* The fog started to disappear in his head. *So, if each individual has accepted an invite to each one of the Gagosian galleries located in eleven different places, then...* He trailed off, unable to link the next bit. These opening nights had to be the opening night of the forthcoming Joseph Legend exhibition, which was due to start on 4 January. That gave Danny less than twelve days from now to save these people and stop this tragedy from happening. 'How the hell will I know which person will be where?' Danny was acutely aware he was talking to himself; looking around, such behaviour appeared to be allowed in art galleries.

Snapping out of his dream mode. He needed to find out the exact timings. Staring at the circles, willing to seek out Hafiz's mind on this one, to get into his mind – a genius's mind, albeit a disturbed one. When confronted with a problem, how would his genius look at it? How many different ways? Genius often came in the form of finding a new perspective that no one else had taken before, which made sense in Hafiz's case as he had become the mastermind behind this by not settling on one perspective. *Geniuses do not merely solve existing problems, they identify new ones. That's it,* he thought, smiling to himself, shaking his head ruefully, acknowledging praise for Hafiz for coming up with something so inventive, but so evil.

Danny sat back and looked around; no security men in white coats were on their way to collar a geezer talking to a painting. He felt clear in his mind that he had solved the puzzle. The use of an edition print was purely a hidden code, a code only for an assassin to understand, to use to carry out his work. It was ironic that Hafiz may once have part-owned thirteen original *Primus Circle* paintings worth millions of pounds and had now downgraded them to mere messages; his ambition degraded down to simply wanting revenge. Danny could only assume the other eleven paintings would be destroyed like the first two. But why destroy them?

Staring at these coloured spots gave him clarity for the first time. Was that their appeal and was that the reason for their creation, even? Just pure simplicity.

Danny knew that secret codes had been used for centuries, with the first known cipher in history developed by the Roman Emperor Julius Caesar, God bless him. His code was very simple: he just replaced one letter of the alphabet with another and it never changed. Luckily for him – in the beginning of course – his enemies didn't catch on very quickly. A code was still a new idea and the Romans were pioneers in their game of war.

People became smarter about the idea of codes. Harder ciphers were developed, for instance by an Italian named Leon Battista Alberti, who made a new invention called a Cipher Wheel. This had two circles, both engraved with alphabet letters, and when you matched each wheel in a certain way, a code could be created and cracked. The point being, if the enemy didn't know where to match the wheel, you could hide some pretty big secrets, even if they had a similar wheel.

As time has progressed, codes and ciphers have become much more sophisticated, and technology has transformed to make much more complicated codes used by everyday folk and not just James Bond or the military. So now you can put a secret code together with only the people at the receiving end knowing the formula and then – bosh! – orders or messages can be communicated without detection. The *Chemical Warfare* image can be researched online from anywhere around the world.

Now that Danny knew there was a code formulated – which was hard enough to trace in the first place – he had to analyse how the murder in London differed from the murder in Miami. Confirming that forensics found a segment of paper with a red spot on, which matched Derek Clarke's original Legend painting. With nothing discovered at the murder scene in Miami. Maybe it was destroyed along with Durand's charred body, or maybe it could have been sent by another means of visual communication… *The first murder must have been a rehearsal to see if Hafiz's code worked precisely as he planned.* However, fundamentally, the end result has been achieved. A harrowing death – the hard bit now would be cracking the code… and in so doing, preventing Hafiz from plotting his deadly revenge.

SEVENTEEN

——— • ———

Hafiz and Marina were sat in complete silence in his study room of his apartment. With just the sound of a vintage carriage clock ticking, the pendulum, swinging left to right, punctuated the air as Hafiz went through the final details of the codes, ensuring each and every one was perfect. There was no room for error.

Marina was relaxed, sitting back in her chair with a glass of red wine, watching him affectionately yet in a rather disturbing, strange way, too, considering he was always so aloof, unkind, unappreciative, unloving and – worst of all, some might say – presently putting together a set of deadly instructions that would be used by equally disturbed individuals to carry out a brutal crusade on his behalf. The atrocious acts of violence that Hafiz was planning were aimed at the remaining eleven people who had screwed him over.

It was sad to see someone so beautiful so screwed up over the likes of Hafiz. Even as she watched, he threw another tissue into the pile of scrunched-up bloodied tissues already in the wastepaper basket beside his desk. His mental condition was worsening and taking its toll on his body. Still, he continued to deny the basic fact that addiction and cancer were eating away at him from the inside out. He simply refused to be stopped.

Careful, meticulous, a clinical modus operandi, a master at his desk, scribbling down his configurations on his A4 sketchpad, placing the chosen colours into the appropriate empty circles, he built up the intricate code that in turn would translate into his personal evil. The only time he raised his head was to laugh out loud; uncontrollably as he referred to his collection of encrypted algorithms; they gave him the chain of calculations that determined in what ways the inputted plain text would be transformed into the output cipher text.

'You're all going to wish you never double-crossed me'. He spoke with a demonic look.

By using the mass amount of circles visible in each of the original paintings, with the absolute control of the key painting *Chemical Warfare* as the master sheet, he was able to generate extremely complicated algorithms to achieve the complex ciphers.

Encrypted algorithms fell into two basic categories: symmetric and asymmetric key algorithms, which to the untrained naked eye looked like doodles on paper. Everyone loves to doodle; that moment when one is bored, waiting, preparing, or stressed, with a piece of paper in front of them, it draws one to it and cannot stay un-scribbled-upon. What one chooses to doodle apparently reveals volumes about one's personality and mood, as does why one doodles in the first instance, which is usually with only a half-conscious knowledge of what one is drawing... meaning everyone's inner preoccupations surface on paper.

Hafiz was unhinged from normality. He continued to construct notes and implement insane methods to kill like a mad professor on overdrive. His creation was a sequence of colours combined with numbers then letters. It was a code that intricately took shape, starting with the name of the victim followed by the day of the hit, then the date, the exact time, the geographical location and method of death. In addition, all this was hidden within a painting that you wouldn't really have noticed at first glance.

He started speaking animatedly. 'I have taken into consideration the global time difference'.

'Genius', she replied, raising her glass of wine in salute.

'By the time this all happens, there will be so much chaos that no one will realise what's happening across each gallery', he said, elated.

Every so often, the demented Hafiz would look up to the ceiling for inspiration and take a deep breath, cross-referencing the original circle painting images that he had from the original gallery that accompanied the auction brochures of when they were originally purchased. Along with his notes that he took while at the Tate Modern gallery. He worked in a slow and precise manner: he could not afford to make any mistakes. His life depended on it, as just one error could bring down his whole operation.

At this point, it would be easy to conclude that maybe death on such a huge scale had always been in the back of his mind. Maybe even years back, as a sort of premeditated insurance policy on his business. Was his life in such a state of paranoia even then for him to have created such a tool to be used? A man of such intelligence and status would surely have made up some sort of contractual agreement between parties as opposed to relying on a gentlemen's handshake; or could he have been that stupid? Is this revenge about the loss of monetary value to his estate, or is it about the morality and principality of trust and friendship and executing those he found lacking? Maybe his mental instability combined with the cocktail of drugs he had taken over the years had overshadowed his conscious ability to judge.

Hafiz paused momentarily and stood up. The sudden movement and interruption to the steady rhythm of his work made Marina look up. 'You okay, darling?' she asked – she was totally ignored. Quickly walking into his bedroom, closing the door behind him. He took out a little sachet of cocaine from the drawer of his bedside cabinet. He tipped a generous sprinkle on the back of his hand then leant forward and sniffed the contents deep into his nose in one intake of breath, pinching his nose afterwards to clear his nostrils as the drug attacked his brain like a bolt of euphoria. He stabilised himself by the cabinet, his mind aching in pain, when suddenly a combination of excitement and depression overwhelmed him. Battling with each emotion, reminiscing on the past that had brought him to this place in time, justifying his mind-set to get rid of everyone who used that incident at the party as the perfect excuse to abandon him instead of helping him. He shut his eyes and saw them in his inner vision. *They have only greed on their minds, but I will have their blood on my hands*, he thought to himself as he viewed the sachet. 'Fuck it, another for luck', he whispered. He took another pinch of the white powder, inhaling only once and rubbing the residue from his fingers on his gums.

Rejoining Marina back in the study. She had helped herself to another large glass of red wine in his absence but he didn't mind; he smiled at her as he sat down, recognising the little 'pick-me-up' had recharged his batteries and concentration. Rejuvenated, he continued with his detailed encryptions, sweat appearing on his brow as his head heated up. Despite the energy given to him by the drugs, he felt as if his brain was going to explode, deranged.

Marina looked at him steadily, assessing his appearance. 'Darling, why not take a break for a while? Please? For me?'

'I can't. I'm in the zone', he replied without looking at her, which was a good thing as he rather resembled something from well under Middle-earth, should it exist. With total crazed determination, his inner mind captured that single moment of rejection in the Hamptons and used it as a focus. It acted like a black-and-white photograph imprinted onto the forefront of his mind, the rows of disgusted porcelain faces motivating his commitment to his cause.

'Finished!' Hafiz dropped his pen onto the desk, closing his A4 sketchpad with a sigh of relief. He leant back casually in his chair, placing his hands behind his head. He didn't need to look at his work to be pleased with it, and a deep breath of satisfaction left him, removing the weight of the whole world from his shoulders. 'They say self-praise has no recommendation, however', he said aloud, with an amused, self-satisfied air of arrogance, and looked across at Marina. The disturbed mastermind started to laugh to himself.

'Over to you now, darling'. He leant forward and slid the completed sheets of artist's paper over to her to inspect.

Marina had been sitting patiently, watching him work. Now, she took another sip of wine, this one larger than the last, before placing the glass down on the table. Marina was able to lose herself in her own heightened reality. She stood up and walked towards his desk, picking up the sheets of paper and returning to her wine. She sat back down, perusing them individually; proof reading his work whilst enjoying the red berry taste on her lips.

'Perfect', she said in delight. Every now and then as she looked through his coded plans, she gazed up at him and raised her eyebrows with the odd giggle to herself. Her maniacal devotion to Hafiz was always simmering below the surface. Only two demented beings could find the same appreciation of humour in such an orchestrated act of hell on earth.

'I thought you would like that', he said, laughing with her as she read the encryptions that translated into hell that had no boundaries. Pointing at a certain row of circles, she said, 'I'd hate to be there when that happens'. She praised his dark creativity, grinning continuously at how a chosen assassin might carry out his method of destruction on the victim.

Hafiz smiled in quiet admiration as he walked over to the crystal drinks decanter and poured himself a glass of whisky, raising it in celebration of all his work. 'Well, it couldn't happen to a nicer person, I say. Cheers'.

Marina smiled back. 'I'll be back at work in a couple of days so I'll get these printed off and signed off, then I can get them sent off'.

'Fantastic', Hafiz replied. 'Word on the street is that the tragic deaths of Derek and Christopher have sent shivers around the art world'.

'There's nothing like a bit of paranoia to enliven the soul', she said, placing the coded sheets of paper into a large plastic artist's portfolio folder.

Hafiz walked towards the bay window with his glass, in a contemplative mood as he looked outside at the evening's twilight sky, his stance that of a captain of a ship looking out to sea. 'Fear, it would seem, is a powerful primal emotion, so potent it can even make us afraid of something that may not even exist – but, in this case, it does'.

Marina stood up and walked behind him, wrapping her loving arms around his waist and leaning into him, placing her head on his back to hear his heartbeat. 'It certainly does, darling'.

Hafiz placed his hand on hers. Marina laughed lovingly. 'You will always be my sweet Hafiz'. Her laughing changed his mood towards her, though; having phased out from the conversation, being off his face, he assumed she had disrespected him.

He gulped the remaining whisky from his glass and placed it on the sideboard, turning around to face her. Stepping back to give him a better view, he opened her blouse slowly, twisting each button with his thumb and finger. He could see at a glance that she was not wearing a bra; he slowly ran his finger along her breastbone. With her blouse open, he could appreciate her stunning beauty. He caressed her breasts and leant forward to kiss her neckline, then moved down towards her nipples, kissing and biting them before gradually kneeling in front of her, his lips moving slowly down her stomach.

Marina was hot at his touch, aroused by the feeling of vulnerability provoked by standing in front of both the window and him with her bare chest on show. She grabbed his hair and forced him towards her. Her breathing became shallower as he explored her lower body with his lips. He pulled her skirt off aggressively and she lifted her heels obediently one by one to allow the garment to fall to the floor. Then, he ripped the delicate lace of her G-string apart with both hands, tearing it off her before he started kissing her just above her pubic bone.

Marina let out a moan of ecstasy as he continued to kiss her femininity and she groaned louder in the heat of passion, her legs shaking pre-climax as the sexual tension between them unstoppably increased.

Hafiz placed his hands on her waist to pull her down onto the carpet with him, then turned her body around so she faced the floor. Marina moaned as she became defenceless in his harsh grip. He undid his trousers with one hand and grabbed her tightly with the other, gripping her waist to keep her in position. He used his knees to prise open her legs from behind as he gripped her more firmly, digging his fingers into either side of her pubic bone, making her ready for him to take. She struggled in pleasure; he grabbed a handful of her long hair, twisting it in his hands and pushing her face against the floor.

His actions increased the size of his manhood inside her, and in turn his monstrous sexual behaviour turned her on and she begged for more. He pounded his tense body against her, punishing her, using her like a piece of meat, disengaging from emotion. His momentum sped up until he reached a climax, almost bruising her with the depth of his final thrust. Then suddenly he relaxed as all his body weight dropped on top of her. He panted hard, trying to regain his breath.

'You will always be mine', he whispered in her ear, breathing heavily. He gently kissed her cheek, leaving a small residue of blood from his mouth on her skin. Without another word, he got up from her limp body, pulled up his trousers and walked towards the bathroom without looking back.

Marina slowly sat herself up, feeling as if she had just received a large hit of heroin, yet still she longed for his love and affection. She craved it, just like an addict. She'd been with him for too long; the relationship's dynamic had been modified to more closely resemble an unhealthy dependency.

Hafiz returned to the room and sat down beside her on the carpet, apologetic. 'Look, my head is a million miles away. You know what I have to do, and when this is over, we will be free'. He wiped his blood from the side of her face and pulled her in towards his chest to comfort her.

Marina again felt her unchanging desire for his love. She knew this whole situation had taken him from her to the depths of hell and back again; this one act, him embracing her, made her believe that once it was all over they could start a new life, the life of which she had always dreamed. 'Very soon. This will all be over'.

'I understand, darling'. She caressed the side of his face.

'You must understand. My belief is so strong. Greed is so destructive; so many so-called friends have turned against me'.

'Have you still been taking your medication, Hafiz?' she asked lightly.

'Yes, like clockwork', he lied, nodding.

'What about attending your weekly counselling sessions?' She looked at him, assessing his response.

'Yes, of course, I go every week'. He lied again, this time managing a laugh, too.

'Okay. It's just that I care for you, that's all, Hafiz'. She pulled her blouse around her shoulders.

'I know you do, but I will not be able to rest until I have my revenge'. It was said with pure rancour, without emotion, purely as a matter of fact.

EIGHTEEN

——— • ———

Bernadette arrived on cue at the Serpentine Gallery in the affluent area of Kensington Gardens. A creature of routine, she always got to work at 9.30am, giving her enough time to put a fresh pot of coffee on before she opened to the public at 10am sharp. Unlocking the main door and pushing it open, she was greeted as always by the annoying warbling of the security alarm. It was a daily test, whereby she entered the disarm code into the keypad — an eight-digit numeric version of her birthdate – to turn the damn thing off.

The gallery was dimly lit by only a touch of natural light from the main door until she flicked the switch to the main gallery lights which illuminated the impressive works of art. Her final job was activating the electric blinds, which allowed the morning sunlight to flood in; the mixture of natural and false light.

She quickly popped her head around the corner to take in the glory of her workspace: it was still a highlight of her working day, appreciating her favourite pieces of artwork which adorned the walls around her desk. Even as she took the coffee from the fridge, her senses were stimulated with sight, colour and the aroma of freshly ground coffee beans.

As she placed a filter paper in the coffee machine and poured out enough coffee for the day, she heard the main door open in the other room and for a flickering second remembered Danny's comment about being all alone in the gallery without security. She shouted towards the door, 'Sorry, we are not open until ten!' Whoever it was should have known better than to enter anyway: the opening times were on the bloody door.

'Bernadette?' a familiar voice called out from the doorway. 'Or should I rephrase that: Harriet?'

She stopped in her tracks, squeezing the seal on the bag of coffee a little too tightly. Taking a deep breath, she put the bag down and walked slowly into the main gallery room. She thought she knew that voice... Unfortunately, she was correct. 'Thom'. It was just one word, but her surprise was evident in her tone. 'I thought you were—'

'Dead?' He interrupted her, noting the shock on her face. 'Me too, but you can't keep an old dog down'. He walked fully into the gallery, making sure the door was closed behind him.

'If it's coffee you want, there is a café nearby'. She watched him step slowly towards her. 'You know I'm finished with all this shit, Thom. It was a long time ago and I've started a new life since leaving Moscow'. She stood still with her arms folded across her chest defiantly.

He laughed. 'Really? Well, you never really leave the Establishment, you know; you simply go to sleep for a while. Come on, Harry, you know the score'. Reluctantly, she took a seat behind her desk, her facial expression suggesting that she didn't give a fuck about the Establishment, with or without his broom-up-his-ass tone.

'I take it you don't want to buy any art, then?' She looked up and was greeted by his blank stare.

'What do you actually want, Thom?' She was dry, stern and aware of the time.

'We have gathered intelligence, locally and from our friends across the pond, that Hafiz de Mercurio is planning an imminent attack with his sleeper cell somewhere in Europe – perhaps even here on British soil'. He sat down across the desk from her.

'I know you are undermanned, Thom, but really? Surely you can put someone on the inside, given that you know he's not been an active target for a long time now, nor is there substantial evidence he is even connected to an extremist group'. She leaned forward across the desk, locking eyes with him to make her point. 'Unless you know something I don't, of course; you always did have a habit of keeping things to yourself'. She oozed sarcasm as she turned away from him to switch on her computer.

'Ouch – and true. But time is of the essence here and we don't have much of it'. Thom glanced around, looking at the works of art that hung around the gallery. 'The war we face now is far more complicated than in your day. The global face-off has changed; there is something inhumane in its approach now'.

'Are you trying to tell me something I don't already know, Thom?' she replied tartly, standing up with anger both in her tone and in her stance.

'All of us face an existential threat on a daily basis. There is not a single day that goes by when I am not reminded of what terror is out there. You know what I went through....'. Thom stood in front of her: no artifice now, just truth.

She stared at him, fighting to blink back her tears as her anger built further. 'The major difference nowadays is that the antagonists are far more ruthless and despicable', she spat out. 'They wouldn't think twice about parading you on YouTube as they take your fucking head off'.

Thom saw the tears but was unable to react as he would have liked. 'There was nothing you or anybody could have done; we have both lost some good friends—' he began.

'Don't patronise me, Thom'. She turned her back on him and looked up at a large, yellow-painted-canvas by the New York conceptual artist Cory Arcangel. It gave her a sense of peace: she took a deep breath and sighed as she placed her hands on her hips and surveyed it.

Thom continued. 'There are no romantic dimensions to being a spy as the movies portray, Harriet. When you get that tap on the shoulder, you know what you are getting into. As do I, as do we all. The business of spying is a deadly game'.

'I wish that you hadn't tapped my shoulder that day at university'. She turned as she said it and caught his eye. A sudden spark of amusement flared between them, the banter of old colleagues, and her mood changed towards him.

'You were one of my best'. He said it proudly. The moment seemed to get to him as he moved towards one of the paintings in front of him, breaking the bond between them. As she watched, Thom stopped in his tracks, clearly confused. He was admiring a painting in front of him and tilted his head inquisitively; he leaned forward to inspect the piece more closely. 'Is that supposed to be a picture of what I think it is?' he asked, shaking his head in disbelief. 'Walt Disney will be turning in his grave'.

Bernadette laughed and shook her head, too. Knowing he hadn't got a clue about art gave her the upper hand again and she walked back behind her desk to a position of power. Yet it was Thom who spoke next.

'Do you have anything on Hafiz?' he asked.

She was peripheral. 'Nothing really', with an extended pause, 'actually, he does seem excited about the forthcoming Joseph Legend exhibition, but that's it'.

'Excited? In what way?' Thom was alerted. Silence.

Bernadette shrugged, disinterested. 'Not sure, he gets like this now and then with a certain artist, but this just seems different'.

'Different?' Thom wasn't letting it go.

'He appears to have a real interest in the whole situation, maybe because it's the first time ever an artist of such high calibre has done something like this worldwide'.

Thom nodded, not convinced. 'I'd be grateful if you could let me know of anything out of the ordinary'.

Bernadette didn't answer him; she looked straight through him…

'Well, I'll leave it with you, shall I?' He raised his eyebrows smugly.

She looked at him, exasperated. 'Listen, Thom, when innocent lives are at risk, I don't withhold information as some people do'. It was a sarcastic dig.

He rolled his eyes. 'You know how to contact me'. He approached the door and looked down at his watch. 'You can open now', he added, with a sarcastic smile. 'Coffee smells good, too'.

'Bye, Thom'. Bernadette didn't even look up from her papers until she heard the door open; it jangled merrily.

'Bye, Harry'. Thom smirked, tipping his hat at her and left.

NINETEEN

— • —

Back home in Milton Keynes. There was a winter chill in the air that gave a certain clarity to everything. Danny needed his space to assess everything, to recover from yet another interesting visit to the capital: he was determined to try and interpret Hafiz's code into a readable language and free his haunt of those coloured circles. Time was running out. Death threats, including his, gave him surreal feelings. This was all too real. It wasn't a rehearsal; he had to get it right first time.

Danny printed off a large A1-size image of the *Chemical Warfare Primus Circle* painting, exactly like the one hanging in the Tate Modern. Hanging it above his fireplace, suddenly he found it to be rather appealing in an aesthetic way.

Nevertheless, the head scratching started up again as he stared at the police report on the assassination of Derek Clarke. He quickly decided his first objective was to use the information found at the murder scene in Lancaster Gates in London as a baseline. The instructions for the hit must have been in Clarke's own circle painting. Once he'd worked the format out, he'd gain a lead on the other assassination codes hidden in other paintings – and thus the knowledge to stop the future hits. The plan sounded good in Danny's head, at least.

'Okay, here we go', he said out loud to remain focused as the Pet Shop Boys played on his stereo in the background. Music always stimulated his creative side and that was exactly what he had to use right now.

Standing up, with his notebook in his hand, he was taken back to a quote he'd heard years ago, that had always stuck in his mind: *Don't bother hiding; death will always find you.* Danny agreed with the ideology – but he hoped he could buy this lot more time.

Steadily, he went through the gathered intelligence; his lounge floor the usual kaleidoscope of coloured paper, images, lists, reports and paintings. Danny began. *Opium* belonged to Derek Clarke and *Anthrax* belonged to Christopher Durand from Miami. Blocking out the images of their deaths, instead, he went through the series of lists he had made, looking at list 'Number One', wondering how the bloody hell he ought to pronounce this lot: *N-Methyl, L-Aspartic, Vespula Vidua, Curare, Norcamphor, Chloroform, Antimony, Amatoxin, S-Lactoylglutathione, Sulphuric Acid* and *Cyanide*: eleven titles of eleven original Primus paintings.

List 'Number Two' was the eleven names of the owners of the paintings, who had all loaned them to the galleries at Madison Avenue in New York, West 24th Street and West 21st Street (both also New York), Beverly Hills, Paris, Rome, Athens, Geneva, Hong Kong and finally at Britannia Street and Davies Street in London, UK.

Holy shit, he thought to himself, *this is quite impressive.* You know you have made the big time to be able to put on an event on this scale. He ripped off strips of paper from his notepad and wrote down each of the gallery opening timings, cross-referencing the city abbreviation codes that were written next to their names, connecting them with the exact gallery addresses. Matching which painting would be exhibited at what gallery, names and details for each spot painting, and who owned each one.

Placing each piece of paper alongside the printed spot images on the floor, making a mental note not to slip on them. Looking at each image, he wrote down which colours were used and counted the circles horizontally, diagonally and vertically, then calculated how many matched on each of the paintings, calculating the diameter of each circle by referring to the master key painting of *Chemical Warfare*. Danny checked the colours next to the letters of the alphabet and numbers, checking primary, secondary and intermediate colours against warm, cool and monochromatic, and not forgetting analogous, complimentary double, Tetradic, and splitting tertiary colours.

The mental strain on his flow of concentration was difficult. His mind kept drifting, despite the overwhelming fatigue closing in, which meant he had to keep going backwards to keep everything fresh in his head. Rubbing his eyes. Each letter had a number from 1 to 9 and 0 combined with twenty-six letters of the alphabet, but he had the intel as to which colour was used in sequence.

Then he drew lines horizontally and vertically next to each row of circles, giving him a six by six grid; totalling thirty-six squares. For example, using Blue 1 x Orange C is either a primary or a secondary colour type which will give you a letter D that in turn is a pale-green spot. He made the names by calculating which number was with each letter, then multiplying the numbers to give the colour specific to the edition of the original, continuing by dividing a complementary colour, using the diagonal circle to give you a location, a vertical for a time where 0 (zero) or the letter O could be used for zero hour. Each encryption was image-specific but still implemented the same instructions for the specific assassin: a code, which was hidden within.

Danny was seriously talking to himself to focus and for his sanity's sake. Assessing his findings. Already the variations of each of the encryptions expanded exponentially. His eyes felt on fire and his brain really ached from constantly staring at spots. *Thank God I'm not colour blind; I would be fucked*, he thought jokingly.

Cross-referencing his calculations using the key painting *Chemical Warfare* against critical points that he had taken from the detailed police reports that he'd received from Thom. Studying the sequence of events of that dreadful massacre in detail. He then should be able to place the events into sequence as if he were the assassin. Danny read the report closely and it stated that a black cab driver dropped off our *femme fatale* at the Lancaster Gates Apartments at approximately 17:30 hours. With this arrival time, that gave her a thirty-minute window to achieve her aim, as the coroner's report stated an approximate time of death of 18:00 hours for most of the victims, give or take five minutes or so.

He jotted down every detail in his notebook: the method of transport to the address, the timings, the type of weapon used and, of course, the victims: Derek Clarke and the three other victims in the apartment, plus the security guard down in reception. Derek Clarke was confirmed as an ex-associate of Hafiz, whilst the others were purely in the wrong place at the wrong time or, in layman's terms, 'unlucky'. 'Do ya think?' he said to himself with black humour.

Then matching everything with Derek Clarke's original *Opium* spot painting, trying to see if coded instructions were hidden within the coloured circles. At the same time, checking his theory against Christopher Durand's original *Anthrax* circle painting. He had a gut feeling it was the complexity of encryption that translated the method of death that was to be used by the assassin.

Looking down at his watch, it was already 7pm. He couldn't believe what the fuck he had got himself into. He created a few paintings and by pure happenstance, this shit happens.

The *Opium* image had ninety different coloured circles: nine circles across, ten deep. His eyes were naturally drawn into the centre of the image. Suddenly... 'Fuck me, that's it!' he exclaimed. Looking at all the images and the centre circle of each painting as if it were a clock face. Did this circle perhaps confirm what time Hafiz had instructed the assassin to strike? With a ruler, he drew two lines on *Opium* to give the time, and then calculated which coloured circle the two lines travelled through. '*Here fucking goes...*'

Derek Clarke was murdered at 18:00 hours. He therefore drew two lines to point to six o'clock, the first line on the 12 position (the minute hand) and the second on the 6 position (the hour hand). Immediately, Danny noticed that the line on the hour position ended on a black spot; *this must differentiate whether it was am-or-pm. The line also passed through a primary colour, and in this case, he thought it would be the colour yellow – to show the colour of a sunset at 18:00 hours –* but just to piss him off, there was not a yellow but a red, as primary colours are not a fundamental property of light and are related to the physiological response of the eye to light.

Frustratingly, Danny wrote down all options: *black for night-time, meaning pm, also depending on what position the black spot was in compared to the yellow spot, which is for sunset or sunrise.* Walking up and down his living room speaking out loud: 'There are twenty-four hours in a day;

the day is divided into daytime and night-time; daytime is from sunrise, approximately 06:00 hours, varying slightly, and sunset from 18:00 hours, with similar variety, depending on where you are geographically'. What conclusions can he draw from this? He was trying to stay in the moment and draw into the equation night-time being from sunset to sunrise; he also realised there were two twelve-hour sequences to play with.

A thought struck him that he needed to think like Hafiz, *dear fucked-up Hafiz*. He stared at the circles of colour, promising himself that the next painting he did would involve squares, *lots of fucking squares*. Hafiz would think intellectually, utilising and visualising art... *Why, why, why* was he now remembering walking through the National Gallery in London and recalling Hafiz's comments on *The Death of Procris* by Piero di Cosimo? Her jealous husband killed Procris. Closing his eyes for a second, breathing three times loudly to remain sane, he went back to the basic theory of encryption. Danny multiplied, divided... and he came up with Selene. What the fuck? His love of Greek mythology?'Crazy brilliant bastard', he said aloud with grudging respect.

Selene was the goddess of the moon, daughter of the Titans Hyperion and Theia, sister of the sun god Helios and of Eos, goddess of the dawn. She drove her moon chariot across the heavens, and several lovers were attributed to her in various myths, including Zeus, Pan and the mortal Endymion. In classical times, Selene was often identified with Artemis, much as her brother Helios was identified with Apollo, and both Selene and Artemis were also associated with Hecate: all three were regarded as lunar goddesses, although only Selene was regarded as the personification of the moon itself. Selene's Roman equivalent was Luna, meaning evening.

He was still thinking of the two twelve-hour sequences, *for if there was a moon, there was also a sun.* He decoded Hafiz's method for timings. *He was using the Greek goddesses within his code. Selene's counterpart would be Aurora, the goddess of the dawn. Aurora was Latin for dawn; she was a goddess in Roman mythology and Latin poetry. Like the Greek Eos and Rig Veda Ushas, possibly even the Germanic Ostara, Aurora continued the name of an earlier Indo-European dawn goddess, Hausos.*

Danny was now sure Hafiz would put into his encryption parts of the day starting from dawn, sunrise, morning and daytime through to evening, sunset, twilight, dusk and night. He could just imagine all the variations of colour the genius could use to denote these times. All these stages could be translated into mythical names which in turn could be translated into certain shades of colour that represented times of the day; a code used in conjunction with the master key painting *Chemical Warfare*.

It was certain he had to dig deep because he knew somewhere in this complicated algorithm was the encryption formulated for the method of death. The type of weapon was the simplest but most dangerous part of the entire structure, but necessary to its execution. *'No pun intended'. How were these instructions communicated?* A voice in his head reminded him that Hafiz had said, *'Black is the colour of death, obviously'*, when he'd recently preached to him about art in one of his fazed-out moments. Noting the colours that passed through the sundial line he had created, he could see burgundy, yellow and blue. By referring back to the key painting, he saw that these colours spelt out *SIG* from the letters by the circles. This was the type of weapon described by the forensics team that had been used in the apartment to murder the victims. 'Fuck!' He shuddered the proverbial pun of someone having just walked over his grave; he hoped not.

It suddenly hit him: the Sig pistol he had in his possession may have been the same one that murdered all those at Lancaster Gates, and forensics could match the ballistics to that weapon.

Digesting the positive feedback of his findings, it was literally as if time flew by. Danny was on a mission that by bedtime, he would have cracked Hafiz's code. He was thrilled to identify which type of weapon would be used on the remaining potential victims. Danny felt mentally drained, prompted by a combination of insanity and excitement. Everything seemed to coalesce; now all he had to do was to decode the eleven images.

Separating the eleven circle paintings that he uniformly laid down on the floor, armed with various coloured marker pens, he began. Focused, he followed the algorithms; *letters and colours multiplied by strategic numbers equals the place, type of travel and time. Adrenalin kicked up a notch. The cold colours divided by horizontal primary colours equals random neutral and opalescent configurations leading to black equals the weapon used on the target.*

Content but knackered, he closed his eyes. Random colours generated secondary colours and that was it. *Holy shit, that's it; I've cracked the code.* He thought he'd be more in the *'Wow'* moment, but he was literally numb at the sea of colour on the floor and the step-by-step instructions to kill.

He urgently needed to phone Thom. He hauled his torpid body up from the floor and picked up his iPhone from off the coffee table, pressing Call. It rang and rang then voicemail. 'Hello, unfortunately I cannot take your call at the moment. Please leave a message.'

'Are you fucking kidding me?' he said as he left his message: 'Hi, Thom. Danny here. Can you give me a call; it's urgent.' Glancing down at his watch, it was two-thirty in the morning. 'So much for having my back. I do hope I didn't wake you.' He said more loudly: 'Have my back my arse, just as long as it's not at an awkward hour.' It was time for bed; he was talking to himself too much. He tossed his phone onto the sofa beside him.

Slumped back, and exhausted, drawn to all the sea of images and research that lay down on the floor. He needed to ensure he was one hundred per cent correct, and there was no room for error. Confident and satisfied. He couldn't help but yawn. His mind was drained. Bed was calling him, but this needed to be finished. He stood up to make a coffee and heard a bleep from his iPhone. *It must be a text from Thom*, he thought.

Danny was mistaken; it was from Bernadette. He was surprised to hear from her at this unearthly hour in the morning. *Hi. When are you next in London? Need to speak to you face-to-face.*

That sounds important and ominous, he thought, but he was just too bolloxed to worry and didn't want to get into anything other than his pit right there and then. *I will be travelling down tomorrow or the next day*, he replied, intrigued by her message.

See you then X. She signed out swiftly, giving nothing else away.

TWENTY

— • —

Danny stood with a sense of solace waiting for the 05:04 service direct to London King's Cross. It was interrupted only by his constant checking for a message back or missed call from Thom. Surrounded by the silence of an empty platform always felt tranquil; the leftover energies of departures, arrivals, meetings, greetings and goodbyes having dissipated into the air. He watched the weak morning sunrise struggle to blister through the grey clouds overhead. Danny could smell the imminent rain in the air and wondered if the sun would break through successfully in London; he hated the damp. Waiting patiently on Platform 3 with his weekend bag beside him, and his laptop bag draped over his shoulder.

Mercifully, it wasn't long before he was sat in the quiet coach, staring out of the window as the scenery changed from static station to green countryside. It whizzed past and he observed it in a state of heightened readiness, imagining a TV screen in permanent fast forward. Tilting his head downwards, looking at the speckles of rain now sticking to the windows, directionally moving like blood in a vein as the train picked up speed. He looked down at the parallel railway lines in an almost hypnotic state of consciousness. Danny's mind was never far away from Hafiz, and a vibration of success flowed through him for having pretty much cracked the mission given to him; he just needed to get hold of Thom, pass it all over to him and pick up that alluring paintbrush of his.

He hadn't managed to get much sleep and again the negative thoughts now crept in as he assessed what could go wrong with his plan. *What if the codes have already been printed off and dispatched to the sleeper cells? Am I too late?* he wondered. *Does anyone else know and does anyone but me even give a shit?* he thought as he tried to call Thom again, straight to answerphone. *Fuck's sake, Thom, answer.* This was beginning to feel like a solo mission and he continued to think all sorts of crap, trying to convince himself that it was the weekend and he still had time to intercept the coded edition prints. Yet something told Danny terrorists didn't keep to office hours.

The official 'Tannoy voice' piped up over the system. 'Ladies and gentlemen', the voice announced, 'your next stop is London King's Cross. Please take all your belongings with you...' Danny mentally switched off before hearing about 'reporting any suspicious packages at the other end' and the rather too obvious warning to 'wait for the train to stop before disembarking, mind the gap', and so on.

He grabbed his stuff from the storage rack as the train glided to a gentle halt inside the newly renovated station. Looking out of the window, he could see there was more life on the platform than on the train, with groups of morning commuters waiting to board, though his route through the ticket barrier and onwards to the ATM was quiet and free of pushing and shoving. Nevertheless, his outlook started heading downwards as he got out cash for the cab journey, the damp air surrounding the machine sinking his spirits. His hope for no rain in London, despite its sporadic appearances on the journey, was now well stuffed. Danny could feel it beating down the back of his neck, causing his shoulders to create an impromptu hunchback as he turned up the collar of his favourite winter coat. Heading directly towards an array of people looking for a taxi to flag down; it was like a mid-air dogfight, precision manoeuvring versus bad manners.

He didn't need reception to tell him he was too early to get into his room. Danny checked in and the concierge organised for his belongings to be left in the storeroom for an afternoon retrieval. So, he decided to head across town towards Hafiz's place to surprise him and offer to buy breakfast. His hunchback waned as the rain eased off – a definite bonus when travelling on foot without a brolly – and the route across town was festive still with Christmas in the air and all around. Cutting through one of the numerous side streets of London, he turned one of the numerous corners that followed suit. Now close to Hafiz's apartment, suddenly clocking him about a hundred metres away. Danny slowed his pace as he registered that he was openly laughing and joking around with a tall, attractive, dark-haired woman outside his apartment. At this point, he didn't think it was anything other than a typical display of tactile behaviour from Hafiz with any beautiful woman.

Deciding that he needed a bit longer to observe them, stopping near the wall of a Georgian terraced building and ostensibly tying his shoelace as he watched them embrace. Arm in arm, he observed the way they smiled and laughed together, trying to clearly identify her. Danny thought she looked very familiar, but she was wearing large blacked-out sunglasses. He wasn't too sure if she was the woman from the exhibition night or even the crazy bitch who tried to kill him. He watched them kiss passionately. He began walking towards them, hoping to catch them out. *Looks like he got lucky last night*, he thought as he gained speed and closed the gap between them.

Watching her turn away from Hafiz to open the door to the black Audi parked on the road; the boot was open at the rear and Hafiz smoothly lifted her luggage off the porch and placed it inside, shutting it quickly. Danny decided it was time to deliver his line, but he was spoilt for choice with amusing openers. In the end, he opted for a normal, 'Hey, Hafiz!' He was still walking towards them, gaining ground all the time, but this was the first time Hafiz had noticed him, close by them, so he had no idea what Danny might have seen.

'Hey, Danny, what are you doing here?' Hafiz looked at him quizzically, pure shock written all over his face. It was backed up quickly with an awkward sheepish manner, as if Danny had disturbed a weak moment in his armour or seen something furtively. His body language suggested he had been surprised all right. So, being a sarcastic git, Danny started up a conversation to make it even more uneasy for him.

'I travelled down to do some last-minute Christmas shopping, my friend, and thought you might fancy joining me for breakfast before

I headed for the shops'. Displaying his cheekiest grin, enjoying every moment, especially when he turned to the sex goddess, who was all legs, holding out his hand towards her even as he held his smile. 'Hi, I'm Danny, pleased to meet you'.

She was standing by the car door, as expressionless as the black paint, and he couldn't work out if she too felt awkward at the situation, with a touch of annoyance. She reciprocated his handshake nonetheless, and more firmly than he'd anticipated.

'It's a pleasure, Danny. I've heard so much about you', she said overzealously.

'You look very familiar; do I know you from somewhere?' Danny replied, smugly, hoping she would remove her sunglasses.

'No, I don't think so. I would have remembered'. Smirking at him in defiance.

'This is my lovely Marina, and you're going to be late, my darling,' Hafiz said, intentionally interrupting them.

Danny stared at her intently, as she sent a look of haughty disdain back. He was suspicious and he didn't bother covering it up. She was the woman in the photographs that Thom had shown him all right, and he was sure she was the one who gave Hafiz the brown envelope at the Anish Kapoor exhibition, maybe the girl who also tried to kill him. This was his first chance to stand so close to her, or was it?

'Right, you best get a move on'. Hafiz moved towards her.

She climbed elegantly into the driver's seat, closing the door; the engine started as she drew the seat belt across her body. Danny noticed a large black artist's portfolio folder sat on the back seat. Instantly, his thoughts were of the codes; gut feeling.

She lowered the car window. 'I'll let you know when I arrive', she said to Hafiz, then a quick nod of her head in Danny's direction, which he reciprocated.

'Let me know how things go'. Hafiz touched her hand; she smiled at him in response.

'Bye, darling'. She drove off as Danny clocked the registration plate as it disappeared into the morning traffic. Danny was pretty sure the black artist's portfolio's folder had to contain the encryptions and that she was heading to where she worked right now to prepare for printing and to get them sent off to the sleeper cells. There was no time to waste. *This is one of the times I'd like my back protected, Thom*, he thought. The military man in him wanted to follow her, but that would look lame bearing in mind he'd just invited Hafiz for some seasonal retail therapy.

Danny apologised to Hafiz: 'I should have phoned or texted you yesterday, but it was a sort of last-minute decision to get last-minute Christmas gifts for the family and all, so I can relax and enjoy the true meaning', he said with a look of sorrow on his face.

'Please come on inside, get out of the cold'. He clapped him on the back and guided him inside. *Is that a gesture of friendship or a recce for a knife?* Danny thought suspiciously. He followed him into his apartment and sat down on a seat in his living room – rather wearily, as yesterday's abnormal office hours and his red-eye train were taking their toll on him.

'So, how long are you down here for?' he asked.

'Not sure yet'. Scanning his living room for more signs or clues, but as always it was immaculate. 'So, that's Marina, then. Is she the one who works at that art factory you often refer to? She's bloody gorgeous'. Danny decided obvious adoration for his missus would flatter his ego.

'Yes, the one in Gloucestershire. She's the love of my life, a beautiful girl with a heart of hearts'.

'They don't make them like that over here, mate'. They both laughed.

Danny tried not to display that he knew that the Method Ltd factory belonged to the renowned artist Joseph Legend, who was based there. He spoke with unusual genuine affection but his mind was clearly not on Marina.

'Do you have a list, Danny?' Hafiz looked steadily at him. He paused, uncertain. Danny had several lists; none of them he'd like Hafiz to see.

'List? What do you mean, "list"?' he asked, deliberately looking confused.

'A Christmas list. Gifts for your friends and family?' he replied, laughing wildly.

'Um, oh no, I haven't', he stuttered, shaking his head, laughing jovially at his own stupidity, but suspicious.

'You would forget your head, Danny, if it wasn't attached'. He carried on laughing to himself as he disappeared into his study, returning seconds later with an A4-sized notepad and pencil. 'There you go, start writing your list. You do know how to spell my name, don't you? I find in capitals and bold makes it jump off the paper more!' He laughed with a cheeky grin on his face. 'Oh, and that is a capital B for Bottega Veneta, size nine of course'. He broke into giggles as he walked towards his bedroom. 'So, breakfast is on me this time, Danny', he shouted from the doorway. 'You got it last time if my memory serves me correctly. I'll just grab my keys and coat; it's a bit nippy out there today'.

'Don't worry about it', Danny replied, about his offer to pay. 'Let's go Dutch on breakfast'. Opening the notepad as he left the room.

Danny looked down at the A4 pad on his lap and twirled the pencil in his hand. He was doomed to write out a half-hypothetical, half-real Christmas list in Hafiz's living room. He was poised to commence with an important heading – *Danny's Christmas List* – when he noticed that there were several indentations all across the top of the page, showing letters and circles. Instinctively, he gently touched the paper with his fingertips, slowly gliding over the braille that had been created. He tilted the pad so the morning sunshine caught the markings inscribed. But neither his fingers nor the sun could reveal their meaning. What was written previously on Hafiz's notepad?

Danny was taken back to primary school in his mind, specifically to the lessons on 'bark rubbings', where they had put a piece of paper over the bark of a tree and rubbed it with pencils to bring up the patterns beneath. Bark rubbings were awesome, he remembered; one could make the rubbings into works of art using different colours. Memories took him back to feeling the bark beneath the paper, all the pits, ridges and bumps of the tree that would be transferred onto the paper in creative permutations.

Using the pencil, he now shaded the paper before him using the same method, gently pressing over the indentations – but he wasn't going to create an artwork. Right now, he hoped his shading would reveal Hafiz's heavy-handed inscriptions. Danny desperately wanted something to back up his theory he worked out yesterday. This primitive art could be it. He barely breathed as the shading revealed a perfect series of circles next to a series of letters and numbers. He was practically giddy, buzzing as though with a shot of adrenalin. Hafiz had used this very pad to work out the codes. *Amateur or arrogant? It seems he doesn't care he's given me his notepad*, he thought. Quickly, he tore the top few pages off, folding them carefully before placing them inside his coat pocket.

Working at speed before Hafiz emerged from the bedroom, he then hurriedly wrote down a random Christmas list, with no thought at all as to any real gift ideas for any of his friends and family. He just needed to write something, anything, so Hafiz could see him writing. By the time he returned from his bedroom, Danny had a half-decent list assembled that at least looked convincing to the casual eye.

'Do you mind if I rip this page out, mate?' he asked, to cover his tracks, given he'd already torn out the other pages. Glancing up at him innocently, only to do a double-take: he was dressed as if expecting a new ice age in his top-of-the-range Moncler designer ski jacket. Danny sighed, only half in jest. 'You do have a habit of making me look like a down-and-out bum, you know, Hafiz. Do you iron yourself as well as your clothes?'

Hafiz laughed out loud at his words. 'Of course not, Danny'. He said – in response to his initial question – 'Rip away'. He grabbed his man bag and put on a woolly hat as Danny ripped the page out. Then placing his notepad and pencil on the coffee table next to his array of art and photography books; Hafiz didn't seem to notice anything was awry.

'Well, that's me sorted', he announced, 'all Christmassed up and on a mission'. *A double meaning to that, he knows*, he thought to himself. Danny stood up and headed towards the door. They walked out into a morning chill that hit them immediately. Feeling thankful for their winter coats, they headed towards Knightsbridge.

Starting on Oxford Street, followed by the King's Road in Chelsea for the designer boutiques if they had time; a final destination that was more Hafiz's idea than Danny's. Shopping wouldn't be complete without Harrods and Selfridges, and at Christmas time they were in direct competition. From Oxford Street via Regent Street they went to Covent Garden and then Bond Street; Danny's credit card took more of a battering than he did the other night, both of which he would have to worry about in the New Year.

'Considering we missed breakfast, how about we get some lunch?' he suggested, famished.

'Great idea, Danny'.

They found a nice restaurant in Sloane Square, a favourite amongst the area's posh crowds with its quirky décor inside. They ordered one of their signature sandwiches with a well-deserved bottle of wine.

Danny was midway through munching a piece of cucumber that had escaped from his wonderfully crafted sandwich when a text came through on Hafiz's iPhone. It was sat face up on the table between them. It read: *That's me at location; I will update you once completed. M x.* Danny assumed this was from Marina. Was she at Method Ltd or was another murder going down?

Hafiz read the text whilst appreciating the glass of white wine in his hand. He swirled the liquid around in a world of his own when he suddenly realised Danny could also see the text. Abruptly, he put the glass in his view and grabbed his iPhone, turning it over to hide the screen. Simultaneously, Danny looked away quickly, as if he hadn't seen the message at all. Using the awkward moment to offer a 'cheers', appreciation of the wine, holding up his glass, he reciprocated.

'Well, I'm going to tuck in'. Danny moved a few spiced chips onto his plate and put his head down to eat, hoping to disguise he wasn't interested in his personal texts. It was at this moment that Danny realised they were poles apart; it was simply his path and Danny never judged his journey. *Is he radically motivated? Could he aspire to kill anyway?* Danny wondered, always cautious.

The troubling question was, how? How did he get these individuals to act out such terror? Had he manipulated his own power within the ranks of the Islamic extremist group to convince the sleepers these acts were for Islam? But really this vendetta was personal. How would they know anyway as the sleepers would be unknown to him; they just receive their instructions. How would the truth go down with the extremists if they found out, or would they relish any attack against the West, regardless of their operatives' true motivation?

Danny was suddenly snapped out of his deep thoughts by the sound of Hafiz dramatically coughing and choking. Watching him struggle to breathe normally and regain his composure, he became worried as his eyes filled with water and panic.

'Are you okay, mate?' Danny leaned forward, passing him a glass of water, wondering if a good slap on the back was required as he held a white napkin over his mouth, trying to clear his throat. Looking at Danny, nodding in response, his eyes relaxing, telling him he was okay. One final cough cleared his throat and he wiped his mouth delicately before grabbing the glass of water. He took a few sips to clear his throat further and breathed normally at last in relief. But he was the only one who felt relief. Danny felt a whole different maelstrom of emotions as he looked down at the napkin in his hand and was startled to see it was covered in blood.

Danny leaned in close, confidentially. 'You're bleeding from the mouth'. Pointing at his stained napkin; there came a lengthy silence. Hafiz looked around the room to see if anyone else had observed him as the situation unfolded. In his agitation, more coughing ensued and he rolled up the napkin swiftly to conceal the blood, placing it inside his blazer jacket, out of sight. He continued to sip more water to clear the residual blood from his teeth and mouth. Attentively, Danny filled up his glass from the jug of water on the table.

'I'm okay, I'm fine. I've not been well of late'. Informing him eventually, shaking his head with a look of anguish in his eyes.

'Listen to me, Hafiz, you need to get yourself to the doctor's. It looks serious', he replied, knowing that he wasn't all right. Danny had seen enough blood from enough different orifices and body parts to know that this was obviously something serious.

'I'm sick of seeing doctors and counsellors', he confessed. 'They all think they know what's best for me'. He sounded pissed off, as though it was all a big inconvenience.

'It looks serious enough to me. Do you take medication? Do you want to talk about it?' He had always had a cast-iron stomach when it came to injury and death. He also liked to think he was right about Hafiz being a killer, too, but nonetheless, he didn't particularly want to watch him drop down dead in front of him right now, so he was solicitous. If he wanted him taken out, he'd do it quickly and simply instead. And so, attending to his needs, Danny poured even more water into his glass. 'Keep drinking the water', he encouraged. 'It will clear your throat'.

'Yes, I take pills', he said briefly at last, in response to his questions. 'I'm sick of talking about it; let's just enjoy the day'. He spoke angrily, in frustration, trying to dismiss the whole thing.

'Okay, mate. Don't forget you're a friend; you would have the same concerns as me if it was one of your friends', Danny replied. Despite his knowledge of his heinous plans, he felt weirdly compassionate and compelled to help him.

'I know and I appreciate your concerns, but I'm okay'. He spoke now with sadness in his voice.

The incident calmed down, the tension vanished, and without the aid of any man hugs, they broke into laughter for no apparent reason other than to clear the air. Outside, they headed by foot towards Hyde Park. The winter afternoon was a picture in central London, beautiful with its borderless flow of clarity: the vast, seemingly empty sky stretched out for infinity and the scent of rain was in the air again, always near.

'I'm going to check into my hotel now', Danny said, yawning. 'I'll grab some rest, too, as that early train journey has really caught up with me now; I'm shattered'.

'I bet you are. Okay, my friend', Hafiz replied happily.

'Go and see a doctor and get checked out', Danny suggested compassionately.

'I will! I'm fine; I'll take a few pills and get some rest'. Hafiz was trying to pacify him, but he already knew he wouldn't do any of that. Something was driving that man more than life, for sure, and taking a few pills seemed far down his to-do list.

TWENTY-ONE

—— • ——

Danny headed in the opposite direction, towards his hotel, wondering, *what is medically wrong with him?* He was well overdue a meeting with Thom and now, more than ever, he needed to get more intel on Hafiz. Danny bent his head down to get out of the blistering cold, keeping his counter-surveillance techniques in the forefront of his mind.

In the warmth of his hotel room, heading directly to the mini bar. Grabbing the remote control en route, pointing it at the TV which was hung on the wall, wanting to get an update on the world's news. Then tossing the remote onto the bed and selecting his drink, he could hear the correspondent's voice on the TV saying, 'These horrific images come from the aftermath of a suicide bombing. The bomber detonated a device, killing himself today outside a busy shopping centre in Belgium, also killing sixteen other people and injuring thirty whilst they were innocently out Christmas shopping.'

Danny turned and faced the TV in disgust as he poured himself a drink. The live film footage on the screen brought back the harsh reality of what he was really dealing with. *My mind cannot be clouded by his trickery,* he thought to himself as he tried to switch off from Hafiz's condition, *why didn't he mention his medical condition earlier? On the other hand, why didn't he want me to know in the first place?*

The news immediately brought Danny back to the reality of Hafiz and his associates being cold-blooded killers. Symbolically, Hafiz was the perfect onion: you stripped away the layers to reveal a dead heart, a superficial appearance hiding a horrific, unpleasant truth.

Danny walked over to the window, pulling the blind to one side as he looked down on to the city street below in contemplation. Remembering a lecture he attended shortly after the 9/11 attacks. They stated that suicide terrorists were psychologically normal, and that they were no different to anyone else who would give up their lives for a cause. It simply meant they were willing to die for what they believed in and they were not crazed extremists; this was just normal behaviour.

The declaration was a load of bollocks, Danny pondered. This wasn't normal behaviour by any means. These self-destructive killers must have had prior suicidal tendencies. They kill themselves to escape their own personal pain, lacking a sense of belonging within today's society. They want to believe they have heroic desires to carry out such glorious martyrdom operations.

Terrorist leaders have strategic reasons for recruiting such vulnerable individuals, knowing that the litany of fear and anger drives them to carry out such evil, considering suicide is explicitly condemned in Islam and guarantees an eternity in hell. Martyrs, on the other hand, can go to paradise and get to shag seventy-two virgins. *Good luck with that*, he thought, chuckling to himself.

Danny picked up his iPhone to call Thom; yet again, straight to voicemail. Tired, stressed and pissed off, 'Thom, can you call me? This is urgent. I have an important lead and we need to act fast'. He practically gritted his teeth in pronouncing 'urgent', just before he ended the call. 'And can you find out if H is being treated for any serious medical conditions? Get back to me soonest'. He ended the call.

'Ping!' A text came through on his iPhone. Picking it up, it was from Thom and it read: *Dealing with something very important now can't call and yes H has cancer and is on post-treatment medication. – I will update you more once I receive more information. T.*

Staring down at his iPhone in disbelief, there were no words but he tried a few anyway. 'What the fuck? He can't call now? This is the time for my back, Thom'. Raising his voice at the ceiling, sighing heavily, shaking his head. He typed back: *Thom, this is urgent call me.* Nothing.

Danny placed his iPhone down on the desk, then leaned back in his chair, taking a deep breath. 'For Chrissake', he said in frustration. *Bloody hell, cancer, that's serious. No wonder he's on a path to self-destruction. Is he running out of time?* he thought. Danny knew he was and was forced to do something about it.

He was now becoming frustratingly concerned as to why Thom hadn't called him back since yesterday. Without delay, he quickly walked over to his bag to take out the loaded pistol. He got out his laptop, too, and placed them both on the desk. Switching on the laptop, he downed his Coke in one, taking his thirst away, and then took a seat behind the desk, linking up to the hotel's internet.

Danny needed to put his Google fingers to work again to research Method Ltd. Something told him he was going to have to make a journey to the factory to see if the mighty Marina had the encryptions. He typed Method Ltd into the search engine. Momentarily, the page appeared: Method Ltd., an art factory in Stroud. This meant nothing to him. He looked up Stroud. A lovely market town located in the county of Gloucestershire. Stroud being approximately 107 miles from the capital, he calculated it should take him just over two hours to get there.

Danny went back to Method Ltd. He noticed it was situated on the edge of an industrial estate with other business units within its vicinity, which is always good for cover.

Then he searched for car rentals and reserved a car from Avis in preparation for his journey west across the country, selecting it to be delivered to the hotel in the early hours; less witnesses, less traffic and this would give him enough time to research and prepare.

Clicking on Google Earth then typing in the area of interest around Method Ltd. A bird's-eye view of the location and buildings would give him a pretty accurate idea of what to expect and prepare for. Sketchbook and pencil at the ready, he started sketching a detailed map of the area for reference.

Zooming in on the factory itself and its perimeter walls, he could identify its entrances and exits and study each road and side road leading to the main factory building. Once he was in the area, he'd get a better ground appreciation, and he could properly assess what he assumed would be a sophisticated security CCTV system; he also expected manned guarding.

This was a phase-by-phase operation and Danny had no room for error. He simply could not afford to be compromised. So, step by step, he started putting his plan together. Once again, he went through the deciphered codes from Hafiz's workings, examining each and every one again in detail, so he knew in his mind he was one hundred per cent sure of what he had to do.

Danny started thinking about Bernadette and her last message. *Damn*, he suddenly remembered; she wanted to see him face-to-face, and urgently. He picked up his iPhone again, scrolling down to her name in his address book. His thumb hovered over her number. *Should I call her? I really want to see her but I can't right now*, he thought. So, placing the phone down with a thump in his heart, *I'll phone her when I get back.*

Marina was already on the case and he knew he had only a small window of opportunity to intercept her. Plus, this afternoon's revelations had made him realise that Hafiz was on fast-forward. Yet he couldn't tell Bernadette what was going on; Danny didn't want to get her involved in all of this. If the shit hit the fan, it wouldn't be fair on her.

Right, it's going to be a busy thirty-six hours ahead, he thought, knowing he would be visiting the beautiful countryside of Gloucestershire.

•

He could not believe it was 03:00 hours. No matter how much he prepared for an early start, it always kicked him in the bollocks when he tried to get out of his warm bed. Darkness whispered the crazy predicament he was solely facing: *Thanks, Thom.* He needed to get to the factory where Marina worked, and Danny needed those codes... *And then what?* he thought; he would figure that out when he got there. That was impetus enough to get him up. Switching on his bedside lamp, visions of the devastation terrorists were capable of wreaking took him in search of hotel-room coffee.

Outside, the frosty morning greeted him. Dressed in a pair of black Nike trainers, black combat-style trousers and a black sweatshirt. Looking up at a clear moonlit sky with a million stars looking down on him; with every exhalation he made, his icy breath floated away into the darkness. He loaded his equipment bag into the rear passenger seat of his Volvo V60 hire car, having one last cursory look around before he set off.

The equipment bag had everything he needed for the task ahead: spare clothes, binoculars, a small head torch, a basic multi-tool, a small camper's rubber roll mat, some food, snacks, water and of course a urination bottle; Danny tended to keep that fact a secret from social conversations. He double-checked for the pistol, which he hoped he wouldn't have to use. He decided to keep his eleven encryptions and the sketches of the area on his person just in case he had to leave the car at any time.

He couldn't afford to stand out to whom or what he was watching. Danny knew from experience that a person who sees someone repeatedly over time in different environments or who clocks a shifty stranger, can assume they may be under surveillance. Basically, staying the "grey man" is the key to blending into nothingness. He had to limit any excuse for being confronted, which could have fatal results. Reading the police reports from Thom, he knew Marina could take him out quicker than a heartbeat – his last – if he didn't watch his back; in the absence of Thom.

Danny was also still getting his head around this highly trained cold-blooded assassin Marina versus the playful kitten he'd seen with Hafiz. She was bound to suspect that she and the whole of the terrorist network cell she worked with might be under some sort of surveillance; Danny was not taking any chances.

Looking up to the sky, instinctively hoping he might spot a shooting star to make a wish upon before he departed, but even the sky was asleep. He jumped into the driver's seat and started the engine, trying to make himself comfortable by turning on the heaters to full blast. Soon he heard the whoosh of tepid air fill the cabin, the artificial heat helping to get rid of the surface frost on the windows. Before driving off, he waited until the engine was warm and the air corresponded nicely.

Danny typed the area of interest into the satnav. The reality of what he was about to do set in. He knew it was essential to keep his nerves under control; they needed to be razor-sharp. Despite all his experience, there was always a feeling of apprehension. Glancing in the rear-view mirror, he couldn't help but notice his bloodshot eyes. The stress on his face was obvious to him, so it must be to others. Danny enjoyed driving, but today he was pleased to have an automatic so his brain could concentrate solely on the job. Leaving the affluent area of Mayfair, his direction of travel was west, heading out of the capital to join the M4 motorway towards Reading. Whilst undertaking several textbook manoeuvres designed to shake any surveillance, Danny quickly pulled over into a darkened lay-by and got out of the car. He smeared mud onto the number plates to make them indecipherable. The upside of a 03.30 start was hardly any traffic. Every now and then, he passed alongside a long-distance haulage driver and imagined him wearing slippers with a pet dog beside him, given they practically lived in their illuminated cabs.

The cat's eyes made him feel drowsy so his spirits were raised as he took the exit A419 to Cirencester, leaving the flicker of signs behind him. Slowing down, he lowered the window, then the feeling of cold air smashed into his face, waking him up. Taking a few deep breaths as he rolled his head around from side to side to loosen his stiff neck, pushing his body back into the seat, trying to stretch out after the journey. Fresh air over, putting the window up, a heavy silence settled inside the car until his iTunes selected another album. As the beat kicked in, he saw a signpost for Stroud – *Not long now* – and adrenalin started to pump through his veins.

His main purpose for conducting a close target recce (CTR) was to obtain a progressive amount of information, which meant searching for vulnerabilities during the best cover of darkness. Danny didn't have time for a daylight operation, and he didn't have men under his command to cover a wide area either. He was reassured by remembering what his ex-captain said once: *Every safety net has a hole in it.*

Not bad timing. After two hours ten minutes on the road, he was travelling down twisting country lanes, taking it easy, making sure no one was following him; well, why would they? They were all asleep. Slowing right down to just under 15mph. Back down went the window so he had a clear view of the area and his target building. Cruising slowly, allowing his eyes to adjust to the natural darkness. The area was silent of traffic and was dimly lit against the pitch black of the sky. The only sound that reached him was the rustle of the trees and overgrown bushes moving in the wind.

TWENTY-TWO

—— • ——

Turning a slight corner on the approach road to the start of the Method Ltd. complex; it was on his right-hand side, on the edge of an industrial estate, mainly surrounded by woods and fields with a river running parallel behind the buildings. The main building was a dirty shade of white which had faded over time due to the harsh British weather. It had a contemporary design, a contrast to the traditional Cotswold-stone buildings in and around the area, with an apex roof on the gable end. A large car park led to the loading bay, with two white delivery access shutters. Both had down lights situated above them. Three huge cylindrical black security bollards protruding out of the floor preceded one shutter. A six-foot wooden fence around the perimeter obscured all views from the road; access was gained through the fence via a wooden gate situated in the right-hand corner.

As the road curved around to the right, the fence turned into a stone wall with a wooden fence running along the top of it. It was effective; Danny couldn't see shit of what was behind it. Approximately 100 metres away, there was a cylindrical-shaped building with a conical roof and a large chimney, just across from a T-junction amongst a row of trees and overgrown bushes. To the left, within its grounds, was a beautiful weeping willow. He knew there were three main approach roads to the complex which travelled in and out of the vicinity of the main target building, so Danny decided to explore all of them.

He gradually stopped at the T-junction without indicating and took a right turn along the fence line, which bordered another traditional Cotswold-stone two-storey building; a property that maybe had a basement. An old black-painted iron fence protected the front of the building, whilst the windows gave a different sort of defence. In the glare of his headlights he could see that all the ground-floor windows were stained glass, decorated with a pattern featuring butterflies and blacked out from behind with a sort of black boarding so that the public couldn't see inside the premises. Danny was instantly suspicious. *I wonder what they are hiding*, he thought.

Continuing along the road. There was a large aperture in the stone building that seemed to provide some sort of pedestrian access to the main building. *It must be the workers' entrance*, he thought. It had two large pinewood doors and two Gothic-style windows on either side on the wall; again, they were blacked out. The road snaked around to the right, a junction peeled off to the left – one he could take to bring him back down on himself in the opposite direction. The whole area comprised lots of different types of industrial units within the obvious mill buildings.

Coming back around on himself, turning left, he saw a bridge next to a small fishing lake. There were a few cars scattered at the side of the road near private cottages, and white lines were situated around; obviously for workers' cars when they arrived. Danny parked in one of the vacant spaces that gave him a clear line of sight of the main workers' entrance and each entry road.

Danny clocked where the security lights were. It would be an indication for overt or covert CCTV cameras. He spotted a few dome cameras strategically placed on the walls. Obviously, the owners didn't want to bring attention to the building; standard practice against criminals. He knew from his research that at the back of the whole industrial estate was an active railway line for the Stroud to London Paddington train. Danny reckoned that a comprehensive security vulnerability assessment and risk analysis would have been conducted prior to Mr Legend moving in for insurance purposes. Therefore, he was guessing that there would be between two to four guards operating on a twelve-hour shift pattern, with the main CCTV operations incident room manned 24/7 and the odd roaming foot patrol to check to see if there were any signs of forced entry.

He was cold so he put his window back up. Fidgeting, adjusting his chair right back to make him inconspicuous, lowering his head and upper torso from view. He turned the car lights off but kept the engine running with the heater blowing full on; the last thing he needed was condensation building up on the windows or, more importantly, cold toes.

Trying to decide what his next step should be, he got his binoculars and gloves and slowly scanned the area in detail to see if there was a better position for him to move to outside the car. If he were to be compromised by Marina, his life would end parked outside this poor bastard's cottage. He was going to have to get down and dirty, *old school*.

Just across the main A road, he noticed an overgrown wooded hedge line, comprising a mixture of trees, brambles, bushes, nettles and wild ivy approximately fifty metres away. It was perfect. It would give a great line of sight as well as concealment, apart from a few private properties nearby which he could handle. The sun was about to rise so he had to get a move on. Danny couldn't help but appreciate the pale purples, pinks and blues that were painting the morning canvas as they moved across the windy skies to ease him slowly into the day ahead. The odd bird beginning to tweet in the background told him nature was waking up, too. *If only I was a fucking artist today*, he thought, mourning the artistic opportunity to capture this on canvas.

Danny grimly slipped on his black baseball cap so that the peak formed a shadow that would obscure his facial features. Reluctantly turning off the engine from much-needed heat, he decided it was time to move; getting out the car, he threw his bag over his shoulder. Shutting the door quietly behind him, he hoped he would get the chance to open it again when all this was over.

Shrouded in the shadows, he looked both ways. A car drove past. Its headlights could be seen long before it drove along the quiet road and left it in darkness. Scarpering over towards the woodland, pushing his way through the tightly grown foliage in front of him. *Clearly, no one uses this path for a country walk*, he thought as he trampled his way through the bushes to make an entry point. The odd thorn dug into and scratched his skin, making him flinch; a large thorn pierced his glove and wedged itself

174

nicely into his hand. 'Little bastard', he whispered to himself. He didn't waste time and got it out; it bloody hurt. Grabbing bunches of bramble branches and arranging them close together, dog-legging the position to masquerade where he entered, so that no one could see anything had been disturbed in the outer hedge line. Completely covered by the undergrowth, pushing forward to the other side of the wooded strip so that he could see the main building and the entrance Marina would use. Pulling down more bushes and branches as if making a giant birds' nest; to give space so he could sit or lie down. Taking out the camper's mat, unrolling it flat on the floor. He was allergic to a wet arse and frankly it was more comfortable.

He put his black jacket on before he got too chilly and swapped his cap for a nice black woolly beanie for warm ears from the wind that was whistling through the trees, delivering the damp scent of the woodland to his nostrils. Daylight was starting to creep in, so he took five minutes to secure his position. The birds were orchestrating the beginning of a timeously practised classic: the dawn chorus; listening to their melody, content, sitting in the cold waiting for staff to arrive... *When, exactly?*

There was no movement anywhere near the building. Looking down at his watch: it was 06:17 hours. The wind was blowing up, reminding him he was already fed up. To distract himself, he sipped from his water bottle and tucked into a protein bar for breakfast.

Despite the miserable conditions, he appreciated his surroundings, contrasting with the tiny roads and decorative cottages. The serenity of his mind slipped back to serving in the Close Observation Platoon, South Armagh; Bandit Country. The country covert den he was sitting in was a direct contrast to the imposing Slieve Gullion mountain, which overlooked some hardline terrorist targets. Spying on some of the most dangerously notorious men and women in the IRA.

Intelligence gathered on known targets from Republican strongholds of South Armagh would be passed to members of the RUC Special Branch. Unfortunately, the bonus was that they became prime targets for the IRA, the missions so secret neither Danny nor any of his men were given the full intelligence picture. They depended on intel from agents who had infiltrated the IRA; the smallest of breaches would cost them their lives.

It was ironic that all these years later, he was again lying in wet undergrowth, simply with a different target. Historically back then, his job was to kill in defence regardless; now he'd be stopping that process.

07:30 hours: the sky was very overcast and it was even windier. Traffic began to travel on the main road as well as the smaller B roads joining it from all around him. He knew that above him and to his right was a private property, and that directly to his left was a church and graveyard. He tried not to seek out chilling Gothic headstones with dark gargoyles ornately gathered in a semi-circle; they had this awful habit of really staring back.

Suddenly there was a mass of activity: cars were pulling in towards the mill buildings from his left and from his right, parking up everywhere they could. The sound of male voices drifted over to him: men chatting and laughing amongst themselves, they walked in several groups. Danny could smell cigarette smoke. Three guards dressed in identical uniforms walked towards the building with the two pine doors: the logo on their chest pockets said G7 *Security* in bright orange writing. *Now we are cooking,* he thought. They were wearing dark navy-blue bomber jackets, black V-neck jumpers, white shirts, black trousers and black military-style boots. All of them carried a military rucksack over their shoulders. He was willing to bet these were the guys he needed to observe, and observe well.

As he followed them in his sights, two of them were practically chain-smoking, the tips of their cigarettes glowing brightly with each deep breath they took, each man desperate to cram the nicotine into his lungs before he started his shift. One by one, they flicked their fag ends into the air like two tiny fireworks; clearly, they had no consideration as to where their pollution might land. *Disgusting creatures,* he thought. Wondering if they were from around these parts of obvious natural beauty; their behaviour suggested not.

Another time check: 07:44 hours. Danny knew guards typically arrived approximately fifteen minutes before their shift was about to start. Given a twelve-hour shift was likely, he now knew the next changeover would take place this evening at 20:00 hours. These guys were obviously retired ex-army, overweight, likely paid the minimum wage with enough war stories to put a glass eye to sleep.

Danny intently watched them go inside the access area of the building towards the main double pine doors in front of them. One of the guards pressed a button on the intercom system on the left-hand side on the wall. Moments later, the left door only opened to reveal a plump-looking guard with dark hair sticking up. By the looks of him, he had just woken up; he had puffy eyes and a useless dimwit look about him. Danny tried to focus beyond him to the background and the interior of the building, but the lighting was bad and the inside seemed like a bloody cave. As he reshuffled his position, hoping for better light, he reflected that he could only imagine how boring and monotonous their job must be – but that would be a plus for him. Their basic drills were likely to be slack and relaxed. In addition, why would they suspect an individual to break in, not to steal anything directly from Joseph Legend but to steal from Marina Khan? One by one, they disappeared inside as the last man closed the door behind him.

The sounds of the birds had by now been replaced by the serious cranking up of traffic movement everywhere. There were buses, cars, motorbikes and cyclists, not to mention lorries that defied all common sense to assert their rights on roads that were clearly not big enough. Danny had lost count of the number of Land Rover Defenders he had seen, commercial and private. He thought they were only for horsey types and large farming communities, but apparently not: it was the obvious Cotswold vehicle of choice.

Thirty minutes later, the target pine door reopened to reveal three uniformed guards, including the little plump guard who still had sticky-up hair. The trio were scruffier than the first lot after a long twelve-hour night shift. They shouted behind them as they left, 'See you later, fellas!' 'Stag on, and enjoy your shift!' Sarcasm oozed as the door closed shut with a loud thud.

If that was their handover/takeover period complete, with day shift secured and night shift departed, Danny started to think his job might not be as difficult as he'd thought. Just as he was wondering if the same guards rotated week on week off, the plump guard stopped as the other two carried on walking. He took out a packet of Benson & Hedges, removing a cigarette and scrambling in his trouser pocket for his lighter. He sparked up, but then paused and looked around, as though aware he was being watched. Danny sat motionless, wondering if he had seen him or suspected someone might be hidden nearby. He breathed out to alleviate the feeling of paranoia that came hand in hand with this job, watching him draw on his cigarette. He clearly enjoyed the smoke, leaving his mouth like the Flying Scotsman; it showed in which direction the wind was travelling: right back at him. *Fucking gross*, he couldn't help but think. Yet the smoke seemed to have settled his nerves. 'Wait up, guys!' he shouted, picking up his pace and his fat body, shuffling forward to catch them up, his rucksack bouncing on his shoulder.

Watching them walk out of sight, Danny evaluated their potential efficiency in a face-off. Knowing some of the guards, on both shifts, smoked was a critical piece of knowledge. Apart from being unfit, their addiction would need them to exit the building throughout the day and night to feed their nicotine habit, which in Danny's eyes left a convenient hole in the safety net of security; *Capt. was right.*

Shortly after, he could hear another group of people chatting amongst themselves approaching his location, from both his left- and right-hand side. Male and female voices, with the aroma of a woman's perfume brushing past his nose. Watching patiently. He counted six people aged between twenty and thirty, all student types. Three males, three females, all dressed in civilian clothing, all carrying some sort of rucksack or satchel; some wearing trainers, some boots, some jeans, and all wearing waterproof jackets. Only the females were wearing woolly hats; one male was wearing a baseball cap. There was no sign of Marina. *Fuck's sake*, he thought frustratingly. *Where the hell is she? I hope I'm not wrong…*

They waited in the access areas of the building to protect themselves from the wind, slowly filtering inside one by one. He noticed that on their jeans and footwear there were numerous splashes and strikes of paint; these were Legend's art workers all right. The moment they disappeared he heard yet more voices coming from his right. 'Bingo', he whispered. 'Marina'. He got maximum clarity on his binoculars so he could get a proper look at her without his awkward position turning him to stone. *How can something so beautiful be so deadly?* he asked himself, observing her every movement and her impeccable style. She was wearing brown cowboy boots and blue skinny jeans, also covered in paint. She was carrying a black rucksack and the large artist's portfolio which had been sitting on the back seat of her Audi. Adrenalin started to pump through his core.

She was walking in between two females who were dressed very similarly. They hunched up together, protecting themselves from the elements, leaning into the blistering wind. A few 'Good mornings' echoed out as they squeezed into the access area. They shuffled over to make room for one another to get inside and moments later the same pine door opened. This time he didn't see who'd pressed the intercom system and he was unable to see the guard as his view was obscured. The interior was still dark and shadowy. They all disappeared inside Method Ltd. as the door shut with another thud, then silence reigned.

Those must be all the Legend workers, he thought to himself as he rearranged his butt and knees; both had lost all feeling. Staring into a drizzly mist, he had no idea why he suddenly thought of *Charlie and the Chocolate Factory* and the Oompa Loompa workers, but he did and the connotation made him smile. The mist turned to rain. Hearing the fat raindrops pat against the leaves around him, he pulled himself together and did another time check: 08:40 hours. It was going to be a long day, but at least Marina was confirmed inside the target building.

TWENTY-THREE

———— • ————

Silently, like a shadow. Motionless, observing through a mass of foliage, lying in the prone position. Danny was rather comfortable, relaxed and dry despite the rain cascading down heavily. The expanse of moisture in the air turned everything a darker shade, as the sweet surrendering scent of rain intensified the aroma of vegetation surrounding him.

Suddenly he was alerted to the sound of footsteps approaching from his right-hand side, together with a jingle of a chain. *Fuck, a dog,* he instantly thought, looking around for the obvious. If anything might discover him, it would be a mutt on a walk. Slowly moving towards the sound of the noise, he saw an old man in his late seventies wearing Epsom-green Hunter wellingtons, blue cords, and a traditional brown wax jacket with its collar turned up and an argyle-patterned flat cap. *Very dapper,* he thought, yet quite traditional for such an area. He was holding a chain dog lead but he didn't see any dog. *Bollocks.* He started to tense himself for an obvious compromise as he watched him pass his position without alert – but where was his hound? Long seconds went by and then he heard the sound of a frantically panting dog. It wasn't long before he came into view: he was a drenched and very dirty Springer Spaniel. He was definitely a he, and he was scenting for something, constantly following his owner, ten yards behind.

Unfortunately, as he paused by a drainpipe, he looked over towards Danny's position. *Dammit, has he seen me or sensed me?* he wondered, holding his breath, lying perfectly still like an ice sculpture. Yet as quickly as he had looked in his direction, he looked away again, his head down as he continued to sniff frantically. He cocked his right leg up but nothing came out, as a grumpy voice called out: 'Buckley! – Get here!' A command endorsed by a loud whistle. Buckley stopped to note where misery-guts was and then scarpered towards him.

In his den of wooded hedge line, the essence of winter romance had blossomed and his mind was almost at one with his enchanted hideout. *Fuck,* he thought, aghast at his train of thought; if he saw fairies next, then he'd be informing Thom he was out. It was an occupational hazard to daydream a lot to pass the time. Danny was catapulted back to his decision to leave the military and become an artist. *'So, how's that going for me then?' 'Not very well because I'm sat in a bush in the sodding rain, waiting for a psychotic killer to leave her "painting by numbers" job so I can sneak in'.*

As the minutes ticked by slowly, his mind went in and out of consciousness, a lucid dream mode as fatigue set in. His eyelids felt heavy. He focused on looking down at his watch: 11:45 hours. Then he felt the vibration of his iPhone in his upper jacket pocket. Slowly taking it out, shadowing the glare from the screen with his hand. It was a text message from Bernadette that read: *Hey handsome, I hear you're back in London, pop round when you're free for that chat X.* Danny looked at the iPhone and thought, *Bollocks, what I'd give to be there right now,* but, *I'm watching an old university friend of yours!*

Texting back – *Hello gorgeous* – He tried to make the text sound upbeat. *Yes, I'm back down in the smoke, not feeling great at the moment, just resting, think it's something I ate, just my luck, I'll call you later X.* Send. His inner strength took a pang of guilt: He felt bad about lying, but that was the only excuse he could come up with. His iPhone vibrated again and another message was received from her, reading: *OK, darling, let me know if you want Dr Bernadette to look after you X.* Shaking his head, smiling, texting back: *Tease X.* Send.

Lunchtime was another protein bar and water. The sound of a train from London Paddington to Stroud prompted him to have a nosey with the binoculars around the area. Waiting patiently for the cover of darkness to come to his advantage, as that was when he was 'going in', as the military say. There was an hour or so of darkness before the door opened, which gave him plenty of time for his eyes to adjust.

•

Standby, standby – The pine door opened, the light from inside escaped, beaming out, illuminating the whole access area. Two female workers from this morning were both coating up in the doorway: they hesitated, briefly waving and saying goodnight to their colleagues, before leaving the building. A uniformed guard closed the door behind them. *Interesting,* he thought, *looks like it is the norm to escort staff in and out. Must be home time,* he wondered.

That leaves ten inside: three guards and seven workers, including Marina, he thought to himself. It had been a long day and he was beginning to feel anxious. *I hope that's them starting to finish off for their day.* Optimistically.

Danny's spirits perked up with the onset of more movement from the target building. Raising his game a gear to high alert; the two gals who had just left were the same two who had accompanied Marina either side of her earlier. *Why wasn't she leaving with them?* They continued to talk to each other as they walked to the right of his position, away from sight.

Moments later, the pine door reopened. This time, it was the three males and two of the females from the larger group leaving, those who had been first to arrive for work this morning. They exited the building and proceeded to walk to the left-hand side of his position and then quickly out of sight. *Okay, that now leaves two other females and Marina, plus the guards.*

Frantically clock-watching. He glanced down at his watch and he didn't even acknowledge the time. Danny had to look again, yearning only to see the minute hand move. Looking again and again, until, some forty minutes later, the door reopened. *At last!* He sighed with relief, simultaneously holding up the binoculars to focus. This time, one of the uniformed guards walked out from the building towards the road, but stayed inside the covered access area. He looked up and down the street, putting his hand out to see if he could feel any rain. Danny gave him a good scanning, making a thorough assessment. He was in his early fifties with a beer belly he had obviously worked hard for, and a handlebar moustache.

More movement and the other female emerged from the doorway: long hair, brunette, late thirties, same athletic build as Marina. He couldn't see her face as it was obscured by the guard in front of her. Marina came out immediately behind her, and as both put on their coats and hats, the guard turned to go back inside; stopping off for a flirt, Danny reckoned. He could tell by his body language that he thought he was God's gift and in with a chance. 'Are you kidding me?' Danny whispered. *They are way out of your league, son.* He tittered to himself at his belief in himself, at his audacity in trying. Even from this distance, he could identify the awkwardness between him and the women, the cringing in the girls' facial expressions on whatever line he was delivering. They fast-forwarded their goodnights in an attempt to get away, leaving him to head inside casually, looking all smug. As he closed the door, he once more snuck one last seedy look at them. *What a twat.*

Danny focused on Marina and noticed that she didn't have her portfolio folder any more. *Thank fuck for that,* he thought as he continued to zoom in; she did still have her black rucksack from earlier hung over her shoulder, though. *They don't seem to be in a rush to leave,* he mused. They were standing close together, chatting and laughing, rearranging their coats and hats. The other female had her back to him, leaving him a good view of Marina, who was seriously a flawless beauty. Finally, they both exited from under the cover of the doorway and moved onto the pathway.

They headed the same way they had approached that morning. When they were almost out of sight, the other woman suddenly looked back over her shoulder, providing Danny with the perfect chance to zoom in with his binoculars to identify her. For a split second, he saw what looked like a healed cut with slight bruising over her left eye – and a very familiar face. *Jesus Christ!* he thought. *Is that the crazy bitch who tried to kill me in London?* He tried to identify her more accurately, but she had turned away once more. Following them through the binoculars until they were out of sight, he asked himself if his mind was playing tricks. After all, he was shattered. Nevertheless, he was going with his gut feeling.

Danny took a minute. *How is she involved? Is she involved, or was it just a random attack?* Nevertheless, that seemed unlikely. He was sure Marina the Manipulator had a persuasive enough hand to make anyone buckle, shaking his head in a little disbelief.

•

Darkness now had seriously set in, the wind had picked up and the scent of dried logs burning close by let him imagine his cheeks all cosy and rosy from sitting in front of the fire. He was still holding on to the assumption that security installations protected by manned guards were at their most vulnerable at the guard shift changeover – just like the one that was about to happen in less than two hours' time, to be precise. The handover period was the weakest time in terms of alertness and human reaction times, especially for those coming off guard shift. They just wanted to give a quick brief intel update, sign over equipment, which he hoped in this case was just torches and radios, grab their belongings and get the fuck out of there for home or a quickie at the local Dog and Duck pub en route. However, Danny knew how dangerous assumptions could be.

The incoming guard shift can never really be arsed either. Knowing the long twelve-hour shift is ahead, in this case night shift, they've been dreading it for the previous twelve hours, despite it being more of a regimented procedure when settling in for a night of watching movies, eating rubbish food and falling asleep in the chair facing the CCTV monitors: a repetitive, monotonous routine which all the movies get right, in the sense that you always know something is about to go down – and, this time, it really fucking was.

Checking his surroundings as he quietly moved to lift himself up into the kneeling position, but his body rejected his attempts uncooperatively; it was in a deadweight mode, aching from lying in the prone position for the majority of the day. *God, I'm getting too old for this shit*, Danny thought to himself, screwing up his face.

Taking off his jacket, rolling it up into a ball and stuffing it deep inside his bag. Then taking out his torch and multi-tool, placing them strategically into separate pockets. Finally, he took out the pistol, hoping he wouldn't need it, yet knowing that he might. He shoved it securely inside his belt, beneath his combat trousers, concealing it by placing his sweatshirt over the exposed pistol grip. Glancing unsentimentally at his faithful ground mat, rolling it up into another tight ball, it also went inside his bag, the straps of which he tightened securely before placing it over his shoulder. All this activity gave his body plenty of notice to get into the crouching position, from which he took one last look around, checking the floor was clear of his presence and nothing had been left behind.

Pushing his way through in the direction from which he had entered the hedge line this morning. He looked up and down the road through the cover of the leaves for any passing vehicles or pedestrians: nothing, so he pulled apart the brambles of the hedgerow, whilst still staying inside its cover. He took one last look around before exiting, making sure all the foliage sprang back into place, leaving no proof of him ever having been there.

Danny speedily ran across the road towards his car, trying to be inconspicuous and stay in the shadows; purposely keeping away from any of the street lights he passed en route. Once clear of the light, he walked normally and confidently. Removing his bag from off his shoulder then opening the car door, he got inside, placing the bag on the floor behind the front passenger seat. He couldn't wait to start the engine and experience long-awaited hot air; admittedly, it was like a warm fart at first, but he was optimistic it would soon improve as he left the lights off and blasted the heaters to full throttle.

Once his body temperature had risen to an agreeable warmth that his body could sustain, he drove away without indicators or headlights. Then accelerating a good couple of metres before flicking on the lights, which exhilarated his spirits as he moved away from darkness and luxuriated in feeling the warmth around him. Danny had to remind himself that although he was really exhausted, this was not a cup of tea. He had to keep alert and switched on if he was going to deceive the enemy.

He drove up the road for approximately 800 metres – still observant in case he was being followed – at which juncture he spotted a nice little position down a small side road leading off to some woods. It passed by a large farmhouse made of stone, but the habitation was silent and still. Turning off the main lights before he drove down the lane, parking tightly against a stone wall, which was set deep in the shadows under a large oak tree.

He knew the night shift would be arriving very shortly so he reluctantly killed the engine. Warmth was already starting to fade as he got out of the car, straight into a blast of chilly air. Quietly closing the door, he quickly headed back to the target area, warming up as adrenalin was now kicking in. Staying in the shadows like a prowling black cat, out of sight, yet with plenty of notice of oncoming cars, which made him scramble head first into dark hedges; otherwise, he'd have been illuminated like a motionless rabbit, blinded in beams of light.

Danny noticed a small overgrown bushy area in a corner of the Method Ltd. complex, facing the car park that was within the compounds of the industrial units of the mill and used by workers of the area. He quickly made his way to some large blue industrial waste bins. Several cats scattered in all directions as they heard him approach, darting beneath a number of parked cars. Crouching down behind the bins, allowing his eyes to adjust to the gloom, focussing on the main entrance area. Tuning into the silence around him, he could hear the sound of people chatting and the noise of machinery from within the units nearby.

Deciding to ditch the pistol: removing it from his belt, placing it in a seemingly tailor-made gap within the dry-stone wall beside him, concealed out of sight. If the shit really hit the fan, he knew he could extract back to this location and retrieve it. If the shit really got bad and the police caught him with a firearm, then he'd be going down for a long time for possession; knowing Thom would deny all knowledge of his existence, framing his arse in favour of his own agenda, for sure. This was his contingency plan if it all went south.

His deep thoughts were interrupted by the onset of loud thumping from the bass of a car stereo, followed by sudden headlights arriving, lighting up the entrance area of the car park. Shrinking behind the bins. It would have to be the stereotypical black BMW 3 Series that winged its way around the corner, parking parallel to a white transit van already there. The engine cut out. The silence was appreciated momentarily as three doors were suddenly flung open simultaneously. As quick as the uniformed guards got out, the doors were slammed shut, rather disrespectfully.

It was the same dudes from this morning, including the little plump one with sticky-up hair; though clearly, he had found time for Brylcreem during his time out. He didn't look smart, just a tad more respectable, though no doubt after a night shift he would regain the bag-of-shit look Danny had seen that morning. They all gathered together by the front of the Beemer, as the owner pointed his keys towards it – 'Beep!' – initiating the car lock as they continued chatting, making their way out of the parking area and towards the main entrance.

With them now out of sight, his adrenalin said, '*Right, let's go*'. He knew that once they were inside, they would be conducting the handover for possibly twenty to twenty-five minutes. The security would be at its weakest as they would be too busy chatting to each other rather than doing their jobs, which would give Danny enough time to get inside the perimeter walls and scout around without being detected. He knew darkness on any covert operation gave him safety. With this plan in mind, he ran swiftly towards the other side of the car park, keeping low at all times within the shadows of the wall and the overhanging branches, knowing that this part of the compound was furthest away from the main Method Ltd. building and its security cameras.

TWENTY-FOUR

——— • ———

He leapt up, putting both hands on the wall, and hauled himself up whilst keeping low and tight against it, so he didn't silhouette, looking left to right to investigate the layout beyond. On his highest alert now, where forward was the only option. There were six entry/exit doors with all the downstairs windows blacked out, identical to the ones at the front that he'd clocked that morning. Two parts of the Method Ltd. complex were contemporary modern-builds that were attached to the traditional Cotswold-stone main building. There were only two windows lit up from within; one of them was a small window open – *Maybe a toilet window or storeroom?* he thought. Four dimly lit down lights were also on, illuminating the doorways. Deciding to drop off the wall outside the perimeter and stealthily make a dash for it, crouching low following the six-foot stone wall along the rear of the compound, making his entry point easier away from the obvious main building.

Five minutes later, he estimated he was at his required position: against the wall with a large wooded area behind him. The only sound was the rustling of trees and nocturnal wildlife, already up and about. Pausing to get his bearings, listening into the darkness, straining to hear if anyone had seen him or was following him. Silence and darkness were his friends, it seemed; primed, ready to go.

Placing both hands up on the wall again. Using his upper body strength, he pulled himself up onto the top of the wall. Checking every direction, leaning his body right over and then, by placing one hand on the wall, he threw himself over in a gate-style vault, landing two-footed on the concrete in front of him, then immediately ducking down into the prone position, minimising his size, disappearing from sight.

Confident in the knowledge he was difficult to spot if anyone happened to glance around, he looked around for movement, listening intently for any suspicious sounds. Reaching down into his pocket slowly for his binoculars and scanning the security systems around the rear of the building, approximately seventy-five yards away. Counting six visible dome-style CCTV cameras, with three of them having passive infra-red motion sensors: these faced the doors of interest. *Bollocks, as if it would be that easy,* he thought. These types of sensors could either set off an alarm an intruder was not aware of or switch on a security light which would Guy Fawkes up a certain area that the guards could then detect on their CCTV monitors. *Bollocks indeed.*

Danny kept scanning left to right and saw four drainpipes that ran from floor to roof, with two within reaching distance of windows. There were also two large green wheelie bins right next to one of the entry/exit doors, with a metal bucket on the other side. He deduced that this must be where the workers or guards took their rubbish.

Crouching down, cautiously making a dash towards the corner of the building. His heart was racing, adrenalin pumping; he was getting hot as he kept his breathing shallow and as silent as possible. Kneeling down, out of view, he was at least ten feet away from the door. Taking another look around from his new position and double-checking how he'd got there for retraction purposes.

Suddenly the door next to the wheelie bins fully opened, releasing light onto the courtyard. Two of the guards emerged from the doorway mid-conversation, including his old friend 'Sticky-up Stumpy', which by his calculations left one guard inside, who was more than likely sat in front of the CCTV monitors. The day-shift guards would have left by now.

Observing Stumpy digging deep into his trouser pockets, dragging out a gold packet of Benson & Hedges and a cheap disposable lighter. He offered the other guard a fag and lit him up as they leant into each other; the other guard inhaled as if he had been off the nicotine for months. Slowly peering around the corner edge of the building, he saw that the door behind them led into a bright corridor. Stumpy lit up his own fag and they both puffed away, disappearing behind swirling layers of smoke that stayed around them, hovering, seemingly confused as to which direction to take into the evening wind. Despite gasping for breath from the pollution, like prize dunces they continued to smoke and chat.

'Did you watch the Chelsea game?' he overheard the first guard saying.

'Nah, mate – what was the score?' Stumpy replied, shaking his head.

'4-1 to Chelsea'. He heaved a long sigh.

'They must have been playing against a blind team', Stumpy commented, dismissively.

'It's bloody Baltic out here, fella'.

'Did you see that bird the other night?' his mate asked, ignoring him.

'Which one?' he said, chuckling sarcastically.

'Which one? You know which one. The one that works behind the bar, at the Dog and Duck; the one with the big...' The guard laughed, gesturing.

'Yes, I certainly did...' Stumpy grinned, like a dog on heat job.

'You're a lucky sod'. The guard made smoke circles as he exhaled.

'Fuck this, mate', Stumpy said, sucking the final drags from his fag, 'it's bloody freezing; I'm going inside'.

'A warm soldier is a happy soldier', he added, as he stood shivering.

'Good idea. I'm going to watch that new *Planet of the Apes* film tonight; I only downloaded it yesterday. Then I think I'll stuff my face with cheese and onion crisps'.

'Once you have finished, lend it to me after', requested Stumpy. 'I wanted to see that at the cinema but my missus didn't want to watch it'.

'Will do. What other new films you got?' he asked.

'I got shitloads, mate. They are all on my external hard drive'.

Stumpy turned towards the door as they both drew the final poison from their fags, rubbing the ends against the wall, making little sparks of embers cascade down the wall, before dropping the nub ends into the metal bucket. Finally, they both stepped back inside, still talking movies, as their voices faded, then to silence as the door closed.

Throwing Danny into darkness again and making him incognito once more. The door was an emergency fire exit that had a large metal push-down lever handle across the inside to open it; to close it, you needed to pull and lift up the bar, then press down so it initiated the locking mechanism. He was hopeful they might not have pressed it into place, but even these dimwits managed to get it right. The building was secure once again – except for that one open window...

Standing with his back against the wall, he looked once more at the locations of the cameras and motion sensors. Steering well clear of them, he crouched and darted towards the small window that had been left ajar. Gently lifting the latch from underneath, he slowly opened it outwards, peering in to see a store cupboard with floor-to-ceiling metal shelving on both sides of the room. He gave it the once-over for a few seconds and identified boxes of paper, a variety of stationery, books, cleaning materials and a big yellow mop and bucket on wheels by the door. The lights were off and no one was inside. Extending the window fully, diving in head first, falling inside in a controlled manner, without noise. Then he closed the window slightly, putting it back on its latch, taking a moment to think in the silence, listening for any signs of compromise.

Looking around the room, he took in everything he could – and quickly. There was a large air vent access panel on the ceiling, which was clearly part of the main ventilation system. For a split second, he considered taking that route, crawling through the air vents to get into the main area of the building, but without knowledge of the building's full layout, he couldn't take the risk. The last thing he needed or wanted was to be jammed in a pipe.

Instead, he walked over to the door. Kneeling down on the right-hand side, slowly turning the round handle anti-clockwise, releasing the catch and pulling the door slightly open. He'd been hoping to observe whatever lay beyond through the tiny slit he had made, but those hopes were in vain: the slit just revealed blackness as there were no lights. As his eyes adjusted, he could see some sort of corridor. He made a bigger gap with the door so he could use the light from the store behind him. Now, he could see two doors with signs on: the first read 'The Laboratory' and the other 'Security Office'. From the latter, he could hear the muffled sounds of a TV, guards' voices and laughter. *Think I'll pin 'No Entry' on that door, then,* he thought cheekily, just as it opened, blasting the sound of the TV louder into the corridor, along with the guards' voices.

'Fuck!' He quickly closed the door. Standing up in a rush, he hid behind a large, neatly stacked pile of A4 paper boxes. Standing still like a statue; his heart was pounding so loud he was sure it could be heard. The storeroom door opened and footsteps headed towards him, stopping in front of him. Someone was shuffling around, searching the shelves close by. Preparing to be compromised and to physically take on the guard, when suddenly he shouted, scaring the fuck out of him.

'Clive, where are the pens kept?' His loud voice unnerving: Danny hadn't realised quite how close he was. Flinching, he prepared himself to attack, if he was compromised.

'On the shelf, next to the notepads', a disinterested voice shouted back from the Security Office.

'Where? I can't see them!' the guard replied, annoyed, shuffling and moving items around on the shelves. Danny heard the footsteps of another guard entering the room. Silently, like a shadow. Watching them.

For fuck's sake, he thought, *now there are two of them to deal with. Man, it's going to get messy in here.*

'Yo. Look. There you go: right under your bloody nose'. The rescue guard spat sarcasm, taking a handful of yellow Post-it notes for himself as he exited the room.

'Thanks, mate'. 'Useless' grabbed the pens and switched off the light as he left, closing the door behind him.

Danny was relieved, *dreading the sound of a door being locked,* he thought, but instead he heaved a sigh of relief as no tell-tale click came. Tension released from his body and he started to breathe normally again, composing himself. *Fuck, that was close,* he thought, listening intently. There was nothing worse than a fight against two large lumps in a small confined space; it would be too much fat ricocheting around.

Time check: 20:45 hours. After the near miss, Danny decided he'd leave it a while and wait for the guards to get settled and bored before he went looking for these all-important codes.

TWENTY-FIVE

——— • ———

Time check: 01:09 hours. Danny decided that the guards had had enough time. Switching his torch on, shielding the beam to a minimum. He walked towards the door quietly, turning the handle, then opening it slowly. At this point, he was tempted to shout, '*Boo!*' just for the fuck of it to see what kicked off, but he resisted, tuning into the muffled sound of the guards' TV instead. There were no voices at this hour, which suggested they had indeed settled in for the night.

The beam of light from his torch guided him to the door marked 'The Laboratory'. Turning the handle cautiously... *Bollocks, it's locked*, he thought. He knelt down and pointed the torch at the lock to identify its type; luckily, it was a simple pin-in tumbler lock, the sort that was relatively easy to open using a pick and wrench. *Oh look, here's one I made earlier:* he mimicked *Blue Peter* in his head as he found his multi-combination tool *avec* a few personal adjustments he'd installed to assist him in times like these. It was amazing how severe fatigue allowed you to walk the fine line between sanity and insanity.

The art of unlocking locked doors without the original key isn't only a learning curve for criminals; it's also a skill you learn for any covert operation. *It's amazing what courses the military put you on; it's a bit stupid of them really,* he thought, concentrating.

With the torch in his mouth aimed at the door handle, he was totally hands-free to place the L-shaped tension wrench into the base of the keyhole. With a little pressure on the lock cylinder and a bit of fiddling around, you could often feel the piece of metal with a bend on the end, feel the pins spring up, resetting, locking into place. One by one, he released them whilst turning the tension wrench anti-clockwise. The cylinder turned, opening the lock. 'Voila –' click '– and bingo'. *It never fails*, he thought, slowly pushing the door open, removing the torch from his mouth and replacing his multi-tool back in his pocket, still listening for any signs of movement from the Security Office. There were none.

Once inside 'The Laboratory', Danny closed the door behind him, pointing the torch in all directions to get an idea of the layout. The room he was in could only be described as the world's largest artist's studio. He looked to his right-hand side and saw three offices stretching the length of the main studio area; the first office was without a door. Redirecting his torch to his left-hand side, he saw two large square wooden boxes on stilts, covered in different colours of paint. Inside each of the boxes was a large wooden disc, like a record player. *This must be where he makes his spiral paintings*, he thought. Imagining the studio of *Blue Peter* again, with scatter cushions and a dog named 'Shep', the Border Collie rubbing his arse on the carpet.

Danny walked two or three paces towards the first office door on his right, then suddenly lights within the whole studio came flickering on. *Fuck!* Startled, he froze automatically, assuming he had been compromised. Confused as to what was happening. He quickly looked around and noticed no guards – but just above the door was a passive infra-red sensor that turned the lights on and off accordingly. Relieved, taking the opportunity to digest his bright surroundings, waiting to hear if there were any sounds from the security guards, no visible signs of any CCTV cameras. Moment of panic over. Quickly running forward to crouch down behind a large stack of white canvases. Nothing followed: only silence accompanied his brilliant vision of everything around him.

Reassured that he hadn't been compromised – but his movement was also akin to a standing ovation. Danny's first impression as he stared around the studio was 'WOW', he experience an overwhelming feeling that flooded his soul, amazed. He felt as if he was in the mind of the creator himself, re-enacting the mundane black-and-white world of *The Wizard of Oz* before the mammoth twister sent Dorothy and Toto into the colour of the diegetic world. *We are definitely not in Kansas any more, Danny,* he whispered to himself. This studio was now that world. Large bright industrial lights shining down on the clinical look of the scientist's laboratory, a row of white coats hanging on infinite rails next to the offices, splashes of spilt paint everywhere. It looked as if it had been done on purpose and in synchronicity.

God knows how dumbfounded Danny must have looked if there were CCTV cameras aimed at him. Giddy with the kaleidoscope of colours, he took his time. The awe of its scale took his breath away, comparing it to his rickety studio in his garage. Slowly walking around, totally forgetting his combat intentions; he felt as if he had been given a special 'Golden Ticket' privilege pass to wander around at his leisure.

There were works of art on the walls around him – some complete, some not – sketches of sharks, flies, skulls, parrots, ashtrays and several of monkeys. A giant seven-foot pink love heart with scattered butterflies, titled *Daddy's Girl*, was hung up to dry by some heaters, identified by a yellow Post-it note written in pencil. Next to this were several large spin paintings, all with explosions of psychedelic colours partly covered in butterflies, whilst jars filled with paintbrushes and piles of pots of paint were everywhere, all around the studio, together with rolls of canvas and different sheets of high quality artist's paper.

Looking towards the back of the studio, he could see a ledge, just below a large blacked-out window. There was a selection of human skulls meticulously placed alongside several half-finished sculptures of angels that were made out of stone. On a large table nearby were several sketches of human foetuses, mystical sea creatures, bugs and insects. Another table had a selection of surgical instruments: scalpels, syringes, saws and other medical tools used in surgery. Several medicine cabinets stretched along the back wall that stood half filled with pharmaceutical packaging. He could see why people either loved Legend or hated him.

Taking one last look around, absorbing the inside of the mind of a genius, he decided he needed to get back to why he was really here. Quickly heading towards the first room to his right. Inside, there were four large artists' desks, all with paper and art materials on them, appropriate chairs, together with various kinds of personal belongings: framed photos, cuddly toys, diaries and personalised mugs. *How communal*, he thought, as he hunted around each of the desks for anything connected with Marina; an item with her name on it or even the artist's portfolio *carrying case*. Nothing.

'Fuck's sake. Where is it?' he muttered in frustration, quickly retreating to the next room; it was in total darkness. Pushing the door open gently, he switched his torch on, closing the door quietly behind him, scanning around each footstep in front of him as his eyes followed the beam. He had half-hoped motion sensors would turn on the lights here, too, as before, but his luck was not in. Pointing the torch beam at the door, he found the light switches to the left-hand side. Switching them on, five industrial strip lights flickered on the ceiling and the first thing he saw was a large silk-screen printing machine. There were two digital printing machines at the back of the room, and along the wall to his right was a long sideboard, stretching all the way from one side of the room to the other. There was also a Belfast sink at one end together with a coffee machine and cups, with a small fridge underneath; his yearning for coffee gave him a nervous facial twitch.

Resisting caffeine, he continued to clock everything. Besides each printing machine was a varied selection of different tins of paint, covering every colour created. Two large desks with facing chairs stood at the far rear of the room, laden with art materials, stationery and computers, which he assumed were linked to the digital printers.

Once again, Danny searched frantically for signs of Marina. Nothing. 'For Chrissake', he whispered to himself. Doubting his own collated intelligence now; *who would employ me? ... Oh yeah, Thom*; he was certainly ready for his retirement fund to 'paint by numbers'. Just as he was about to leave, he spotted an artist's carrying case in his peripheral vision. He'd almost missed it. It was placed between the desk and some boxes of art materials. His heart started beating with anticipation and its fair share of frustration as the adrenalin shot through him. 'Please. Come on', he said as he picked it up and put it down on the desk in front of him.

Unzipping the top, looking inside, carefully removing a pile of quality artist's papers... He dared to think, to dream... it was the codes. *Bingo! That's them; thank God for that.* Excitement overwhelmed him. A few controlled deep breaths allowed him to stabilise. Slowly, he went through them individually, in detail. Simultaneously, Danny pulled out his own pile of deciphered codes and the A4-coloured photocopy of the *Chemical Warfare* spot painting he had concealed about his person. Placing everything down on the table in front of him, running his forefinger down each of his findings, comparing his projected ciphers to Marina's original scripts. *'Spot on'* – pun intended.

Rearranging her work alongside his, neatly in a row, one by one, Danny matched them to each encryption and to each of the deciphered codes. He counted twelve encryptions from Marina's artist portfolio case. *Eh? What the fuck?* He was puzzled: there were only eleven names left on the hit list. Counting them again, shaking his head, convinced it was a mistake. Had one been repeated, or maybe he'd finally fallen asleep and this was a dream… but twelve encryptions stared back at him. Ignoring the mysterious twelfth code – he reasoned there would be time enough to look at it later, pushing it aside, he went back to the eleven that he knew needed his attention right away.

Time check: 02:37 hours. With the night passing swiftly, he was under pressure – it didn't help that he felt sick with fatigue. Every now and then, he would pause for a moment to listen out for any movement from the guards; he was on edge. Drawing deeper inside himself for strength, needing to stay alert and crack this bitch before the guard shift changed over – not to mention to find a way out before sunrise.

Danny was drawn to four large metal drying racks that were placed beside the printing machines, having recently discovered these were used by printers and artists for artwork to dry evenly and not be damaged or smudged before being sent out to customers or galleries. Removing each screen print from its drying compartment. As he did so, his eyes were damned again by circles, sleep deprived; all the coloured circles seriously didn't help. Placing the pictures from the drying racks carefully on the extended sideboard in a neat row, counting eleven; which once again made him think the twelfth encryption in the folder was a mistake.

Matching all eleven of the encryption sketches made by Hafiz in Marina's case with the A3-size prints that he'd just removed from the drying racks. They were all different circle compositions and different sizes, dependent on what original circle painting the individual on the hit list actually owned. Some had 180 coloured spots, some had 90 and some editions had the spots strategically placed together inside to form a larger circle or a triangle. Danny simultaneously cross-referenced that his deciphered codes were one hundred per cent correct and matching.

These drying copies were definitely the ones ready to be sent to the assassins. For the first time, he knew he had truly cracked his code. *So, what the fuck now?* he thought.

He needed to know how much time was left. He quickly walked over to the door. He opened it slightly to have a peek out into the studio, which was back in total darkness. Listening carefully, straining to hear anything, but only silence emanated from the guards' room: movies, food, boredom and slumber had hopefully rendered them useless. Another time check: 02:57 hours. Closing the door quietly again.

Danny got out his iPhone; he had to call Thom. It rang and rang; the same voicemail message. He tried again. *Come on, Thom. For Chrissake, answer your fucking phone!* He frustratingly whispered into the phone voicemail: 'Thom, call me now. It's urgent'. Keeping his voice down, Danny ended the call imagining throttling Thom for an answer. *Why won't he bloody answer?* Putting the phone back in his pocket, now was not the time to leave it behind. He stood and stared at the limited edition prints and the deciphered codes, deliberating his next move... *Which is?*

Looking at the silk-screen printing machine, Thom's plan... which was? Danny's plan, any plan, was screwed. Danny hadn't a fucking clue how to use it and even if he did, the noise would alert the guards. He scratched his head, which still didn't work on any level. Protocol in any solo covert operation was to have a Plan B. He contemplated destroying the codes, but that would only delay the inevitable. Danny needed to change the codes... to what? Drawing deep into his knowledge of Hafiz's psyche over the months, Danny had a genius idea, speedier than he gave himself credit for.

Picking up an unused paintbrush, selecting the paints he'd need. *I'm going to be an artist after all,* he thought, *no pressure if I get it wrong, just a lot of innocent people will be annihilated, that's fucking all.*

Danny chose a titanium white acrylic paint to start his own interpretation on *Primus Circles*. Dipping the brush in, removing the excess paint with precision, then delicately painting over the specific colours of the encryptions, slowly contouring the edges of the circles, filling in the spots. With a steady hand being guided by his other hand, one by one he completed each of the eleven circle prints, cross-referencing each of the ciphers, ensuring every encryption was erased. Allowing them to dry.

Time check: 04:04 hours. He needed the new codes for each edition. Danny hastily dotted about the studio, gathering up in his arms tubes of pyrrole red, cadmium orange, ultramarine violet, cerulean blue, good old olive green and lemon yellow. He felt like an *Oompa Loompa* worker. Laughing at his own jokes, blaming a Molotov cocktail of fatigue, hunger, spots and paint fumes.

Another time check – 04:44 hours – was a stability slap: he got new paintbrushes quick sharp. 'Okay, my devilish friends, now for a few minor adjustments', he announced quietly, as he went back to the first print to see if the titanium white acrylic had dried. It was perfect; he was perfect: you wouldn't have had a clue the circles had been changed. His new best friend was acrylic paint for drying fast compared to oil paints. Then he patiently covered the white spots with his specific encrypted colours, two steady hands leaving no trace of change. As he worked, he observed his artistry lovingly, but with each stroke he could feel the fatigue setting in a bit more. He had to stretch his arms and neck regularly. Mentally exhausted as he leant over the table.

However, as the saying goes: '*If it's the last thing I do…*' He checked each print carefully before lifting ten of the newly configured editions off the table and placing them back in the drying racks in the exact same order he had removed them. 'Finished', he whispered in accomplishment, with not a lot of energy left. Finally, the last one – number eleven – was completed and stowed away. He placed his paintbrush down with a sense of grim satisfaction. Standing up and taking a much-needed stretch.

Again, he stared at the drying racks, thinking how ironic this whole situation was. Then he suddenly felt a big wave of sorrow for Hafiz: how he had thwarted his plans. What would have happened if he hadn't met Hafiz and coincidentally bumped into Thom; though Thom had pretty much bumped into him. Would anyone else have been able to stop him?

We sometimes ask esoterically why someone comes into our life and contemplate: is it for a reason? Usually, it's to meet a need you have expressed in your mind and thought only in the subconscious world.

'They' – whoever 'they' are – have come to assist us through a difficulty, to provide us with guidance, support, to aid us physically, emotionally or spiritually. 'They' may seem like an angel sent from God in times of need and maybe they are. 'They' are there for a reason; we need them to be there, whether we are conscious of needing the help or not.

So, where the hell does that leave Hafiz, Thom and me? he pondered. Then remembered the time when Hafiz once told him that the colour black always described death, always black. Almost trance-like, Danny reached over to the drying rack and removed the eleventh circle edition, placing it back down. He picked up a tin of Mars black acrylic paint and lowered another paintbrush into the dense-looking paint, watching the bristles sink in the liquid, absorbing the colour.

With precision, he painted over the blood-red coloured spot with the black; that specific spot signified the method of death. It was conveniently positioned dead centre of the image. Pausing for a moment, looking down at the final completed edition, wondering, guessing; then he gently picked it up and placed it back on the drying rack. *Doing bad things for good reasons, think of the greater good.*

The lights started to dim in his head: his body was shutting down. Time check 05:07 hours: 'Right: time to get out of here', he said to himself, putting everything back as he had found it. Grabbing an old cloth from the sink, he meticulously cleaned the brushes before going to the rubbish bin, where he pulled the existing rubbish to one side so he could push the cloth and brushes he'd used to the bottom of the bin, undetected, to camouflage them back over.

Carefully, he put Marina's encryptions back into her artist's carry case exactly how he'd found them. To ensure he hadn't left anything behind, he checked the floors and tables: Danny didn't want to leave any ground trace that might make Marina suspect someone had been in the room. Concealing his deciphered codes under his sweatshirt.

Time check: 05:37 hours. *Time to go; it's rude to outstay one's welcome.*

TWENTY-SIX

———— • ————

Switching off the main lights in the side room, then slowly opening the door to the main studio to check that all was clear: clear it was. He left the room quietly, almost imperceptibly, closing the door behind him. Feeling oddly calm: the studio was in total darkness and the motion detectors hadn't clocked him. Cautiously staying out of the path of the infra-red motion detectors. Crouching down near the door, he could see the infra-red motion detectors above; Danny was practically splatted against the wall. Softly, slowly, gently turning the door handle to open it slightly to look into the hall and at the Security Office. *Coast is clear…* he thought, with caution.

Quietly leaving the room, turning the catch on the inside of the handle, ensuring it would lock once closed. A satisfying click as he pulls it to, successfully covering his tracks. Tentatively pausing for a moment to listen for any movement from inside the Security Office: silence. Growing steadily more confident, he headed towards the storeroom. As he turned the handle, he was beginning to feel the need to rush, to get the hell out of there. Safely inside, closing the door, the lights were still off. He could now see the window he had come in through, still pitch black outside. Pushing it fully open in an upright motion, he secured it with the long-arm latch to make sure he could squeeze his body through it without the window slamming shut; the last thing he needed was to be stuck arse inwards to the enemy.

Stretching himself up as high as he could on his toes, looking out to check for a clear exit. *It's clear*, he thought, pulling himself up onto the ledge, leaning forward head first through the window, followed by his torso, then trying hard with an unsightly wiggle to fall out of the window without injury or too much noise. Managing a sort of vault motion, but not without a few grazes and scrapes to his shins. 'Bastard', he whispered as the pain of the metal latch scraped down his leg on the way out, but gravity took over with no possibility of wiggling back. Landing on the ground, rubbing the wound immediately whilst looking around for signs of movement, listening for sounds. Clear. He stood up and closed the window gently. Unbelievably, he was almost home and dry.

'Can I help you, fella?' An aggressive voice with a touch of sarcasm suddenly came from behind. Danny was startled and he quickly turned around to look directly at who it was.

'*Fuck!*' It was Stumpy, the little plump guard with sticky-up hair, hand in hand with his early morning fag, that was clearly also breakfast. *He really needs to address his diet*, Danny thought, but – much more importantly – he wondered: *Where the fuck did he come from?*

Instinctively, Danny said, 'I'm with him', pointing right behind him, over his shoulder, having paused to dust down his trousers in a nonchalant fashion, by which two gestures he was both reassured and made curious, so he momentarily looked around to see what Danny had been pointing at. It was the oldest trick in the book – but it worked a treat, the poor sucker. The instant he looked around, Danny made his move, wrapping his right arm around the front of his neck, putting pressure on his Adam's apple and carotid artery. Extending his arm forward, he put it in the elbow pit of his left arm, tightly squeezing inwards. Linking arms in that position, looping his left arm to the back of his head, pulling him down to the floor in a controlled manner. He tried to struggle free so Danny applied more pressure in the precise hold, whispering to him, 'Don't fight it, mate'. In that second, he drifted off to sleep and he knew he had just a few seconds before he woke up.

Given the suddenly pressing timescale, in his panicked state, Danny decided to disregard his sleek stealthy panther prowess and simply sprint like fuck towards the perimeter wall closest to him. Leaping up and grabbing hold of the top, pulling himself up and forward; suddenly he felt a large hand grab his left ankle. *Fuck*, he thought, startled, trying to shake it off. Luckily, his weight and momentum took him over the wall, making his grip release him. Landing on the grass on the other side, he glanced over his shoulder to see a larger dark figure clambering on top of the wall.

'Oi! You, you little fucker!' Another aggressive voice shouted in his direction.

Adrenalin was causing a speed-freak momentum in his movements; he legged it towards the car park and the industrial bins, accurately removing the pistol from the wall, shoving it down the belt of his trousers. Then running full pelt through the car park in the general direction of his car. Then out of the shadows another large figure came crashing into the side of him, knocking him off his feet, forcing him to tumble violently to the floor, in sheer agony.

'Gotcha! You little bastard', he said menacingly.

Slightly winded and grazed, trying to control his gasping breath whilst on all fours on the floor, charging towards Danny like a fierce rhino, launching his right foot deep into the pit of his stomach. Taking his breath fully; the excruciating pain made him feel nauseous. Danny keeled over onto his side, panicking for air.

With a maniacal laugh: 'You little bastards think you can break in and steal people's property. The lads are going to love this. Lads, lads, he's over here, I'm in the car park'. He shouted in excitement over to the others. Chuffed that he had incapacitated him. Turning his Maglite torch on, pointing the beam in Danny's direction. Instantly, Danny held his hand up to his face to protect his night vision.

Still trying to compose himself, taking deep breaths, quickly getting up, shocked, afraid, trying to figure a way out of this mess. Danny knew he couldn't afford to be apprehended by this lot; being handed over to the authorities would ruin everything. For a split second, his hand moved to the pistol in his belt…

'You're not going anywhere, you're mine', he growled. 'Lads on me, I've captured the little fucker'. Holding his arms out to corner Danny form escaping.

Just before he lunged at him again, Danny managed to step to the side, transferring his weight to palm heel him direct to his nose with his right hand: whack! With devastating effect, it forced his head back on impact. Instantly, precision timing allowed Danny to send a vicious knuckle strike to his larynx with his left hand. Sending him immediately down onto his knees in excruciating pain, choking, instantly releasing the torch by his side as he clamped his hands around his throat.

Danny kicked the torch well away from their position. In the chaos and fear, he ran like fuck whilst he had the chance, still catching his breath, making his way out of the car park. Looking over his shoulder.

'He's heading that way, lads', the guard attempted to shout, but his voice was raspy and broken: holding his throat with one hand and pointing with the other. Danny could feel them chasing him. The sound of his heartbeat filled his ears, adrenalin pumping like ice in his veins, Danny's instincts screaming at him to do nothing but run. This was the hunt, and Danny was the prey.

Sheer shock and survival helped him make good distance. He knew they had given up trying to chase him after about 800 metres. Danny shot into some bushes close to some nearby garages and knelt down, deep in the shadows, trying to control his breathing, observing. His heart was literally racing and it took time to recoup and breathe. His senses were back on high alert as he scanned around and waited.

From this elevated new position, Danny saw two of the guards in the workers' car park with large Maglite torches. Beams of light were frantically pointing in all directions, followed by Stumpy and the other guard both looking like they hurt a lot; it was his *good manners that left them both still alive*, he thought. He waited to see if they were planning to pursue again but they went back inside – to his immense relief. Game over; for now, anyway.

•

Back in London – a location Danny would not normally think was the best place ever – in his hotel room and more specifically about to get into an amazing hot bath. For the first time ever, he skipped his religious OCD toe-digging, carpet-pile ritual and made straight for soapy suds and 38-degree water. Nevertheless – call it ESP or paranoia from the last twenty-four hours – suddenly he sensed someone had been or was still in his room.

Pausing for a moment, something was wrong, something was skew-whiff. Despite all his training, he still opted first for the 'feet sticking out from beneath the closed drapes' scenario, before he slowly scanned around further, looking for signs as to what was out of place. And there it was: on the desk, next to the telephone was a silver room-service tray with a padded couriered envelope. He did a double-take, bearing in mind the number of envelopes he had seen recently, but this one certainly was a new acquisition. Glancing quickly into the bathroom to check it was secure, he walked towards the desk. Opening the seal, he found, tucked inside, another brown envelope addressed with the letter T. Another twenty grand of fifties grinned at him when he peered inside. *Nice one, I think I do deserve this*, he thought, but he was confused as to why Thom still hadn't got back to him. *No phone calls or texts on any progress, what the hell?*

The bath scalded his skin as each part of his ice-cold body entered the depths, real slow. Welcoming the peaceful warmth of this ritual, allowing the hot water to sink deep into his pores, tiny ripples accessing his body before totally submerging, like the tide coming in, causing water to bubble up under the sand ahead, massaging his tired aching muscles.

Steam rose towards the ceiling and he watched it glaze over the mirrors and windows, relaxing in the comforting knowledge that he had nothing else to scrutinise in his surroundings: the freedom of safe peripheral vision. A sudden awareness of pain made him look down at the grazes on his shin, as the heat and water intensified the ache at the location of the injury. Inspecting his recent war wounds.

From somewhere within his ecstatic state of *nothing to worry about here*, he heard the buzz of the vibration of his iPhone. Somewhat reluctantly, semi-flopping himself out of the bath to get it from his combat trouser pocket. Settling back into the water, he saw he had a text from Bernadette.

Time check: 10:36 hours. *Morning, handsome. How you feeling today? Bernie X.*

Blimey, he thought, he hadn't clocked that it was morning; he'd lost track of time. Danny wanted to sleep but he didn't feel tired; he guessed he'd crossed that pain threshold of fatigue that often comes with doing covert ops; perk of the job, in some ways. He texted back: *I'm feeling much better, thanks, fancy meeting for lunch today?*

Seconds later, her reply arrived: *Yes please, I can't wait to see you. Shall we say 2pm? Meet me at the gallery.*

Danny replied quickly: *Can't wait X.*

TWENTY-SEVEN

——— • ———

The wind had now dropped to a whisper as he arrived at their agreed meeting place early, as usual, which gave Danny time for some rather more pleasurable secret covert work. Mesmerised by his date, he watched her through the gallery window; her beauty meant he saw only her as the afternoon light caught her hair, making it shimmer like a spectrum of colour passing through. Oblivious to his presence, she pottered around the gallery tidying up, moving magazines and books, her silk white blouse clinging to her sensual body, her black pencil skirt emphasising every movement and the contours of her beauty.

Bernadette turned to face the window and Danny waved over at her. Standing at her desk, she now had that look of demanding his physical attention. Her tight rose-coloured lips pursed in anticipation, the moisture on her lips glistening in the light, beckoning to him, inviting him to lean in and press firmly against them in the perfect kiss. Smitten and spellbound, he caught her eye. They smiled in harmony as she commanded him with one finger to come inside.

Danny smiled then walked towards the door. As he did, she opened the door and curtsied, tilting her head downwards meekly, gesturing to hold out a pretend flowing skirt. In reality, nothing could get in between that pencil skirt and her skin apart from fresh air. 'Hello, sir', she played.

After the last twenty-four hours, he could cope with a bit of *foreplay*… He meant *role-play*. 'Mademoiselle'. He tilted an imaginary hat with one suggestive wiggle of his eyebrows as he walked past her, hearing her close the door behind him. Alone at last.

'Come here, you'. Danny turned and took hold of her waist, manning up, pulling her into him as her body submitted to his.

'Sir, this isn't one of those establishments; you will have to go to the other side of town'. She attempted to pull away, then flickered her lashes at him and breathed, 'Unfortunately'. Provocatively, she leant back into Danny, mirroring his smile, staring deep into his eyes.

He was on a roll. 'Damn, I do apologise, *jolie jeune femme*; my sense of direction is somewhat terrible', he replied with a smile on his face.

'Umm… The last time you were here, sir, you knew exactly which direction to go'. She winked, biting her lip, blushing. Their shared laugh didn't last long; he strengthened his hold around her waist, the scent of her perfume intoxicating him, making his desire uncontrollable, especially when she closed her eyes and pushed into him. Finally, she opened those soft glossed lips and they kissed passionately at the door with the world walking by outside.

There is something timeless about kissing for literally minutes but when they stopped and she looked deep into his eyes, with a sense of sorrow, something distant in the windows of her soul – he knew something was wrong and that was confirmed when she suddenly held him tighter, placing her head on his chest in an unusually tender moment. Danny wrapped her up tight, waiting for her to speak.

'I've missed you', she said, placing her perfectly manicured hands on his chest.

'I've missed you, too'. There: he'd said it, it was out. 'You had something important to tell me?' he prompted. 'What's up?' Looking down at her enquiringly.

She looked back up at him endearingly and he stepped back, trying to read the emotion in her eyes but, unlike Hafiz's codes, it was indecipherable.

'I just want to be honest with you and let you know a bit more about me', she said with a look of apprehension.

'Hey, listen, we all have skeletons in our closets'. He wasn't sure where this was going.

'True', then she paused for a moment, struggling to get the words out. Finally, she blurted out: 'I used to be married and my husband died'.

'Oh. I guessed that. Hafiz sort of told me'. Not fazed by her statement.

'What the! Hafiz? How?' she gasped. Her face unexpectedly turned a crimson red; she became fearfully angry. He needed to smooth this over.

'No, no, not that you were married, that you had a double-barreled name, so putting two and two together, or like some people prefer to have their family names like that'. He was better off in a hostile bush than dealing with this.

'Oh, right, yes; sorry, of course'. She didn't understand; it was as if her brain had short-circuited and needed to be rebooted. She exhaled in relief then smiled. He could tell his mistake had hit a nerve.

'Hey, look, I know it must have been a difficult time for you, but this and us, we will just take it easy'. Trying to reassuring her but she just stared at him; like she was holding back tears. *Why don't men just shut up when they are out of their depth, like now?* he thought. 'Then as things progress between us I'm sure we will open up a bit more, if either of us wants to of course, I mean, if it's relevant to our future'. He wasn't sure that the babble registered much.

'Yes, you're right, Danny, of course I just don't take things for granted, especially with people I care about'.

'Well, I'm here for you if ever you want to talk', he simply said.

'I hope so'. She turned away abruptly, walking towards the area out the back, then returning momentarily, wearing her navy-blue Prada trench coat, carrying her Louis Vuitton handbag, before turning on her heels and going back out again.

Well, what did she mean by all that? He fidgeted around. *Maybe she just wanted to get that off her chest*; distracting himself by admiring the art on display to think.

Bernadette returned once more, this time doing up her belt on her coat and clutching her bag in one hand, then grabbing a bunch of keys from her desk, and turning to Danny, she said, 'Ready?'

'Always ready', he said, nodding.

I will be after a stiff drink, he thought, but said nothing. Smiling as he opened the door for her. She walked over to the security system, keyed in a multi-digit number; the alarm beeped several times, then silence. She reversed the sign on the door to read CLOSED, then, to his surprise, reached up on tiptoe to peck his cheek. Smiling as she passed by him. Even though the kiss was affectionate, he still felt strangely tense.

'So, where are we going?' he asked, taking her by the hand as he fell into step with her, not knowing what direction to go. She slowed down, surprised, staring down at their hands. Squeezing her hand tighter. This was freaking him out. *She will either pull away or affirm this relationship*, he thought.

'I have booked a table at Scott's restaurant in Mayfair'. She smiled, pulling herself closer towards him. They continued chatting through the busy street.

•

After his drink and drug-fuelled night at the last exhibition, Danny was now aware that Hafiz was definitely an Arabic-speaking Muslim, albeit presently a fully westernised one. Learning from Thom that he had been orphaned after an airstrike that killed his parents and he was shipped off to his uncle's home in Dubai concerned him, as that wasn't the skiing accident Hafiz led him to believe. Then being perfectly strategically placed within the United Arab Emirates to recruit individuals for their perpetual fight against the Western world.

It is widely known to the powers-that-be that terrorists share similar psychological profiles. *Yes, they are fucking nuts*, he thought, but one common trait they all share is a faulty belief system. So not only do they possess a radical religious faith, they are also mentally bludgeoned into believing that they can manipulate the will of their enemies, stopping them from accomplishing their goals through horrendous fear tactics. Terrorists believe they are quite justified in using any means to change society, to make the world obey their own warped fundamentalism. *So they think.*

Sadly, the terrorists in the Middle East were predominantly children, deceived by their elders. This was the case with Hafiz: he was dictated to and groomed for the Taliban by Uncle Mullah Mohammed Omar. At the time, he was most vulnerable, traumatised by the death of his parents; his head was quickly filled with hate. A scholar who could easily adopt the cosmopolitan way of the UAE, Hafiz subsequently gained the perfect education and upbringing to enable him to blend into any environment, ultimately America and the UK.

It wasn't long before Hafiz was able to climb up within the high ranks of the Taliban. Soon he had enough power and manipulative abilities to make important strategic decisions to rage the now-constant war against the West himself. Having had many years to blend in and create an illustrious career, he was now about to tap into his privileged terrorist military existence.

The sleeper is society's deadliest chameleon, dormant in wait.

•

Breakfast time was always a hive of activity at Cody Elmont's house. He had worked at the same bank for fifteen years, where he regularly doodled at his cashier's desk, daydreaming. He was happily married to Christine. His home life, in fact, could not have been more perfect: Christine was a brilliant housewife, she and Cody were childhood sweethearts and they also had the 2:2 lifestyle with two young twin girls.

This particular morning, Christine was making pancakes, the girls demanding multiple crépes with syrup. Coffee sat close by on the boil. The radio was on in the background to phase out the sound of the girls drumming impatiently on the table beside Cody. School time couldn't come soon enough for either parent. Christine was looking messily cute, her hair tied up, dressed in a scruffy dressing gown that she really should launder. She was already talking out loud dreamily about meeting her friends at the local Starbucks straight after the school run.

Cody tried to sit quietly in his business suit at arm's length from the girls' sticky syrup spoons, reading his newspaper, eating toast with one hand and sipping a hot coffee with the other. *It sure is funny how marriage can make you complacent*, he thought as he agreed to every word Christine was saying without really registering the content. 'Yes, darling, that will be nice', should have been written into his marriage vows. He smiled at his girls proudly, watching the mess two tiny people can make eating and wondering at the scale of it.

'Don't forget we have to see my parents this weekend'. Christine talked over her shoulder in the general direction of the dining table as she stood at the stove.

'Oh, I'd kind of hoped it was cancelled…' Cody replied with a wink at his wife and a big grin on his face, to let her know he was only kidding. He glanced up at the kitchen clock. 'Right, girls, I better get moving so I'll miss the traffic'. Christine walked over and kissed him on the cheek. 'Okay, my little monsters', he said to the twins, 'Daddy's got to go to work. Love you all millions'.

'Love you too, Daddy!' they both replied simultaneously, giggling melodiously, a sticky mess all over their mouths. He kissed them one by one, not caring.

'Be good at school, girls'. He grabbed his car keys and briefcase from the sideboard and left the house. Closing the front door behind him, he looked up at the beautiful blue sky above and took a deep breath of fresh morning air. He put his key into the door of his car, got inside and started the engine. At that moment, the music came on. As the sound of Bob Marley and the Wailers' *No Woman, No Cry* resonated around the car, he joined in with the lyrics, smiling happily, and duly set off for work.

•

Portia Brandt-Harley was the original posh totty. Though she was admittedly hard-working, she was privileged nonetheless. A likeable person of average attractiveness, she had aspirations to become a professional show jumper, but in the meantime, it was just a hobby. Her day job was grooming horses for the local celebrities with titles; not that she needed the cash, of course. Given that, one definitely couldn't call her lazy.

It was 9am; she had been up for three hours already and had just arrived at a local unaffiliated one-day event with her lovely 16-hand black gelding who was raring to go, according to the cameras in the cab of her lorry. Mummy and Daddy were with her, along with the family Labradors who had managed to curl up behind the front seats on the elevated storage area. Even though her mother had packed flasks of coffee and a hamper full of goodies, Portia couldn't wait for a crunchy bacon butty from the outside catering units. She wouldn't normally eat before eventing but she had a good time slot of 11.05am, giving her plenty of time to eat and warm up 'Ever So Softly', stable name 'Mr Softy'.

'I'm going to find Chantal and the gang after, Mummy', she called as she got out of the cab. 'Can you help with the door, Daddy?' Her father walked around to the back of the lorry with her and together they started the fiddly process of unhinging the back door, which meant a lot of standing on her tippy-toes to reach the complex locks!

'There you are!' She suddenly heard a voice behind her. 'Nice joddys, bitch; are they brand new?' Her best friend, Chantal, appeared with Dominic, Benjy and Tabitha in tow: the gang was complete. 'How did he travel?' Chantal asked. She walked up the ramp and started petting a still-excited Mr Softy, who whinnied at everything with four legs passing by the horsebox.

'He was fab. I'll get him out, actually'. Portia untied her beloved horse and walked him down the ramp and then around the side of the lorry, where her mother had just tied up the hay net brought from home for him.

'He looks stunning, Portia'. Dominic gave Portia and Mr Softy a brief cuddle before turning to much more important matters. 'Who wants a butty, then? I'm starving!' In his eagerness, Dominic started walking off the ramp backwards, very nearly colliding with Portia's father... who was used to it.

'Get one for me and Mother! We will stay and let the dogs have a run around – and we'll keep an eye on Mr Softy'. Portia's father let the Labradors out of the cab.

'Can you walk him around too, please, Daddy?' Portia asked. Her father acquiesced with an indulgent nod as she set off with the gang towards the catering caravan, feeling a bit nervous but also quite happy about the ground and the weather; it was going to be a great day.

•

Li Yun-Wing was a senior project manager for an executive car design company. Right at that moment, life was good, really good. He sat perched at a long table, flicking his pen around his fingers. 'So, ladies and gentlemen, any questions so far? No? Good, then that concludes the meeting for today'. He pushed his chair back and stretched his arms, straightening his back as the team of seven left the room.

'Hey, Li, are we going for dinner after the gallery event later or what?' Li's girlfriend, Chin, got up and started collecting her paperwork; she was a designer at the company and showed a talent belying her young age.

'Of course, what time do you think?' Li replied, standing up and crossing the room – but he didn't head towards her. Instead, he made a beeline for his design board.

'We could try for a table for eight-thirty, which should give us enough time to get across town after the opening?' Chin suggested. She was standing in front of Li, but he barely looked at her.

'Great, look forward to it', he replied distractedly. He didn't look up or around at her as he sketched a new shape – a concept car – on his design board.

Always the workaholic, Chin thought as she left the room quietly.

TWENTY-EIGHT

—— • ——

Hafiz was in his apartment, deep in the midst of another mental meltdown. The signs that he needed help were already there: window blinds drawn. Tiny beams of daylight squeezed through into the room but other than these, he had had no contact with the outside world for over forty-eight hours. Instead, he sat alone. He was still wearing his nightclothes, which he'd first worn to bed two days ago: a sweat-stained T-shirt and urine-stained grey shorts were now his habitual uniform. He was unshaven with bloodshot eyes, his only companion paranoia and the resident voices in his head, which penetrated his mind, whispering repetitively:

'*Trust no one*.'

'*Everyone abandons you*.'

'*Revenge is the only way*.'

Repeatedly, the whispers echoed in his mind, with the occasional shout. Holding his head in his hands, he screamed out as the pain of his lack of control drilled deep. He scrunched his hair in anger, trying to inflict pain on himself, so that at least he had controlled something. Tears rolled down his face, whilst the overwhelming negativity caused uncontrollable sobbing, so much so that he struggled to breathe. Some hypnotic trance music was bellowing out on a loop, somewhat appeasing his warped mind; lines of cocaine, crushed tablets and crystal meth were his flatmates and some still lay on top of his coffee table, lording it over the multiple bottles of whisky that lay upon the floor.

The room stank and was a mess: a beautiful crystal glass near Hafiz was cloudy with the residue of narcotic powder and alcohol; it was placed beside a £20 note and a credit card. Hafiz stared at the floor, incapable of focusing on anything in particular. He couldn't get up; his body was unsteady and swayed around if he tried, so he stayed put in a slumped state. Leaning back in the chair, he drifted off into a comatose sleep, blood dripping unchecked from his nose.

•

The sound of a joyful jingle penetrated the misery that had moved into his apartment. It continued trilling happily around him as the light from his phone accompanied the melody, lighting up the room. The constant, persistent noise forced him to open his eyes, but the sudden consciousness was confusing and he registered nothing, looking dazed as if he had just unexpectedly won an award; his drug-fuelled mind was still in bye-bye land.

At last, he was drawn to look at his phone, still lighting up with every ring... or had it stopped? He had no idea. He leant forward to pick it up, holding the screen up close to his face, forcing his eyes to focus. Even though his hand was shaking, he could see it was Marina calling him. He sighed, gingerly, as he rolled his eyes before resentfully lifting his phone to his ear and eventually answering.

'Hello', he said groggily, coughing to try to clear his throat.

'Hafiz, I've been trying to call you! I've left texts and messages.' She attacked without missing a beat, worried sick, a tone of anger and frustration in her voice.

'What time is it?' he asked with his head in his hands, his phone barely held to his ear.

'It's nine-thirty'. She was irritable with him, he could tell, as he sat forward, right to the edge of his chair. Lifting his head, he saw the mess around his living room and sighed.

'What? Nine-thirty in the morning?' he asked as he looked around, still confused.

'No! It's evening time; what the hell? Look, I just wanted to confirm that everything is complete and now the sky has a rainbow'. She wanted to scream the shit out of him, but she lowered her tone, being very ambiguous in her choice of words, just in case they were being listened to by intelligence agencies. Hafiz sat in silence listening to her voice, which was all he was good for just now. 'Where the hell have you been all day?' she went on. 'I've been worried sick. You cannot keep doing this to me, Hafiz. Hafiz? Are you listening to me?' The anger increased in her voice.

'I'm okay, I'm fine', he responded at last. 'I've been sick; I went to see my doctor'. He realised what she had just said a few moments before, his brain moving sluggishly a few steps behind: his masterpiece was almost complete. This new information suddenly energised him. 'Tell me again, tell me again'. He sat up straight, audibly more alert.

'Tell you what again?' Now she was pissed off; she feared the worst: him taking drink and drugs again.

'That everything is good to go'. He tried to snap out of his drug- and drink-fuelled state.

'Yes, yes, everything is completed my side'. What she wanted to say was that all the encrypted circle editions had been completed, as per his instructions, and had been packaged and sent off to the sleepers, but she couldn't be bothered. She was also still unsure of any intelligence surveillance that might be happening. 'Listen, once this is over, we will go away somewhere, just the two of us'. Her voice calmed as she spoke: she appreciated the stress and torment that he was going through. For herself, for him, she had to believe there was something to live for around the corner.

'Yes, yes! That's a fantastic idea, darling, you have done me proud. Thank you. We can just sit back and watch our work unfold now and justice will be done'. His mind came to the realisation that he was totally out of it; he saw the residue of his drugs and empty whisky bottles scattered around. He stood up, unsteady on his feet, feeling light-headed, and walked towards the window, bumping into furniture on his way, somehow stepping over everything that was scattered all over the floor. He pulled the cord to one of the blinds, raising it fully, and opened a window, allowing cold fresh air to circulate around the room. He closed his eyes and breathed in the cleanliness of the air as though it could heal him, gradually noticing the yellow glare from the lampposts outside that subtly filled the room. It really was evening.

'Please get some rest, Hafiz, and some decent food inside you; and take your medication: it's there to help'. Marina was still talking, trying the motherly approach. 'Right, I've got to go'.

'I will, I will. Stop worrying, I'm fine. I'll be in touch'. He ended the call, sitting back down in the chair feeling relieved. More than relieved: a sense of euphoria rushed through his entire body. He smiled in total awe of what he had achieved even at this stage of his planned reign of terror. He tilted his head back onto the headrest, looking up to the ceiling. He raised both his hands in the air, shouting the words, 'Allah Akbar' in Arabic, meaning 'God is greater'. Total happiness and relief spread over his face.

•

8am the following morning, his living room was spotless. There was neither a speck of dust nor a hint of seedy behaviour anywhere. The apartment was back to its normal, immaculate show-home self, oozing elegance and wealth; the only standards acceptable to the rich and famous. The floors sparkled in the morning sunshine as the rays of light bounced down through the two large windows; the glass top of the coffee table was wiped clean, not a smudge or fingerprint upon it; a superb inverted mirror. The art and photography books were placed back with precision on the table, velvet cushions sat in regimented rows along the back of the antique settee, his silk Arabic rug sat perfectly near his antique table, and the crystal from the lamp holder sparkled, showcasing a million colours.

From the silence of the hallway came a shout to Hafiz, who was in his bedroom. 'Adios, Hafiz, everywhere is clean and tidy. See you next time you need me!' Valentina, his trusted cleaner since the day he'd moved to London, bade him goodbye.

'Muchas gracias, Valentina', Hafiz shouted from his bedroom; he was grateful to her and he did tip well. He would have needed to, given the state of the place, but now she would not need to provide treacherous eyes and ears on him to the outside world. To secure that kind of loyalty was worth a tip.

He closed the mirrored door to his bathroom cabinet that reverberated his usual Adonic masculinity, cleanly shaven. With his hair sitting perfectly, he looked directly at his reflection, all model-like; it would be hard to even suspect he was an addict on self-destruct, dying of cancer. He wore the finest of threads direct from Mr Porter, a Givenchy sweater, Thom Browne chinos, finishing off as though ready for the catwalk; black and white Balenciaga trainers. The look was complemented by a splash of Penhaligon aftershave, Gucci winter jacket, Burberry scarf and a Valentino man bag.

He planned to walk around his favourite art galleries to ease his body and soul and finish with retail therapy and fine dining. No matter how badly his demons punished him, he had an image to keep up.

•

Unfortunately, Danny was still recoiling in disbelief at Hafiz's alter ego. He did indeed have a network of sleeper agents that were imminently about to wake up: eleven psychotic highly trained individuals whose identities were unknown, even to Hafiz himself. These individuals had infiltrated into society or were already in society, having been radicalised for reasons one couldn't understand. The same question pops up: *Why do these men and woman decide to kill?* Danny pondered confusingly. There is one path to radicalisation and that is: everyone must have an inner issue with today's society to be persuaded to defect from it.

However, are there reasons why some brainwashed moron picks up a gun or blows himself up, from the command to *'DO IT'*? Is it electable personal reasons, born variously of grievance, frustration, religious piety or the desire for systematic socio-economic change, irredentist conviction or commitment to revolution?

Just to help keep our security forces on the ball, there is no universal terrorist personality; no single, broadly applicable profile has ever been produced – but there are things one does know. Terrorists are generally motivated by a profound sense of misguided altruism and deep feelings of self-defence; they are religiously observant, devout with an abiding, unswerving commitment to their faith and the conviction that their violence is theologically justified and divinely commanded. *Oh, shit yes.*

So, in that list of anyone, one concurs that a terrorist could be a loving father, husband, wife, daughter, girlfriend, boyfriend, extended member of the family, friend, colleague; the list is infinite, so how will you know who can be trusted? After a horrific terrorist attack, even whilst people are recoiling from the horrendous atrocities, each and every time you will hear endorsements of the terrorist directly from witnesses and reported by the news correspondents:

'He was a lovely gentleman; he was a real part of the community'. The next door neighbour sits in the doorway of her house.

'I can't believe it; she was an absolutely model student'. Bound with shock.

It's equally hard to understand that these unfortunately controlled beings, these sleeper terrorists or assassins, have simply 'gone to sleep', often for many years. They get on with everyday normal life until someone wakes them up; in this case with a gift of a manipulated limited-edition circle print.

All terrorists fundamentally see themselves as humanitarians, incontestably believing that they are serving a good cause designed to achieve a greater good for a wider constituency, whether real or imagined; the terrorist, his organisation or cell purport to represent such constituencies. Which is why Danny kept asking the same questions, combined with Thom's theory: how had Hafiz manipulated his sleepers because this wasn't religiously motivated? These crazy individuals were showing their dedication – but were dedicated to what cause?

There could be many reasons to this. However, to point out the basic factors that make a human turn terrorist could be lack of empathy. People fail as parents in providing their children with humanitarian values, instead, motivate them to become religious and be known by that identity first. Terrorists are attracted and justified to violence in different ways, and it is precisely this sense of self-righteous commitment, self-sacrifice even, that draws people into each terrorist group, giving them a collective meaning and cumulative power. They are reluctant warriors, cast perpetually on the defensive, forced to take up arms to protect themselves and their community. They view themselves as driven by desperation and lacking any viable alternative against a repressive state, a predatory rival ethnic, a nationalist group or an unresponsive international order. So, which was the answer in the case of Hafiz's sleeper cells?

Danny knew the sleepers were being deceived by Hafiz, the real reasons for their sacrifice unknown to them.

TWENTY-NINE

———— • ————

Cody felt at his best when spending blissful time with his family, enjoying the repetitive and slightly surreal existence of the daily routine. He liked nothing better than the beginning and the end of the day, sitting in his kitchen amidst a swirl of activity that would make most people giddy.

This particular morning was much the same, keeping an eye on his twins' breakfast habits whilst reading a pristinely flat newspaper. He wouldn't be at all surprised if he discovered his wife actually ironed it for him.

The doorbell rang, shattering his bliss. He sipped coffee to wake himself up, to make himself move. Finally, putting his mug down, he stood up to answer the door.

'There's somebody at the door, Daddy', one of the twins informed him. He loved the way children always told you the obvious, as though one couldn't work it out for oneself.

'I'll get it!' his wife shouted out; she was on her way downstairs holding a laundry basket. Cody sat back down; he really wasn't quite ready to make logical decisions right now. His wife put the laundry basket down on the floor, near the cabinet of proudly framed and arranged family photographs, then peeped through the security hole in the door.

'It's a delivery guy', she announced. Removing the chain from its latch, unlocking the door, she opened it to see a rather attractive young man greeting her with a lovely smile. In his late twenties, he was wearing a blue FedEx uniform; his grey Transit delivery van was parked on the driveway behind the family cars. Still smiling, he proffered a large brown cardboard tube towards her. It was covered in stamps and stickers, suggesting it had made a long journey; the addressee's name – her husband's – was clearly written on the side in black marker pen, so she smiled happily back.

'Good morning, madam, I have a parcel for Mr Cody Elmont'. He handed over the package, along with a small digital box which had a pen attached to it by a plastic spring-coiled cable. 'Just sign above the black line, ma'am, please'.

She stood the tube upright on the floor next to the door and tried to write her name on the device. 'No matter how you try, it always looks like a two-year-old has signed for it', she said with a giggle, passing it back to the man of her dreams – fifteen years ago – he laughed with her.

'To tell you the truth, ma'am, I don't think they even register what's on the digital receipt. I get people writing weird quotes about the meaning of life sometimes! Have a good day'. He turned away, tilting his baseball cap towards her politely, and got in his van.

'You too!' she said dreamily.

Christine closed the door, thinking how very handsome the delivery guy was. Grabbing the laundry basket once again, she put it on the floor by the washing machine and handed over the parcel to Cody. 'Not another piece of art, hun', she said with just a touch of good-natured disapproval. She poured herself a coffee, looking at him, waiting patiently to see what was inside.

'I think Daddy needs to build more walls for his art collection, girls'.

'Why do our drawings only go on the fridge, Mummy?' Melanie asked.

Cody ignored the teasing, which he was sure was actually a genuine complaint on his wife's part, and placed his half-munched piece of toast down on his plate. The twins stopped eating too and stared at him inquisitively as he held up the large cardboard tube. Children love opening parcels, even when they're not theirs. 'What's that, Daddy?' they asked in unison. Both of them were fidgeting, desperate to tear open the packaging.

All this interference went over his head. Revealing new art required a respectful sense of ceremony so he tuned them out. Reverentially, he peeled off the brown parcel tape, revealing a white plastic lid. Taking it off, he put it by his mug. Looking inside, he took a moment to register the contents. It certainly was art: circular rolls of white paper obscured by patterned tissue paper. His family watched as the excitement slowly appeared on his face: his eyes lit up and opened wider with anticipation; they had seen this look many times before. The girls resumed eating and his wife sighed in frustration at his slow speed; she would have popped the artwork out of the container a long time ago.

However, Cody took his time. He reached inside the tube, gently pulling the contents out for fear of tearing them. Slowly, the large rolled-up sheet was released from the tubular shape it had arrived in and steadily unfurled. Cody checked inside one last time before placing the cardboard tube on the floor by his chair.

'You going to be long, hun?' Christine was getting impatient; he was like this at Christmas.

He looked through his wife like glass, grinning back to the sheet he'd taken from the tube, carefully unrolling the tissue paper and smoothing down the print, laying it on the table away from all the mess around him. Placing an object in each corner to stop it rolling inwards, he stared at it intently.

'Spots, Daddy!' Nancy laughed in delight.

'You had spots, Nancy', Melanie announced.

'No, I didn't. They were chickenpox'.

The argument had started; it was too good to be true that they had managed this far without squabbling. Christine was now full-on bored at her husband's delay; she needed to get on with her chores. She walked over to Cody, who was still staring at the print in a trance. She was struck by the expression on his face – she'd not seen that particular look before – but she really didn't give a damn. She checked the clock: she needed to move; they all needed to move. She placed her hand on his shoulder.

'Whatever keeps you happy, darling', Christine said forgivingly, before clicking her fingers at the children, which meant 'Let's go!' She giggled suddenly, looking at the painting over his shoulder. 'You call that one art, hun; I could do better with one of Melanie's crayons'. Whilst the girls ran for their coats, she stayed by the sink, taking a moment to pour her unfinished coffee away.

Cody's expression was quite serious, transfixed by the 90 x 90 spot painting: a signed limited edition. 'You wouldn't understand what art is really about; not this one anyway', he said, somewhat hypnotically, defending his art collection whilst gently touching random spots on the paper, still utterly mesmerised.

•

An array of guests had gathered in the large farmhouse kitchen, all grouped around the rustic French antique table that held a beautifully personalised birthday cake. The recipient, standing next to her mum and sister, stood proudly by with a knife, hovering ready, waiting to carve the cake into thick slices. Portia Brandt-Harley touched the white icing base delicately, tracing her fingers over the horse-and-rider figure depicted in a cantering scene on top.

The words *Happy Birthday Portia* were iced underneath the figure; the cake also boasted fake grass and flowers, also made from specialised candy, to complete the horse-riding scene.

'Oh, look at the horse! It's Mr Softy, isn't it?' Portia exclaimed, turning to her mum.

'Your sister made it', her mum said, winking at Eleanor.

'You can eat the horse, too', Eleanor added, smiling.

'Never! I'm keeping it forever'. Portia gave Eleanor and her mother a hug.

They lit the candles and the pressure was on Portia to blow them out. You would think she was too old for this at twenty, but her parents had a compulsion to spoil, and spoil they did, bigger and better than anyone else. She took in a bigger and better breath and managed to blow them out in one to a mammoth round of applause.

'Make a wish, make a wish', the guests demanded. Portia closed her eyes and crossed her fingers, holding them up.

'I wish, I wish…' She paused and opened her eyes, only to see everyone waiting in anticipation. 'Well, I'm not going to tell you!' She laughed along with everyone else.

Alice Brandt-Harley cut the first piece of cake, placing it on one of the Wedgwood floral plates and handing it to her daughter, as she did so, licking off the excess icing that had fallen onto her finger. Portia took one of the William Turner silverware cake forks that had been arranged in a fan on the table and tucked in, savouring the sponge. It tasted fantastic and her face showed it. Her mother continued to cut and share out the cake to everyone, and for a few moments, the atmosphere was one of simply sublime savouring.

Eleanor handed Portia her first birthday gift from a pile that was also on the kitchen table, next to her cards.

'Happy Birthday, Sis. Love you'. She leant in towards her and kissed her on her cheek.

'Thanks, babes, love you too'. Portia was thrilled: unwrapping the large box and removing the lid, she espied a fantastic pair of Italian De Niro riding boots. 'OMG, Sis! OMG, they are just perfect. I needed new ones – but seriously?' She practically screamed her way across the room for a massive sibling cuddle. Eleanor ate her cake afterwards quite smugly, certain that the boots must be the best gift on the table.

'Speech! Speech!' the guests chanted. Portia looked at her family, smiling appreciatively. As the guests continued to chorus, Alice went over to the seventeenth-century mahogany sideboard and started to pour the chilled Pol Roger champagne into the waiting Waterford crystal-cut champagne coupes.

'Okay, okay!' Portia beamed, red with embarrassment. She looked around the room momentarily, as her fingers absentmindedly combed her long fringe away from her eyes. Feeling embraced by love and friendship. She cleared her throat in preparation for saying a few words. She spoke animatingly. 'Thank you all for being here today. It really does mean the world to me, especially those of you who have stuck by me through some pretty tough times; well, you know who you are'. Facial expressions in the room changed to express solicitude and knowing. 'All remember the mystery of human existence lies not in just staying alive, but in finding something to live for in the afterlife'. An awkward silence followed, fuelled by confusion and weird bad timing, as people tried hard not to look at each other.

'Everyone, please raise your glass to Portia and wish her happy birthday'. Alice interrupted the silence and everyone duly toasted her daughter with a dutiful 'Cheers and happy birthday!'

More mingling and sipping of champagne took place in the kitchen and conservatory as Portia now looked through her cards, deciding to open the gifts after the guests had left; it would be rude not to. 'Open this one, please; I want to see your face!' A long-standing family friend handed her a large silver sparkling gift bag that contained a white pair of Beats headphones.

'Thank you, Evie, just what I needed'. She leaned towards her conspiratorially. 'It's nice to get non-horsey gifts sometimes, too'.

Benjamin Brandt-Harley, her father, entered the room with style and timing, holding a very large rectangular-shaped object wrapped in Liberty paper. 'There you go, my little princess, happy birthday', he announced. He put the large gift on the table, holding it upright. Portia stood by in amazement – whatever next? The guests gathered around, all of them intrigued by the gift; Benjamin was a very well-off investor and he did nothing by halves.

She pushed her forefinger delicately through the reverse of the wrapping paper, piercing a small hole before ripping it apart from the back so as to preserve the gorgeous Liberty paper. There were gasps in the room as the paper fell off, revealing a large limited-edition circle painting, professionally float-mounted on a white-card border with museum-quality glass and a thick white wooden frame setting it off exquisitely.

'Bloody hell, Ben. Is that a Legend?' Evie's husband enquired. Ben smiled, nodding his head slowly, confirming smugly that, yes; he not only loved to have the best himself but to share it, too.

Portia's reaction was one of total shock. Her mouth dropped open, her eyes transfixed by the image held by her father. She was overwhelmed, speechless.

'It was delivered to the house the other morning, sweetie, when you were at the stables with Eleanor. Mummy signed for it so we thought it would be a fab surprise to get it professionally framed for your birthday'. Benjamin felt awkward, concerned at his daughter's silence. 'Nigel Robertson did it for us and you know how good he is at framing'. Portia reached out and touched certain spots behind the glass. We didn't know you were into art…? Princess?' he questioned, receiving no response.

Alice stepped forward, suddenly worried they had done the wrong thing. 'Do you like it, sweetie?' Her mother placed her arm maternally around her daughter's shoulders, squeezing her tightly. She tilted her head at the painting, trying to appreciate it, but on this occasion, she found that hard to do – she didn't always 'get' the things that came into their house. At times, they were just an endless list of expensive things she paid the cleaner to dust.

Portia snapped out of her trance. 'Yes, yes, I love it. It's beautiful, thank you so much'. She moved away from the glazed array of coloured circles and Alice and Benjamin looked at each other in relief, nodding in agreement. Eleanor, too, nodded with satisfaction: she knew from her sister's face that the De Niros were the best gift of the day. *Smashed it*, she thought, smiling to herself.

Portia stepped away, seeking privacy. 'Will you all excuse me for a moment, please; all this excitement is overwhelming'. She left the room, contemplating.

•

In most large organisations with dedicated employees situated on several floors, there is a mail room, where the incoming mail is sorted by not-so-dedicated staff; after all, who wants to be a bloody mail boy or girl whizzing around with a trolley, dropping off wanted and unwanted envelopes into pigeonholes and onto desks? Such jobs come with a big staff turnover as a penalty for not paying attention in class. However, to most employees who work in such buildings, these dudes are the unrecognised foundation stones of the office block – and Renan was one of those dudes. In his mid-twenties, he had worked for the company for a few years in order to pay his bills whilst studying at night school to become a car designer. He already had his eye on getting a job right here where he worked – just a little higher up the food chain. To add to his impressive résumé, he was now senior mail boy, in charge of three dudes, one dudess and all the internal mail; man, he was on fire.

'Morning, Li. I've got some deliveries for you!' Renan breezed into Li Yun-Wing's office waving a large file of mail, stopping his trolley just outside the office door. Li had one of those glass-partitioned, floor-to-ceiling offices that reminded him of a fish bowl. Renan told himself frequently that he was going to have one of those offices one day.

'Morning, Renan, how are you today?' Li was sitting behind his technical artist's desk, intensity clear in his stance and with good reason: he was working on a new project. He lifted his head up, turning around on his swivel stool and lowering his spectacles on his nose. Patiently, he watched Renan sort the mail into the designated piles that Li had requested; he liked Renan, for there was something cutting edge about him.

'Hey, I'm good, thanks. How was your weekend?' Renan finished sorting the piles. 'Do you want this lot on your desk or over there?' Li signalled to put them on his desk and Renan obliged. Then he hesitated, as a large brown cardboard tube caught his eye. 'What about this one, Li, there or here?'

Li leaned forward for a closer look, placing his glasses back in position to gain focus. 'Can I have that one here, please?' he said.

Renan walked over and handed Li the tube. The designer continued sitting on his stool, resting the parcel up against his desk. 'How long have you been working here now, Renan?' he asked, biting the end of his pencil, pausing as though a thought had struck him.

'Three years'. Renan rearranged the space on the top section of his trolley to accommodate the remaining mail.

'Great – so when are you going to oil that squeaky wheel?' Li moved his glasses to the end of his nose in amusement, pointing at the offending form of transport.

Renan laughed. 'I'm not! I'm keeping it for nostalgic purposes to remind me how many miles I've travelled; plus, it lets people know I'm on my way so I don't have to be scarred by office gossip!' Renan waved to Li as he left for next door.

'See you tomorrow'. Li laughed as he looked curiously at the brown cardboard tube, examining the various stamps and stickers. With a letter opener, he sliced into the parcel tape, balling it up and throwing it into the bin across by his other desk. 'Shot', he said, as he looked inside the container. He took a moment and smiled. This moment had been long awaited.

He walked over to his other desk, sat down and took another moment. Then, using his thumb and forefinger, he pulled out a large rolled-up sheet of paper wrapped in patterned tissue paper, which was intertwined with a large sheet of artist's paper. Separating them, he placed all the packaging at the top end of his desk. He took a deep breath and unrolled the sheet, securing each corner with bulldog clips, revealing a limited-edition circle painting: an assortment of different coloured spots, each individually and strategically placed to form a large triangular shape. He was fixated, hypnotised. 'There must be at least three hundred spots here', he said to himself. Sporadically reaching forward to gently touch several of the embossed colours that drew him to them, naturally attracting his eye.

•

Danny looked back on the war on terrorism over the past ten years when the enemy as one knew it was clearly in one's sights: identified, expected and in uniform. But now everything is blurred, unidentified, unexpected. Huge terrorist organisations are born, one unit situated mostly within the Middle East, led by an identifiable leader. But that's no longer the case.

One doesn't recognise human chameleons living within today's society. One doesn't see deadly sleepers like Cody, the hard-working family man dressed in a suit carrying a briefcase to work every morning; Portia Brandt-Harley, the posh spoilt princess with two event horses and Daddy's credit card; Li Yun-Wing, a successful car designer with the world at his feet. One also doesn't see Billy, the telecoms-engineer with a wife and three children; Rosie, the retired librarian; Nick, a reporter from the *Evening Echo*; Dr Ayman Zawahiri, a paediatric surgeon; Mohammed, the owner of the local pharmacy; Adrian, an ambulance driver; Darren, an air traffic controller; and Claire, an interior designer. One just does not see them, but we question, what motivates them. *And why?*

This sleeper list is eleven, but in reality, a sleeper list is endless, which means danger. However, not as much as having a substantial understanding of the nature, the function and even the intelligence gathered. Intelligence has built an effective defence against previous threats, but now everyone's challenge is to develop new defences counteracting the more amorphous ones. Considering there are well over 7 billion people on the planet, it's like finding a fart when you're blow-drying your hair… Danny has had to use a type of acceptable terror to fight terror to stop the abominations scheduled for the 4 January 2012, which he can live with, when it's all in the name of art…

But can he? And is it?

THIRTY

——— • ———

New Year's Eve celebrations were kicking off big time around the world, and in all their different time zones people were marking the arrival of 2012. In London, high-flying people were impressing at the exclusive members-only Groucho Club in Soho: it was the who's who of parties amongst the creative sorts and sickly rich and, this year, Danny was one of them. He was impressed by this yearly prestigious event, hosting the likes of critics, agents, gallery owners, artists, singers, musicians, actors, models and authors. Danny was not sure how he fitted in with the shoulders he was rubbing alongside; it was crowded and he hadn't exactly managed to launch himself as the budding artist he had hoped to become, thanks to a black Ford Transit van, Thom and a psychotic, rejected art dealer.

This venue was full of glitz, glamour, elegance and class; the women wearing designer party gowns, providing a palette of colour besides the traditional white and black tuxedos of their male counterparts. Tonight could be the Oscars for all the flutes and coupes of Dom floating around, which were helping to wash down the salmon and caviar canapés circulating on large silver platters. The loud hum of conversation was fighting against the DJ's efforts in the corner; spinning the finest of bar grooves.

There was no time to feel isolated, inconspicuous or dateless; there were so many egos in the room it was clear no one really gave a shit about anyone else but themselves. Danny looked around the crowded room, scrutinising the faces and the pockets of space to see if he could spot Hafiz, who had assured him he would be attending. But he couldn't see anyone he recognised.

Suddenly from around the side of a waiter, a figure moved his way: radiant and beautiful, stalking like a panther, effortlessly sexy, wearing a Dior haute couture black dress which clung to her like a second skin; nothing moved but her body. Bernadette. She glided across the room in her expensive heels, as if she was born in them. Her angelic beauty of course stunned him; her red glossed lips smiling at him, oozing elegance and sex appeal. Hypnotised and aware of his sexual urges flowing through him as she leant in to kiss him on the cheek; frankly, he was tempted to borrow a silver tray to conceal his body's natural reaction.

'So, Mr Swift, at least I will see in the New Year with you then', she said, with glistening lips.

'You certainly will. You look stunning', he complemented, staring deep into her eyes with a glint in his, gently touching her on her very pert behind. In the background came a timed 'Five, four, three, two, one!' then jubilant screams and a chorus of 'Happy New Year!' There was clapping and party poppers landing on the heads of very pissed-up partygoers, who were trying to drink their champagne despite the coloured streamers that had landed in their glasses. At the bar, an octet of businessmen recited a version of *Auld Lang Syne*, surrounded by their groupies: young ladies who clearly didn't know the words. As they finished, there were more cheers and the sound of corks popping, silencing the DJ into submission.

It's funny how in the first five minutes of the New Year, some people use the perfect excuse of being totally trollied to snog the face off a stranger, or a known victim, whilst others just stare into nothing in the drunken knowledge that, having successfully made it to this hour, they now really want to fuck off and go to bed.

Being a gentleman, Danny toasted a decadent New Year with his date, cross-linking arms romantically, and without spillage. Then he kissed her gently on her lips – just as Hafiz approached them, dressed in his trademark black Zegna tuxedo, his signature untied bow tie draped around his neck and the top button of his shirt undone. His gait had unmistakably developed a slight wobble. As Bernadette and Danny pulled apart, Hafiz was holding a half-full coupe of champagne in one hand and a bottle in the other. His eyes were bloodshot, almost devil-like, with his pupils dilated. That and his continuous sniffing were a dead giveaway that he was truly wired up on coke.

'Hey! I knew you two would get together: my two dearest friends. In fact, you know what?' He leaned in between them. 'Someone should paint this moment'. Bernadette and Danny just smiled at each other, the perfect *Mr and Mrs* contestants – Was Danny being paranoid that his presence had changed things between them? Raising their champagne-filled glasses to him, smiling.

'Happy New Year, Hafiz, all the best for 2012', Danny said. Holding out his hand to shake his, which stupefied him for a second, given his hands were full. Bernadette took the champagne bottle from him to alleviate his spaced-out confusion.

'2012 will be my year, that's for sure, my friend', he replied, shaking hands. Looking into Danny's eyes, his grip tightened and he leaned in to whisper. 'When you have something special in your life, you protect it with all your power and wisdom', Hafiz said, then pulled away, barely focussing, and tapped Danny's shoulder in a friendly manner. Danny didn't have the slightest idea to what or whom he was referring; there was no sense to what he was trying to say, but given what he knew of his plans, he made his body language demonstrate that he wasn't the enemy but his friend.

'Whatever it takes, mate'. Looking at him until he gained some form of facial control to meet his stare. He laughed, looking happy at both, choosing to downplay his comment.

'So, Danny, when is this exhibition of yours going to take place?' Bernadette asked.

'I do apologise, guys. I was going to mention it earlier, but as you have both been really busy, I didn't want to bother you. I just got on with it. You know the amount of work and effort it takes to organise an exhibition'. He exhaled slowly.

'I certainly do. I remember you mentioning it to me. I didn't think you had it sorted already', Hafiz said, looking surprisingly intrigued, excited.

'Yes, it's all sorted, all organised and it's going to be hosted near the London docks area in an unused warehouse'.

'Wow, I like it', Bernadette said excitedly. She leaned in to peck him on the cheek. 'Have you given the show a name?' she added, looking at him adoringly. He couldn't tell her the truth. Never more so than now did he need to keep his enemies close; she wasn't his enemy and she didn't need to know.

'Yes, the exhibition is going to be called, "How the Eighties broke my heart"', Danny said, looking pleased with himself.

'Congratulations, Danny. I'm so sorry I couldn't help more with the organising of things', Hafiz said, slurring, taking another sip.

'Listen, you have both been great, but I just wanted to do this myself. I've made enough contacts here in London to make it happen'.

They both nodded in appreciation of his efforts. 'For any creative, the biggest catastrophe is not having something to show. So it's a kind of relief to have my paintings ready and to prove to the world that they exist, they are a tangible thing'.

'I totally agree with you, Danny. When is the opening night?' Hafiz asked, patting him on his shoulder.

'Doors will open at 7pm on the 4th January, so please come along as soon as'. He watched Hafiz.

'The 4th? This Wednesday?' Bernadette asked, looking slightly concerned.

'Yes, that's right', he replied, nodding.

'Darling, I'm really sorry. The 4th, I can't make it as it's Legend's opening night and I have clients to meet at the gallery prior'. She spoke with a look of regret on her face.

'Hey honestly, don't worry. I knew it was Legend's opening night and you would both be busy there; your work comes first', he said, hugging her as he studied Hafiz's response.

'You make me feel bad now'. Bernadette was genuinely sad but he couldn't tell her the truth.

'Please don't feel bad. My show will run till Friday, so there will be plenty of time'.

'I'll try to pop over, but it may be late', she added. Pecking him on the cheek.

'That's fine; there's no rush. No wonder I got the venue really cheap, everyone will be at the Legend exhibition, while I'm eating vol-au-vents and sausage rolls by myself', Danny said jokingly, laughing. 'What about you, Hafiz?' he asked.

'I wouldn't miss it for the world, Danny. Don't forget you can count on me', Hafiz said with an excited breath, raising his glass in salute.

'Appreciate that, mate'. He reciprocated the gesture.

'I have something to do beforehand but I'll be there, just after eight'. Hafiz looked preoccupied.

'I'll wait a few days before I go to see Legend's work. I don't know what all the fuss is about, will let the crowds die down'. Hafiz laughed, taking a large gulp of champagne. *Wonder if there was a pun in there somewhere,* Danny thought.

'Okay, great; I'll text you both all the details, shall I?'

'Yes, please do', they both said, nodding.

'It's going to be a great year for us'. Hafiz finished his glass, at once signalling to one of the waitresses floating around the room to come over with another tray of drinks. Bernadette held up the bottle of champagne he'd already brought, attempting to wave it in his face and catch his attention, but there were no signs of life. She topped herself up instead, amused at Hafiz being in what she considered to be a perfectly acceptable state given the season. Spotting some associates in the crowd, she waved to a group of dealers nearby.

Hafiz was about to walk off. Instinctively, Danny grabbed his forearm and smiled. 'It will be a great year, mate, we all make choices', he said with compassion in his eyes, 'but we can sometimes stop what we are doing and make a change for the better'. For a split second, he was hoping he could break through to who he thought he was, so he would stop his plan, but it was ingrained in him, like a prehistoric fossil.

'Trust me: I love art, not people. It will be a good year for both of us, whatever happens'. He delivered his line whilst looking around, smiling at every female that edged past, and Danny knew it was too late. Reading between the lines to see his commitment to take revenge against those who had double-crossed him.

'I'm sure it will be', Danny replied, just as a waitress arrived with a tray of coupes and flutes of champagne. Hafiz sank the rest of his glass in one before putting it down, replenishing his stock with two more coupes from the tray: one for each hand. Hafiz winked at the waitress, whilst Danny took another glass for himself and Bernadette, who surrendered the bottle to the waitress. The girl took it, glancing somewhat pitifully at a dribbling, winking Hafiz as she walked away; not one of his most attractive moments.

'What's your plan for this year, then?' Danny asked intriguingly, knowing the first bit anyway and wondering if his lie would reflect this. He saw before him, on the surface at least, a reputable art dealer and critic, but at the centre of his truth was the opposite kind of figure, and he knew exactly what he was really all about.

Yet he merely laughed, not really taking his bait, speaking only ambiguously. 'I predict big changes within the art world this year', was all he said. He added, perhaps a touch more darkly, 'About time, too. Don't you both agree? So, watch this space.'

Bernadette seemed to have patiently taken this opportunity to guzzle champers whilst Danny interrogated Hafiz, for she didn't engage in the conversation at all. By now, Hafiz was running out of champagne again and he started to look agitated; clearly too much talking was a load on his nerves, which looked as if they needed calming chemically.

'Right, I will leave you two lovebirds to it.' He rudely looked over their shoulders as he spoke, simultaneously sighting someone he knew, and he walked off without waiting for a reply. Danny glanced over to see who it was.

Marina was near the bar, dressed in an extremely racy red Alexander McQueen silk wrap gown, which showed off every centimetre of her phenomenal frame. Danny could only imagine what she was like behind closed doors. His distraction spoke volumes, considering the beauty of Bernadette in front of him, whom he had blatantly just ignored.

'Oh, look, there's Marina.' Bernadette pointed, clearly having clocked his interest; she waved and Marina casually held up her glass in salutation.

'She needs to put a cardigan on or she'll catch a death', Danny suggested, defusing the situation, yet laughing to himself, too – *if only* – at the thought that the precise line of work this particular red praying mantis was in, must indeed come with the threat of death sooner rather than later. Bernadette looked at him, trying not to smile at his strange sense of humour. 'I find their relationship very strange, don't you?' He carried on looking at Marina and Hafiz. Their body language was louder than the DJ's tunes. The icy face of Marina wasn't too pleased with him. She had clearly noticed what had gone into Hafiz's bloodstream that night – and it was not a soda fountain syrup, that was for sure – she clearly disapproved.

'What makes you say that?' Bernadette flattened Danny's white square pocket-handkerchief in his tuxedo chest pocket with the palm of her hand, half interested in his answer, seductive: a woman with a plan. They shared a moment, but despite her many charms, he was more interested in the scene that was about to kick off in front of them.

He tried to explain. 'Just… well, it's like they both want to be together but won't allow themselves to be, if that makes sense'. Danny wondered what Bernadette knew of their set-up.

'Maybe the time just isn't right for them', Bernadette said, looking over, which kind of gave him permission to do so, too. Marina's body language was becoming tenser: her arms were folded defiantly and her eyes stared into her drink; she was clearly not listening to his excuses. *They have known each other for many years; what's left of their original romance?* he asked himself. Leaning into him, pulling down on his shoulder, Bernadette suddenly whispered directly in his ear, 'Happy New Year, Danny. Oh, by the way, I'm not wearing any underwear'.

THIRTY-ONE

———— • ————

9am, Tuesday 3 January 2012. It was the first day back at work for all the reluctant Oompa Loompas at Method Ltd. and their motivation was not apparent after a splendid Christmas and New Year break. It didn't help that everyone had been thrown straight into the all-important final preparations for the forthcoming global *Primus Circle* paintings exhibitions, which were being coordinated from their head office. Everything was to be of the highest standard for the world's eyes.

Marina sat at her desk, busily calling all the owners of the original *Primus Circle* paintings that had been loaned by them to the galleries for this unusual extravaganza. She needed to confirm with them one by one that they would be attending the opening day of the exhibition for the exclusive opening ceremony.

'Hello! Good morning, this is Charlotte Cunningham from Method Ltd. Just a courtesy call really; to just confirm that your client will be joining us on the 4th January for the opening presentation?' She circled the last name on her list of eleven. 'That's fantastic', she said to the PA on the other end of the phone, 'we look forward to seeing them both'. She ticked off the name efficiently. 'And please reassure the client that his original circle painting arrived on time and is now on display, all ready.

Goodbye'. Marina placed down the phone, feeling very happy as she folded up her list and placed it inside the back pocket of her jeans.

Only a few minutes later, one of her male co-workers popped his head around the office door of the open area where she and her colleagues worked.

'Hey, girls, there is an important security meeting in the studio right now. The Head of Security wants us all to be there', he said, raising his eyebrows knowingly as the lecherous guards always wanted the girls to join them, pulling a funny face as though to make a joke of it. His tone, however, suggested that there was some urgency to the unscheduled company meeting. Marina and the other woman sitting opposite her looked at each other with enquiring eyes.

'Must be about the exhibitions', the girl said to Marina as they downed tools and headed into the main studio room. Everyone was gathered around, forming a half-circle that faced inwards towards a well-dressed gentleman in his late fifties. He had a receding hairline and was smartly dressed, wearing a navy-blue suit with one of those "I used to be in the Metropolitan Police" ties with matching cufflinks. Marina assumed an irritated and bored expression at the very sight of him, defiant even before he'd opened his mouth.

'Okay, gather around, can you all hear me?' he said loudly in a broad Scottish accent. Everyone but Marina replied, 'Yes', as they shuffled into position so they could see him, more out of curiosity than obedience.

'Right, listen up. I'm Albert, your Head of Security; some of you may have seen me before, floating around, and some of you may not'. He looked around at the blank faces staring back at him. 'It is my job to let you know that there was an attempted break-in just before Christmas'. He rubbed his hands together, enjoying his captive audience; Marina thought he looked like a lame game show host. 'Unfortunately, this matter has only just been brought to my attention today: we have two security guards off on sick leave who have only just informed me they were both jumped upon by about three suspected criminals who were trying to gain entry through one of the rear windows'. He shook his head. 'This matter should have been reported immediately, but it wasn't'.

Finally, Albert had got her interest. Marina put her hand up, just like a schoolchild, and he turned his attention towards her.

'Yes?' he said, pointing at Marina.

'Did they gain entry into the main factory area or offices? I mean, were they on their way in or out?' she asked, and then continued before receiving a response. 'Did the CCTV pick up anything? Can you confirm there were three of them? Did the factory alarms go off?'

Albert was annoyed; he had not expected a barrage of stupid questions. Now, everyone was looking at Marina awkwardly.

'As far as we can tell, these criminals didn't gain entry into the main factory area or the offices.' He folded his arms defensively; Albert didn't like anyone questioning his security team, especially when it looked as if someone might have fucked up.

Marina was now seriously irritated. 'As far as you can tell'. The statement was loaded and aimed at Albert; a few of the staff started to laugh at her intrusive attitude, which took them by surprise.

Albert squared up to her, which was probably a mistake. 'Listen, luv', he said patronisingly, raising his deep voice to shut her up.

'I'm certainly not that'. Marina was by now looking quite severe, causing Albert to grimace, but he continued with his thread on the matter nonetheless.

'Nothing is on our CCTV recording system that signifies anyone gained entry. We have checked all the locks and there are no signs of forced entry to any of the main areas of value, including here. However, I have spoken to your management team and ordered a full accountability check to be conducted by all departments. I ask that you report back to me ASAP with any discrepancies'. He looked at Marina in particular. 'If any discrepancies are found, we will investigate further, but I think it highly unlikely that will happen, luv'. He shot her a dirty look before turning his head to look at the others.

'Yeah, right'. Marina whispered the last word, laughing to herself even as the group appeared uncomfortable and confused at her in-depth interest in the possible break-in. 'We have all put in a lot of hard work and effort to ensure this is of the highest standards, and to let some creeps ruin it for us really upsets me', she said, looking around at the group, diverting any sort of suspicion, as they all nodded in recognition.

Albert continued, 'Okay, folks; that will be all. You may return to work now'. Albert left the security briefing with one of the managers from

Method Ltd. as the group dispersed back to their various tasks, chatting together about Marina's showdown with the Head of Security.

Marina planned to head directly to her office, yet she paused on the way to look around the printing studio room, staring oddly at the artist materials spread all around. For some reason, she was drawn to the paint pots and piles of paper stored there, and wondered why she felt she must check the stock. Confused and not knowing what she was looking for, she scanned to see if anything was missing or out of place. She walked over to the piles of new and used paintbrushes, which were sitting amongst an array of art materials, running her eyes over them, looking for an anomaly. She was content that nothing was missing or out of place. But her gut feeling was now making her think the worst. Marina frantically hunted for her phone – it was not in her pocket – quickening her pace as she entered her office. Plucking it off her desk with relief, she headed straight towards the main exit and gently knocked on the door of the nearby Security Office.

'Come on in', a voice of authority from behind the door shouted, and she slowly pushed the door open.

'Hi, can you let me out please? I need to make an urgent phone call'. She glanced at the nearest security guard who was in the middle of reading *Bravo Two Zero*. 'It's my sister; she's in hospital, pregnant and about to drop. I just want to see if I'm an auntie yet'. She smiled flirtatiously.

'Hey, sure, you bet'. He put down the book and stood up obediently, feeling compassion for her situation. Opening the security door for her, he naturally felt it was also his job to check out her ass as she walked past him. 'Just knock on the door when you're finished, darling'. He closed the door with a final wink at her.

Marina smiled back, gritting her teeth. Saying 'wanker' under her breath, she walked swiftly away from the building until she was out of earshot. Scrolling down through her iPhone address book, she found HAFIZ and pressed call. As she held her phone to her ear, the connection was made and it started ringing. 'Answer the bloody phone, Hafiz', she muttered. It rang and rang and she tapped her foot impatiently; more ringing, then directly to voicemail. 'For fuck's sake, answer, Hafiz'. She redialled and walked around in a circle whilst it rang again.

'Hello'. Hafiz sounded as though he was eating something. Normally, she got pissed off that he didn't personalise from 'Hell fucking lo' when he answered her calls, but today she had more important shit to moan about and she went straight into the topic without an introduction.

'They are saying that there was an attempted break-in at the factory just before Christmas', she said frantically, looking around to see if there was anyone nearby who might hear her conversation. 'What if they're on to us?' She was panicky and stressed.

'Calm down, just calm down', Hafiz replied, audibly placing his fork down on his plate. 'What exactly has been said?' He spoke in a stern voice of authority to grab her attention; she had certainly grabbed his.

'Some retired asshole from the Met says there were three of them, that they tried to break in and put two of the security guards in hospital'. Marina caught her breath in panic.

'What about the CCTV footage, Marina? Was anything picked up on that?' Hafiz asked, worried.

'He reckons there was nothing on the CCTV recording system and no signs of forced entry'. She was becoming frustrated with Hafiz for not being as worried as she was.

'So, there is nothing to worry about, then. Everything was completed and sent off?' Hafiz waited for her answer, trying to reassure her.

'Yes, everything was completed as per your instructions'. Yet Marina still wasn't convinced. 'Something just doesn't seem right'. She lowered her voice. 'Hafiz, what if we have been compromised? What if I have been compromised?'

'You would have been arrested by now. Trust me; just relax'.

'Easy for you to say', she said sarcastically, realising just how not involved Hafiz sounded.

'For the love of Allah! Will you just stop panicking, Marina? The man you work for pickles the body parts of animals, and not for the purpose of them ending up in a bloody corned beef tin, either. It was probably some drunken idiots wanting to take a sneaky peek or local journalists trying to report on anything new from the factory'. Hafiz cleared his throat. 'Listen, just go back to work and let me know if you hear anything else. You know what to do. We are so close now. Nothing will go wrong; it's practically bombproof'. Hafiz reassured her again. 'Everyone has received their instructions and we will have enough witnesses spotting us on the night when we are at my counselling session to make sure we are home and dry, never even under suspicion'.

Marina closed her eyes and took a deep, long breath. 'Yes, I know, darling' – sighing – 'we have come this far with no problems. But I just want it to be over so we can start up a new life together'. Marina finished the call. His calming words had some effect; she went back inside the factory.

In London, Hafiz looked gloomily at his unfinished scrambled eggs and fresh salmon as he finished the call with Marina. Pushing the plate away, he threw his phone down too, deciding the uncertain news had put him off his food. Now paranoia and doubt began to agitate him. He picked up his phone and scrolled down to Bernadette's name. As he called her, he got up and crossed to the window of his apartment. Looking out at the street, he wondered if anyone close to him could possibly be suspicious of his activities. Marina's call had unsettled him.

'Hello', Bernadette answered breezily, too preoccupied with her work to notice who was calling.

'Hey, how are you doing?' Hafiz sounded upbeat.

'Ah, Hafiz! How are you?' Bernadette stopped typing when she realised whom it was, and the clatter of keys down the line ceased.

'I'm good, thanks. Fancy meeting for a late lunch today?' he asked in a jovial manner. She looked down at her diary, checking her availability.

'Umm, yes, that would be fantastic, darling. What time?' She spoke lightly, but she was curious: why did he want to meet up out of the blue?

'Excellent, meet me at Claridge's at two o'clock. I have a couple of Russian art collectors in town that I want to push your way. I'll update you on what they like before I send them into the gallery'. Hafiz relaxed and took a sip of his orange juice.

'Fabulous, Hafiz, that's great'. She ended the call, already envisioning the potential commission that could be made from sales to the vodka-drinking rich Russians of London and feeling grateful to Hafiz for the introduction. She shook her head to clear it, looking around her dream workplace, her gallery.

Hafiz was about to place his phone back down on the table when he suddenly paused in thought. He scrolled down to another contact. Pressing Call, he sat back deep into his chair. 'Yes?' A deep foreign voice answered.

'Were my suspicions correct?' Hafiz asked with a sombre look on his face.

'Yes. I will send you the details'. The call was ended abruptly; no time for pleasantries and no time for tracing.

Hafiz leant further back, stretching his legs, deep in thought. This was the final hurdle and no one would get in his way; of that he was determined. After all, he had painted a masterpiece. Now, all he had to do was wait patiently for the oil paint to dry before he could reveal it to the world.

THIRTY-TWO

———— • ————

Claridge's is set in the heart of London's Mayfair. It epitomises timeless elegance and is considered to be one of the best five-star luxury hotels in the world. The ethos of the hotel is that it is proud to have preserved both physical and spiritual aspects of its unique heritage, whilst adding all the modern luxury flourishes that guests demand, all bound together, of course, by impeccable service. Hafiz did indeed require, demand and expect such service.

'Hello, darling! How are you?' Hafiz stood up flamboyantly, his arms open wide to greet Bernadette as she approached him. He was dressed immaculately, his outfit more suited to Monaco than the middle of winter in the English capital. He expressed his happiness at seeing his old friend with the customary European pecking of both cheeks before pulling Bernadette's chair out, signalling for her to sit down.

'Please take a seat'. He waved in his usual suave, sophisticated manner, oblivious to the handsome French waiter. Bernadette wasn't oblivious, however, and smiled appreciatively at Pierre a few times.

'Great to see you, Hafiz'. Bernadette kept her voice low and intimate. Beautifully dressed in black and white Chanel, she hesitated as she glanced at him, noticing he looked gaunt and unwell, and hollow-eyed, bloodshot;

reminding her of the state he was in on New Year's Eve. She decided to address it. 'So, you looked a little worse for wear at New Year, Hafiz'. She placed her bag down on the floor by her legs, adjusting the chair to get comfortable.

'If you can't enjoy New Year's Eve celebrations, what can you enjoy?' he said, laughing, whilst signalling over to Pierre to serve him, pouring a glass of water to start. Hafiz's hands were shaking nervously as he picked up his glass to take a sip. A cold sweat appeared on his brow that she chose not to notice.

'That is, of course, true, darling, but Marina didn't look as though she shared your views on officially timed merriment; I definitely saw a look of her not being impressed'. She spoke laughingly but there was an edge to her voice. At that moment, however, the waiter appeared at Hafiz's side, ready to take his wine order.

'Red or white?' Hafiz asked, peering over the wine menu at her.

'White, please'. She looked around the half-packed room of suits, who were taking in their daily business lunch of wine and gossip. She observed that a few women entrepreneurs were in today, too.

'Marina was fine, she... women just get like that now and then'. He laughed, too, taking the criticism on the chin, knowing full well he had been off his face and wired up on everything, yet not conceding Marina had the right to admonish him. 'I'll take a bottle of the Blondelet Pouilly-Fumé Millésime 2003', he added to Pierre, giving a quick nod and smile before he walked off.

'So then, how's Danny?' he asked her with a big grin on his face and noticed her blush; he knew what was coming.

'Danny's okay'. She was taken aback at the sudden question, having expected to be briefed on the Russians' art requirements. She momentarily thought back to kicking Danny out of bed this morning before she'd gone to the gallery and he'd set off back home, but more arresting was the image of their passion before he'd left. She was aware of Hafiz waiting for a more detailed answer and felt flustered and hot. 'Sorry, I was miles away then. Well... yes, Danny, well, I enjoy his company and he makes me laugh; he has a worldly passion and loves art. I find him quite fascinating, really'. She decided to play it down, be aloof and coy. 'He's excited about his forthcoming exhibition', she added, extremely happy for him.

'I have great hopes for him in the future. I'm sure his exhibition will be a great success', Hafiz agreed.

'If you're involved, Hafiz, I'm sure it will', she praised Hafiz.

'I will do my best. He has a long way to go. I'll be there to support him', he said smugly…

'He has great respect for you and is grateful for the knowledge you pass on to him', she added.

Hafiz was distracted by the chilled bottle being brought for his inspection. Pierre poured a small taster into the pristine crystal glass and they both watched Hafiz perform his ritual of breathing in the aroma and tilting the glass for tasting. He confirmed his delight to Pierre: 'Yes, it's good'. Bernadette accepted her full glass from the attentive waiter and as she did, Hafiz stared at her intently.

'So, what do you know about him?' Hafiz selected a green olive with a cocktail stick from a variety of olives and pickled raw vegetables displayed on the table. Popping it into his mouth, he scrutinised Bernadette's reaction. She, in turn, was aware she had a spotlight aimed at her, but why?

'Probably as much as you, to be honest, or perhaps less. He's very private, wants very much to make it as an artist. He's told me a little about his family, where he's travelled to, what he used to do for a living but he doesn't still have his uniform… unfortunately'. She made it a joke but it didn't even get a facial twitch from Hafiz. 'Anyway, not really very much as it's all about the here and now with him. We all have skeletons in the closet, I guess, but that doesn't mean we have to stay at home dusting them'. She sipped her wine. 'This is excellent wine, Hafiz'.

He looked sternly at her. 'Skeletons are easy to find if you look hard enough'. He seemed to be urging her to tell him something, yet at the same time he seemed to want to tell her something that no one else should or would know. He drained his glass and she found herself wishing he would just spit it out: the intel, not the wine. 'Time can be ruthless with reputation', he said at last, sitting back and folding his arms.

'Maybe; providing there is a reputation'. She wondered what the hell he was trying to say. 'Oh, and of course', she added, remembering, 'he mentioned how he met you, which is fantastic; otherwise, Danny and I wouldn't ever have met'. She successfully diverted the conversation back to Hafiz.

'Well, I'm happy for you both'. Momentarily, he looked sincere, until he started to cough badly. He took a good drink of water, trying to clear his throat, placing the napkin over his mouth.

'Are you okay?' She looked on in concern. There were coughs and there were more than coughs. She was increasingly worried at the length of time it took for him to calm his breathing and at the severity of the cough. Hafiz pointed down at the bowl on the table, suggesting the olive was to blame.

'Sorry about that, must have gone down the wrong way'. Quickly wiping his mouth, taking another sip of water, placing the napkin down on the table near the neatly arranged silverware. Yet Bernadette caught a glimpse of blood on the napkin. As she looked away quickly, shocked, Hafiz concealed it on his lap, hoping she hadn't seen it.

'You don't look too good, Hafiz', was all she said. She reached down for her bag and took out a box of painkillers. 'Here, take these. They're just painkillers; well, anti-inflammatories, really. You've probably caught a winter bug or something. Loads of people have it; I blame the air conditioning in the shops, unhealthy places, you know'. Hafiz took two of the proffered tablets with a glass of water.

'Thank you for your concern but I'm fine, honestly. I'll just stay off the olives; tricky little blighters when you have a sore throat'. He called Pierre over to order their food as they continued to drink the superb wine and chat like the old friends they were.

The food arrived timeously with the standard 'Bon appétit' from Pierre, a throwaway comment that made Bernadette confirm her belief that the French accent had got to be the sexiest around, hands down. The food provided a distraction. The foyer and reading room food was impressive: Cornish lobster risotto. The aroma steamed its way up from the pure white crockery and fluttered around their nostrils.

'I'm famished, Teatro! A work of art'. Hafiz said grinning to himself as he satisfied his hunger in part by the presentation on his plate alone. As he began to eat, he barely touched on the subject of Danny any more. Instead, he frowned seriously. 'As I mentioned to you earlier, hence this meeting, the Russians are in town, Bernadette. Nikolai Berzeitis and Vasily Rybalko are regular visitors to London and I have previously advised them and sold them art. They have shitloads of cash and not a lot of direction. I have recommended you to them and told them what's best to invest in at your gallery or with your sources. Heads up for you, though, they are presently fascinated with Emin and Yiadom-Boakye, and if you can throw in Gabriel Orozco, too, you will have a tidy commission.'

Bernadette paused, covering up her confusion by playing with the rice. Where did she know those names, Berzeitis, Nikolai Berzeitis, and why was Hafiz throwing this her way? He could snap this up himself. 'Of course, that would be fantastic. I could meet them this afternoon after we finish here?' She tried to alleviate her suspicions by dreaming of what a good result could buy her: the latest Louis Vuitton bag in Harrods.

'Unfortunately, they are in meetings and only available on Wednesday. Any good?' Hafiz was more than aware that that was the opening day of the Joseph Legend exhibitions.

'Great, Hafiz!' Bernadette reached for her diary in her bag. 'Here we are, oh, Wednesday is the 4th?' she read out loud. 'Hafiz, I'm fully booked, it's the Legend opening night. I'll move stuff around. What time suits?' She nibbled the end of her Mont Blanc pen.

'It will be around six-thirty, as they will not be finished until late.' Hafiz pretended to look sympathetic, knowing full well that the gallery closed at 6pm on the dot on Wednesdays, unless she was exhibiting. She looked down at the page, disappointed, tapping her pen.

'Okay', she said finally, 'I'll keep the gallery open, but please let me know soonest if they can't make it, and the earlier the better as I'm booked to meet with other clients at Legend's opening night on Davies Street.' She made it obvious she was reluctant to agree, yet she knew the Russians could spend some serious money so she had to compromise.

'Don't worry, darling, I will be accompanying them myself to the gallery'. Hafiz lied without hesitation, knowing he would actually be on the other side of town, meeting with Marina. 'You know, you are right: I am not feeling so well and those painkillers haven't really had much effect. I think I'm going to head home now and get some rest if you don't mind'. He didn't need to act to look like shit this time. He could finally give in to it: his job was done; Bernadette would be at the gallery on Wednesday.

'That's fine, darling, you go ahead. I totally understand, be well'. Bernadette looked concerned.

'Please stay here without me and finish off the bottle of wine, though; a good wine should never go to waste'. He signalled for Pierre, taking out his Bottega Veneta wallet and placing his Centurion credit card on the silver tray presented, without even looking at the amount. He stood up, not exactly strong on his feet, wobbling as if he was intoxicated, though he had only had one glass of wine. He used the table to steady himself. Bernadette instinctively stood up at the same time.

'Do you want me to walk you back home, Hafiz?'

'No, no, I'm fine, darling. I believe the fresh air will do me good'. He took a few deep breaths and started to leave.

'There are drivers outside the main door, should you wish for a cab, sir'. Pierre handed him back his card and cleared the table courteously, leaving the wine and rearranging it in the ice bucket, just as Hafiz had directed. As Hafiz walked away, Bernadette sat back down, wondering what could be wrong with him. Pierre poured a fresh glass for her and she said thank you automatically, smiling at him, and then turned her attention back to her diary, reaffirming how busy she was.

A familiar voice made her smile disappear.

'He doesn't look well, does he?'

'Thom. I thought I could smell something, a decaying scent, almost rodent-like'. She shook her head, sighing heavily; accepting her day had just turned bad. 'What do you want this time?' she said testily.

'Now, now, you humble me with such niceties'. He brushed off her cutting words and presumptively took a place opposite her. 'May I?' It wasn't a question as he helped himself to a glass of wine; Pierre had smoothly appeared with a fresh glass and Thom nodded appreciatively. Bernadette, however, was not at all appreciative. *I've just sat with someone who looked like death warmed up, and now I've got someone who actually is death*, she thought as she flashed him a look saturated in annoyance and irritation. Thom sipped the wine and tucked into the olives.

'He's got cancer'. Thom nodded at the door through which Hafiz had exited. Bernadette didn't say anything for a while, in shock. She just watched as Thom carelessly kept eating and the olives disappeared.

'Cancer. Are you sure?' She took a deep breath, trying to settle her nerves. She had a weird feeling of Hafiz being on both ends of a seesaw: at one end, he was strangely kind, a friend in many ways; and at the other, he was known for being a maniacal individual who had once been connected with an Islamic extremist terrorist group. Unorthodox heartstrings sat over the crucial tilt of the seesaw. Would the cancer kill him before the suggested intelligence activities did?

'That explains why he looks like shit and some of why he is acting the way he is', she said, shaking her head in sympathy at his obvious suffering. 'Poor bastard. What stage is it? How long has he got?'

'We have checked his medical records; from the medication he has been prescribed of late, our physician reckons eight months-tops without proper treatment'. Thom topped up Bernadette's glass; she looked like she needed it.

'He hasn't mentioned anything. But then, why would he? He has been his normal self: you know, one minute a nice person then the next in self-destruct mode, getting high on drink and I assume drugs; now I know why. I'd probably be the same. How awful', she said, worried.

'But this is why it is imperative to find out what he is up to ASAP!' Thom emphasised the urgency of the situation.

'Thom, I haven't seen or heard anything that points me in that direction. I told you before: I haven't seen any behaviour that indicates he is involved in anything terrorist-orientated at this time'. She kept her voice low, looking around, and Thom studied her body language, aware she was about to confide something. 'Just before you arrived, he informed me he is bringing two Russian art collectors into my gallery'. Bernadette finished her glass and poured another; frankly, she felt like having another bottle.

'Russians... did he say – who?' Thom looked intrigued, holding up his glass for a refresher, too, and chomping thoughtfully on the last olive.

'Nikolai Berzeitis and Vasily Rybalko'. Suddenly the penny dropped and she closed her eyes, berating herself in realisation. 'Of course', she remembered who Berzeitis was now: he was connected to the Russian mafia, known for selling guns to terrorist organisations within the Middle East. Thom picked up on the name simultaneously.

'Nikolai Berzeitis! And you still think he has nothing to do with terrorists?' he said, in that authoritative voice. Thom barely held it together in such formal surroundings: now he knew he was on to something serious with such a big-time player being in the city. 'He's a gun dealer, for fuck's sake, Harry'. Bernadette looked away, annoyed with herself for not realising who the Russian was earlier. Thom leaned forward across the table and lowered his voice, suddenly aware of the other diners around them.

'Let me remind you that Berzeitis's family were well known for selling weapons and ammo on the black market after the fall of the Soviet Union at the end of the Cold War. His father was a high-ranking general in the Russian military and reports led us to believe he was assassinated by MI6, but that wasn't the case, he just disappeared. After the correct amount of time to let the dust settle, he emerged with an unfathomable surplus of armaments in military storage, from machine guns to components for nuclear weapons, and the Russian mafia has taken to selling them to anyone who has the money'. He paused to sink the last of his wine.

Noticing the wine had been consumed, with characteristically impeccable timing Pierre proudly approached the table with a half-bottle of the Château d'Yquem Sauternes 96. 'The gentleman ordered this especially for the occasion before you arrived, mademoiselle', he announced.

Bernadette viewed the bottle, impressed. 'Excellent indeed. Thank you, Pierre'. He took the liberty of pouring the liquid into two exquisite glasses he'd brought with him and left.

Thom couldn't help but notice the new arrival on the table: 'What's with the small portions?' He referred to the size of the dessert-wine glasses. Bernadette simply closed her eyes, repulsed at his lack of finesse, as he continued his sarcastic rundown of the global terrorist situation.

'Agencies such as ours have drawn connections between these former Soviet weapons caches to the arms used by terrorist organisations in the Middle East, all provided by the fucking mafia. This illustrates the epidemic we are up against, which still persists'. He sat back in his chair, looking around for any signs of anyone taking in the intel, but the businessmen were all too caught up in their self-importance. 'Just find out what you can', he said dismissively, shaking his head in a patronising manner and raising one eyebrow in disbelief at her ignorance in not identifying Berzeitis.

As he knocked back his wine, Bernadette tapped her fingers, patiently waiting for the obvious to hit the moron. There it was: he visibly winced at the sack of syrup his ignorant palate felt he had just drunk. She chortled into her glass, demonstrating how to drink a dessert wine correctly.

'That's a dessert wine, by the way, Thom, and I know who he is, and it just slipped my mind. Added to which, you know what, Thom? It isn't our agency any more, it's yours. And it's Bernadette'. She spat the words at him yet still maintained a ladylike manner. Nevertheless, she was clearly furious with him; her eyes narrowed and her teeth clenched together, her hands curled into fists with rage. She felt as if a long-overdue punch in his smug face would help. She looked around to make sure no one overheard. 'And don't fucking patronise me. Let's face it: we all stood at the funerals, including yours, but unfortunately somehow you're still here'. His nerve enraged her. Picking up her bag from the floor, she threw her diary and pen inside in one shot, clearly preparing to depart.

Thom leaned forward to stop her next move. 'For some reason, you're blaming me for that day in Kabul. Once that front gate was hit and the insurgents entered, people were going to die. You knew that, you knew the risks; it's the nature of our business'. Thom felt pain that the reality of this life was not common knowledge; he sighed angrily, looking around the room awkwardly. 'You know the protocol: when the shit hits the fan, I am immediately extracted'. His face tightened uncomfortably; he looked guilty, even.

'Well, what a load of shit hit that particular fan, Thom. We were dealing with mass casualties. No one knew you'd been extracted; you were pronounced missing, assumed to have been vaporised in the initial blast, yet that piece-of-shit explanation just doesn't add up, and especially considering you're sat across from me right now. It really doesn't fucking add up'.

Thom stared deep into her eyes, listening uncomfortably to her diatribe as he glanced around the room. Abruptly, he diverted the conversation away from his own behaviour. 'Everyone knew about your relationship with Steve; nothing is a secret in the agency. I get it; you are full of pain and anger. But there was nothing you or anyone else could have done to prevent that day from happening'.

In her mind's eye, Bernadette left the room. She headed back to the sounds of explosions and chaos, to screams of horror and orders, then to Steve; her husband dying in her arms, to her begging him to stay with her, to stay alive. Her eyes filled with tears, glistening in the light from the chandeliers above. Thom had hit a nerve, but ever since that had happened, Bernadette didn't like pain; she couldn't bear it.

Standing up, looking furiously down at him, she now decided a showdown would be good. The commotion and tension between them was plain in her body language, and the other guests glanced over in that polite yet desperately nosy British manner.

With great style and purpose, she placed her right hand into her bag and pulled it back out slowly. 'Oh, you dropped these, Thom', she said carelessly, before waving two rigid fingers in his face and storming off, leaving him sat at the table with embarrassed diners around him, all assuming they were a couple who had had an argument. On her way out, she tipped Pierre generously, telling him to keep the rest of the dessert wine himself. She received a courteous bow in response.

'Mademoiselle'. He opened the door for her and she swished through it on her way out.

THIRTY-THREE

———— • ————

4th January 2012 had been etched on Danny's mind for months and no more so than today, the day it had finally arrived. His anxiety levels were off the scale, and he didn't know if it was because he was nervous of fucking up or high as a kite at succeeding. Still needing to speak to Thom to brief him of everything. Slightly worried his plan wasn't foolproof, worried an attack of sorts was imminent today on each Gagosian gallery. Knowing he couldn't put that over the network in an unsecured text.

Danny had all the details practically etched in his mind. Wealthy private sources and public institutions had lent the paintings in the exhibition; there were more than 150 of them from twenty countries, yet Hafiz and Danny were interested in only eleven of them... Not that he knew that Danny knew.

As people prepared to walk through the doors of each gallery, the finishing touches were made. Each had a clinical touch to its décor, complementing all the different variations of the *Primus Circle* paintings: white walls and highly polished floors. Each edition had been strategically placed to be seen from every angle, so that the variety of coloured circles danced and pulsated gently, drawing your eyes into a 1960s BIBA poster.

In London, Hafiz forced all his optical muscles to open his eyes, wincing at the natural light piercing through the window. His dominant thought on waking, as usual, was one of confusion, of trying to make sense of what had happened last night. His mind was messy, his head thumping as he slowly sat up and looked around the bedroom, anxious at what he might see.

He became aware of someone lying in the bed next to him, and he quickly tried to identify the clothes untidily scattered on the floor. Yet as he looked to the body beside him, its familiar form, naked limbs intertwined with the white Egyptian cotton sheets, pacified him. Nevertheless, he sighed, annoyed that he felt too fucked up to do anything about appreciating her sensual curves. It wasn't only his hangover: as his illness had grown more serious, the regularity of his manly dawn o'clock hard-on had decreased exponentially.

Sitting up, he swung his feet out onto the floor, steadying himself. The intense pain in his head gave him the feeling of still being drunk, yet without the euphoria and escapism. He suddenly collapsed with his head in his hands, hating his pathetic state: the alcohol and drugs debilitated him more than the cancer. He took deep breaths to compose himself as the blood rushed to his head. Rubbing his eyes, he dragged the skin down on his face; he looked and felt like shit.

'Good morning, darling', Marina whispered behind him, stretching out her body as she woke. Shuffling and fidgeting, she dragged a couple of pillows up against the headboard, wanting to sit up in comfort.

'Good morning'. His voice sounded hoarse and as shitty as he felt. Stretching his arms over his head, he tried to put his flashbacks in sequence, willing his memories to come to the surface, wanting to recall their night of celebration. 'What a night'. He released a deep breath from the pit of his stomach, preparing himself once more to stand up. This time, he made it. Naked and unsteady on his feet, he wandered into the bathroom to empty his bladder, a move that was well overdue.

'It certainly was, my Adonis'. Marina heard the toilet flush and tried not to think about the emotional roller coaster she went through every time they were together, enjoying the feeling of being wanted yet again, and then trying to ignore the pain of the instant rejection afterwards.

Hafiz appeared at the door of the en suite brushing his teeth. 'Right, you know the plan, don't you? Today is the day and our people will be in place by late afternoon.'

It wasn't exactly easy to decipher his words with a mouth full of white, foamed-up toothpaste, but she got the general gist as she secured her hair in a ponytail. She sighed in irritation. 'Hafiz, I said I'd be there at seven-thirty on the dot and I will. Stop worrying, darling. You're the genius; you have everything covered and they won't be laughing at you later – or ever again.' She wished he'd play another record as he gargled, rinsed and re-entered the room, this time with a white towel wrapped around his waist.

'Good,' he said bluntly. 'You know I'm not a fan of these group sessions; they're full of all sorts of crazy people, fucked-up people, even, but needs must; and more importantly, we will be seen together when we make art history.

•

It was an event that represented the epitome of the high life. Men, women, children, art enthusiasts, acclaimed critics, collectors, reporters, photographers, notorieties and the occasional celebrity had travelled the globe to see the 300 variations of Joseph Legend's *Primus Circle* paintings on display at one of the eleven Gagosian galleries. It was mind-boggling to think that this was only a fraction of the number of circle paintings produced by Legend.

Now awake. Mobile towards their predetermined positions, using various forms of transport in preparation for the arrival of their targets. Human chameleons blending into society thanks to their nebulous construction, their own physical instruments they are living in. Like an insidious disease.

One either likes metros, subways and undergrounds or hates them. They are a particular acquired taste. The doors slide open efficiently and hundreds of people forming one blob burst out, as though a hole has been blown in a dam. In these underground mole holes, there are no manners, nor recognition of the frailty of men, women and children; there are no lifeboat ethics here, it's everyone for themselves, all trying to resist responding to the ignorant Neanderthal behaviour which may result in you being trampled.

Cody was experiencing just that feeling, but at no point did he arouse the suspicions of the authorities or his fellow passengers leaving the underground. Dressed in his usual business suit, carrying his briefcase just like any ordinary day on his way to work. His survival technique was to allow himself to be carried by the flow of pedestrians towards the exit. He observed the families around him enjoying their time together. The memory of Christine and the twins made him well up and he winced; he quickly buried the thoughts deep and turned to the sinister job in hand.

Meanwhile, Rosie, late 50s – who resembled the typical librarian, inconspicuous – took a cab from the airport to the city centre to roughly where she needed to be. She'd decided on that itinerary so she could take in some sightseeing and was thoroughly enjoying her casual stroll, undaunted by the busy streets, though she could not believe the height of the buildings all around her. It was difficult to see the sky, and there was a wind route that hit her whenever she crossed the side streets, no longer protected by the giant architecture that blocked the wind in its path.

Another sleeper was overwhelmed at the size of the city and by the number of people who didn't make eye contact with him: they clearly didn't give a shit who he was so long as he got out of their way. Talking wasn't an option, so he shrouded himself in a quiet shop doorway, barely visible. Scanning the streets for any signs of being followed. He found solace in tracking where he needed to be as per his ruthless instructions.

•

Danny couldn't get today out of his head. It had been such a long time coming. He was feeling incredibly excited yet contented at the same time. The only way he found he could relax was with music or by painting or both, so he sat back, listening to one of his favourite albums and reminiscing, with his sketchbook on his lap, pen poised. However, he found he was unable to describe the feeling with words, let alone pictures.

Danny walked into the kitchen to make a brew. As he did so, he noticed his coat hanging up on its hook out of the corner of his eye. Suddenly he had a vision of tearing off pages from Hafiz's A4 notebook when he was sitting in his apartment; they were still neatly folded inside the pocket.

Taking them out, he flattened them down on his dining room table. 'For Chrissake!' He'd forgotten all about them, and deciphering what they meant. Running upstairs to his bedroom, fetching his weekend bag; he needed the plastic folder containing all of his research on the circle paintings and the deciphered codes. Back downstairs, he couldn't believe he was looking at spots again.

Off he went, again, shading evenly over the top of the page with his 7B graphite. Gradually, as if by magic, it exposed circles, then letters followed by numbers from the indentations made on the paper by Hafiz. Danny's mind kicked in… again. 'Oh, bollocks', he said in frustration, closing his eyes, rubbing his neck as he felt the tension already start to grip it. Now he remembered the night he'd broken into Method Ltd. and found the codes in Marina's carry case – including the unexpected twelfth code. 'For fuck's sake, what was it? What was the twelfth code?' He spoke with abject failure. Back to pacing and scratching his head, worrying himself sick. Danny couldn't believe he'd left it behind. Suddenly he was thinking all kinds of shit… again.

Is there such a thing as a controlled panic? If so, Danny was having one. He got his code deciphers out and started cross-referencing each one… again. 'No, no, no; not that one; or that'. Finding it helped to talk to himself… again. Ticking the codes off one by one, slowly going through each of the eleven in front of him and comparing them with Hafiz's codes on the shaded paper. Repeatedly, assessing them in fine detail, confirming he hadn't made any mistakes, wanting to take away the crippling fear that in changing the paintings he had made things worse. 'Get a fucking grip', he told himself. He was confident he hadn't.

Placing the *Chemical Warfare* photocopy in front of him, writing down all the information, numbers and letters, the number of circles and how he had configured the code. Pausing in thought, trying to clear his mind. 'What the fuck is this one all about then?' He spoke to the twelfth code in his head, remembering eleven on the drying racks. He cross-referenced each circle, rotating the pages, looking horizontally, diagonally, going through every combination. Staring at the walls afterwards, trying to blink the spots from his eyes. 'It doesn't make sense, but maybe it's nothing'. Questioning himself. Yet he shook his head at that. His gut feeling said: 'It means something'. He'd heard of writer's block and experienced painter's block, but this was a lot worse. Not to mention it was now four forty-five in the afternoon; it was a tad inconvenient, given the timing of a rather large incident scheduled to occur later that day.

As though an angel had entered his kitchen, the afternoon sun beamed through the window. Danny took a moment and got a glass of water to remedy the dry mouth that this thinking shit had given him. Turning back to the table, the sun seemed to glow poignantly over the table – and only on the table, like a spotlight highlighting the root of his misery. Sitting down, bewildered. 'You're a wanker, Hafiz'. He looked at the sun and the table, back and forth, as though he was praying for intervention. Moments passed, then – wham – he jumped up, picked up the shaded page and held it up to the large mirror on the wall.

Well, fuck me. Everything is opposite, Danny realised; it was a mirror image. It made sense given that Hafiz practically lived his life staring into a mirror. Cross-referencing it now started to make sense, so Danny wrote down the twelve deciphered codes one by one.

Okay, here we go... again. Working out the first part. There were twelve spots in total: two yellow, two red (a large and small each), five black (two large, three small) and a cream-coloured spot with overlapping spots. Referencing against the *Chemical Warfare* key code, he knew immediately this layout of spots meant the location was London, so he wrote it down. Then he deciphered the following codes: RODENT, GORGON and GHOST. Now Danny was confused. Rodent, frankly, described what he thought the original circle looked like – so much vermin – whilst Gorgon described him, shaking his head with a blank, staring look. Ghost clearly had nothing to do with the afterlife. This was not the usual circle painting Legend had produced over the years; surely, this was new.

After more puffing and blowing, he got the numbers 040120127 and the letters NYX, which he knew were the date and time. NYX meant the goddess of night, so the numbers meant the 4th day of the first month of 2012 at 7pm. As he looked down at his watch, his heart pounded. 'Holy shit, something is going to happen in less than two hours' time. Are you fucking kidding me?' he said aloud. 'What the fuck is happening?' The only way to find out the answer was to crack the code... again. A nervous hit of adrenalin flowed through his body. He couldn't believe he had to race against the clock again. *Fuck, I have to speak to Thom,* he thought. If more shit was going down in London imminently, he needed to let him know.

Perseus flashed into his mind, a mythical character in *The Clash of the Titans*. Danny needed to emulate him right at this moment. Taking a step back – cue more neck rubbing – looking at the coding again, trying hard to concentrate afresh. *Come on, Danny! Screw the nut! Concentrate.*

The answer came to him almost as an angel's voice inside his head, as though the sunshine was still beaming in. Hafiz used ancient mythology in his codes and this one wouldn't be any different. Getting his laptop, he Googled for Gorgon. The page loaded. A Gorgon was a female creature, also meaning dreadful. The descriptions of Gorgons vary in Greek literature, yet the term commonly refers to any of three sisters who had hair made of living venomous snakes, as in the best-known sister, Medusa.

Great, so it's a female with snakes. But that couldn't be right. His mind dug deep for this cryptic message. He looked for the method of death, typing in Perseus, who had fought Medusa by using the reflective underside of his shield to deceive her, then decapitated her, collecting her head for a trophy and possible further use. Thinking how Hafiz's logic had perfectly chosen this figure of Greek mythology for his reflected-image code. Then: was this the method of death? What a barbaric fuck. *Do these people ever evolve from such cavemen-with-sticks-rooted behaviour?* he wondered, disgusted.

Danny was left with a rodent and a female with snakes being beheaded on British soil. He could barely bring himself to phone Thom with that classic *whofuckingdunnit* mystery to top off the weekend of terror in London. Realising he'd have to explain his fucking circle theories would take forever.

Reading up on the previous research, he saw the iconic Disney character Mickey Mouse in the style of a circle painting was to be auctioned at Christie's. Mice are rodents; you're a moron! But it took him longer to get it; then a while longer to realise where he had seen that image recently. Yet he was still stuck on the Gorgon, the female with snakes. 'Come on, Danny, think!' he said in frustration. 'Snakes are reptiles, they're… they're serpents'. At that moment, Danny froze from the inside out. 'Fuck! The Serpentine Gallery'. He couldn't move, in mourning mode, then he rushed to his phone, scrolling down, down. *It's BERNADETTE, the female is Bernadette* was the only thought racing through his head, even as the phone rang. 'Pick up the phone, babe, pick up the phone'. It went to answerphone; he rang again. 'Pick up, pick up...' Answerphone again. Danny left a message, even as he was trying to get the gallery's number from the now remarkably quick 'internet'.

'Bernadette, it's me. Please call me ASAP; it's urgent. Stay away from the gallery today. Stay away tonight, please. I'll explain later'. Sending her a text to duplicate the message, his fingers shaking.

The number of the gallery popped up on his laptop, calling the landline, but once again, there was no answer: straight to answerphone. 'Bollocks!' *Maybe she's not gone into work today...* Danny could only hope.

Urgently, he called Thom, but his phone was conveniently switched off. 'Fucking wanker'. He was in too much of a panic to imagine shooting him in the arse as he was clearly doing to him.

Running upstairs, opening his cupboard door, reaching behind the false piece of plasterboard and punching through several shoeboxes, placed strategically to conceal the pistol, thinking of Thom's head with every thump. It was now wrapped in an old Arabic shemagh scarf to deceive any onlookers, and it held an ironic note as he held it with his right hand. Using his left thumb and forefinger, fully cocking the weapon, allowing a round to go into the chamber, then half-cocking it so he could visibly see a round in the breach. Letting the top slide go forward under its own steam, applying the safety catch, finally placing it inside his belt on his jeans, then he ran back down the stairs, taking them four at a time. Ramming his trainers on, grabbing his jacket and car keys, locking the door and practically parachuting into his car.

The engine screamed to save him the trouble as he put his foot down hard on the accelerator. He was a man on a mission, fully focused, knowing he could make it to London in just over an hour. It was now five-thirty in the evening and nightfall had truly arrived. Danny squealed out of his driveway, his iPhone automatically linked up to the hands-free Bluetooth system. Again, he tried Bernadette and Thom. Again: stalemate. 'Fuck', he said, slamming the steering wheel with his hands in frustration. *I can't even get a fucking police escort when I need one*, he thought, panicking.

THIRTY-FOUR

——— • ———

Bernadette was sat down behind her desk in the Serpentine Gallery, looking rather pissed off with Hafiz for promising to be at the gallery with the two Russians at six-thirty. She should have known better, should have told him no way; the Joseph Legend opening on Davies Street was so important for her and it should have been for him, too, especially given the way he had pestered her for the exhibition dates. At this point in time, she had no sympathy or empathy for Hafiz, despite her recent knowledge of his impending departure from this earth; the guy was a wild card. She glanced up at the clock on the wall above her desk: six fifty-five. Double-checking this with her watch, she confirmed the asshole was a no-show. He was probably getting pissed on vodka with his Kremlin buddies whilst she kept the gallery open.

Two big sighs later, she threw her pen down onto her desk, shaking her head in disgust. She shut down her computer and headed out to the back office, switching the rear gallery lights off on her way before tidying up before closing. Still cussing, she heard the main gallery door open, then close. 'Oh, only thirty bloody minutes late then', she muttered, drying the last coffee cup. As she walked back into the gallery, she shouted out, 'Good evening, Hafiz. I guess nobly late is better than never!' However, there was no one there.

Confused, she stood still, rooted to the spot. She scanned around, convinced she had heard the door open. 'Hello?' She raised her voice, wondering if someone had gone straight down to the other side of the gallery looking for her. No answer. She tuned into the silence, unsettled by the eerie feeling someone was inside. Twirling around, slowly, she thought she heard something from the back end of the gallery.

'Sorry, the gallery is closed', she shouted, her loud voice carrying through the entire exhibition space. She walked around, traversing around the partitioned walls of art, large sculptures and installations, hands on her hips. Yet she saw no one. Silence.

'I must be going mad', she said to herself, turning back around to grab the keys and lock up. As she did so, she jumped in shock to see Marina stood directly in front of her; she had come from nowhere.

'Marina?' She felt unnerved and wasn't sure why; her sudden appearance without Hafiz, probably, let alone without the Russians. 'What are you doing here? You just scared the shit out of me! Where is Hafiz? I was expecting him – and two clients'. Bernadette looked at Marina and noticed her contemptuous expression towards her as she stood in a shadow. As Bernadette shifted her weight, trying to see her in a better light, Marina didn't look herself: her eyes were bloodshot, dilated and staring, and she didn't answer or respond to anything Bernadette had said. 'Is everything okay?' she asked. Bernadette felt vulnerable. She walked towards her desk, wanting to get the hell out of there, and Marina stepped to the side and obstructed her.

'Marina, what are you doing?' Bernadette drew a deep breath, feeling defensive, trying to prepare for any eventuality because she felt that something was seriously wrong. Confused but wary, she stepped back, putting distance between them, remembering her training. Marina reached into her jacket pocket and pulled out her iPhone. Pressing the screen to summon an image, she confrontationally held it up to Bernadette's face.

'Do you have one of these?' Marina asked in a patronising way, knowing full well she did. Bernadette pretended to study the image on the phone, despite having recognised it straight away; she wanted to buy herself time to assess Marina's behaviour.

'What, an iPhone or a Joseph Legend?' Bernadette asked cheekily, watching Marina's reaction, noting the aggression in her stance. 'I have an iPhone and a Mickey. It's actually on display at the front of the gallery; it's on loan before it goes to auction.' Bernadette wondered for a quick second if Marina was actually going to steal a painting. 'But what is this really all about, Marina?' Marina ignored her, placing her iPhone back in her pocket, and Bernadette chose that moment to push past her, politely but firmly.

'Now, if you will excuse me, I've got a shitload to do, including closing the gallery. Having waited for your boyfriend to stand me up, I'm now late, so go play your silly games elsewhere.' Bernadette headed towards her desk defiantly; she wasn't in the mood for Hafiz and co.

Behind her back, Marina pulled out a large, dazzlingly sharp kitchen carving knife and held it down by her side.

'Harriet Chadwyck-Healey', Marina casually called out.

Bernadette was stunned. Barely believing what she had just heard, she stopped on the spot and closed her eyes, taking a brief moment in disbelief. Breathing out slowly, she feared the worse and, reluctantly, accessed the military bitch in her.

'Sorry?' Bernadette played dumb but it was not meant to fool. She turned around just in time to see Marina charging at her with wild ferocity, holding a large blade aimed right at her chest.

Thom was right: you never retire. She blocked her strike with her left forearm instinctively then whacked a direct hit square in Marina's face with her right fist. Her assailant went down with a sudden burst of blood spraying out of her nose; she covered her lower face, holding her hand over her nose, as the thumping sound of her body's shock and adrenalin filled her head, the impact giving her blurred vision.

Timeously using the stunning result of her punch, Bernadette kicked the knife out of Marina's hand and it slid across the gallery floor. Marina composed herself surprisingly quickly. Wiping the blood off her mouth with her jacket sleeve, she got up furiously, throwing well-aimed punches to Bernadette's face and body. Whack, whack: Bernadette was hit in the head and stomach. She dropped to her knees, emptying her lungs in a dizzying explosion of pain. Bernadette couldn't stop the terrible convulsive pain as her body struggled to breathe, trying not to panic as she fought for air. 'You fucking bitch. I've never liked you', Marina yelled, with a maniacal laugh. Toying with her prey. She raised her foot and kicked

Bernadette in the stomach again, blow after blow, winding her again as Bernadette clutched her guts, falling on her right side and assuming the foetal position in a vain attempt to give herself some protection, even as she retched for air. Occasions such as these were the only time Marina was ever in control in her life and she liked it very much, asserting pain, eradicating others; causing the same pain she felt at not having her love. 'So, Harriet, all these years we have known you, and you were working for the fucking British Intelligence!' she screamed demonically at Bernadette, walking over to the knife on the floor.

Bernadette took a deep breath. Finding the fortitude and determination to get up, she attacked Marina from behind, landing a pissed-off punch to her kidneys. Marina arched her back in agony, screaming out in pain. Bernadette spat at her as adrenalin became her saviour. Channelling it, using it to give her strength, she grabbed at Marina's perfectly coiffed ponytail, pulling her downwards at the same time as kneeing her hard in the face, followed by a punishing kick to the chest. Still holding her ponytail, which she'd been grasping to give her absolute precision for her hits, she finally let it go, discarding Marina as she fell to her knees screaming in agony, coughing up blood.

'You fucking bitch', Marina snarled, trying to assert control.

'Funnily enough, I've never liked you either; you're as fake as your collection of handbags... bitch'. Bernadette viciously struck her hard in the face, putting her flat on the deck.

Marina got back up and started delivering a barrage of kicks and punches to Bernadette, who took a couple of blows to the arms and ribs, retaliating with several right and left hooks towards Marina's now rather messed-up face. Unfortunately, Marina ducked down to avoid them, following up with an upper-cut blow to Bernadette's chin which devastatingly knocked her onto her back, so that she whacked her head on the gallery floor, rendering her unconscious for a few seconds.

When she came to, it was with dark thoughts. Given her former occupation of covert and frontline operations, Bernadette had often wondered how she might die. Was this the moment? Dazed and confused, she couldn't hear anything in the room, just deathly silence. Her ears still ringing, she didn't hear Marina's footsteps on the floor as she walked over to pick up the knife from off the floor. She didn't hear as she walked back.

But, slowly, she became aware of Marina's presence as she grew closer and closer to her, as she walked towards her with a disturbed evil look on her face. Bernadette's lip was cut and she tasted her own blood as Marina's face loomed into her vision and she stood dominantly over her.

Marina stared down at Bernadette in murderous blood lust. Then she sat on top of her body, knees either side of her torso, dropping her weight on her to push the oxygen out. Bernadette screamed as her lungs drained. Marina grabbed a fistful of her hair. Lifting her head off the floor, as she was breathing in shallow gulps, frightened. Marina's right hand coolly positioned the blade to slice through her throat. She was making ready to decapitate her, just as the method of death instructed.

Bernadette may have wondered how she would die – but it wasn't going to be today. She somehow drew on reserves of strength in her body she didn't know she had and managed to grab the hand holding the knife, before sinking her teeth carnivorously into the flesh. Marina screamed like a bitch from hell, instantly releasing the knife onto the floor beside them. Bernadette spat blood and skin at Marina's face, temporarily blinding her, before grabbing her clothing with both hands to secure the perfect headbutt to her face, knocking her out cold. Marina flopped, a dead weight, right on top of her.

With the adrenalin still peaking within her, Bernadette pushed Marina's limp body off her own and onto the floor in a heap. Her laboured breathing sped up as the pain circulated around her body. Wobbly from shock, she managed to get up off the floor, still holding her battered stomach, and stumbled towards her desk. She tried to focus on her bag to find her phone. Taking it out, she saw several missed calls and texts from Danny. Tears filled her eyes as shock was setting in. She tried to call Thom but his phone was off, as usual. She stood still, wavering slightly on her feet, taking a moment to work out what the fuck had just happened.

Suddenly the gallery door burst open, and Danny ran through the door holding a Sig pistol in the aiming position, safety catch off. Bernadette turned to look at him in complete shock as he pointed the barrel at her. She closed her eyes, silently admitting defeat. *So, this is it. So, this is how I die*, she imagined, concluding that Danny must be involved with Marina and had come to finish what his partner had started. Her life flashed on a screen behind her eyes in the darkness of her solitude. Anticipating merely the bludgeon of the bullets to pierce through her.

Thud. Thud. Danny squeezed the trigger, firing off two precision-aimed shots. Bernadette flinched with each loud onslaught... as the bullets passed by her left shoulder. She thought Danny had missed – but he hadn't. The first round penetrated Marina's chest, blowing her heart out of her back. The second penetrated her forehead; bone and brains projected out of the rear as she dropped to the floor. Her body convulsed with a final gasp of air. Marina had been standing directly behind Bernadette with the knife in both hands, the blade raised ready to strike above her head. She had been seconds from driving the cold blade deep into Bernadette's skull.

•

Covered in blood, cut and swollen lip, bruised eye. She caught Danny looking at her in concern, placing the safety catch back on the pistol then tucking it into his belt.

'I thought I'd lost you'. Gently hugging her as carefully as he could, knowing she had to hurt everywhere, given both the state of Marina and his own knowledge of what that bitch could do.

'So, you're the Ghost', he said to her, smiling and wiping the blood from her face with a tissue from the box on her desk. She looked at him, knowing from his words that he now knew she was an ex-spook.

'I'm just so glad you are here right now; I'm a bit rusty for this shit'. Bernadette's voice quavered on the edge of tears.

He sat her down in the chair opposite her desk. 'Everything will be all right now', reassuring her, giving her a kiss on the forehead. Then he walked over to where Marina's dead body lay on the floor, a pool of blood pouring out from underneath her from the two exit wounds. As he knelt down to assess the scenario, he could hear the vibration of her mobile phone, which was obviously on silent. Danny zoned into where it was on her body and removed it from her jacket pocket; it was illuminating with each ring. Danny smiled, nodding almost imperceptibly when he saw it was Hafiz calling.

THIRTY-FIVE

———— • ————

Eleven owners stood proudly in their respective galleries worldwide, holding their own special VIP invitations. Elevated up their own asses, they had indulged their trusted entourages of PAs, family, friends and business associates with an invitation to this special event, too, an invitation engineered to ensure that their entourages must stand staring at them – and at their original circle paintings on display. They had constantly reminded everyone on their speed dial that their originals had been graciously loaned out for this Joseph Legend extravaganza and wanted to soak up the associated glory. Now, they were waiting patiently for their ever-so-exclusive gift in return for such a favour from the illustrious artist himself.

In London, the temperature outside was below freezing and although Hafiz was desperate to get out of the cold, he wasn't overly fond of what was behind the door through which he was entering. 'Here we go again', he muttered, shaking his head, noticing with irritation that there was no one on reception. 'I have to sit in here and listen to these crazy fuckers'. He walked through the corridor to the main meeting room, irritated again to realise he wasn't the first to arrive. Still, at least it would help with his alibi. As he entered the cold room, he felt a further rush of irritation. *They couldn't even put the fucking heating on*, he thought.

Looking around, he took a seat on a grey polyprop chair close to the window, conscious that if he didn't choose that location he would get claustrophobia: another ailment to add to the list of many with regards to his mental health. The chairs had all been arranged in a full circle, typical for such sessions, yet annoying to him. He disliked group therapy; he preferred one-to-one as it was easier to manipulate the outcome his way. He had no patience for this group-dynamics style of therapy: he wasn't interested in everyone telling everyone else how fucking mad they were, what drugs they took, how many times they had tried to commit suicide... A problem shared was not a problem halved in Hafiz's world; it was gossip, and he preferred to deny his problems than admit them.

He tried to remain calm in the face of his own mental agony and boredom, knowing that at the very least his presence here ensured witnesses and alibis, a thought that brought him back to the question at the forefront of his mind: *Where the fuck is Marina?*

Two men and a woman were already sitting in complete silence across from each other, the woman playing on her mobile phone. One guy was in a suit, sat somewhat sternly, his arms crossed, staring into nothingness, whilst the other was biting his nails and was sat anxiously on the edge of his chair. Hafiz could almost prescribe what he needed. They all glanced over to see who he was and he tried to make himself comfortable in the face of their scrutiny by taking out his mobile phone and checking the time on the screen against that on his Audemars Piguet wristwatch. Marina was late – very late.

Looking around the room, Hafiz saw it was a stereotypical setting for a British National Health Service activity; only a grade better than the normal community sports halls that might host such events. Yet it was cold and decrepit, with a layer of dust on the parquet-style wooden floor. Three large windows, which looked out on a side street that faced an old derelict pub, dominated the room – as did the draught that came from them. In such rooms, there is always a wooden table against the wall somewhere, and in this one, it was under the central window. It displayed the omnipresent large silver hot water urn: the tiny plume of steam wasn't inviting, nor were the box of teabags, jar of coffee, upturned teacups and large plate of stale-looking digestive biscuits.

Public information posters that lined the walls were a constant reminder of the emergency helplines available for addicts, people with anxiety, depression, and schizophrenia, which no one ever phoned. Amidst the blanket of posters was a large wall-mounted clock: its annoying ticking sound served only to reinforce his anxiety – so much so that he almost missed the sound of the door opening and three more people entering: two men and a woman. The silence amongst them continued as the new arrivals sat down, looking apprehensive, fidgeting, unnerved.

The occasional exchange of eye contact, with a nod or forced smile or sometimes nothing. *It's a wonder people don't go mad within the first five minutes of these counselling sessions,* Hafiz thought, the awkward sighs of irritation, yawning, tapping of feet, fidgeting and forced coughing niggling him. Noticeably, one young woman was completely spaced out, rocking her body back and forth in time with whatever it was she was listening to; she also looked like she hadn't slept properly in weeks. *No wonder, if she's always plugged into those bloody earphones,* Hafiz thought; he wasn't a fan of such devices.

Hafiz fitted in perfectly by obsessively checking the time on his watch, then mobile phone, then on the clock. He nervously rubbed his sweaty palms onto his jeans whilst trying to psychoanalyse everyone in the room. Two more men entered the room in silence: one sat beside the woman with earphones and the other, unfortunately, sat beside Hafiz. As he gave a nod, he announced in an oriental accent, apropos of nothing, 'I like London. I travelled to London in a taxi', staring strangely at him, spaced out.

Hafiz was now beginning to freak out: he had this lunatic sitting next to him and not Marina. This wasn't how it was supposed to be. He turned away from the crazy fuck's constant stare and checked his watch again: seven twenty-five; she should have been here by now. He mentally commanded the door to open – there were only a few seats left – and sent her a text message: *Where the hell are you? Call me.*

The man next to him shifted nervously in his chair, his hands intertwining with each other. He was fidgeting, digging his nails deep into the skin on the back of his hands, and also constantly checking his watch; Hafiz should have been happy he had someone to play nicely with, with the same anxieties as him. The face-frozen man in the suit got up abruptly and walked over to the makeshift refreshments table to get a coffee. Then, suddenly the door swung open and an old lady came into the room with a maniacal energy about her, totally changing the dynamics of this quiet, anxious environment. 'Hello, hello, I'm Rosie. Hello there, everybody'. She acknowledged the people sitting in the circle en route to her chair; they responded by ignoring her with blank faces.

The circle was now almost formed. She took her canvas bag from her shoulder and placed it on the floor under her chair, talking to herself as no one else could be enticed into conversation. Yet she continued to smile at everyone, happy with her day so far, but the others just didn't engage. The majority flashed her dirty looks, irritated by her extrovert behaviour, shaking their heads in judgement. Hafiz wondered idly if she had learning difficulties – she seemed so ignorant of the social dynamics of the room – as he mentally dissected her. Unperturbed by the silence surrounding her, she continued to describe her day so far out loud; from the running monologue, she seemed infatuated with British ideals, the sort the British take for granted. Hafiz was tempted to tell her to shut the fuck up, but as she was more entertaining than the rest of them, he desisted and turned to look out of the window instead.

The door opened again and a trendy middle-aged couple entered the room holding hands. They seemed to have taken supporting each other to a whole new level as they were wearing dapper designer gear with matching leather coats. Hafiz rolled his eyes. He was now royally pissed off and all the chairs in the room were taken. He took a moment to clock that: *It's unusually busy this session*, he thought. He didn't recognise any of these people as being the usual fucking nutcases that attended, but that was sometimes the way: society fucked up so many people that there were always new faces needing help.

To distract himself from the ticking clock and his building anxiety about Marina's unexplained absence, he played a game: imagining the identities of his co-patients, wondering what they did for a living. It amused him, especially knowing that, whoever they were and whatever they did, they didn't have a clue that they were sat with a mastermind, nor an inkling of what was about to happen around the world on this day... Eleven times to be precise. Hafiz exhaled again, fighting the urge to check his watch but he couldn't resist: 19:28. 'Marina, where the fuck are you?' He said it out loud in his frustration, but no one blinked an eyelid: his mad exclamation fitted into the general dysfunctional atmosphere in the room. He phoned Marina, holding his phone up to his ear, his other hand over the mouthpiece so no one could hear what he was saying.

'Marina, where are you? Call me ASAP. You should be here already; the session is going to start in fifteen minutes'. Finishing the call, he saw a few more people entering the room. He yearned for Marina to arrive. Uncharacteristically, he decided she could have his chair when she arrived; whatever it took, just so long as she was by his side.

19:29. Demented, Hafiz stared at the second hand on his watch. It cost enough so it was big enough, but he couldn't believe the time it was telling. He stood up, impatiently walking over to the window, looking outside in search of her. Tick, tick, tick: the minute hand flew to 19:30. Once more he called Marina, closing his eyes to calm himself as he listened to the ringing, the endless ringing.

He was just about to hang up when it suddenly stopped. She had answered! Yet that wasn't Marina: he heard a voice on the end that clearly wasn't Marina... With his heart pounding, his mind confused, his peace of earlier shattered and his mind overloading, he stupidly asked for her nonetheless.

•

Danny answered Marina's phone and heard Hafiz sounding less than composed – even more so than usual.

'Hello...'

'Marina?' he asked, as his heart was consumed by utter desolation.

'No, it's Danny. Marina is dead', he replied calmly, with an air of authority.

Hafiz shut up for the first time – vocally and in his own head – stunned into silence. Listening with avalanching dismay to Danny's voice. Trying to convince himself that he didn't hear that, that Marina wasn't dead – but Marina wasn't here, with him, where she should have been. The shock that Danny had her phone ripped through his heart with a feeling of complete confusion and despair, worse than ever before. He glanced down at his watch: 19:31. His body started to tremble as the adrenalin pumped through his collapsed, overused veins, releasing a cold sweat over his entire body. Acid rose in his throat as his heart began beating hard, pounding deafeningly in his ears. Robbed of words, nothing came out.

Suddenly the room was filled with tumultuous chaos, as confusion rapidly unfolded in the room. He detected the atmosphere was changing by the second from anxious waiting to petrified urgency. There were no more awkward silences. Nervous fidgeting changed to people actually getting up off their chairs, as though preparing for something; a feeling of turmoil and desperation replaced basic boredom and annoyance. Hafiz froze as everyone picked up their belongings simultaneously to reach for their specific *Primus Circle* edition pictures. A look of puzzlement crossed his face, instantly giving way to imminent fear of what was unfolding in front of him.

They all started yelling, to absolutely no effect. All in turn, confused, trying to take command of the situation. Seriously arguing, exposing their weapons, shouting aggressively at each other, chairs being kicked over in anger and frustration. Desperately trying to reason with each other, knowing instinctively that this was not the plan. Like Skinner's laboratory rats on acid, their conditioning plan had changed and they became erratic and brutal. Violently pushing each other away in a heightened state of desperation, scuffles were breaking out, whilst two men in the corner fiercely compared their *Primus Circle* prints, both convinced that each was the other's victim.

The old woman, Rosie, was still deliriously talking to herself. She gaily reached into her canvas bag, taking out the large folded piece of white artist's paper, yet as she quickly recognised that it was a *Primus Circle* edition like the rest in the room, she stopped being happy and psychotically changed to victim mode. 'This can't be right', she said sadly, taking in the chaos around her.

The young woman with the earphones looked up at her and then down at her own Primus edition. Her panicky eyes slid instantly towards the old woman. She quickly walked over and held her print up against Rosie's to see if they matched. In a heartbeat, Rosie's victim mode changed to that of a killer: she pulled out her Browning 9mm pistol and cocked the weapon, aiming directly at her chest.

At the sound of the pistol being cocked, the rest of the assassins in the room, being basically controlled sheep, copycat a chain reaction of activating their own weapon systems. Hafiz actually could not move or breathe or activate any weapon, let alone his body. Hafiz counted the people in the room, frantically, his head moving left to right: eight, nine, ten and eleven. Of course. He closed his eyes, tilting his head back as the full horror of it hit him. Knowing. *'Fuck! How can this be happening?'*

'No. No, it's a set-up! Everyone, listen: it's all fucking wrong'. Hafiz screamed out loud, pleading, desperately through the noise and chaos that surrounded him, but nothing.

Yet they ignored him. The girl with earphones screamed out frantically, and her shock manifested itself physically. Pulling out a large knife from her bag, she attempted to put her training into practice but it was too late: Rosie squeezed the trigger, emptying the whole magazine into Portia's chest. Crack, crack, crack. As the rounds severely pierced her body, blood sprayed everywhere from her exit wounds, killing her instantly, before her frail body hit the floor with a deadened thump and the screams of utter panic and confusion in the room escalated to devastating war mode.

Hafiz crouched down, his hands trembling, cowering for his life, still with the phone against his ear. Danny heard the inhuman screams and chaos echo down the phone with the traditional screams of *'Allah Akbar'* heard in the background. Wondering if Hafiz was dead, trying to decipher individual voices in the crazy scenario that he had engineered.

A wave of sudden nausea, of betrayal, almost choked Hafiz. 'What the fucking hell is happening?' he asked, so quiet almost inaudible. Crying into the phone.

'I cracked your code', Danny said as he was still kneeling over Marina's dead body, checking her pockets.

'I knew from your diary that every Wednesday you attended counselling sessions'.

'What code? What are you on about?' Objecting vehemently to what he had just heard.

'Hafiz – don't be so fucking stupid as well as evil', Danny replied, immediately on the offensive.

'Who are you, really?' Hafiz asked, defeated and numb.

'I'm just an artist', he simply replied.

Unbeknown to Danny, the man who had been sitting next to Hafiz now revealed a Heckler and Koch 53 semi-automatic sub-machine gun.

The crazed excitement, the fear, the rush as he switched the safety catch to fire; he set the weapon off on automatic in every direction, screaming deliriously, accepting his fate and entering into it willingly.

The sound of a sub-machine gun on automatic was deafening, as the bullets penetrated people and stonework, ricocheting around the room – Danny knew the score and the damage those weapons could inflict – but the bullets came so thick and fast, it was impossible. 'Hafiz, LISTEN!' Danny commanded into the phone, military-style, to grab his attention.

'I'm listening. Please, please help, please'. Hafiz just pleaded; he really couldn't hear what was being said to him, yet hope still lingered: was his old friend Danny going to get him out of this?

'I told you I promised I'd be with you until the end'. As he said it, Danny stood up from Marina's prone body, looking at Bernadette, and she got it, she understood: Hafiz closed his eyes – as if that was going to change things.

'Yes, yes, you did, that's right, you did'. Desperately pleading, grovelling on his hands and knees emotionally in hope.

'But the end is now dead before me', Danny said, with harshness and finality in his tone.

Amongst the chaos, still standing by the refreshments table, Cody, who at this point was injured, was struggling to stay stood up. Slowly, he reached into his pocket, taking out the remote-control detonator, which was linked to his briefcase still under his chair. Flicking the switch to green, arming the device, he held both arms out like a crucifix, and prepared to die.

The pair of trendies who were now injured took action at that moment, following his lead; not surprising as they didn't appear to do anything individually, looking at each other and then over to the impromptu Jesus by the table. In synchronicity, they opened their heavy coats which concealed the fact they were wearing explosive vests.

Cody closed his eyes, adrenalin at its highest – pumping, committed, but crying for his wife and children, his tears running into his mouth, salty and strangely warm. He screamed out loud, 'Allah Akbar, Allah Akbar' – God is great – and pressed the Pressel switch with his thumb – simultaneously, just as the trendies did, their hands interlinked, detonating their deadly vests. Seeing a blinding white light, followed by a hailstorm of death, annihilating everything in its path.

The phone went silent, cut dead. Danny stared at Bernadette, contemplating the assassins' end; Hafiz's end. It is never an easy moment and it wasn't now, for Danny or Bernadette. The sound of the devastating explosion that ripped through the building could be heard across the city; the walls of the gallery shivered from the deadly energy of the shockwaves from the blast.

Don't bother hiding, death will always find you, Danny thought, reminiscing.

Danny placed Marina's phone down on her blood-soaked chest, then walked over to Bernadette as she sat there; emotional debris whirled around her. Then tears finally burst through her iron curtain. As he tended to her, smiling gently, knowing that he himself was still shaken from what had happened. But as a military man, he knew he must man up: Danny flashed her one of his winks and smiled. 'You will be fine, it's just a scratch', he said humorously.

THIRTY-SIX

— • —

London, predictably, returned to normality only a few days after the explosion that ripped through an isolated old council building in Hammersmith. Nevertheless, the uncertainty caused by the explosion was a perfect opportunity for every other known terror group to hop onto the old bandwagon and phone in lots of security alerts, probably for the laugh of the major inconvenience they caused. Two weeks on and the city at large still remained in a heightened state of alert. Nevertheless, life, as they always say it does, went on.

Danny was stood outside the Serpentine Gallery, pausing for a moment in thought, as usual, staring into the gallery to observe the lady within. He hugged his coat around him as tightly as possible, trying to stop the heat escaping, just when he thought he was about to expire from the cold.

He suddenly realised it wasn't Bernadette inside the gallery, but someone else. Baffled as to whom it was, he quickly walked towards the entrance to go in and investigate. *Where's Bernadette?*

'Hello there, can I help you?' the woman asked, smiling, whilst she was sat down behind the desk, glancing up over her laptop just as Danny walked into the gallery. He paused momentarily, glancing around to see if he could see her.

'Hi, is Bernadette here?' he asked, still peering around the gallery.

'No. Sorry. Unfortunately, Bernadette no longer works here any more. Can I help you with anything?'

'What…? Doesn't work here any more? Since when?' he asked sharply, shaking his head, confused.

'Since two days ago. I got the call from our head office, to stand in until they find a permanent replacement', she said, somewhat sympathetic.

'Oh. Right. She hadn't mentioned anything to me', he added, shaking his head.

'Do you want to leave a message for her? Was she dealing with any purchases on your behalf?'

'No, no. It's okay; I'll give her a call', he replied, knowing from her body language something wasn't right. Then, after a long pregnant pause of silence:

'Look. Is your name Danny Swift by any chance?' she asked, analysing him.

'Yes, it is. Why?' he replied, nodding, looking rather puzzled.

'Bernadette gave me your name and description. She did say that you would probably pop in and ask for her. She asked me to give you this', the woman said, handing over a white sealed envelope with his name written on it.

Danny took the envelope from her hand then he sheepishly smiles. 'Thanks', he said in return. 'Did she say anything else?'

'No, nothing… Erm, she seemed to be in a hurry. I'm sorry, that's all the information I have', she added, nodding towards the envelope.

Without another word, Danny exits the gallery, expecting the worst.

He stands outside, morosely contemplating. Sighing, with a gut feeling in the pit of his stomach. He carefully opened the letter, and it reads:

My dearest Danny,

If you're reading this letter, it means that I have made one of the hardest decisions. With recent events, I have decided to leave this life to start another. Somewhere I can live without risking the lives of people I love. That day you walked into the gallery reminded me of what I once had. However, the path I had chosen is a direction I wish I hadn't, but I have no choice but to be that Ghost once again. I couldn't always express my innermost thoughts as accurately as I wanted to at that moment. Each time I search for love, God has a funny way of taking it away from me, so I stay two steps ahead of him. Incessantly, I will cherish our memories, your touch, your humour and your affectionate solitude.

Intelligence without ambition is a bird without wings.

Bernadette x

Danny paused in thought. Trying to absorb what he'd just read. Immediately, he pulled out his mobile phone from his coat pocket to call her. Pressing Call, he waited. 'Sorry, but the number you have dialled has not been recognised. Please check the number and try again'. Danny repeated this several times. He even turned his phone off and on again, confused. *What the fuck?* he thought.

Immediately, he started to run in the direction of her apartment, hoping to see her. To stop her from leaving, to change her mind. Anything?

When he arrived at her apartment, he frantically banged on the door. 'Bernadette, are you there? It's me, Danny, hello! Are you there?' he shouted repeatedly. Nothing. He peered through the living room window to discover that inside was empty and all her belongings had gone.

Danny's heart sank as he stood still on the path, shaking his head in disbelief. He turned to face out towards Hyde Park, gutted. Knowing that she had truly gone. Disappeared without an explanation or saying goodbye... Momentarily, the magnificent image of the Queen's Life Guard mounted on immaculately groomed horses riding tantivy past. Their breastplates shining in the afternoon sun, with a roar, like thunder resonating across the skies.

Although Danny was numb and upset, he started to smile in admiration for her. The euphoria of the moment turned his smiles into laughter. *Where has she gone? I hope she finds solace,* he thought.

•

There is something very British about a village green fringing period houses. When set in a beautiful area of unspoilt natural beauty, it radiates an aura of peace and serenity: birds chirping, scattered tall trees towering over the entire village, pearl-coloured buildings sparkling majestically in the sun. The icing on the cake is a stream babbling through the village, little rainbow fish flowing through it rhythmically, making this the perfect tranquil setting for any act of creation.

Located at the back of the large manor house that fronted on to this particular village green stood an old white servants building with a black door and two small windows either side. Inside, visitors were greeted by the aroma of paint and thinners, and the sight of piles of stretched canvas leaning against the walls; half-finished artworks hung where space allowed. A large old oak table boasted six small CCTV monitors, providing a 24-hour live feed direct to the main studio and offices at Method Ltd. On one of the screens, at that very moment, several figures moved.

Dressed in old jeans and a white T-shirt, which were covered in a multitude of paint colours, the artist sat in front of a canvas, the radio playing in the background, his T-shirt serving the purpose of a towel. The classic wooden easel held a masterpiece that was almost complete. Against a dominant white background, multiple coloured circles were organised mathematically, in perfect symmetry. They stared back at him as his hand dipped the tip of a fresh paintbrush into a large tub of Mars black paint. Transfixed by the sheen of black oily liquid, he tapped the brush on the side of the tin as it emerged from the inky depths. Scraping the brush along the edge of the tin to remove the excess paint, with a steady hand, he delicately, intricately, traced around the edge of the contours of the final circle, the final spot. After another little dip into the paint, made with the same regimental formality, he filled in the remainder of the circle.

He leant back in his chair momentarily, admiring the finished product, literally watching the paint dry, sealing his creation. Then, placing the brush down, he stood up and leaned forward, unscrewing the locking nut on the easel, lifting the finished canvas off with both hands. Carefully, he walked over to the other side of the studio, as protective as a father with a newborn baby in his arms. He attached the painting to the wall almost reverentially, where it hung next to another similar creation; both contained a black spot. Hands on hips, he stood before them, almost in awe as he looked from one to the other.

His hands were covered in paint. He picked up a cloth from the table and poured white spirit onto it. Taking several skull-shaped rings off his fingers, then dropping them into a jar filled with paint thinners. Then he cleaned his hands, still staring at his circle paintings and checking the stage the chemical reaction was at by removing the residue of paint from his rings.

Suddenly there was a knock on the door.

'Yes?' he shouted, which also meant: 'Come in'. The door opened and a familiar figure entered. 'Ah, hello! How's it going?' Then he pointed towards the artwork on the wall. 'What do you think, Thom?' he asked.

'It's going well, thanks'. Closing the door behind him. 'They're looking good'. He dutifully admired the work opposite and on display around the studio. 'I just thought I'd make contact to let you know everything has been taken care of'. He pushed his glasses up higher on his nose with his forefinger, leaning forward, admiring the painting, arms across his chest for something to do; he wasn't a fan of chatting or art.

'That's fantastic'. He smiled. Finishing with the cloth, he threw it down on the table.

'Are those the two replacements?' Thom asked.

'Yeah, no one would know', he replied, nodding in amusement, then quoting a favourite philosopher of his, Thomas Hobbes. '*No arts; no letters; no society; and which is worst of all, continual fear, and danger of violent death: and the life of man – solitary, poor, nasty, brutish and short.* Especially for critics', he added, now laughing to himself, as he was the only one who 'got' it. He fished his skull rings out of the jar, 'But anyway, thanks, Thom. As per our agreement, you will find it has now been honoured'. He rinsed the rings under the tap, wiping them dry before putting them back on. 'Oh, before I forget... how's Danny?'

'He's fine, thanks, Joseph'.